Praise fo

DEATH AT THE
DRESS REHEARSAL

The first Lowe and Le Breton mystery

"*Death at the Dress Rehearsal* is certain to find a place in the hearts
of cosy crime readers everywhere, with its breezy prose, its witty
observations and the often hilarious interplay between its two thespian
leads – not to mention the cracking mystery at its heart. Stuart Douglas
has just delivered the best cosy crime novel since *The Appeal*."

George Mann, author of the Newbury & Hobbes series

"It was a joy to be in the company of these *Dad's Army* detectives. I
read the whole book in one sitting. Hugely enjoyable and lots of fun."

Nev Fountain, author of *The Fan Who Knew Too Much*

"Glorious and ingenious. What a lovely start to
what I hope will be a long-running series!"

Paul Magrs, author of *Exchange*

"*Death at the Dress Rehearsal* is a real tootsy-pop of a mystery
thriller, with an irresistible conceit and enough twists and turns
to bamboozle the most conscientious of armchair sleuths. Think
you won't love it? *Who do you think you are kidding…?*"

Steve Cole, author of the Young Bond series

"Holmes and Watson by way of Arthur Lowe and John Le Mesurier; a
wonderfully mismatched duo who you can't help falling in love with."

Trans-Scribe

Also by Stuart Douglas and available from Titan Books

DEATH AT THE DRESS REHEARSAL

The first Lowe and Le Breton mystery

STUART DOUGLAS

TITAN BOOKS

Death at the Dress Rehearsal: the first Lowe and Le Breton mystery
Print edition ISBN: 9781803368207
E-book edition ISBN: 9781803368214

Published by Titan Books
A division of Titan Publishing Group Ltd.
144 Southwark Street, London SE1 0UP

First edition: June 2024
10 9 8 7 6 5 4 3 2 1

A CIP catalogue record for this title is available from the British Library.

Printed and bound by CPI Group (UK) Ltd, Croydon CR0 4YY.

For Julie, Scott and Paul.

And for my Uncle Eddie, who I
promised I'd put in my next book.

PROLOGUE

The taste of blood in her mouth reminded her of childhood; a fall from a swing and a sharp blow to her chin which had rattled her infant teeth. Then, her father had caught her up in his arms and carried her away, cleaned her up and given her ice cream and orange juice. But there would no such rescue this time.

Instead, she stumbled through the thick gorse, alone and aware of the closeness of her attacker, only a few yards behind her. She could hear breathing at her heels and a soft voice calling her name. "Give up, Alice, there's nowhere to go."

Whether that was true or not, she didn't know. She could only hope she would come to a road, and that a car would pass and miraculously she would be saved.

When she had fled from the car park, away into the darkness, she had been heading uphill, and now she crested a small peak and, to her delight, made out a faint glow a hundred yards or so ahead. She risked a glance back, but the blackness of the countryside was so complete that she could see nothing, only hear the steady tread of someone close behind her, in no hurry to catch up. The certainty in that tread, the conviction that her capture was inevitable, was almost enough to break her, but instead she forced herself to increase speed, tripping and half falling as she pressed onwards, wondering if she might somehow fashion a weapon from something lying about. Anything to gain enough time to reach the lights.

But she knew the moors from her father's descriptions, and knew the ground was scrubby gorse for miles around. There was barely a tree that might have shed a handy branch, and if there were any heavy rocks to hand... well, unless she tripped over them, they would go unseen. And she could feel her strength fading, her lungs tightening as terror-filled panic and unexpected exertion combined to rob her of breath. Perhaps it had been a mistake to try to go faster? Perhaps she should turn and fight? No, better to get to the lights and, if necessary, make her stand there.

Fifty yards, forty, thirty...

She almost fell as she left the rough ground and stepped onto the narrow, dimly lit path. Viewed up close, she could see these were not the streetlights she had hoped for. She felt her stomach sink as she realised they were simply small electric handlights, strung in haphazard fashion along a fence that skirted the far side of the path. She stopped and stared stupidly at the topmost metal cord of the fence, one of three lines of thin steel wire which stretched between wooden stanchions off into the darkness in either direction. A cold wind blew in her face. She realised the sounds of pursuit had ceased, and knew, as a cornered animal does, her pursuer was directly behind her.

She clenched her fists and tensed the muscles in her arms and legs, ready to spin around and launch herself at the figure to her rear. She pressed the balls of her feet down onto the gravel and prepared to turn…

The blow, when it arrived out of the blackness, was hard and heavy. It connected with the side of her head so swiftly that, for a moment, she wasn't even aware she'd been hit. Her body continued to move, twisting around to attack even as the strength in her arms suddenly disappeared, while her head was forced in the opposite direction by the force of the blow. She felt muscles tear in her neck before she felt the huge, dull pain in her head, and then her legs went from under her and she staggered to the left, and collapsed on wet grass. Her eyes were open but she was incapable of focusing them, so she felt rather than saw her attacker grab her beneath the arms and haul her along the ground, then heave her to her feet and prop her against something hard but yielding, which dug into her side and shoulder. She opened her mouth to speak, to ask why this was happening, but no words came out, only blood and a few indistinct, wet sounds. She felt something press against her lips and smelled spirits, and then something slap against her chest, and she willed her hands to come up and grab whatever it was, but try as she might, they remained uselessly limp at her side.

There was surprisingly little pain, she realised.

The pressure on her chest eased, then ceased altogether and, for a second, everything was silent and still. She sagged backwards gratefully, and sucked cold air into her lungs... then, as though from a great distance away, she heard someone say her name – *Alice* – and felt hands grasp her ankles. Her head fell backwards as her legs were lifted into the air until a tipping point was reached, and suddenly there was nothing to support her.

Without a sound, she tumbled into space. She had time to trace a half turn in the air, then she struck water colder than any she had ever known before and was engulfed in its freezing embrace.

1

Edward Lowe let the witless tittle-tattle wash over him and tried to pay it no attention. It was the same every morning. He would arrive with a copy of *The Times*, take a seat beside John Le Breton, and pointedly and noisily open it. The implication was obvious, surely? That he had no desire for conversation and would appreciate a little silence in which to read the news, first thing in the morning.

And yet, without fail, he would get no further than the first paragraph of the first column before John and whichever girl was doing his make-up would start. Such-and-such was seeing so-and-so, whatshisname was putting on weight, and you-know-who was rumoured to be about to be shifted to a new show on account of his dislike of one of the new producers. It was the banality which grated most – that, and the way in which his girl would invariably get involved. Within two minutes, she would stop mid-application and, in a tone he felt was better suited to

Norman Evans gossiping over the garden wall, say, "Well, what do you think of that, Mr. Lowe?"

It really was too much.

"Do you think we could have a little quiet for once!" he snapped, then immediately regretted it.

Everyone was looking at him. It would have been preferable if they'd snapped back, but the closest any of them got was John's raised eyebrow, and even that was accompanied by that infuriating half smile of his. The girls just giggled. They were used to his occasional outbursts, he supposed. He'd heard one of them say, "you have to make allowances for them, they're that old" once, and the memory rankled afresh.

"I think we're done now, in any case," he grumbled, and pushed himself to his feet, pulling the tissue from his collar and dropping it on the floor. He'd had enough for one morning. He needed some air.

Without another word, he tramped down the stairs of the make-up van and left them to their gossip. There was a bitter wind blowing from the reservoir and it was still an hour before he was needed for shooting, but it would be better to wander across the freezing moorland than stay inside in an awkward atmosphere. He buttoned his coat up, buried his chin in its collar, and set off along the path around the water, away from everybody.

The worst of it was, he knew he was at fault. His mood had been foul since the previous day, when the show's producer, David Birt, had leaned over the top of the chair in which

Edward was almost napping and informed him that the following day's shooting had been changed.

"Apparently, there's a problem with the swimming pool we were intending to use, so we're going to do the scene at a reservoir up the road instead," he'd explained, with a tiny shrug. Then he'd handed over a thick sheaf of paper. "I know this isn't going to make you happy, Edward, and believe me, I'd prefer not to be doing it, but there are new lines to be learned, I'm afraid."

Even if the last-minute change hadn't been enough to sour his mood, that little dig about new lines would have riled him. He knew it annoyed the others, his refusal to allow work to intrude on his private life. But he was damned if he was going to waste his evenings – which should be spent in front of the fire, with a glass of something decent and good music playing on the stereo – muttering lines to himself, with the script face-down in his hand, like some grubby schoolchild cramming for an examination. Even here, on location for *Floggit and Leggit* (and what a ridiculous title that was!), he refused to spend his evenings committing tripe to heart as though it were Shakespeare. Close enough was good enough for this kind of thing.

"It's really not on, David," he'd remonstrated, knowing it was a futile exercise, but unwilling to let the change pass without protest. "This is the second time in this run, you know? What was the excuse last time? The costumes weren't ready, wasn't it?"

"The costume girl's mother died, Edward."

"I know that, David! Though you'd never know we employed anyone to look after that side of things, given the shoddy state of some of the props. The antique miniature I was supposed to be appraising last week was a photograph of Guernsey in a plastic frame! As for the costumes…"

His voice had trailed off into ill-tempered silence and he'd taken refuge in lighting a cigarette, conscious that to say anything else on the subject would be to place himself in an invidious light.

"Well, if you could look over the new pages, Edward…" Birt had motioned towards the papers which Edward had already dumped on the table. "Of course, nobody expects you to be word-perfect tomorrow!"

He'd smiled, but Edward had been having none of it. He'd made as non-committal a sound as he could manage and nodded once, almost imperceptibly. Birt had stood for a second, then, evidently deciding no more need be said, smiled again and headed for the bar, leaving Edward to stare at the script with a baleful eye.

Learning lines had been easier when he was younger, of course. When he was doing rep, he'd only needed to look at a script once for it to become lodged in his head forever. He could still quote chunks of any number of long-forgotten plays, whole convoluted speeches which nobody else remembered, or would ever speak again.

Irritated, he peered at the top page of the new script. With a sigh, he skimmed through the episode synopsis.

THAT SINKING FEELING. Wetherby convinces Archie and the shopkeepers to test out a collection of vintage diving gear at the local reservoir. High jinks ensue when Wetherby ends up adrift in a rubber dinghy and Archie attempts to rescue him in a moth-eaten diving suit.

About par for the course, really. Last week it had been Joe Riley, who played local councillor Brian Clancy, and Donald Roberts, as the incontinent Vicar, trapped in a pub cellar with no access to a lavatory. He'd almost called his agent when he'd seen the episode was called "Bottoms Up". High jinks, indeed. It was just another word for unnecessarily coarse behaviour, in his opinion.

He hadn't called, of course. He knew exactly what his agent would have said. That *Floggit and Leggit* was his biggest break in years and that, after a professional lifetime spent as a supporting actor, this was his chance to play the lead on television.

The question he had to ask himself – that he *had* asked himself every day since he'd signed the contract – was whether being the star of a cheap-as-chips BBC series in which the elderly shop owners of Groat Street Market got into allegedly hilarious scrapes was really the height of his professional ambitions.

He'd really thought that by this stage in his career he might be doing better than playing George Wetherby, the self-important owner of a provincial antique shop in a slightly vulgar situation comedy. If 1972 was anything to go by, this was going to be a tedious decade, professionally speaking.

And it wasn't as though he didn't learn his lines, was it? Most of them, anyway. Birt and Bobby McMahon, the writer, could hardly expect perfection straight off the bat, not when he was only given one evening to learn page after page of arrant rubbish. Because the quality didn't help. Of course, it didn't. *Give me* Hamlet *or* Lear, Edward thought with a burst of fresh irritation, and it would stick like glue. But "hand me that chamber pot, Archie," and "where have your trousers gone, Malcolm?" Not exactly the Bard, was it?

Perhaps he should just retire and accept his glory days (such as they'd been!) were behind him. He wasn't the only one, either. Joe Riley might bleat on about working with Hitchcock and his days at the Old Vic, but there was a reason he was reduced to playing a sour-tempered local-government man. And as for Donald Roberts...

He shook his head and smiled to himself, bad temper all but forgotten as he recalled old Donald remarking mildly that, after a lifetime in the business, all he'd be remembered for after this was Malcolm the Vicar's allegedly hilariously weak bladder and propensity for misplacing his trousers.

At least Wetherby was only the guiding force of the Groat Street pensioners, and not quite one himself.

The thought that, even in his sixties, he was still one of the younger cast members served to dissipate the last vestiges of ill-humour from Edward's mind, and he finally looked up from the ground to discover where his angry steps had taken him – just in time to stand in something soft and wet. He jumped to one side automatically, but the damage was done. He lifted the offending boot and peered myopically down at it.

Well, that was a relief. No sign of dog's mess, at least.

He glared at the path and discovered the source of his momentary confusion. A grubby rag had been flattened against the gravel by the pressure of his boot, squeezing a pale, watery liquid into a puddle around it. A little of the liquid had darkened the bottom of his boot, but running the sole across some of the ever-present gorse quickly removed all trace of that.

For the first time since he'd stomped out of the make-up tent, Edward spent a moment taking in his immediate surroundings. His foul mood had evidently caused him to quicken his pace, he realised, for the set was sufficiently far away that he could make out only lorries and a tent, with the figures hurrying around them as indistinct and blurred as if he'd removed his spectacles. Otherwise, there was little to see. Ahead, the path disappeared around a bend and to the right the gorse extended across a field until it too vanished at the horizon.

Which left only the reservoir itself, ringed to his left by a low fence and, here and there, isolated stunted trees which bent at unnatural angles where the wind had buffeted them throughout their existence. No matter where he looked, there was nothing interesting to see. Not that it mattered. He should really be getting back to the set, in any case.

He turned on his heel, bored now of both his bad mood and the cold wind, and, in doing so, inadvertently caught the rag with the toe of his boot. It unfolded with a wet slapping sound, and lay flat on the grey pebbles, a sodden white square, unexpectedly edged with intricate lace and exuding a familiar odour.

Brandy.

Curious, Edward knelt down to examine it more closely, but immediately froze in shock. Crouching low, he could now see underneath the nearest bush. And there he could clearly make out two fists clenched tight upon clumps of grass and, between them, the pale face of a young woman, whose blank, staring eyes and slack mouth left no doubt she was dead.

For all that he'd spent much of the time working in radar and had never seen action, he *had* been posted out East during the last war, and he'd seen his fair share of dead bodies. So perhaps it was the juxtaposition of English countryside and wide-eyed corpse that caused him to shiver with shock. For several long seconds he stayed painfully crunched on his haunches, until, with a start, he scrambled backwards, falling hard onto the path, scratching his hands on the gravel. His eyes never left those of the dead woman.

There were white ice crystals in her long eyelashes and in her dark hair, and, as he crawled slowly towards her, he could see her lips were a pale blue. There was something familiar about those eyes, though, something hovering on the tip of his tongue. But even as he thought about it, it was gone, and he was tearing his gaze away. Over her shoulder, he could see the inadequate fence directly behind her was damaged. Had she fallen in the reservoir, perhaps, and dragged herself out, only to succumb here, frozen and without the strength to go any further?

He levered himself to his feet and, touching nothing, leaned forward to get a better look. The fencing around the water consisted of wooden poles, probably rotten, spaced out every dozen yards or so, with thin metal wire strung through each pole at three points, equally spread up the wood. The top wire behind the dead woman had been pulled back towards the reservoir, causing the poles on either side to lean in towards one another at a steep angle.

She'd gripped onto the metal and pulled herself out of the water that way, he realised, with a muted approval. *Never give up* was a mantra he'd always embraced, ever since he'd returned from the War, a short, stocky northerner with a receding hairline and bad eyesight, and decided he wanted to be an actor. He had never quit on anything, and it seemed this poor woman had been the same, at least while her strength lasted.

He was looking around for something he might use to cover her up and restore a little of her dignity when he became aware of a figure running towards him from the direction of the set.

"You're wanted, Mr. Lowe," the young man (Edward had no idea what his name was, but he'd seen him around) shouted as soon as he was within earshot. When Edward made no move towards him, or even acknowledged his existence, he repeated the shout, then, when the distance between them was sufficiently small that shouting would be both unnecessary and rude, said in a quieter voice, "David says could you come back, please, Mr. Lowe? You're wanted on set. Dress rehearsal is about to start and David's worried you're not in costume yet."

Edward looked at him blankly, the words making no sense – or rather, communicating nothing of importance. He pointed downwards, underneath the bush. "I think you'd best go back and tell David there'll be no filming today," he said, finally.

2

The rest of the morning was spent in a series of meetings and interviews, in which Edward was forced to repeat the same brief tale over and over again to a variety of official – and unofficial, but just as interested – parties.

"I have already explained all of this to your colleague," he found himself saying to a police inspector who had been called in from the city. Constable Primrose, the bobby in the local village of Ironbridge, had been deemed too inexperienced to investigate a sudden death on his own.

The inspector nodded. "I'm aware of that, sir," he said, "but in cases like this, I prefer to hear any recollection first-hand."

Edward bit off a sigh. The man was only doing his job after all, and, even if it was annoying to constantly repeat oneself, he supposed he should be pleased the police were being so thorough. For the umpteenth time, he cast his mind back to that morning.

He had remained by the body while the young assistant had run back to tell everyone what had happened, and to phone the authorities. Within a few minutes, David Birt, Bobby McMahon and one or two of the cast had arrived. The youngest of the actors, Jimmy Rae (who played Wetherby's idle son, and had hair as long as a girl's), had brought a blanket, which he and John Le Breton had draped over the dead woman.

That had been the first time he'd had to tell his story, such as it was; how he'd walked for a bit and kicked the white handkerchief...

The handkerchief. He'd forgotten all about that.

"As I told your colleague, I'd forgotten all about the hankie until then, you see," he said to the inspector. "It was only when I was telling everyone about finding the body that I remembered why I'd bent down in the first place."

It had been in the exact same position. Through sheer good luck, nobody had disturbed it as they came running up, every man somehow contriving to step over or around it. He'd stooped low and poked the sodden fabric with a pencil. A fresh trickle of what he was now sure was brandy oozed from it.

"That's what made me check it, you see," he said. "That and the fact I could see the lace trim. It seemed an odd thing to be lying on the path, out there in the middle of nowhere."

"Could be a clue," Jimmy Rae had said.

"A clue to what exactly?" Edward had asked, testily. Jimmy seemed a nice enough boy and had been fine so far playing the series' youthful heartthrob, but he was inclined to the melodramatic. He had a background in experimental theatre, apparently. All foul language and insufficient underwear, he shouldn't wonder. "Clearly, the poor woman fell in the water last night and, though she managed to pull herself out, she hadn't the energy to get any further."

"So, what's with the hankie, then?" Rae had pressed. "How did it get over there, and why's it soaked in drink? I reckon there's been *foul play* here."

Edward had heard the relish with which he'd said *foul play*, like a detective in a Bulldog Drummond movie. Before he could say anything, though, John had interrupted, in his usual mild, slightly distracted tone. "It could be purely coincidental, I'd have thought." He smiled and waved one hand in Edward's direction. "Just because it prompted Edward to... hmmm... squat down, doesn't mean it has anything to do with this poor lady's fate."

"John plays Archie Russell, who works in my antique shop on the show," Edward explained to the inspector. "He's had a reasonable career, of course – made some films and spent time in America, I believe – but he can be a bit vague at times. He has a tendency to fall back on an 'oh my, I don't know how to tie my shoelaces, won't someone find Nanny to do it for me' little boy routine at the drop of a hat. But there was no denying the sense in what he'd said, so we decided the best thing to do was to leave the handkerchief where it was, until your lot arrived."

"Quite right too, sir," the inspector nodded. "So, you moved nothing until Constable Primrose arrived? Which would be approximately twenty minutes later?"

"About that, yes. We did wonder if perhaps we should head back to the village, but it seemed disrespectful to the dead woman to leave, and I knew someone would want to speak to me."

"You did the right thing," the inspector said.

It had been bitterly cold. The chill wind had grown stronger and a dirty drizzle had set in, not too heavy, but incessant. There was nowhere to shelter, but Edward had been certain the police would arrive very soon, and so had insisted on staying put. Later, he'd wondered why he hadn't gone back to the set at least, and sheltered in the food tent, but the thought hadn't occurred at the time, and because he was staying, the others did too. David Birt had left instructions that one of the crew was to guide the police to the body when they arrived.

"But no, nobody moved anything before the constable turned up. He was the first person to touch the body. He was the one who found the paint, in fact."

Constable Primrose was a skinny beanpole of a man, in his early twenties, at a guess, with already thinning fair hair and a wispy moustache. He was ridiculously young to be the only policeman for miles around, in Edward's opinion, but still, for reasons he'd never been able to explain, he had taken an immediate liking to the boy and was careful to portray him in as favourable a light as possible to his superior.

"He took in the scene very commendably, you know," said Edward, leaning forward slightly and tapping on the inspector's notebook, as though reminding him to write it down. "He had us all move well back, then he checked the poor woman over thoroughly and realised there was something on her blouse."

In reality, the tall constable had stood indecisively for some time, rubbing his fingers on his chin and glancing repeatedly from the body to the group of actors. It was only when John had murmured, "perhaps you should, you know…" and indicated the corpse, that he had nervously knelt down.

"Ooh, she smells of drink something terrible," Primrose had said, as he turned the woman over onto her back. "And there's something on her top," he'd gone on, then yelped in alarm. "It's coming off on my hands!"

He jumped up and showed them his palms. They were covered in small white flakes, like dandruff. Primrose had rubbed his hands on his official police black trousers, leaving faint smears down each thigh.

As if released from a trance by his actions, the others had surged forward as one and crowded around the body. Viewed from the comfortable position of the hotel bar, with the inspector seated across from him and a glass of passable Merlot in hand, Edward thought that perhaps he had not been quite so quick as the others to gape mawkishly at the poor woman. John Le Breton, however, had been very much to the fore.

"I do believe it's paint." Edward had never previously heard John express any emotion stronger than wry amusement, but there was a definite note of interest in his voice as he pointed at the policeman's leg. "Look, there's a patch of it on the front of the poor woman's top."

The inspector coughed and shook his head slightly. "Actually, it turns out it's not paint. We think it's some kind of face powder, probably from a compact she had in her pocket. It must have partially dissolved in the water and soaked through the dead lady's clothing." He smiled, but there was no warmth in it. "It's a bit of a lucky break, actually. The fact it only partially dissolved shows she wasn't in the water long."

"I thought that must be the case," Edward agreed. "I said as much at the time, when we took a closer look."

Primrose had at least closed her eyes, Edward was pleased to see. He'd pushed his way past David Birt and peered down at the girl. She was brunette, around thirty, he would guess, fashionably dressed in a bulky jacket and blue slacks. A pale cream shirt was visible beneath the jacket, the pocket stained. The knees of her trousers were filthy. Her shoes, he noticed absently, were missing, presumably lost at the bottom of the reservoir. Her bare toes pointed back towards the water.

"Rather a pretty girl," John had murmured softly at his side.

Edward had whipped his head around, a reminder on his tongue that there was such a thing as decorum, but the look on the other man's face was so maudlin that he bit off the remonstration, and left it unsaid.

"Yes," he'd said instead. "She was. She can't have been in the water long, or… you know…"

He let his voice trail off as an image skittered across the edges of his mind. There was something wrong about this… something not as it should be…

Whatever it was, it remained frustratingly out of reach. The instant he'd tried to concentrate on the wispy half-thought, it was gone, and he was left still staring at John.

"And then PC Primrose covered her with his coat, and asked us all to go with him, back to the filming area," Edward concluded, suddenly keen for the inspector to be on his way. He drained his glass, troubled by that final momentary sense of familiarity. "After that, you chaps took over," he said. "That's all I can tell you, I'm afraid."

"You've been very helpful, Mr. Lowe," the inspector said. He scribbled a last line in his notebook and folded it shut. He glanced around quickly and lowered his voice. "Unofficially, I can tell you that we believe that the lady was out hiking and fell into the reservoir while under the influence of alcohol. The smashed remains of a half-bottle of brandy – the label was in perfect condition, so recently dropped there, and therefore we believe linked to the drink-soaked hankie you found – was discovered near her body. That's not something to be shared at present, though," he cautioned. "We've not spoken to her next of kin yet, you understand."

"Ah, so you know who she is, then?"

"We do. Ironbridge isn't a big place, Mr. Lowe, and PC Primrose was able to supply a list of the bed-and-breakfast establishments at which the lady might have stayed. Mrs. Alice Burke, her name is. *Was*. She was a guest at the second one we tried. The landlady said she arrived yesterday morning, on a hiking holiday, one small rucksack, no suitcase. Come to see the area her family comes from, apparently." He shook his head. "She went out last night at about nine, passed the landlady on the stairs. Said she was going for a stroll. The landlady warned her to stay to the roads and reminded her the door was locked at midnight. That's the last anyone saw of her alive."

He leaned in closer and lowered his voice. "It's enough of an open-and-shut case that I'll be leaving tonight, in fact, and writing up my report back home. To be honest, in the force, we refer to my visit as a box-ticking exercise. Sadly, Mrs. Burke's death was a tragic accident, caused by a combination of unfamiliarity with the area and strong drink."

"Are you certain of that? It's just…" Edward reddened. Suddenly, he was unsure how to go on. He didn't have strong suspicions, after all. In fact, until that very moment, he hadn't been aware he had suspicions at all. Just a nagging sense that something at the reservoir had been amiss.

The inspector was looking at him curiously, waiting for him to continue. When the silence between them had lasted a second too long, he filled it with a gentle prompt.

"Just…?"

What could he say? That her eyes had unearthed a memory – half a memory, not even that, not even a memory at all, really – and that it had made him uneasy? He shook his head, covered his embarrassment by lighting a cigarette and letting the smoke form a cloud in front of his face. "Oh, nothing. Nothing at all. Forget I said anything, Inspector."

There was understanding, but also a degree of condescension, in the inspector's voice when he spoke. "I know it can be traumatic, seeing death up close, especially when you're not used to it. But sometimes accidents happen." He smiled as he clipped his pen to the inside pocket of his sports coat. "There's not always a bogeyman in the background, thankfully."

He drained the last of his lemonade and carefully placed the glass back on the table. "Please do remember what I said about not discussing anything I've said with your colleagues. Best all round if you just forget it ever happened, and go back to making everyone laugh. Leave the policing to the police, and we'll leave the funny business to you lot." He stood and offered his hand in farewell. "I shouldn't really be telling you any of this, but given the circumstances, it can't do any harm. And well, the wife and I are looking forward to seeing the new show. She'll be chuffed when I tell her where I've been today."

Which was pleasing, of course, but experience had taught Edward it was best to say as little as possible when a member of the public mentioned work. You could never stop some of the buggers talking once they got started, and they all ended up thinking they were your best friend after two minutes of chat. "That's very gratifying to hear..." he began, but the inspector, it seemed, was not finished speaking.

"Oh aye, a big fan of Mr. Le Breton, the wife is. Always has been."

Edward's smile never flickered, he was pleased to note, and his handshake could not be criticised for a lack of good fellowship. He watched the policemen walk out of the room and waved to the barman to bring over another bottle of Merlot.

3

John Le Breton couldn't decide if he actually liked Edward Lowe or not.

He certainly didn't *dis*like him. There were very few people John did dislike, really. A housemaster at Sherborne (long since in his grave, he suspected, and felt a shiver of guilt for thinking ill of the dead) and a theatre manager in... Darlington, was it? Or perhaps Doncaster. But that was about it.

Edward wasn't a *great* friend, of course. John had worked with far too many actors to be great friends with them all, even if they'd been uniformly charming and the best of company. Which, whatever other sterling qualities he might have, Edward definitely was not. He was pompous and prickly, and quick to take offence (and not backwards in giving it either, John thought with a smile, remembering his reaction to one request for an autograph).

Take that morning, for instance. Of course, he'd been rattled to stumble upon a dead body. Who wouldn't be?

Even in the War, when one rather expected to do so now and again, it had been a terrible experience, but in the incongruous setting of the English countryside, a quarter of a century later? Of course he'd been rattled.

Even so, the way he'd elbowed everyone out of the way to look at the poor woman's paint-stained blouse had been a bit off. There were definite traces of George Wetherby in Edward Lowe, in John's opinion.

"Which is not entirely bad, to be fair," he murmured to himself, a habit he'd picked up while staying alone in digs across the country.

Clive Briggs, who was playing the local ironmonger in the show and who he'd known for years, looked up from his paper, assuming he was being addressed. "What's that?" he asked.

"Oh, nothing." John smiled and drained his glass, wiggled it in the direction of his friend. "Another one, Clive?"

He didn't wait for an answer – what else was there to do on a rainy Monday night in Ironbridge, after all? – but gathered up Clive's empty glass and headed for the bar. Edward looked up as he passed. The policeman he'd been speaking to had just left, and John wondered what he'd said.

"Can I get you a drink, Edward?" he asked, on impulse.

"No, no thank you. I've just ordered this," he said, indicating the bottle of house red on the table. "Perhaps you'd join me, though? There's something that's been bothering me, and I'd appreciate your opinion on the matter."

John glanced across at Clive, but he was laughing and waving his arms in front of Jimmy Rae, evidently already deep in some hilarious anecdote or other.

"Why not?" he said and slipped into the seat opposite Edward, as the little man gestured to the barman to bring over another glass.

Once he had his drink and Edward had replenished his, he cocked an eyebrow quizzically. "So, what's bothering you, old chum?"

He suspected it was something to do with the policeman's visit, and was pleased when Edward bent forward and, in an undertone he could barely hear, confirmed that suspicion. "The police are treating the death as accidental, you know?"

"So I heard. The constable told Jimmy they think she was out walking and fell into the reservoir. Poor woman heaved herself out, but froze to death overnight."

Edward nodded. "Exactly. The inspector didn't say that in so many words, but still, it was pretty plain that was what he meant." He frowned. "Blithering idiot. There's obviously more to it than meets the eye."

Now, that was unexpected. This could turn out to be far more entertaining than he'd expected. "Really?" John said in as flat a voice as he could manage. "Wasn't that exactly what you said earlier on?"

"I did." Edward paused, leaving John with the impression he was making his mind up about something important. Finally, he said, "But I've since changed my opinion. I think something untoward occurred, even if the police don't."

"I must say, I thought it was all rather cut and dried," John replied.

Edward drained his glass and refilled it, scowled, began to speak, then stopped and shrugged instead.

"Lack of imagination, that's the problem," he grunted.

John wondered if he meant the police or himself.

"Well, what do you think happened, Edward? What do you think they've missed?" he asked finally. Across the bar, he could see Clive Briggs arm-wrestling the barman, and Jimmy Rae slapping a pound note down between the two men, obviously betting on the outcome.

"I can't say precisely," Edward replied after a moment. "There's something nagging at me, something I can't quite put my finger on. And I don't have the *access…*"

Evidently he thought that was sufficient explanation, for he moodily sipped at his wine and said nothing more.

It would have been simplest for John to leave it at that, and rejoin Clive and Jimmy. In many ways that would have been more in character, too. And, later, he could not have explained exactly why he didn't. Instead, he tutted and shook his head.

"What sort of access?" he asked.

"To everything, of course!" Edward's words were a little slurred, but what they lacked in clarity they more than made up for in volume.

John held a warning finger to his lips before he could shout anything else.

"To the body," the little man repeated more quietly. "To the area where it was found. To everything." He lit another cigarette and blew smoke at the ceiling. "I'm not one for astrology and palm reading and all that heathen mumbo-jumbo, but there was a look in her eyes. A look that said, *help me*." He reddened a little and squinted through his glasses. "I know I sound like I've lost my marbles, but I'm telling you, the police have missed something. I'm not saying she was murdered, necessarily…" He broke off, as though saying the word for the first time had surprised even him (it had certainly surprised – and delighted – John), but, after a sip of his wine, concluded, "…but I'd be astonished if it were the simple mishap the authorities believe."

That was the moment at which John should have definitely made his apologies and rejoined the others at the bar. But instead, he grinned wolfishly at Edward and said, "David says we'll not be able to film for a few days, and there's not much to do round here, lovely old dump though it is. So why don't we see if we can identify this troubling something while we wait?"

Even after several months of working together, John didn't know if he liked Edward Lowe, but there was a look in the other man's eyes just now that promised some entertainment over the next few days, and he decided that was enough to be going on with.

He twisted in his seat and waved to the barman. "Another bottle of this frightful plonk, when you have a moment, please," he called, and drained his glass.

* * *

It was such a shame that, unlike trumpet players and malt whisky, hangovers did not improve with age.

John groaned as he gingerly rolled onto his side, trying to find the one spot on the pillow where his head was not pounding with an insistent beat and his stomach wasn't cartwheeling like a particularly inept circus acrobat. He opened his eyes, but only reluctantly and with difficulty, checking quickly whether there was anyone unexpected lying beside him. There was not, which was both a relief and a disappointment, but he could see his cigarette packet lying on the bedside table. As he reached shakily for it, the events of last night began to trickle back to mind.

It had begun quite promisingly, at least. Edward Lowe was stubborn, fussy and convinced he was always right – just the sort to think he knew better than the police, in fact – but he was also surprisingly good company once a few glasses of atrocious red had loosened the permanent stick up his back.

"The thing is…" he had said (*probably* said, John mentally corrected himself; he wouldn't be willing to swear in court to anything Edward had said after his sixth drink). "The thing is, there is a… *discrepancy*… which the police have failed to identify."

Edward had definitely sat back after that, his hands crossed over his ample stomach, his face flushed red, cigarette ash falling on his waistcoat, looking quite Dickensian in a Joan Littlewood sort of way.

"So you said," John had replied, a little unsteady himself. "But what is it specifically?"

"Ah…" Edward had sighed. "I'm not absolutely certain of that."

He had no memory of the period immediately afterwards, but he suspected they had sat in the silence of the just-beyond tipsy, that wonderful extended moment when there was sufficient alcohol in the blood to lend a rosy glow to the world, but not quite enough to set the room spinning.

He did remember the barman standing by the table, informing them firmly that he needed to close the bar. Other than that, the evening was composed of fragments, tiny shards of memory which he found difficult to place in order; they were too brief and too similar, with too little information to create a useful timeline.

Edward tearing the label from the wine bottle and sketching on the back of it in pencil. Something to do with silver and ice. Jimmy Rae throwing bags of crisps across from the bar. Himself telling Edward about Sally, his ex-wife and – he could admit this only to himself and nobody else – the real love of his life, and how he'd missed her when she left him for the bloody insurance man. Edward thumping his hand on the table, over and over again…

Actually, no, that wasn't right. That wasn't from last night. That was happening now.

John opened his eyes and carefully turned them towards the door. It shook on its hinges as someone outside kicked it and shouted his name.

"John! John! Let me in! I've figured out what they missed!"

Of course it was Edward. Who else would be so cruel as to deliberately wake a hungover man at such a tragically early hour?

"Come in," he called weakly, then stubbed out his cigarette and arranged himself in a manner which he hoped indicated a sick man best spoken to quickly and quietly, then left alone. He doubted Edward would even notice, though.

And so it proved.

"It's not the missing shoes!" Edward exclaimed without preamble. "It's the missing socks!"

John's head – his health, even – was far too precariously balanced for guesswork. "What's that, old boy?" he asked. "Missing socks? What missing socks?" He pressed a wan hand to his forehead and gave a small, but audible, groan. "You mean our late lamented lady friend of yesterday? But she wasn't even wearing shoes, far less socks."

"Exactly!" Edward strode across the room and stood over John's bed. For the first time he seemed to notice the condition of its occupant. His nose wrinkled in disgust. "Shouldn't you be up by now?" he said; then, clearly determined not to be distracted, continued, "You remember I said there was something they'd missed? That's it. The police believe she kicked her footwear off in the water. But if she'd been hiking, or even walking by the reservoir, she would have been wearing boots." He peered at John's face, his eyes screwed tight behind his glasses, as though willing him to understand. "Or stout shoes, at the very least. Don't you see? Nobody wears those kinds of shoes without socks. It just isn't done. The only kind of shoe a woman would wear without socks or stockings is one with a heel! And who in their right mind would voluntarily walk across the moors in heels?"

It was a good point. Even in his current state, John had to admit that. He wasn't convinced it was one that justified being roused from what he feared might turn out to be his death bed, though.

"So, she didn't walk across the damned moors," he said, and winced at his own sharp tone. Regardless of his possibly imminent expiration, there was no excuse for rudeness. "Perhaps she drove?" he continued, more gently.

"But she had to come across the moors," Edward countered, becoming more animated as he paced around the small room. "Look, I'll show you."

From the pocket of his dressing gown – only now did John notice that he was still in his pyjamas – he pulled out a map. That was reason enough to take him seriously, or to admit that Edward was taking things seriously, in any event. John had never seen the man anything other than fully dressed before. The removal of his jacket and tie was, for him, akin to indulging in the sybaritic rites of the Polynesian natives. To appear in the bedroom of one of his colleagues in carpet slippers and dressing gown was a sign of previously unimagined agitation.

Edward spread the map – one of the colourful ones of the village which sat in a plastic container at reception – on John's bed and traced a route with his finger. "You see? There's no road she could have taken that leads to the reservoir other than this one, the one we came up yesterday morning. And that was closed on the night she died, so the scenery chaps could leave their lorries and whatnot parked and ready for shooting."

John pulled the map closer and studied it for a second. He indicated a thinner, shorter line to the northwest of the town. "What about this one here, though?" he said, running his finger along its length to a small rectangle halfway between Ironbridge and the reservoir. In spite of himself, he was growing interested again. He peered down at the map key. "That's a B road, and it ends in a car park," he observed. "Perhaps she drove there, then decided to go for a moorland stroll?"

Edward shook his head emphatically. "I don't think so. See, there's a track marked as a scenic walk leading north from that car park. Why the devil would she ignore that and head west across the moors to the reservoir instead? No," he declared firmly. "She must have walked across that unmarked and muddy moorland in footwear entirely unfitted to the job, and I refuse to believe that was done voluntarily. Something's definitely not right here, John. I'm sure of it."

John had no doubt there were several perfectly good explanations, but in his current condition, he couldn't put his finger on one. In any case, even on their relatively short acquaintance, he'd come to know that tone of voice well enough to understand that Edward would not be swayed by anything so tiresome as mere argument.

Besides, it *was* odd.

So, he nodded and waved a hand towards the door. "Then why don't we both get dressed and take a trip up to the moor?" He smiled and winced a little as the pain in his head flared up. "After breakfast and a couple of aspirin, that is."

4

The morning was damp and cold, but Edward had woken up in an unexpectedly good mood. Generally, rising early left him irritable and ill-tempered, especially when, as now, he was involved in sub-par sitcom rubbish like *Floggit and Leggit*.

The reason for his good humour was obvious, of course. The previous night had been a waste of his time, it was true, and he wasn't even sure why he'd asked John to join him. But the second he had opened his eyes, the matter which had been on the tip of his tongue all evening had miraculously shifted itself to the front of his brain, where it sat, fully formed and ready for expression.

He'd been delighted to discover that his brain hadn't entirely atrophied after weeks of spouting the writers' gormless claptrap. He was a little concerned, however, that he'd allowed excitement to overtake him to such an extent that he'd crossed the landing to John's room without dressing, far less shaving.

It was a one off, though, not a sign of slipping standards. He finished his delayed shave, wiped his face and straightened his tie. He wasn't sure yet exactly what the missing socks and shoes signified, but as soon as they'd popped into his head, he'd felt a strange pressure in his chest, tight but not unpleasant. They signified *something* important, he was certain, and that was a starting point, at least.

So good was his mood, in fact, that when he made his way downstairs to the George Hotel dining room, he was barely put out by the absence of kippers on the breakfast menu.

"Are the sausages fresh?" he asked.

"Just arrived from the butcher, Mr. Lowe."

"Well, I suppose they'll have to do. If you could make sure to have kippers tomorrow, though. Proper kippers, mind. None of that boil-in-the bag muck." He wiggled his hand in mimicry of a kipper swimming upstream.

For once, they were quick to get his food out, and he was just about to tuck into the sausages, with bacon and mushrooms and two rounds of toast, when John walked in.

"John," he beckoned, waving a fork in his direction, then, to the little blonde girl taking the breakfast orders, said, "Mr. Le Breton will be joining me. He'll require cutlery."

"If that's not too much of a bother, my dear," John clarified, as he slipped into the seat opposite Edward. "And I'll just have toast and butter, and a coffee, when you've got a second."

It was a measure of Edward's current equanimity that he felt no annoyance when the girl beamed at John and bustled off to get his toast. *It took her ten minutes yesterday to find out whether the ham was on the bone*, he thought indignantly, but decided not to let that spoil his mood either.

"I've been thinking about the missing shoes," he said, as the girl reappeared at John's elbow and slid a mug of coffee in front of him. "We should trace her steps across the moor. Start at the car park and head straight for where I found the body." The bacon was more fatty than he liked and he pushed it to the side of his plate with a scowl. "I looked at the map before I came down, and it can't be more than a half-hour walk."

The girl was back again, John's toast in hand, and he took the opportunity to point out the failings of the bacon and request an extra sausage. He shook his head as he watched her wander off towards the kitchen. He'd have finished his breakfast by the time she came back, he was sure of it. But if *John* had asked… he gave a mental shrug. He would be the bigger man. Nothing could be allowed to derail this morning. Not when they had so interesting an expedition planned.

He'd always been fascinated by detectives, and policework in general. Since he was a boy, he'd been a keen student of famous cases. And when hostilities broke out in '39, he'd spent a short time working with the military police before he'd been transferred to radio work and shipped out to Egypt. He often wondered how his life would have turned out had he kept working with the MPs. Would he have even gone into acting? Perhaps he would have stayed on past demob. Perhaps he might even have ended as something higher than a sergeant?

He allowed himself a small smile. He didn't think a military career would have suited him, not really, but he would have liked to finish the War as an officer, rather than an NCO. Captain Lowe did have a ring to it.

"…boots with me, but Madge from wardrobe volunteered to look out wellington boots for the pair of us."

John had been speaking, he realised, but he'd been paying no attention. Luckily, his meaning was clear enough.

"Splendid!" he agreed, with enthusiasm. "We should collect them, and then borrow a car and drive to the car park."

John nodded. "Fine by me," he mumbled through a mouthful of toast. "Madge said she'd leave the boots at reception. Wonderful girl, that. Such an obliging nature. I might see if she fancies a drink one night." He pushed his plate to one side and lit a cigarette, with the faintest of smiles on his lips. "Though I have to ask – what are we hoping to achieve? Even if the poor woman was wearing heels, and even if they aren't at the bottom of the reservoir, and even if we find them," he went on, more seriously now, "it won't prove any, ah… *skulduggery* has taken place." He coughed as the smoke reached his lungs. "I bumped into David on the way downstairs, by the way, and the police have told him we can recommence shooting the day after tomorrow. They're satisfied it was a terrible accident. The inspector left first thing, apparently. Which does rather beg the question; would we not be better taking the word of the professionals, and leaving this be?"

Edward shook his head. "The police are far too ready to write this off, in my opinion," he declared with a grimace of annoyance. "Typical of the modern world, if you ask me. Everything's so rushed, nobody takes the time to do their jobs properly." He glared at the waitress as she bent over him and removed his plate. *Totally forgot about the replacement sausage*, he thought.

"More coffee, Mr. Le Breton?" she asked, pronouncing it "Le Britain", which gave Edward a momentary stab of pleasure.

The mispronunciation evidently didn't bother John, however. He simply shook his head. "No, thank you, Julie. It's so kind of you to ask, though. I don't know what I'd do without you. And do call me John. All my friends do."

She reddened and smiled at him, then, with a quick wipe of her cloth, flicked a few crumbs from the table to the floor. "Just shout if you change your mind," she said, and moved away towards the other guests.

"Sorry, Edward," John apologised as he lit yet another cigarette and settled further back into his chair. "You were saying?"

"I was saying that the police have been altogether too quick to dismiss this case," Edward replied testily. "If we find the missing shoes, that proves she crossed an area of open moorland in heels and that, for reasons unknown, she discarded those shoes at some point. And then, in bare feet, she didn't return to her car, but instead contrived to reach a fenced-off reservoir and, once there, fall into the water."

"Well, perhaps…" John's tone was doubtful. It was clear it wouldn't take much to quench whatever enthusiasm he had.

"There's no *perhaps* about it," Edward snapped. "Those are the facts of the case – or at least will be, if we find the shoes!"

He peered across at John doubtfully. His colleague's lack of drive was near legendary in the industry. The "Le" in Le Breton stood for Lethargy, a director had once apparently said, but presumably that had been on a day when the actor was feeling particularly energetic. In retrospect, he might have been better to have spoken to one of the more active members of their little group the previous night: Clive Briggs, say, or young Jimmy Rae. But it had been John who had stopped by his table, and so it was John whose spirits he must encourage.

To his credit, he accepted Edward's statement without further complaint. He stubbed out his cigarette and rose to his feet. "If you're so sure," he said, "then I'd best toddle along to reception and pick up our boots. While I'm doing that, why don't you rustle up some transport?"

He gave a little wave to the waitress and slouched off.

Edward untucked the napkin from his collar and considered how best to convince someone to loan him a car. Perhaps he should have asked John to arrange that too.

5

Edward brought the borrowed Vauxhall Viva to a halt next to an old-fashioned Vanguard and pulled hard on the handbrake. He peered out at the grey skies through the flecks of drizzle which spotted the windscreen. Perfect weather for a bracing walk across the moors.

Of course, they were here out of duty and not for pleasure, but he couldn't deny that his main motivation was curiosity. Even as a schoolboy back in Manchester, he'd had an inquisitive nature – nosiness, his teachers had called it, but there was more to it than that. He'd always wanted to know how things worked, always wanted to know the answers, always wanted to make sure things were done properly. And now he wanted to know: what really had happened up at the reservoir?

"Are you certain we need to go out in this deluge?"

The exaggerated dismay in John's voice was enough to jolt Edward from his thoughts and into action. He pushed open the car door and stepped out into the rain.

"Well, are you coming?" he asked, bending down to address his still-seated colleague. "A little bit of rain never killed anyone, you know."

John's brow furrowed in apparent pain, and he sighed, but he also stepped out of the car. "Perhaps not," he grumbled, "but it's never done me much good either." He pulled on his hat and glanced glumly around. "Is this where elderly cars come to die?"

Nobody would enter the car park into a Britain's Most Beautiful Parking Spots competition, Edward admitted to himself. What was once tarmacked road had been so eroded by years of rain that the surface now appeared to be composed of tiny black tarry pellets, which turned underfoot as he walked to its centre and looked around. There was a path on the other side of the parked Vanguard, with a weather-beaten wooden arrow pointing down it. He could just about make out the words *Scenic Route* painted on the arrow, but he could see nothing about the path that looked any more scenic than the landscape in the other directions.

There were three other cars parked as well as their own, but he could think of no way to tell which, if any, might have belonged to the dead woman.

He walked around to the Vanguard and cupped his hands against the glass, the better to see inside.

"What are you even looking for?" John asked.

"I'm not sure yet. Something that says it belongs to the deceased."

"Yes, I understand that, Edward. But what exactly says, 'shoeless corpse in a reservoir'?"

"Shoes and socks on the back seat, perhaps?" Edward replied, with what he hoped was enough acid to be unmissable. "No doubt there'll be others. Perhaps if you were to take a look in one of the other cars, something might suggest itself."

He turned away before John could complain any further.

Inside the Vanguard, all he could see against the brown fabric of the seats (he doubted it was leather) was a copy of the *Daily Mirror* (definitely not leather, then) and a crumpled packet of No.6 cigarettes. The ashtray was overflowing. It certainly didn't feel like a woman's vehicle. He glanced over to where John was peering through the windscreen of a Morris Minor.

"Anything?" he called across.

"I wouldn't have said so, no. Brochure sort of things on the passenger seat, and…" He strolled around to the other side. "…assorted tat in the back. Some kind of salesman's car," he said, ostentatiously wiping rainwater from his face. "Not what we're after, in any case."

Edward agreed, which left only one car to examine, a dirty green Austin Marina parked nearest to the wild moorland that spread out to the north of the car park. But there was nothing at all to be seen inside that. A spotlessly clean interior contrasted with the mud-spattered exterior.

"Could be a woman's," John offered. "Sally always kept our place neat as a pin. It wouldn't have crossed her mind to wash the car, though." He raised his eyebrows thoughtfully. "Nor mine, come to that. Our cars were always *quite* filthy. I remember one time…"

Whatever it was that he remembered, Edward wasn't interested. It was a good point, though. Give a woman somewhere to clean that another woman conceivably might see and they'd have it gleaming. But he'd never seen a woman take so much as a sponge to a car door.

Still, that wasn't proof. The police wouldn't be interested in that. What they needed were the missing shoes. And they could well be on the moor somewhere. He pointed in the direction of the as-yet-unseen reservoir.

"Right, then. No point in wasting any more time. Follow me!" he said, and strode towards the open moor.

It took only five minutes to make their first discovery. Annoyingly, it was John who made it.

"Would you mind popping over here for a moment, Edward?"

He was crouched above the gorse, fishing about in the thick undergrowth, while doing his best not to let his trousers come into contact with the damp ground. By the time Edward hurried back from his forward position, he was already straightening up.

"What have you found? Come on, man, out with it."

"A button."

He held out his hand, palm upwards. Nestled in the centre was a small, brown button, decorated on one side with what might once have been a flower.

"It was just lying in the gorse," John explained.

"Fallen off the woman's coat, perhaps." Edward couldn't for the life of him remember if there'd been any buttons missing from her jacket, but it had been open, hadn't it? Perhaps because a button had come off in a struggle?

"Or been ripped off as she fought for her life."

Really, there was something quite *European* about John at times. He took such relish in the macabre.

"Maybe," he allowed after a moment. "There could have been a struggle." He kicked at the dense plant life underfoot. "Not that you could ever tell in a place like this."

"Shall we go on, Edward?" John asked after a moment. "My feet are like ice, standing here."

"What? Yes, yes, of course." Edward dropped the button into his pocket and gestured for John to take the lead.

Ten minutes later, they found the shoe.

It lay at the base of a small rise, from the top of which it was possible, for the first time, to see the reservoir in the distance.

It was black and had a small heel, Edward was pleased to note. He examined it closely as John climbed the little hill to see if its partner was anywhere to be found.

"I wonder if she saw the lights when she got to the top," he said as the taller man trotted back down the hill towards him, shaking his head. "She saw them and thought she might be safe there. Kicked her shoes off so she could run faster and get there quicker."

It was a melancholy thought, given what had actually happened, and when John asked, "What was that, Edward? I didn't catch it," he didn't repeat it.

"Nothing," he said. "Just idle speculation. No sign of the other one, then?" he asked, keen to change the subject.

"I'm afraid not. There's flat ground from here to the reservoir, too, so you'd think it would stand out if it were there."

That was a shame. A pair would have been far more conclusive. Still, they had come looking for a shoe and they had found a shoe. What were the chances of random footwear turning up in the very place they looked, unless it belonged to the dead woman who was missing them? He said as much to John.

"It's possible," John agreed after a second, but there was still a hint of doubt in his voice. "And if it is her shoe, then you were certainly right. She wasn't hiking." He frowned. "The question is, what to do now?"

"That's obvious, surely."

"Yes, I suppose it is." John scratched at his chin. "Will Constable Primrose be at the station, do you think?"

Edward shook his head firmly. "No, not Primrose. He's a decent lad, but no more suited to a murder investigation than Donald Roberts would be. No, what we want is to go straight to the top. That inspector left his number with reception at the hotel. We can phone him from there."

The look on John's face did not betoken great enthusiasm, Edward thought. But, before he could interject anything too dispiriting, he turned quickly and headed back to the car park. Better to assume agreement, he considered, rather than risk dissent.

* * *

To Edward's fury, the girl at reception proved too idiotic to understand the importance of their discovery.

"So, you found a shoe on the moor? Just the one?" She flicked a stray lock of blonde hair out of her eyes and glanced doubtfully between the two men. "What kind of shoe? Is it in there?" She reached across the desk towards the cloth bag Edward had left there. But, before she could lay a hand on it, he whipped it away.

"That is none of your business, young lady!"

He ignored the receptionist's indignant snort as he bent down to place the bag at his feet – well, what could you expect of a girl who coloured her hair? – and rose slowly, arranging his face into as amicable an expression as he could manage. Immediately, he realised he needn't have bothered.

"If you could just slip us his telephone number, that would be utterly delightful of you."

John was positively simpering as he leaned over the reception desk and let one of his long, pale fingers brush against the girl's hand. "If you could just pop that over, we... *I*... would be terribly grateful."

Edward was reminded of French gigolos plying their murky trade in Paris after the War, but said nothing. They'd slithered around the British nurses like garlic-scented snakes, leaving courteous young men like himself without so much as a look-in.

Even so, there was no denying the effectiveness of the tactic. The girl bobbed her head and fluttered her eyelashes, then pulled a scrap of paper from beneath the desk. She pushed it across to John, with a sly grin. "Only because it's you…" she said, glaring briefly at Edward, before turning the full force of her smile back onto the other man again.

For a second, Edward thought John was going to kiss her hand, but instead he squeezed her fingers and mouthed something which, though he could not be certain, could well have been "you're such a sweetheart". Whatever it was, the girl giggled like an imbecilic child and turned a shade of beetroot-red that merely highlighted her poor complexion.

Did the man have no sense of priorities? Surely he knew they had no time for this sort of foolishness?

"If you're quite finished?" he hissed and picked up the bag in a pointed manner. "We can use the telephone in the television room." He leaned closer. "Away from flapping ears," he whispered, glancing at the receptionist.

She caught his eye and sniffed disdainfully. "I've got no interest in whatever it is you need to confess to the police, I'm sure," she said. "And you need to use the other phone, anyway. The one in reception is for staff only." She picked up a pile of blank hotel notepaper and tapped it on the table to straighten it. "If there's anything else *you* need me for, though, Mr. Le Breton, just you let me know." She flashed him a final smile, then picked up a paperback book from beneath the desk and began to read, her time with the two men obviously at an end.

Edward glowered at her, but if she was aware of his ire, she gave no sign. He'd be having words with Bobby and David about her, but for now he had other, more important, things to be getting on with.

With a nod towards John, he led the way to the television room.

It was not a popular spot with the cast, even though it contained the hotel's only television set. For one thing, it was dingy, dusty and smelled strongly of incontinent cats. The chairs were elderly and uncomfortable, and the windows sufficiently loose-fitting that no seat was safe from a persistent draught. More crucially, apart from Jimmy Rae, none of the cast were of an age where the sight of themselves on the small screen was designed to thrill. Better to do the work, take the cheque and leave others to actually watch the results.

It was, therefore, often empty. To Edward's relief, it was so now. If pressed, he couldn't have explained why, but he had the unshakable sense that their discovery was best kept secret, and the last thing he wanted was an audience for his telephone call to the inspector.

In the event, he needn't have worried. The number the inspector had left, far from being a direct line, merely took him to a switchboard, and a woman on the line who was only marginally more helpful than the little blonde on reception.

"You're through to Ashworth Station. We are here to help however we can. How can we be of assistance?" she said, in a bored monotone that gave the lie to the words she had just spoken.

"Hello, my name is Edward Lowe. I'm phoning from Ironbridge regarding…" He paused, considered for a second. "…a recent case. Can I speak to Inspector—" He cupped the receiver in his hand and turned to John. "Actually, what was his name?"

"Ewart, I think. Or possibly MacDonald. Something Scotch, anyway."

Fortunately, the voice on the phone hadn't waited for a name. "Ironbridge, was it? I'll just check if Inspector Ewing is available," it said, and Edward heard the sound of a receiver being placed on a desk, and the voice shouting something muffled and incomprehensible. Moments later, it spoke again.

"Sorry, the inspector is busy just now. Can I take a message?"

It wasn't ideal. But a woman had been murdered; he was increasingly sure of it. Now was not the time to stand on ceremony.

"We have found a shoe," he said, realising how foolish he sounded even as he said it, but by then it was too late to take the words back.

"A shoe?" The voice at the other end of the line made no effort to disguise its lack of interest.

"And a button," he added weakly, as John coughed a warning at his side.

"A shoe and a button?"

"Yes, the woman wasn't wearing any shoes, you see, and—"

The voice interrupted smoothly, and the sound of dismissal was unmistakable this time. "Well, I'll be sure to pass that on to Inspector Ewing. In the meantime, he says can you address any further enquiries to the local constabulary? Thank you. Goodbye."

Before Edward could say another word, the line had gone dead. He stared at the receiver in his hand, refusing to believe that a discovery of this importance had been dismissed so quickly – and by a switchboard girl, at that. There was no denying it, though. He was not so foolish as to think that the voice on the other end of the line had misrepresented the inspector's level of interest in what he had to say. Clearly, he viewed Edward as a bumptious fool, in over his head, involving himself where he had no right to be, and with nothing of interest, far less importance, to contribute.

John was looking down at him curiously, one eyebrow arched in an overly theatrical manner. "Problems, Edward?" he asked.

"You could say that." His own voice was icily calm, he was pleased to note.

"The inspector's not interested in your shoe, I take it?"

"I didn't get to tell the inspector, as it happens."

"I did wonder."

Edward straightened his glasses carefully. "I think perhaps we should take our discovery to PC Primrose. Local knowledge is terribly important, after all."

6

Village bobby was the ideal occupation for Frank Primrose.

John had thought that the day they met, and nothing he had seen in the period since had caused him to change his mind. In many ways, he was like a character from a TV show, so well did he fit his role. John wasn't alone in thinking that, either.

"He's like a damned caricature," Joe Riley had said at the first day's shooting, rolling both his eyes and his Rs in his exaggerated Scottish fashion. Primrose had just contrived to knock the elderly actor's mug of tea all over his script. "An addle-brained, lanky length of string with a daft wee hat on top."

"That's a little unkind, don't you think?" Donald Roberts had protested, but only mildly. "I'm sure he never meant it." He blinked myopically before returning to his crossword, and John was reminded of Mole from *Wind in the Willows*.

The others had said nothing, but there was no denying the clumsy, cartoon-like qualities of the local forces of law and order. John had rarely seen a man who seemed so clearly to have been created with mockery in mind.

Perhaps if he would just admit defeat with the moustache, he thought, as he followed Edward into the station. There was no shame in it. Not everyone suited facial hair. He had grown a beard himself once, but Sally hadn't liked it at all, and had said it made him look piratical. He smiled at the memory, and the mental image of himself with a gold earring and an eye-patch.

"What are you grinning at? You look like you're about to have a stroke."

The sudden intrusion of Edward's peevish tones caused the image to burst like a soap bubble, and he forced himself to focus on the present and their current errand. *I bet he thinks of it as a mission*, John considered, and smiled again, then quickly composed his features along more serious lines before Edward could comment.

"Sorry, just remembering something somebody once said," he murmured.

He had never been inside a local police station before, but it was much as he'd imagined from the myriad sets on which he'd performed during his years in rep. A cork noticeboard nailed to the wall, complete with notices about a missing dog and an upcoming jumble sale. Two uncomfortable-looking wooden chairs directly beneath the noticeboard, and a long wooden counter with a hatch to one side that faced the entrance. Behind the counter was a closed door, with the words *Official Entry Only* etched in the frosted glass. A small silver bell sat beside the hatch, the only spark of colour in the entire dreary room.

Edward wasted no time. He strode across and firmly pressed down on the bell with the palm of his hand. John wanted to smile again, thinking of Sally and pirates, but then Edward pulled the shoe from the bag under his arm and placed it on the counter, and for all that it was probably nothing to do with the dead woman really, everything suddenly seemed less funny.

"Perhaps you should ring again," he suggested when Primrose failed to appear.

Edward did so, then rapped loudly with his knuckles on the counter. "Shop!" he shouted. "Shop!" He shuffled to one side and tried to see through the frosted-glass door. "He's got until I count to three, then I'm going in," he declared and pushed with his foot at the small door beneath the counter hatch. "One. Two. Thr—"

Bang!

The slam of the door closing behind them made both men jump.

"Sorry about that. It must have caught in the wind."

PC Primrose was eternally apologetic, it sometimes seemed. His face was wet from the drizzle outside, which made it look as though he'd been crying.

"Morning, Mr. Le Breton, Mr. Lowe," he added as he edged past the two men and slipped through the hatch. He pulled the end of his scarf out of his police jacket and wiped his face. When he spoke, it was in a nervous rush of self-justification.

"Is this about the dead lady? Cos I've not heard anything else. I did telephone to ask, but I just got a rude woman who told me to get back to catching boys scrumping apples."

He frowned unhappily and removed his helmet to scratch his head. The resemblance to Stan Laurel was unmissable, and John had to stifle another smile. Why did everything seem so funny today?

Edward, however, evidently saw no humour in the situation.

"I think I spoke to the same woman. I'll be having words with her superiors, I can assure you, Constable. But I didn't come here looking for an update from you. I came to give you one. From me."

He picked up the shoe and held it out, as though that explained everything he had to say.

Primrose peered blankly at it, but made no attempt to take it from him. "It's a shoe."

"Exactly!" The conviction in Edward's voice was as unmistakable as the confusion on Primrose's. "We found it up on the moors," he went on, as the constable's face grew blanker, if such a thing was possible. "We think it belongs to the dead woman."

"Just one shoe?"

"Just one for now, Constable. Mr. Le Breton and myself are keen as mustard to do what we can, but I'd be the first to admit we're not as young as we once were, and we're not the ideal candidates to search a wide area of moorland."

"A wide area…?"

"Of course! The button was found some distance from the shoe, after all!"

"The button?"

John would not have thought it possible for anyone to look as confused as Primrose did at that moment. But it just went to show there was always another level to which one could aspire, if pressed.

"Yes, the button!" Edward fumbled in his pocket and pulled out the little brown disc. "This button here." He placed it on the counter and waved at it as though it explained everything. "Possibly it was wrested from the unfortunate victim's coat in a struggle. Or perhaps it snagged on a tree or bush as she fled across the moor for her life." He cleared his throat and slid the button across to Primrose with one finger. "But that's for you to find out, of course. No doubt you chaps have tests you can do, catalogues you can check, that sort of thing. In the meantime, you'll need to arrange with your superiors to send a team up to the moor where we discovered these items and have them find the other shoe. And who knows what further clues you might find up there."

Primrose looked down at the button uncertainly. "Clues to what, Mr. Lowe?" he asked. "Because, before he left, Inspector Ewing said it was just an accident. There's nothing to find clues *for*."

"Nonsense." Edward was brusque. "No doubt the inspector is a solid enough fellow for the obvious sort of crimes you get in a big city, but exposure to that level of constant violence has left him blinkered to the more subtle signs of villainy." He tapped hard on the counter, the heel of the shoe in his hand leaving a square indentation in the wood. He muttered an apology and placed it carefully down. "Ask yourself this, Primrose. What sort of person goes hiking in heels?" He paused for barely a second. "Nobody. That's who."

"But what makes you think that's one of her heels, Mr. Lowe? Inspector Ewing said she had boots on and they were lost in the reservoir."

"The lack of socks, of course. Do try and keep up, Constable."

"Inspector Ewing also said that I wasn't to encourage civilian fantasy. Even if the civilians are off the telly."

Primrose's voice held a definite, if nervous, hint of defiance, thought John. *He's not as spineless as all that, then.*

"What Edward means," he interrupted, before the little man could react, "is that it seems unlikely the poor woman would have lost both boots and socks while she was in the water. He – *we* – thought it was more likely she was wearing something like that…" He indicated the solitary shoe. "… instead. And when we looked near where the body was found, we, ah, stumbled across this one."

Said aloud, it sounded rather slight, even foolish. What had he let Edward get him into? He shrugged apologetically. "It's got a heel, you see. So, no socks."

"We discovered it between the little car park near Byers Road and the reservoir," Edward clarified impatiently. "It's inconceivable that any sensible woman would choose to go for a stroll across the countryside shod like that." His glasses had slipped down his nose as he spoke and he pushed them back up before concluding, "And if she wasn't walking in the countryside, how did she end up in the water? Answer me that, if you – or the inspector – can."

Primrose was a decent sort, and it was obvious to John that he had no desire to be rude. But it was equally plain that, for a village bobby, the views of an inspector outweighed those of an actor, even the star of a BBC comedy show.

Plus, there was no denying their story was thin. Really, it was hardly a story at all.

"Well," the gangly policeman said after a brief pause, "that's an interesting theory, Mr. Lowe." He screwed his face up in a peculiar manner, and for a moment John wondered if he was in pain. But then he brought his hand up and stroked his thin moustache, and it was clear the policeman wished them to understand that he was deep in thought. "And so you want me to arrange a *search party*" – John could see him savouring the term – "to check the area around the Byers Road car park for another shoe like this one, because you think the dead lady walked from there to the reservoir in high heels and lost them somewhere on the way."

He glanced between the two men.

"I really don't think I'll be allowed to do that, Mr. Lowe. Not with the cuts and whatnot. I wasn't even allowed to replace the stapler when I dropped it down the facilities." He held his arms out and shrugged. "And besides, even if you're right about the shoes, who's to say she didn't just have no idea what to wear to go walking? City folk are like that, you know. They think that the moors are the same as a park or something." He shook his head, plainly astonished by the foolishness of city dwellers. "I'll tell you what, though. I can go up myself on my bike this afternoon after I've had my sandwiches and take a look. But that's about all I can do."

John wondered what Edward had actually expected of Primrose. Whatever it was, the offer of a quick scout about after his lunch wasn't it, and the look on his face betrayed his undoubted disappointment.

"Well, if that's the only action you feel able to take, I suppose that'll have to do for now," he said with a scowl. "But it'll be on your head if a murderer goes unpunished because of your lack of foresight."

"A murderer? Who'd want to murder a woman on her holidays, halfway across the country from home, and where nobody even knows who she is?"

Edward was quick to spot the implication in Primrose's words. "Aha! So, you know where she comes from?"

"We do," Primrose replied, pride overcoming his earlier unwillingness to divulge information. "It was me who discovered it. A rucksack in her room at Mrs. Kay's B&B. There was a name tag sown on the inside, with an address too, in case it got lost."

"The inspector did mention how useful you'd been," Edward said, with a smile.

John wondered when that had been, because he hadn't mentioned it before.

"Burke was the name, wasn't it?"

Primrose looked pleased. "Did he say that? He didn't say that to me. He said I'd made a right mess of things, tipping the rucksack out like that."

"No, he said you'd been very helpful. He told me all about it, in fact. How you'd identified Mrs. Burke... now, what did he say her first name was again? Alice, wasn't it?"

"That's right," Primrose agreed. "Alice Burke. Wife of Peter Burke. Fourteen Hamilton Road, Blackburn."

"That's the one. Well remembered, Constable." Edward picked up the shoe and dropped it back into his bag. "We'll take this with us, I think, so as not to clutter up your station. And you will have that button checked?" He pulled back his shirt sleeve and made a show of checking his watch. "We must be on our way, actually. Scripts to memorise and costumes to be fitted, you know how it is."

Without waiting for a reply, he turned on his heel and strode towards the station door. John trailed after him, back out into the fitful rain.

Standing in the street, sheltered by the stone awning which stretched out from the station door, John lit a cigarette and gestured with it in Edward's direction.

"Well done, Edward," he chuckled. "Primrose may not be the sharpest knife in the toolbox, but still... well done." The wind gusted and drove the rain briefly into their sheltered alcove, so both men were forced to turn their collars up. "One thing, though," John continued from the depths of his overcoat. "What do you intend to do with the woman's address now you've got it?"

Edward stared up at him as if he had taken leave of his senses. "Why, go there and speak to her husband, of course. How else will we uncover who might have reason to kill her?"

It was another point at which he might have walked away, and so avoided everything which was to follow, but instead, John again found himself willingly wandering further in. It wasn't as though there was much chance the late Mrs. Burke *had* been murdered. Still, there wasn't anything else to do that promised half as much amusement.

"I suppose so," he said, though in reality he supposed nothing of the sort. "And it's only a couple of hours away. It might be quite jolly to pop off for a bit of a poke around."

Edward had hunched down so low in his coat that only his glasses were visible between his collar and hat, so it was difficult to be sure, but John suspected he was glaring in irritation when he replied, "A bit of a poke around? I hope it'll prove a little more focused than that."

"Oh, I've no doubt it will be, Edward. I'd expect nothing less with you in command."

John was sure Edward would have smiled inside his coat at that. Certainly, all hint of irritation left his voice. "Yes, well, that's good of you to say. One does one's best, of course, but even so…" He paused and considered for a moment, then stepped out into the rain. "In any case, why don't we head back to the hotel and pack a pair of overnight bags? If you could check on train times to Blackburn, I'll let David and Bobby know we'll be away for the day."

There was something endearing in the way Edward came to life when he was ordering people about, John thought. He'd heard it said that the character of George Wetherby had been based on him, and that was the reason he'd been offered the part. He had no idea if that was true, but there was definitely more than a bit of Wetherby in him.

7

It was the sense of entitlement that was most irritating, Edward decided. He peered over the top of *The Times* at John, who lay stretched across all four seats in the small carriage, with his own newspaper draped over his face, and wondered again whether to wake him.

The warmth he had felt towards the man after his kind words outside the police station had entirely dissipated by the time they boarded the train for Blackburn, rubbed away first by John leaving Edward to carry both of their bags onto the train and then by his request that Edward rustle up a cup of tea and a custard cream if the refreshment trolley should go by.

Born with a silver spoon in his mouth, that's his problem, Edward fumed to himself. *Prep school, public school, university, commission in the War, the lot. Never a day's struggle in his life. Straight into movies too, I shouldn't wonder. No apprenticeship in rep in Aldershot and Inverness for Mr. John Le Breton, I'll bet.*

That was *Floggit and Leggit*'s big joke after all. Edward Lowe, the northerner, as the self-educated and fussy antiques expert and shop owner, and the aristocratic southern gentleman John Le Breton as his underling, obeying orders and shifting the stock about, but always effortlessly superior in every other respect to his common little boss.

Almost too common, in fact. He'd heard the whispers; been told them direct to his face too, in fact. How the powers-that-be at the BBC had tried to blackball him for the role of Wetherby. *He's not one of us, is he?* they'd asked, knowing the answer full well. Too ITV, too *commercial* (he could hear them sneering the word).

And so he was, and proud of it. He'd been in some of the most popular shows on television, after all. He'd been in *Coronation Street* and *Emergency Ward 10*. He'd been on the front of the *TV Times*! Just one side of his face in the background of a Corrie cast photograph, admittedly, but that was more than most people could claim. How many other actors could say they'd done as much? Could John? Never mind the fact that he'd appeared in plenty of stuff on ITV himself; he'd even popped up in the same shows as Edward more than once. Still, nobody had said that *he* wasn't good enough for the BBC. Nobody had suggested he wasn't *one of us*.

John had been a captain in the War, apparently, and that still counted for something, even now, a quarter of a century later. Edward himself had never risen to officer rank, of course. He hadn't been to the right schools. But sergeant had been good enough for him. That was where the real authority lay, after all. He smiled, in spite of himself. Maybe there was more than one layer to the joke, after all, he decided, contemplating his sleeping companion.

And it *had* been decent of John to praise his leadership qualities. That couldn't have been easy. Let him sleep on, he decided and settled back into his seat.

The Times was full of Idi Amin, the troubles in Ireland and the apparently never-ending strikes, which were growing more widespread by the day. He sometimes wondered what was happening to the country. Britain had once stood for doing what was right, regardless of the consequences, but nowadays it seemed that everyone was out for himself, and never mind his neighbour. *Twenty-two Arrested as Police Charge Wharf Picket*, he read, and shook his head. They'd end up with that bloody Harold Wilson in charge again, if they weren't careful.

He put the newspaper aside with an irritated grunt. His time would be better spent summarising what they knew about the case so far. He was convinced that Alice Burke had been murdered, even if he couldn't prove it yet. But the conviction was enough. He'd always been that way. Once he was sure something was right, he would fight for it like a terrier, and would not be swayed, no matter the opposition. Never give up, that was the thing. And if some people chose to view that as obstinate or bloody-minded (he'd been called both at one time or other), well, that was their problem, not his.

Besides, they had the shoe, even if Primrose's reaction had suggested it failed, in itself, to carry sufficient weight to convince the authorities of foul play.

Still, he had said they would find a shoe, and find a shoe they had. That meant he was on the right track, he was sure of it.

"And that track leads to Blackburn," he muttered, then quickly glanced across at John, hoping he hadn't heard him speak. It wouldn't do at all to have people thinking one was in the habit of talking to oneself.

Luckily, the other man gave no sign of waking. The newspaper over his face moved slightly but rhythmically as he breathed, but beyond that he was completely still.

Edward had bought a notebook at the station of the sort used by journalists, with plastic rings at the top and pages which flipped up and over. He opened it now and wrote *Alice Burke (Mrs.)* on the first line and then, beneath that, a physical description of the dead woman and of the shoe. That done, he tapped the pen against his teeth and looked out of the window.

So, what do we hope to find in Blackburn? he considered, silently this time. A suspect would be the ideal, of course. Some known enemy, who had sworn bloody vengeance on Mrs. Burke.

Unlikely, of course. But some indication of what had brought her so far from home was surely not too much to ask? After all, if there was one thing the shoe did prove, it was that she was no hiker.

He looked down at the notebook again and wrote *Not a hiker* on the page then, after a second's thought, added *A button (possibly lost in a struggle?)* beneath it. Then, when nothing else came to mind, he stared out at the passing countryside as it sped by and felt his eyes lose focus as the steady rhythm of the train lulled him into a light doze. He dreamed of dead eyes staring at him through the window and woke with a start, just as the train gave a jerk and began to slow. Were they at Blackburn already?

Edward pressed his face against the glass and peered down the track. Sure enough, there was a station coming up. He reached across and pulled the newspaper from John's face.

"Up you get," he said, shaking him by the shoulder. "This is our station."

He slipped the notebook into his jacket pocket and pulled down his case. Alice Burke had been murdered, and he was going to find her killer.

It was years since he'd been in Blackburn, and the railway station had shrunk since its heyday just after the War. Still, it remained a decent size, and there was a taxi rank right outside.

"Shall we pop in somewhere for a spot of lunch and a drink, do you think?" John asked as soon as he was settled in the back of the cab. "I must admit the train journey has left me quite parched. I always find travelling so fatiguing."

Edward said nothing, only leaned forward and gestured to the driver. "We'll be going to Hamilton Road."

He turned back to John. "Best if we strike while the iron's hot, I think. It's a quarter to twelve now, so we should just about have time to speak to Mr. Burke and then stop for lunch after."

"Do you think that's really necessary?" John groaned. "Wouldn't it make more sense to get a bite to eat first, then go and see Mr. Burke? The pubs close at two, and he's not going anywhere, presumably." He smiled suddenly. "Actually, isn't he most likely to be at work just now?"

It was clear from the way he said it that he thought this should clinch the argument, but Edward had half-expected something of the sort and had prepared in advance.

"As it happens, he's off work just now. Hurt his back, I believe." He smiled in return. "I phoned earlier and said we'd be on the 11.45 train, and that'd we'd meet him at his house at midday."

"Did you now? That was frightfully industrious of you, Edward."

There had once been a time when "industrious" and Blackburn had been synonymous, Edward thought, suddenly gloomy, but the abandoned mills along the railway line, all broken glass and rusted metal, made it plain this was no longer the case.

The streets he could see through the taxi windows hadn't changed much since his rep days, though; he doubted they'd changed much in the last century. Row upon row of identical red-brick terraces that reminded him of his childhood, and dirty, grey streets full of dusty little shops.

"How long until we get there, driver?" he asked, keen to get on with things and regain the positivity he'd felt earlier.

"Won't be too long," the driver said. "Five minutes, maybe. Depends on the traffic. But don't you worry, I'll get you there quick as I can, Mr. Lowe," he concluded, with a grin of recognition. "You making a new TV show up here, are you?"

"I stayed there a couple of times," Edward said to John, pointedly ignoring the driver and indicating a squat building at the bottom of the hill onto which they had just turned. "The Carlton, it's called, or was then. When I was touring, that was the place to stay if you were in the business. The whole street around the corner used to be full of very nice motor cars, parked there by acts playing the Cavendish, in town." He laughed, short and sharp. "Not that I ever had a car. It was just a short walk from the train, and a chance to rub shoulders with the stars." He laughed again, thinking of the sort of people he had once considered stars, and the laugh morphed into an extended and painful coughing fit. A smoker's laugh, his doctor called it. "Clodagh Rogers was about as big a name as I saw, though," he concluded, once he'd got his breath back and could speak again. "I said hello, and she told me to bugger off."

He was pleased that John simply chuckled in acknowledgement and made no attempt to trump the story with one of his own. If there was one thing he couldn't abide, it was actors who felt obliged to put on a performance all the time. Do the job and go home, that was his motto. It was a relief to discover that John felt no compulsion to always be on show. Though he never really seemed to act, either. In character or out, on set or in the street, it was always the same performance. John Le Breton every time, only in a different jacket and tie. He reached for his cigarettes and turned back to the window. He had no idea what he intended to say to the grieving Mr. Burke, and he would need the whole five minutes to think of something.

In the event, it was a good fifteen minutes before the two men found themselves standing outside 14 Hamilton Road, with the driver's loud promise to wait for them ringing in their ears.

Now it came to the sticking point, Edward was far more sanguine about the approach he would take. It was always like this; in the half hour before the curtain went up, his stomach churned and tumbled as he convinced himself that today would be the day he made an utter fool of himself. And then, when the moment arrived and he was about to take that first step forward, whatever had been bothering him faded away and he became completely calm.

So it was now. He would offer his condolences, explain that he had found Mrs. Burke's body, and say he had come to pay his respects. Whatever happened after that would take care of itself.

He knocked on the front door.

The man who answered was best described as "gone to seed", with slickly greasy brown hair that reached down to the collar of his shirt at the back and joined up with a heavy, tangled beard to the front. A faint whiff of stale alcohol wafted towards them as air was blown out of the house in their direction. The man peered at Edward and John for a moment, then pushed the door a little more closed.

"I'm not interested in saving my soul, or contributing to the Sally Army," he said, and stepped back into the house, obviously about to shut the door completely.

Without conscious thought, Edward took two steps forward and placed his hand on the closing door. "We're not affiliated with any religious body," he announced firmly. "I telephoned earlier to say we were coming? My name's Lowe. My colleague and I are assisting the police with their enquiries into the death of your wife, Alice Burke."

Where had that come from? He'd heard it said in a hundred variants in a hundred productions, of course, from *The Avengers* to *Z-Cars*, but he'd had no intention of saying anything of the sort himself. He could feel John's mocking smile even without looking.

Still, whatever the reason, it had the desired effect.

"Oh aye, right enough," Mr. Burke said, and slowly reopened the door. "You'd better come in then."

The two men followed him inside, along a short hallway and into an untidy sitting room, where their host cleared piles of books and newspapers from two armchairs and gestured for them to sit.

"Excuse the mess. When the muse is upon me, I tend to forget to clean up. I'd offer you a drink," he said, indicating a selection of bottles on top of a nearby sideboard, "but it's a bit early, I suppose." He paused – in hope of disagreement Edward thought – and only when none was forthcoming did he sit down opposite them.

"I'm not sure what I can tell you, though. Like I told the constable that came round the other day, I don't see Alice as much as I once did."

That was a surprise. "You and she are no longer together?"

"No, though not by my doing. We got divorced years ago. Tell you the truth, we were only married for eighteen months all told, and she was back home for a year of that." He frowned and sniffed.

He couldn't be sure, but Edward thought he might even be blinking away tears.

"We were just children, caught up in the thrill of a forbidden love affair and a secret elopement."

"My goodness, that does sound a frightfully dramatic story. Did you abscond in the dead of night, with a ladder at the lady's bedroom window?"

Trust John. Not a word of help to get in the door, Edward thought with a scowl, but as soon as something with the smack of sex comes up, there he is, derailing the enquiry with his prurient questions. Before Burke could respond in kind, Edward intervened and steered the conversation back to more important matters.

"You haven't kept in touch, yet she still used her married name, and still had this address stitched into her rucksack? Isn't that a trifle odd?"

"Not really. I bought her that rucksack on the day we ran off together, with her new name and address already stitched in place. She thought it was romantic." He smiled weakly. "Plus, it was a good-quality rucksack. Alice always hated waste."

He picked up a glass from the floor and rose to his feet. "If you're sure you'll not join me?" he asked, already pouring himself a large whisky. "It must be five somewhere, as my old dad used to say."

He drained the glass and poured himself another, then resumed his seat with the bottle in his hand. "But I told the constable about the rucksack already. And he said Alice's death was an accident, and that I'd hear no more about it." He leaned forward in his seat. "So what brings two detectives to my door?"

Edward had decided from the off that there was no dishonesty in claiming to be assisting the authorities – after all, the fact the police weren't aware they were being assisted didn't mean that they weren't – but he could not in good conscience allow either of them to be described as detectives.

"Aha," he coughed, "I think there may have been a misunderstanding. We're not detectives, not in the formal sense. In fact, the main reason we're here is that it was I who found your wife's – your *ex*-wife's, I should say – body. I simply wished to come and pay my respects, and my friend here was good enough to accompany me."

Burke squinted at him suspiciously. "But you said you were with the police."

"Not *with* the police. *Assisting* them, I believe I said. With some enquiries relating to Mrs. Burke's death."

"Why?"

"Why what?"

"Why are you assisting them? And why are there further enquiries, come to that? Like I said, the constable who came round said that Alice drowned in some kind of accident and that was all there was to it. Isn't that right then? Are you saying there's more to it than that?" He waved the whisky bottle in Edward's direction, suddenly aggressive, in the way that drinkers of cheap spirits could be. "Just who are you, exactly?"

Flummoxed by the flurry of awkward questions, Edward could feel the situation slipping away from him. He was grateful, therefore, when John took up the conversational baton.

"Mr. Burke… Peter. May I call you Peter? It just sounds so much more friendly, don't you think? Peter… the thing is, we believe that the authorities have been a trifle *premature* in declaring that your ex-wife's death was accidental. We did want to come and pay our respects, of course, but we also thought we might check a few bits and pieces while we were here."

"Kill two birds with one stone, as it were," Edward interrupted, then winced as he heard his own words. "In any case, we wondered if Mrs. Burke might have had any enemies? Anyone who might have wished to do her harm?"

Burke shook his head angrily. "Not that would want to kill her. Of course not." He smiled. "Alice could be stubborn, and she was never shy to speak her mind, but she had no enemies I knew of."

"So, nobody who bore her ill will?"

"I said so, didn't I?"

"Quite." Edward's tone was conciliatory, but he wasn't sure the other man even heard him.

"She was a bloody good woman," Burke went on with a catch in his throat, as he poured himself a third large whisky. "She was the love of my life, you know." His eyes were filled with water, but Edward doubted there was any genuine emotion involved. He'd seen the same rheumy, bloodshot eyes on enough old actors to know a heavy drinker when he saw one. Sentimentality and a love of melodrama was almost as addictive as whisky to both drunks and artists. A combination of the two could be deadly.

"I won't have you have coming here, insinuating people didn't like her!" Burke barked, thrusting his empty glass in Edward's direction. "She was an angel!"

It took all Edward's self-control not to flinch, but even though he remained calm and held Burke's eye, Edward knew they would get no more out of the man. It appeared the investigation had ended before it had properly begun.

"Tony Coe!"

This time Edward did jump. He shifted in his seat and glared at John, who stood by the window holding out a long-playing record that he had, presumably, plucked from the record rack by his side.

"What a delightful player he is, don't you think? So expressive. I saw him perform with Tubby Hayes in, oh, '57 or '58. Even in that company, you could spot the class." He flipped the record over and examined the back cover. "You a bebop man, Peter?"

Edward had no idea who the unkindly named Tubby Hayes might be, far less what bebop entailed, but Burke obviously did. He shuffled across to John and took the record from his hand. "Oh yes," he said. "I've followed him since his army days. This isn't his best work, of course, but I suppose he had to record whatever was popular." He reached down and pulled another record from the rack and handed it to John.

It was clear what John was doing, of course. Engage the man on a topic of mutual interest and build a relationship based on common ground. It was textbook stuff, and Edward was annoyed he hadn't thought to do the same. Though what he might have in common with a slovenly drunk, he really couldn't say.

While the two men discussed jazz musicians, he took the opportunity to look around the room. He had noticed the general untidiness and air of bachelor living straight away, but now he took a closer look, he could see it went far beyond that.

Everywhere Edward looked, he could see signs of neglect. Plates covered in scraps of rotten food and cups furred with mould dotted the floor, with, here and there, a filthy glass half full of murky liquid. There were books and newspapers on every free surface, piled high in precarious towers against walls and on tables, or stuffed into the long French dresser that took up one wall. No television, Edward noted, with a combination of surprise and approval.

"The divorce must have caused you great pain." John's voice rose a little as he asked the question, and Edward turned his attention back to the conversation.

"We never stood a chance, John," Burke replied. "She was to be my Beatrice, and I was going to write great poetry for her. But that swine of a father of hers wouldn't have it. Wouldn't have *me*; that's the truth of it. He wanted her to marry someone who'd come into the business. He wanted a pencil-pusher for a son-in-law, not a poet."

Tears were rolling slowly in fat drops down his face now. He slopped the last of the whisky into his glass and repeated, "We never stood a chance."

"Is her father a local man?" John asked, pulling a handkerchief from his pocket. "I assume the police have let him know about his daughter?"

Burke took the handkerchief and wiped his eyes. "I imagine so. When I told the constable we were divorced, he asked who her next of kin was now, and I told him. Go and see Lowell Edwardsson, I said. See if you can pull his attention away from his ledger books and accounts."

And like that, suddenly, in the interval between one second and the next, the world around Edward shimmered and shifted.

One moment, John was tapping a finger against his top lip, listening to Burke speaking. The handkerchief was knotted in one of Burke's fists, the empty glass in the other. A clock was ticking somewhere in the room and the sun had come out, though its weak light was struggling to penetrate the dirty window on the far wall.

The next moment, separated from the first only by the name *Lowell Edwardsson*, was thirty years previously and relocated to a wooden hut on an army camp outside Aldershot, early in the War. A much younger Edward was seated at a desk, leafing disinterestedly through a pile of papers, reports of infractions committed by soldiers across the country the previous evening. A name caught his eye:

Lowell Edwardsson. A name almost the reverse of his own; otherwise he'd never have noticed it amongst the dozens of malefactors that day. Edwardsson was a young private accused of involvement in an unexplained death. Across the decades, Edward could smell the fresh paint that seemed always to inhabit that office, could hear the clock ticking on the wall and the rain thudding on the window, but could recall nothing else about the case. A dead woman... He closed his eyes and willed the two clocks, the one in Burke's sitting room now and the one in the army office then, to come together. For a long moment it seemed impossible, and all he could see was the backs of his eyelids.

Then the ticks locked in step and, for an instant, he could clearly see the documents laid out on the desk, and the file photographs of the accused man and of the dead woman. His face was that of one more young man in uniform, indistinguishable from a thousand others. Her eyes were lifeless but open, her body lying sprawled on some sort of muddy embankment. "I don't believe it," he said in wonder. "Lowell Edwardsson."

"What's that, Edward?" John asked. He handed the record he was holding to Burke. "You don't know the man, do you?"

"Of course not," Edward replied hurriedly. "It's just the coincidence of the name. It's so similar to mine. Lowell Edwardsson. Edward Lowe."

Burke seemed puzzled and on the verge of speaking, but John smiled and eyed him curiously. "If our friend Peter here is to be believed, Mr. Edwardsson is not as affable a soul as you, however."

"He's a pompous, arrogant philistine," Burke nodded in furious agreement. "He only cares about money and that damned factory of his. He never cared a jot for Alice for herself, only what she could do for the firm."

But Edward was no longer listening. "Do you have an address for your father-in-law?" he asked. He checked his watch. "Will he be at his factory, do you think? Or will he be at home, on account of the tragedy?"

"He won't take time off work, not even for this. He'll be at the factory, mark my words."

"And where would that be?"

Burke shrugged. "I don't know the address, but you can't miss it. Head back towards the train station, cross the river and follow the old road towards Mill Hill. Edwardssons is along there. There's a great big sign on the side of the main building. You can't miss it," he repeated.

Edward rose to his feet and held out his hand. "Thank you for being so helpful, Mr. Burke," he said, already half-turned towards the door. "And condolences again on your sad loss."

"My pleasure," Burke slurred. "And when you see the old bastard, ask him how he felt about Alice leaving the bloody firm."

"Was she leaving?" Edward asked, turning back with renewed interest.

Burke attempted to tap the side of his nose, missed, and poked himself in the cheek. He tottered backwards and fell into his seat. "That's what I heard," he muttered indistinctly. "Setting up on her own, I heard. Ask him."

He closed his eyes and immediately began to snore.

Edward glanced across at John. "I wonder what that was all about?" he shrugged. "Perhaps we'll find out at the factory." He smiled thinly and opened the door. "Assuming the taxi driver can follow Mr. Burke's less-than-precise directions, that is."

8

The driver knew exactly how to get to Edwardssons.

"Told you I'd wait, Mr. Lowe, didn't I?" he said with a grin, as John pulled the taxi door closed behind him.

"You did have the meter turned off, I trust?" Edward asked suspiciously, and John remembered what Sally had once said of him. A man who knew the value of a shilling, she'd said, and though they'd not been working that long, he knew what she meant. Edward wasn't mean; he always stood his round at the bar, for example. But he wasn't one to waste money, either. Careful, he would say. Tight, others might call it.

Regardless, the driver had indeed switched off the meter and was plainly offended to be asked about it. "Don't you worry," he said, his good-natured grin replaced by a frown of displeasure. "I've never charged a penny more than was due." He flipped the meter back on and started the engine. "It's a half-hour drive to Edwardssons from here. It'll be another shilling. Is that alright with you?" he asked.

"Perfectly," Edward replied testily, and leaned forward to slide the little glass divider closed, ending the conversation.

"I can't abide it when staff are overly familiar," he muttered as he settled back in his seat. "Give them an inch and they'll take a mile – and then be straight on the telephone to the *News of the World* if there's any money to be made."

For his part, John was fond of taxi drivers, on the whole. Like chambermaids and barmen, they were good listeners and good talkers, and they crossed paths with lots of interesting people. John liked to chat and he liked to hear about other people's lives. On this occasion, however, he appreciated the need for privacy. There had been recognition in Edward's voice when he'd said the name Lowell Edwardsson, and John wanted to know more, without worrying if the driver was eavesdropping.

"So, why are we paying this chap a visit?" he asked. "His name obviously rang some kind of bell."

Edward nodded. "It did. At least, I think it did. It was during the War, when I was working for the military police, waiting for my travel papers to come through. It was mainly making cups of tea and doing the filing, but one of my jobs was to sort through the day's arrest records. One morning, there was a report about a soldier called Lowell Edwardsson, a private in some regiment or other, I forget which. He'd been accused of murdering a prostitute, I think, but I can't remember a damn thing else. There was a lot going on then, and if it hadn't been for the coincidence of the names, I wouldn't have remembered him at all." He stopped, glanced at the driver and lowered his voice. "The funny thing is, the only other thing I can remember is a photo of the murdered woman that was attached to the report. Her body was found frozen stiff the next morning, with her eyes wide open." He frowned, pulled a cigarette from the packet in his pocket and lit it. "Just like Alice Burke."

"My God!" John preferred to avoid blasphemy – a holdover from his childhood, he supposed, since he was considerably less averse to more Anglo-Saxon forms of cursing – but if anything deserved a call on the Almighty, this surely did. "You mean to say that he might have murdered his daughter as well?"

Edward stared at him as though he had lost his mind. "What? No, of course not. Englishmen don't go around slaughtering their children like Arabian Maharajahs, you know."

"Peter Burke did say that Alice was about to leave her father's firm," John insisted, but with little conviction.

"Even so. It's hardly cause for driving down to Shropshire to throw her into a reservoir, is it?"

John was quiet for a moment. He doubted Edward's reasoning would convince a jury, but that was true of everything he'd said about Alice Burke so far. To be frank, he was finding all this theorising quite dizzying, and increasingly unnerving.

"Well, it is a coincidence, that's all I mean," he said finally, winding the taxi window down half an inch and blowing smoke towards it. "I don't suppose there could be two Lowell Edwardssons?"

"That'd be even more of a coincidence, don't you think?"

Which was a fair point. At the same time, John had a sudden, unpleasant suspicion they were about to move into territory that would be best left unexplored. A day out playing detective was one thing; confronting a complete stranger about his dead daughter and a murdered prostitute was another thing entirely.

"Are we really working on the assumption that…" He paused and let the words trail off. Actually, what were they assuming? For that matter, why should they make any assumptions at all? Wasn't that the police's job?

It seemed Edward felt the same. "Let's not get ahead of ourselves," he said carefully. "Not at this early stage in the investigation." He leaned across and flicked his cigarette butt out of the window.

"Can't remember anything else from the report, can you?" John asked. "Nothing that might provide a stronger link between the cases? No mention of a reservoir, for instance?"

Edward shook his head. "Nothing at all. Though I do think I'd remember if there'd been a reservoir involved. I'll keep thinking, but it was a long time ago and during a very busy period of my life. Of everyone's lives. I may well not even have read the rest of the report."

"Well, keep at it, there's a good chap. I'm as happy as the next man to play Lord Peter Wimsey, but I have to say, I'm a little leery of interrogating a grieving father."

"I think *interrogate* is a bit of an exaggeration," Edward said, but mildly, then looked away.

John hoped he hadn't offended him, but he couldn't escape the feeling that things were getting out of hand. He lit another cigarette, and the two men passed the remainder of the journey in silence.

Edwardssons was large and sprawling, a noisy, dirty expanse of stained brick and grimy glass. Two elderly chimneys belched smoke above a squat, soot-coated factory building, and to the left of that, a collection of many windowed, more modern buildings spread out over an acre of cracked grey concrete.

"This is Edwardssons," said the taxi driver, as they turned into the small car park in front of the main entrance. "Will you be wanting me to wait again?"

Whether it was Edward questioning the status of the fare, or his closing the window between them, it was clear the driver hoped they would say no. He barely met John's eye as he handed over a ten-shilling note to cover the fare, and said nothing else, even when told to keep the change.

"No, thank you," Edward said, as he bustled out of the cab, "I don't think that'll be necessary."

John watched the taxi drive off with some regret. He still had reservations about their plan of action. True, the fact that Lowell Edwardsson's daughter had died in a manner at least reminiscent of that of a woman he himself had once been accused of killing was noteworthy (that thought prompted a further one, which John realised he should have considered before now – had Edwardsson actually been found guilty of the crime?), but did it justify harrying the man like this?

He wished, not for the last time, that he'd stayed in the hotel in Ironbridge. He could be pleasantly half-sozzled by now, sitting in front of the fire with a large drink and a book. Instead – he looked up and realised Edward was already almost at the door marked *Reception*, and hurried to catch up with him – he was about to involve himself in what was certain, at best, to be a frightfully awkward interview. And, he realised with a sudden horrified shudder, what if the man recognised them and knew they were actors? What sort of ghouls would they seem then?

Edward waited at the door for him, then held it open to let him go inside first, as though not trusting him to follow. As he squeezed past, he gave the little man a sour look, but Edward gave no sign he'd noticed it; he closed the door carefully behind himself, and strode towards a cubicle set in the wall, behind the glass of which John could see a uniformed guard hastily pulling on a peaked cap.

"Mornin'," the guard said as he emerged to greet the two men.

He was older than John would have expected from a security guard; in his mid-seventies at least, but tall and thin, with iron-grey hair and a bristling moustache. He straightened his cap and smoothed down the front of his blue uniform, pressing down particularly on a small row of medal ribbons on his left breast.

"Have you got an appointment, gen'lemen?"

His accent was so thick that John had difficulty understanding him, but it seemed Edward had no such trouble.

"Good morning, the name is Lowe, and no, we haven't got an appointment. But if you would be so good as to tell Mr. Edwardsson that we wish to speak to him regarding his daughter, I'd be obliged."

The guard's response required no translation. He scowled deeply. "Mr. Edwardsson's daughter died," he said. "Recent, like."

"I am aware of that," Edward went on, seemingly unperturbed. "In fact, that's why we need to speak to him."

"Ah don't think so." There was no mistaking the animosity in the guard's voice. "Last thing he needs right now is bloody journ'lists botherin' him."

He took a warning step forward and, as though engaged in a formal dance, John took one backwards. Edward, however, stood his ground. He glared at the guard for several seconds and John wondered if, for once, he was at a loss for words. Then he nodded firmly and turned his head in John's direction.

"Take this man's name, Sergeant Bullimore," he snapped.

Had Edward lost his mind? He'd always seemed fairly sensible – too sensible to be any real fun, in John's opinion – but even sensible people could go a bit doolally. He'd read about a man who woke up one morning convinced he was a duck – and he'd been a Church of Scotland minister. Even if Edward had gone a bit funny, though, this was probably not the time to bring it up. Better to go along with him for now.

"Certainly… eh… sir," he said, using a voice he'd once employed when playing an army chaplain in a little film for John Boulting. He knew it wasn't quite right, but it would have to do. He'd never played anyone in the other ranks, after all.

He approached the guard and guided him to one side. "I wonder, my dear chap, do you happen to have a pencil and a piece of paper I might borrow? I seem to have left mine at home, and I shall never remember your name for the captain if I don't write it down."

The guard had been in the middle of bringing his hand up, finger extended, to prod John in the chest, but now he let his hand drop.

"You army?" he said, his tone doubtful, but without aggression.

"Once," John replied truthfully. "Not for a while, though."

"Thought as much. Ye can tell an army man." He dropped his voice. "That yer officer?" he asked.

"In a manner of speaking. Sorry if he came across a little brusque. You know how they can be." John coughed softly and smiled, inviting the guard to agree with him.

"Aye, I do that. Ah was a sergeant meself, back in t'day. Had a few officers like that one."

John's laugh sounded entirely false to his own ears – *some actor you are*, he thought – but it was convincing enough to satisfy the guard.

"What's t'army want with Mr. Edwardsson then? He's a good man, and like ah said, he's mournin' his girl."

"Well, we're not in the army any longer. But we are providing some assistance to the police force in their investigations into Mrs. Burke's tragic demise, and we hoped to ask Mr. Edwardsson a couple of very general questions which will help with that." He smiled again. "Naturally, we'll be sure not to upset him."

The guard wrinkled his brow in thought as he picked through John's words, and glanced across at Edward again. Then he swivelled unsteadily on his heel and crossed back to his cubbyhole. When he re-emerged a minute later, he held a clipboard in his hand, a pen pushed through the metal clip at the top.

"Mr. Edwardsson says he'll speak to you," he said, handing the clipboard to John. "You'll need to sign the list first, though."

John signed for them both, and the guard looked down at the names without interest. "Come wi' me, then. The office is through by."

He led them past his cubicle and along a short corridor painted a fashionable beige and brown, at the end of which stood a glass-fronted door, with Edwardsson's name etched on it above the single word *Proprietor*.

He knocked on the door and then pushed it ajar. "In you go, then," he said and, bowing his head towards John, muttered, "Mind and go easy on him, Sergeant. He's taken the news right bad."

John nodded his understanding and murmured his thanks, then followed Edward inside.

9

Lowell Edwardsson was standing with his back to them, looking out of the long window that took up the entire right side of his office. As they entered, he turned and offered his hand in introduction.

Had John been asked to describe him in advance, he would not necessarily have pictured someone like the man who now stood before them. Of above average height and heavy built, he was unshaven, but with hair so neatly trimmed around his ears that John could tell that wasn't his usual state. The hair was short, turning to grey at the temples, and he had watery-brown eyes which observed them in obvious misery from behind large square spectacles.

"You'll be Lowe?" he said, and shook Edward's hand. "Which means you must be Bullimore," he went on, doing the same to John. His grip was weak for such a big man, and only briefly held. "Harry's good at descriptions." He shrugged listlessly and turned back to the window, a picture of suffering and sorrow.

"He said you've got questions about Alice?" he asked after a minute in which Edward and John stood awkwardly, unsure of how to proceed. He spoke over his shoulder, without looking at the two men, but there was so much pain in his voice as he said his daughter's name that John almost apologised and walked straight out of the room. Instead, he followed Edward's lead and pulled back one of the seats in front of the desk and sat down. Edwardsson turned around, but remained standing, a bank of heavy, dark clouds framing him in the window as though he were wearing them on his shoulders.

"Thank you for seeing us, Mr. Edwardsson. We'll try to take up as little of your time as possible, but we do indeed have some concerns about your daughter's death. To cut a long story short, we think it may not have been an accident." Edward's voice was dignified, quiet and filled with empathy, and John was reminded that his colleague was both a decent human being and an excellent actor. He was not here on an idle whim – at least, not in his own mind – and nor was he some uncaring monster, content to trample on another man's grief for his own entertainment. He genuinely believed Alice Burke had been murdered.

The effect of his words on Lowell Edwardsson was immediate and dramatic. He made a tiny choking sound in the back of his throat and his knees buckled. He collapsed forward as though he had forgotten how his legs worked and clutched at the desk for support.

John poured a glass of water from the jug on the desk and passed it across to him. They waited while he drained the glass with a shaking hand.

"Sorry," he gasped finally. "I don't usually get taken funny like that. It was a shock, that's all, what you said…"

He walked over to a cabinet by the window. He pulled open its two doors and gestured to the array of bottles inside.

"I need something stronger," he said. "Can I get you anything, or are you on duty?"

Edward shook his head, but John took a beer and sat with it in his hand as Edwardsson resumed his seat. He flipped open an onyx cigarette box and swivelled it around to face his two visitors.

"Help yourself," he said. "And call me Lowell. Nobody calls me Mr. Edwardsson."

Rather than doing so, Edward straightened in his seat, and John could tell he was eager to begin asking his questions. Under the desk, unseen by Edwardsson, he pressed a cautionary hand down on his friend's arm. *Let him get his breath back*, he tried to communicate. Edward seemed to understand. His shoulders relaxed and he reached into his jacket for his own cigarettes.

"I'll smoke my own, if you don't mind," he said. "I only ever smoke Craven A."

They smoked in silence until the cigarettes were done. Edwardsson was the first to speak. Plainly, the pause had given him the time he needed.

"You really think someone killed my Alice?" He sounded stronger, but there was still the tiniest wobble in his voice as he said her name.

"Yes, we do," Edward replied with certainty. "And we're hoping you can clear one or two things up for us." He paused for a second, then went on. "Can I ask, Mr. Edwardsson... ah, Lowell... was your daughter a vigorous girl? Keen on the outdoors and that sort of thing?"

Edwardsson frowned. "When she was little, she was," he said, after a moment's consideration. "She was real outdoors type when she was at school. She was one of the first girls to do that Duke of Edinburgh thing, you know." He smiled sadly at the memory. "She complained that the girls didn't get to do everything the boys did."

"Quite so," Edward said with a distracted air, clearly – and quite rudely, in John's opinion – not paying full attention to the reply. What could he be thinking about, staring out of the window at the car park?

Fortunately, Edwardsson was paying as little attention to him. "The other policeman said that Alice..." His voice trembled again as he spoke his daughter's name. "He said that she must have become disoriented and got lost. As if she couldn't walk across a bit of moor without getting turned around." He gestured at the window and the rolling hills beyond, indignant on his daughter's behalf. "We were hiking through those fells together since she was big enough to pull on a pair of boots."

"Ah! So, she would certainly know the appropriate footwear for walking across rough ground?" Edward asked, excitement creeping into his voice.

A look of confusion crossed Edwardsson's face. "Appropriate...? Aye, of course she would. I told you, she knew what she was doing. She'd no more get lost in the countryside than she would in the High Street!"

Edward was beaming at this apparent confirmation of one part of his theory, but John had read enough scripts to know that things were rarely so cut and dried, and never so early. There was always a twist or two. "A bottle of brandy was found at the scene, you know," he interrupted, before Edward could say anything else. "If she'd been drinking…"

"Brandy?" Edwardsson's laugh was harsh. "Not Alice. She didn't drink. I told that idiot of a constable that, but he took no notice. Just wanted to get the job done and get out of here."

So much for cut and dried. "She didn't drink at all?"

"Never touched a drop! I was a drinker when I were younger, you see. Got myself into a bit of trouble. When I married her mother, God rest her soul, she wouldn't have drink in the house, and she made sure Alice knew to stay away from the stuff." He grimaced, and John saw his fingers whiten around the glass he held. "Is some bugger saying she was drunk?"

Edwardsson's face flushed bright-red and a vein throbbed alarmingly in his forehead. John exchanged a quick glance with Edward; he had no desire to question the man any further. A swift escape from this room, and soup and a sandwich from the dining car on the train home, were the height of his ambitions at that moment.

Unfortunately, Edward appeared not to share those ambitions. "Not us," he assured Edwardsson hurriedly.

"But the police did mention it. We're simply passing on the information we were given."

"I thought you were the police? That's what you told Harry, wasn't it?" Far from placating the other man, Edward's slip served only to enrage Edwardsson further. He pushed himself up from his desk and slammed his fists down on top of it, causing a pile of papers to tip and slide in an avalanche to the floor. "Did that bloody fool not ask you for any identification? If you're journalists, I'm telling you now – one of you'll be reporting how the other one ended up in the hospital!"

He strode around the desk, fists clenched, as Edward and John scrambled to their feet. Give him his due, John thought, while considering how best to get to the door: as before, Edward stood his ground as a much larger man loomed threateningly over him.

"We told your guard no such thing," he said with unexpected authority. "The man's obviously completely incompetent. But if you sit back down, I'll be happy to explain." His voice was steady and firm with just a hint of righteous indignation. John recognised it as the one he used in the show whenever Joe Riley's councillor entered the antique shop, hell bent on blocking one of Wetherby's schemes. An all-purpose "how dare you challenge my authority!" tone that invariably got Wetherby nowhere.

Here, though, it was rather more effective. Edwardsson took a step back and stared for a moment at the two men, then slowly returned to the other side of the desk. He didn't sit down, but even so, John was reassured to have a large piece of heavy wooden furniture between them. Clearly, the man had a temper.

"Aye, well, Harry's getting on a bit. But he's been here almost as long as me." Though no longer actively aggressive, Edwardsson unmistakably remained suspicious of his uninvited guests. "But if you're not from the police, who exactly are you then?"

Again, John was impressed by Edward's air of unflustered calm. "We're based in Ironbridge, near the reservoir where your daughter's body was found," he said, as matter-of-fact as you like. "In fact, it was I who found her."

Grief was a funny thing, John thought suddenly. When they had walked through his office door, not five minutes previously, Edwardsson had seemed a broken man, barely able to stand or say his daughter's name out loud. Now, though, as if given fresh energy by the heat of his own anger, he stood straighter and taller, his eyes boring into Edward's, waiting for further explanation. The pain was still there but resignation had been transmuted into a resentful fury that was currently being held at bay solely by Edwardsson's curiosity. It would take only a single misplaced word to bring that fury back to the surface.

"Go on then," he said slowly. "I take it there's more to it than that."

Edward nodded. "There is." He explained about the missing shoes and the discovery of one of them on the moors. "Since the constable was happy to supply us with the name of your former son-in-law, we decided to pay him a visit. And he directed us to you," he went on. "I hesitate to mention it, but Mr. Burke seemed to think there'd been some recent disagreement between you and your daughter? A suggestion she was about to leave the firm?"

For an instant, John saw the anger flare up in Edwardsson's eyes, but then it was gone, and replaced with a cold disdain. "Peter Burke's a drunken waster, and the day he drinks himself to death, the world'll be a better place for it," he said, his voice flat and cold. "He was always pestering her, trying to get her back, even after all this time. As if she'd even look at him! But I can tell you now, the only disagreement between me and Alice was that she was more ambitious for the factory than I was myself."

He spread his arms wide, encompassing the office and, by implication, the factory beyond its walls.

"I won't deny that I work hard – since I lost Alice's mother, I've done not much else but work – nor that I expect those who work for me to work hard too. But I'm content with what I've built here. Edwardssons is a name people trust; nobody who buys from us goes away unhappy. I employ sixty men, and plenty of their fathers worked for me before them. That's enough for me. But Alice is young and she's got the education I never had. She's been to university, you know," he said with a proud smile that faded as quickly as it had appeared. "Anyway, she wants us to expand into other areas, away from souvenirs and that."

He reached beneath his desk. John heard a drawer slide open.

"This is what keeps this factory going year-round," he said, placing three small plastic objects in a neat row on his desk.

John picked up the nearest one, a silver plastic Blackpool Tower, and handed it to Edward, then politely looked over the others, little models of Big Ben and the Palace of Westminster.

"Not exciting, I grant you," Edwardsson admitted, "but steady sellers, twelve months a year, year in, year out. Throw in the Christmas market, and this is a solid business, one that turns a good profit. But Alice thought we could do better." His face fell, as though the muscles had collapsed all at once. "Now I'll never know if she was right."

Edward nodded. "Let's disregard Mr. Burke for now, then. Did Alice still live at home?"

Edwardsson shook his head. "No, she moved into a flat in town a couple of years ago. She was always an independent girl. She'd have gone earlier, but I'm a widower, so she stayed on, to keep an eye on me, like."

"Did you know she was going away this week?"

"I knew she was on holiday. Of course I did; she worked for me, as well as being my daughter. She told me last week she was going away for a few days."

"Did she know the area, do you know?" John asked.

"Not Ironbridge; not there specifically, no. I don't know why she went there. But I grew up in a little place called Bridgemere, just north of there, so maybe that was it."

"Really? I'm from Shrewsbury, myself, though I spent my childhood in Bury St. Edmunds." John smiled. "You've got even less of an accent than I do." It was true. If he'd had to guess, he'd have thought Edwardsson a Yorkshireman by birth.

"Lost the accent in the War," Edwardsson replied with a matching smile of his own. "The army'll do that to you, if it gets you young enough."

From the corner of his eye, he saw Edward stir with interest. With no real effort on their part, it seemed the conversation had naturally come around to the topic they were most interested in. John found that was often the way with conversations.

"That's actually something I hoped to talk to you about, Lowell," Edward said quickly, with an ingratiating smile. A bit too quickly, and a little too ingratiatingly, in John's opinion.

As he spoke, Edwardsson stiffened and cast a suspicious look at the little man. The awkward intrusion of his first name, for all he'd told them to use it, didn't help either. There was a knack to getting people to help you, a rhythm as important as that in a trumpet solo. Edward, for all his abilities on screen, just didn't have it.

"Was it now?" asked Edwardsson carefully, the brief spark of companionship John had fostered snuffed out before it could come to anything.

"If you don't mind, that is. I know the War was a long time ago, of course, and the particular incident I have in mind is one you've possibly tried to forget, but I think it might have significance."

Years previously, John had returned from the War to discover that Sally had graduated from heavy drinker to near-alcoholic while he'd been away. All his fault, of course. Sally had an artistic temperament, and he'd been called up within months of their wedding, and not returned for the best part of six years. It was hardly to be wondered that the poor girl had turned to the bottle in her loneliness. Anyway (he thought with a shudder) the look that crossed Edwardsson's face at that moment was the exact same as that which had disfigured Sally's pretty face whenever she'd been drinking, and it was obvious he knew. An unforgettable mix of guilt, embarrassment and anger at being exposed.

"I know what you're talking about."

There was real menace in Edwardsson's snarled response. He glared across the desk, perhaps deciding whether now was the moment to throw them out into the street. John nervously fiddled with the bottle he still held in his hand, and wondered if any of this was really a good alternative to sitting in his hotel room memorising the following day's scripts. The silence stretched uncomfortably on, and the tension increased.

Finally, Edwardsson appeared to come to a decision. "Sylvia Menzies," he said.

Edward nodded. "If that was the name of the woman you were accused of killing during the War, then yes, that's exactly who we want to talk about."

"You don't know?" Edwardsson was cautious, but not enough to stay silent. "Aye, that was her name. I was a young lad; she was an older woman who was interested in me. It was an exciting time, the War. Full of promise it was. You both must remember – away from home for the first time, a bit of money in your pocket, and the chances of getting killed remote enough that you never gave it much thought. Like a new world for a lad like me, who'd never been far from the little village he was born in.

"And Sylvia was part of that. We were stuck in a place called Balcon, in Cheshire, and Sylvia was a local girl. I say girl, but she was thirty if she was a day, and blowsy, if you know the type. She liked a drink and a dance, and wasn't shy about enjoying other things, if you get my drift. I was going on nineteen, but young for my age; I'd never seen the like before. Her old man was away somewhere, I forget where. Joined up probably, but I didn't ask, so long as he was out the picture. I met her at a dance at the base, something the brass had set up to let the locals know that having the army on their doorstep wasn't as bad as they imagined."

He laughed, a sharp, bitter laugh, with no humour in it. "That didn't work out like they hoped."

"She was married?" Edward asked with a frown. "And that made no difference to you?"

"Like I said, I didn't know where her man was, but she was definitely on her own. Had a kid, and a wedding ring on her finger, but I never heard the husband's name. Or if I did, I don't remember it. Never met the kid, either, but she let slip about him one night. She was raging about that, but it didn't bother me. It wasn't like I was intending to marry her or anything. I was doing my basic training and I reckoned I'd be in France in six months, and then back home by Christmas."

"How long did you know her, before…?"

"Before that night? A month, six weeks maybe. Not much longer than that. I used to meet her in the pub when I could, go back to hers sometimes, or just sit drinking with her and one of her pals, and some of the lads from the base."

"Some of the lads?"

Edwardsson snorted in derision. "You *really* don't know the details, do you? Aye, there was a group of us who hung about together. Mainly conscripts like me, but there were a couple of regulars too. We all tried to get off the base at the same time, head down to the pub, and meet up with Sylvia and any of her pals who were about.

"The night you want to know about, there were six of us, plus Sylvia and her best mate, Lorna. Ritchie, I think her name was, but she was divorced, so that could have been her maiden name. It was one of the lads' birthdays, and he'd had a postal order from home, so we had a bit more money – and a bit more to drink – than usual."

"You were drunk, then?"

"Pretty pie-eyed, most of us. We drank until last orders, then downed a couple of doubles apiece before we left and bought a few bottles to take with us. Little Henry Anderson could barely walk; me and Bert Smith had to half-carry him out the door. Probably the first time he'd ever been properly drunk, the poor sod. But none of us were exactly sober. That's likely why nobody objected when Sylvia said we should go for a drive and Bob noticed there was a jeep just sitting there in the pub car park, begging to be borrowed."

The description brought a smile to John's face. So far, it seemed a good night out and not too dissimilar to several he'd had himself, back then. He caught Edwardsson's eye and nodded encouragingly.

"Well, borrow it we did. The keys were still in the ignition and most of us piled into the back with the girls, while Bob drove and Bert, who knew the area, gave him directions. Ten minutes later, we were out in the country."

Edward shuffled in his seat and began to ask a question, but Edwardsson was lost in his story and not to be distracted. "A lot of us were from the same neck of the woods, roughly, brought up in the same little towns and villages, and it was like being home, sitting out there in an empty field under the stars, drinking and messing about. We left little Henry asleep in the car – he was a city boy, in any case – and spread a couple of coats out for the girls to sit on. It was a bit parky, with a real nip in the air, but with the booze and the excitement of being on a spree, well, you don't notice that sort of thing, do you? Not when you're young.

"We must have sat there for about an hour. By this time it was nearly midnight, and we knew we were all going to be for the high jump when we got back. So, I said it was time we made a move – a mate of mine was on guard duty that night, and if we were lucky, he'd let us sneak back in with nobody any the wiser. Leave it too late and we'd have to face the music in the morning. That didn't matter to Sylvia, though. I don't know who was watching the kid, but she was in no mood to go home, and she wasn't shy about saying so. Lorna had already passed out on the grass and we carried her to the jeep, but Sylvia was having none of it."

Edwardsson sipped at his drink, placed the glass on the table and ran his finger around its rim. "To be honest, thinking about heading back to camp had reminded everyone that we'd pinched a jeep, and that was enough to sober all of us a bit. I tried to tell Sylvia that, but she wasn't having it, and there was a bit of a row. The others were in the jeep by that point, but Sylvia and me were still by the fire, with me trying to convince her to get in or she'd be walking home, and her saying I was just a pathetic little boy who couldn't hold his booze. Which was true, right enough, but nobody wants that said in front of their mates. So I said to her, come now or stay here, but we're leaving anyway. And she slapped me a beauty across the face and stomped off into the darkness."

Edwardsson's attention was no longer on either of his guests. His voice grew quieter as he stared out the window, and his eyes closed as though he could no longer bear to see the world outside.

"Before I could go after her, Lorna was sick all over the jeep, and Bob started the engine and told us to hurry up and get in or we'd both have to walk back. I shouted after Sylvia, but it was pitch-dark once you got away from the fire, just big empty fields, and dirty great hedges, and she never let on. Everyone scattered and had a look, but after five minutes shouting her name, it was obvious she wasn't coming.

"So we jumped into the jeep and drove off, with Sylvia still sulking somewhere in those black fields. We dropped Lorna off in the street outside her house, dumped the jeep down an alleyway and walked back to camp. My mate was on the gate and let us in, and we all thought we'd gotten away with one."

He stopped and drained what was left of his drink. The glass made a quick double-tapping sound as he placed it back on the desk. "Next morning, we heard that Sylvia had been found dead in a ditch at the side of the road, five miles from town. She'd been walking along the road, they reckoned, and either sat down and fallen asleep then rolled into the ditch, or taken a tumble into it in the dark. Either way, she froze to death overnight."

The room had darkened while Edwardsson had been speaking. Heavy raindrops began to thump in an irregular beat against the office window. He sighed, a low, mournful sound that sent a shiver up John's spine.

"And that was that," he said. "We'd been seen leaving the pub together, and Lorna told the MPs we'd left Sylvia behind. Which was true enough, as far as it went, but it's not like anyone expected her to die. She was fine the last time I saw her. It wasn't my fault she didn't have the sense to come when she was called. I told the MPs that – hell, we all told the MPs that – but it made no difference."

"Was there a trial?" Edward asked. "A court martial?"

Edwardsson shook his head. "Not over Sylvia. The last thing the brass wanted was a load of squaddies in the papers for killing a local woman. Like I said, a couple of the boys were long-timers, and most of the rest of us were all but done with our training. Likely we'd have spent a while longer in England, but there was nothing stopping them shipping us out straight away. Within a couple of days they'd split us up, sent us to different camps around the country, and a week after that I was in India. I spent the rest of the War there, and the most dangerous thing I faced was a local tart with the clap."

It was on the tip of John's tongue to point out that he too had spent much of the War in India, but in spite of what he would be the first to admit was an almost pathological desire to be liked, he knew this was not the time.

"I must say, I'm surprised there wasn't an investigation, given the evidence against you," Edward said, with obvious disapproval. "Quite slipshod, don't you think?"

Edwardsson shrugged. "I don't know about that. It might have been better for all of us if we'd been court-martialled. We didn't kill her, did we? We'd have got a couple of months waiting for the trial, maybe a month in the glasshouse each for pinching the jeep then, like as not, sent back to do training over again when that was done. We might not have seen the War up close for years."

"You sound like you didn't have too bad a time of it," Edward snapped, causing John to wince as he waited for Edwardsson to take offence. Fortunately, it seemed the industrialist agreed with his guest.

"I did alright. It worked out good enough for me. But Matty Peel spent years in a Jap POW camp, and I heard a couple of the lads bought it in France."

"You've kept in touch with the others?"

"Not really. I used to get a Christmas card from Matty and a letter now and then, but not for years. It was him that told me young Henry and Bill ended up killed. I've no idea what happened to the rest. Could have died then or since, for all I know."

"Were you all charged? The report I saw only mentioned you."

"So you saw the report at least? Good for you, I was beginning to wonder if you knew a bloody thing about it. But, aye, we were all charged with theft of army property, conduct prejudicial and unauthorised absence. Only I was charged with negligence." He frowned. "But now I've answered your questions, maybe you can answer one of mine. What's this ancient history to do with the death of my lass?"

"I'd rather not go into details just now, Mr… eh, Lowell."

"Is that right? You'd *rather not*?" Edwardsson snarled, his patience evidently at an end. "You come in here and pretend you're police, but I let it go, because you say you know something about my Alice and how she died. Then you dredge up stories from thirty years ago and ask me why I didn't get done for murder. And now you think you can just say you've said enough and leave it at that?"

John's eyes were fixed on the whiteness of Edwardsson's knuckles where they gripped the desk. He wondered if it was too late to steer the conversation back around to their shared service in India, immediately decided that it was, and instead drained the dregs of the bottle of beer he held and slammed it more heavily than he intended onto the table.

Both men turned towards him and, with an effort, he curled his lip into his most hapless smile, the one he used whenever he hoped some kind laundry girl would perhaps do a spot of housekeeping for him.

"The thing is," he began, unsure what the thing actually was, even as he mentioned it, "the thing is we're not with the police in any way. Not even unofficially. In fact, they warned us at the very start not to get involved in this business at all. They actually told us explicitly to keep our noses out of it. So far as they're concerned, Alice is just another city girl who went wandering where she shouldn't with a beltful of booze in her and got herself killed. A damn shame, of course, but there you are. Bad things happen, but it's a straightforward case for them. Open and shut, they called it.

"Everyone except Edward, that is." He nodded at his companion, who was staring at him with understandable alarm. "Edward was the only one who thought it was fishy. He was the one who found Alice's body, and he spotted that she wasn't wearing boots when she should have been. It was Edward who calculated where Alice must have walked from, and Edward who found one of her missing shoes. And maybe her death *was* just a tragic, pointless accident, maybe there is no mystery beyond a misstep in the dark in unfamiliar territory – but when Edward and I told the police what we'd discovered, they still didn't want to know. They were still happy to call it a damn shame and leave it at that.

"But I think Alice deserves more than that. And I assume you do, too."

The look that Lowell Edwardsson gave John then was one that popped into his head several times in the days ahead, in those moments when things looked particularly unpromising. There were still traces of anger and suspicion in there, it was true, but the overwhelming visible emotion was relief. Relief tinged with gratitude and the smallest hint of hope, perhaps. Whatever it was exactly, whatever the precise levels of its various constituent elements, it spoke of a man almost crushed by the weight of a huge, unexpected loss suddenly wondering if there was something in life worth bothering about after all.

"Aye, I do," he said finally. "And that was a good speech. Bloody good, in fact. But it still doesn't answer my question. What's what happened thirty years ago to do with my Alice?"

"To be frank, I'm not entirely sure," Edward admitted. "But both your daughter and Mrs. Menzies died of exposure, having lain overnight in freezing temperatures. That's more than coincidence, I think."

"To you maybe, but not to me. You might as well say that Sylvia died because she cheated on her husband, or because she had a fondness for gin and lemon. Seems to me that you're picking and choosing the facts to fit. Seems to me that maybe you're just two bored old men, looking for something to pass whatever time you've got left."

John supposed that not many fools ended up as successful businessmen.

He realised he'd allowed Edwardsson's grief to colour his opinion of the man. A crude, uneducated local industrialist, running a factory that churned out tat for Blackpool sightseers, he'd thought. A grieving father, crushed by loss. That was all he'd seen when he looked at him. But, clearly, he was no idiot, and Edward's argument was far from convincing.

"But even if you are," Edwardsson went on, "that's not to say you're wrong about everything. And I'll not take the chance you are. You obviously think that what happened in the War is something to do with what happened to Alice. So, I'll ask you one more question, Mr. Lowe. What can I do to help?"

John felt the air involuntarily expel from his lungs in a single long sigh, and realised he'd been holding his breath. It appeared Edward had also been tense, for he blinked rapidly, cleared his throat and pushed his glasses up his nose before he replied.

"Can you remember the names of your fellow soldiers? The others who were there that night."

Edwardsson was doubtful. "Their first names, aye, I can do that. There was Henry, Bill, Bert and Bob – his last name was Murray, I remember – and me and Matty Peel. I think I've got a photograph of the lot of us, back at the house somewhere, taken just before that night. If I remember right, everyone's names are on the back."

"That'd be very useful. I don't suppose you know what happened to any of them? If they survived the War, where they ended up, that sort of thing?"

Edwardsson shook his head doubtfully. "Just that a couple of them never made it. And Matty said in one of his letters he'd heard Bob Murray got caught in a burning tank and spent months in hospital. Melted his face off, Matty said."

He scratched at his rough chin and frowned. "What I need to do now is go home and clean myself up. I've definitely got Matty's address on an old letter, though God alone knows where."

If his anger had injected some life back into Edwardsson, the thought of taking positive action, no matter how small, had put fire into his veins. He pressed his palms on the arms of his chair and threw himself to his feet.

"If you give me a number where I can get you, I'll phone when I find anything. It might take a day or two, mind. I was never the tidiest of men, even when the wife was still alive, and since then... well, let's just say it might take a day or two."

He held out his hand to Edward and John again, but his handshake now was firm.

"Thank you for this. Like you said, maybe it'll turn out to be a wild-goose chase and it really was just an accident. But I don't believe it, and while that's the case, I'll do everything I can to help you both."

There was nothing more to be said. As John pulled the office door closed behind him, he heard Edwardsson on the phone, already barking orders to his secretary.

While they waited for Harry the guard to telephone for a taxi, they discussed what they'd learned in hushed tones.

"Of course, you'll have had the same thought I did?" Edward asked.

"That we should be careful not to raise that poor man's hopes over what might yet turn out to be just a coincidence?"

Edward glared at him. "What? No, don't be obtuse. I meant, why did the killer wait thirty years between his murders?"

"Oh, right."

A pretty brunette girl in a fetching pink skirt and matching cardigan walked past, and John reached across to hold open the door for her. She smiled her thanks sweetly and, as he watched the door slowly swing shut behind her, he found himself thinking again about Alice Burke lying on the grass and the look on Edwardsson's face when he realised there might be something he could do about her death. Perhaps the whole thing *was* poppycock, perhaps the mere chance of Edwardsson's involvement was the only thing that linked 1944 and 1972 – but perhaps there were worse things than raising the man's hopes. He turned back to Edward. "I hadn't thought of that," he said, "but it's something to consider, isn't it?" He clapped the other man on the shoulder. "Jolly well done, Edward."

Edward grunted, and his ears coloured a coral pink. John thought he was about to say something, but instead he closed his mouth and gave an almost imperceptible shake of his head. Harry had reappeared from his cubbyhole to inform them that a taxi was waiting. Apparently, Edward thought it best their conversation did not become public knowledge.

John smiled his thanks at the guard and headed outside. Now he had decided that there was value in continuing with Edward's investigation, regardless of whether it made sense or not, he had no desire to stop in Blackburn for a meal or a drink. A sandwich and a bottle of beer on the train would definitely be enough. Though he barely dared admit it to himself, what had begun as a mere diversion, a way to spend an unexpected day off, had turned into something potentially much bigger.

He glanced across at Edward as he sat back in the taxi seat, eager to talk further, but before he could say a word the little man shook his head again.

"Not yet, if you don't mind," he said. "We've learned a great deal and I'd like some time to think it over before discussing it any further. Tomorrow, perhaps, after filming?"

John nodded. There was no point arguing. "Of course, my dear chap. I think better when I've slept and been fed, in any case."

He lay back in the seat and closed his eyes. Almost in spite of himself, he considered whether they were on the trail of a killer.

It was, he was forced to admit, actually rather exciting.

10

As it happened, the next morning was so busy there was no time to give the case much thought. With the reservoir now officially out of bounds, David Birt had decided to move up a script in which Wetherby believed he'd found some valuable saddles going cheap at a rundown stately home, and so the actors spent the day messing about in a stables, with various short, comic scenes that involved elderly men getting on and off horses.

Edward thought it was terrible.

"What a load of absolute tosh," he complained to Donald Roberts as they sat in folding camp chairs in the lee of a stables wall, out of the wind. It was the only accessible place for miles around that offered enough shelter to light a cigarette, but the smell was appalling.

"Would you say so?" Roberts asked mildly. He did everything mildly, truth be told.

"Wouldn't you? No, I don't suppose you would."

Edward tossed his cigarette butt into the mud and huddled more snugly in his coat. "I've told David I won't be falling off any horses, no matter what it says in the script. That's what we have stuntmen for."

Roberts nodded amiably. "I'm sure you know best. I'm not convinced I can actually get onto a horse nowadays, far less fall off one again." He shifted in his chair and settled himself more comfortably. "Oh, before I forget, I was reminded earlier of something I thought you might find interesting." His smile was uncertain and weak, but he was such a picture of softly spoken innocence that Edward found it impossible to be annoyed with his occasional lapses in concentration.

"Oh really," he said. "What would that be?"

"Well, it's perhaps nothing and I almost didn't mention it at all, but it popped into my head, you see, and I would so hate to have kept quiet then found out later it might have been helpful."

He fell silent, and Edward wondered if he'd nodded off.

"With your murder, I mean," Roberts went on suddenly, just as Edward leaned across to poke him in the knee.

He converted the gesture to an awkward pat and murmured, "Do go on."

Roberts smiled again. "It's rather gruesome, I'm afraid. But John and Joe Riley were chatting on the coach this morning about the Yorkshire chap you met yesterday, and Joe mentioned a role he was offered some time ago, and that reminded me of a book I once read."

He paused again, but this time Edward had no problem waiting for him to speak. Inwardly, he seethed at the thought that John had been unable to keep their progress to himself for even a single morning. It was typical of the man, though. Couldn't bear not to be the centre of attention. And now he'd have to humour Donald in whatever, no doubt unrelated, memory he'd unearthed.

Across the yard, he could see Jimmy Rae waving an obviously fake sword about in cavalier fashion and Clive Briggs, playing the fool as usual, sitting backwards on a horse. The sword bent in the middle as the wind caught it, and Clive had to grab onto the horse's tail in panic as it unexpectedly broke into a trot. Perhaps there were worse ways to spend his time than sitting quietly away from such foolishness, he decided, and lit another cigarette.

The movement was enough to prompt Roberts to resume his story. "It was when I was trying to come up with a follow-up to *The Velvet Web* – a play I wrote between the wars; it was quite a hit at the time – and I wasn't really getting anywhere. I'd spend my days in the local library, looking through histories and memoirs, whatever caught my eye, seeking inspiration but not really finding any. And – and this is the part that I thought might interest you, Edward – one of the books was about murderers who copy other murderers. Copycats, I believe the book called them."

Edward wondered if Roberts's memory was playing him false. "Copy other murderers?" he asked. "How could they manage to do that? For that matter, how would anyone know? Surely a murder's a murder, when all's said and done. You can't really accuse a man who shoots his wife of copying another man who did the same thing the previous week."

"Ah, there you have me, I'm afraid," Roberts apologised. "It was some time ago, and my memory's not what it once was. But I rather think the accusation was based on the precise details of each murder. A playing card left by the body or an unusual type of weapon used, that sort of thing."

Well now, that was more interesting than Edward had expected. Mentally, he created a checklist of similarities between Sylvia Menzies and Alice Burke. Both were women, of course, but that hardly signified – if the front pages of the tabloid newspapers Jimmy Rae left scattered round the hotel were to be believed – women were far more likely to be murdered than men.

But they had frozen to death in similar manners and had been found in suspiciously similar positions, and – for all Lowell Edwardsson's protestations otherwise about his daughter – both had also been drinking on the day they died. Was there anything else? Might there be other similarities? Could someone from the original party have remembered those details and copied them, years later? Might there be two killers after all?

He groaned inwardly. That was far too many questions, and not enough answers. Plus, even allowing that his basic supposition was correct and the murders were linked, why wait so long, and why choose Alice Burke? Presumably there was a rationale behind the killer's actions, but at that moment it eluded Edward.

He thanked Roberts, who seemed already to have nodded off again, and brushed cigarette ash off his trousers before getting to his feet. He needed to speak to Le Breton.

"Edward!"

The sound of the director's voice, calling him to take part in the next scene, meant that would have to wait for now. But this idea of a copycat was certainly worthy of further consideration.

He pulled his riding cap firmly onto his head and, reluctantly, walked towards the horses.

* * *

By the time shooting had finished for the day and Edward was back at the hotel, there was a real temptation to head for a bath, his bed and a good book, and leave speaking to John for the following day. His body ached from the exercise and he was exhausted, plus the entire day had been taken up by slapstick tomfoolery and idiotic visual gags that he had fondly supposed himself to have long since left behind.

But even as he turned towards the stairs which led to his room, he realised Donald Roberts's story was an itch he needed to share, and that he would get no peace until he did so. He spun on his heel and headed back the way he had come, towards the hotel bar.

Fortunately, John was standing at the counter, so he was able to corner him before he rejoined Jimmy Rae and Clive Briggs at a table by the window.

He waited while John took a trayful of drinks to the others, then outlined what Roberts had said.

"Very interesting, Edward," John said thoughtfully, as he finished. "So, what are you thinking?"

To this question, Edward had what he believed was an excellent answer. A *theory*, even. "The missing husband, of course. Sylvia Menzies' husband, that is. He goes off to war, hears his wife's been killed, comes back and discovers how she died, and that the army have hushed the whole thing up. But there's nothing he can do; how's he even to find the men responsible? Years pass, and the knowledge gnaws away at him – until one day he snaps and kills the daughter of the man he blames for the death of his wife, leaving her to die in the same way she did all those years previously."

"A tad melodramatic, don't you think, Edward?" John's eyes sparkled with amusement. "I was half-expecting Tod Slaughter to jump out from behind your chair there. Very humorous. You should offer your services to Bobby and David."

The man's inability to take things seriously was infuriating. "You take my point, though?" said Edward. "Menzies is the only one with any reason to wish to see Alice Burke die in the same manner as Sylvia Menzies. He copied the original death in order that Edwardsson would know!"

John screwed up his face doubtfully. "But he didn't," he said, after a moment's thought. "Know, that is. And there are one or two other problems with your theory, my dear chap. As before, why wait until now? But also, why kill Alice? Why not just kill Edwardsson himself? For that matter, why kill any of them? Sylvia Menzies died of natural causes, when all's said and done."

"Opportunity," Edward declared firmly. "The opportunity may simply not have arisen before now. What if he's not exactly brooded, so much as had the thought of vengeance at the back of his mind all this time? Entirely natural, I think, to plan what you'd do to a man who you blame for the death of a loved one, without ever seriously intending to carry those plans out. And then your path happens to cross that of someone on whom you *can* take your revenge. And you snap and, before you know it, you've done something terrible, from which there's no going back." He looked across to the bar and snapped his fingers to gain the barman's attention. "In my opinion, Alice died because she was unfortunate enough to cross Menzies' path, and she died this week because this week is when she did so. As to why Menzies might blame Edwardsson in the first place – you heard him say he was the only one charged over Sylvia Menzies' death."

"You've got an answer for everything, haven't you?" John's tone was, if not admiring, at least less mocking. His face, however, was horrified. "My God, if what you say is true, Menzies must live in the area!"

"Not necessarily. He might have come across her anywhere and followed her here. Presumably Edwardsson wasn't the only one who knew where she was going on holiday. Or he too might have been passing through Ironbridge and recognised her, or simply heard her name. Perhaps he's been tracking her for years, waiting for the perfect opportunity."

"So we're no closer to finding him, then, assuming your theory's right?" John wrinkled his forehead in thought. "We could hire someone to look for him, I suppose. I do know a chap. He was very helpful in a pal's divorce a few years back."

Of course you do, thought Edward. But, "No, no," he said instead, shaking his head. "There's no need to involve that sort of person. You forget, we can go directly to the police force for assistance."

"That didn't work terribly well last time, did it?"

Was there a hint of a smile on John's lips, Edward wondered, at this reminder of the embarrassing call to Inspector Ewing? Perhaps, but he needed the other man's help and so would be the bigger man, and act as though the comment had been well-intentioned.

"More locally, I meant," he said mildly.

"Primrose, you mean?"

"The very same."

"Hmmm..."

The way in which John pursed his lips and emitted a dubious hum suggested he was not won over. As if to prove it, his thin face twisted into an unmistakable expression of disbelief.

"You think Primrose will be able to track down someone from thirty years ago, in a different county, based only on his surname? And that's if he's even willing to try, which I doubt, since, interesting though your theory is, it presupposes a murder has taken place, rather than proving it has. I hate to say it, because part of me finds this whole affair a splendid break from the tedium of filming – but apart from an old shoe, nothing we've uncovered so far has been what you could call real evidence, has it?"

Perhaps it was the long day, perhaps it was because he'd not eaten for hours, perhaps it was simply that he'd had enough of the fellow's obstructive attitude, but suddenly Edward decided he needed to be somewhere other than in John's company.

"Time I was heading to bed," he announced, standing up so quickly that he pushed over his bar stool. As it fell, it rattled against the brass footrest that ran along the bottom of the bar and everyone in the room turned to look at him. Embarrassed and angry (both at himself and at John), he left it where it lay and stalked out.

Perhaps John was right, and he hadn't proved that Alice Burke had been murdered. But if everyone had that attitude, nobody would ever be caught. That was the problem with people, in his opinion. They were always far too ready to admit defeat, or to give up without even trying.

He was still fuming when he reached the bottom of the stairs, and so almost missed the soft voice of the night porter, calling to him from the reception desk.

"Mr. Lowe! Sorry to bother you, sir, and it can maybe wait until morning, but there's a message for you from a Mr. Edwardsson…"

11

"Is this the car you were talking about, Mr. Lowe?"

PC Primrose pressed his face against the passenger-side window of the Morris Minor and screwed his eyes up tight, the better to see inside. Edward was tempted to ask if he thought it likely there were two such cars, each of them with sales brochures and samples on the rear seat, in this little car park. But sarcasm was hardly likely to encourage continued police cooperation. So he simply agreed that, yes, he believed it was, and joined the policeman at the car door.

"As I said at the station, Lowell Edwardsson telephoned the hotel last night and left a message for me, with a description of his daughter's car. He also said there was usually some stock in the back, in case she came across a potential customer." Edward pressed a finger against the glass. "Things like that little plastic castle, there." He took his hat off and used it to shield the window so the constable could see the interior more clearly. "And though it's mainly hidden, I think I'm right in saying those are the letters SSONS peeking out from the top of that pile of papers. Part," he explained more slowly than was strictly necessary, "of the name Edwardssons."

"Golly, I think you're right."

It had been surprisingly easy to convince Primrose to accompany him to the car park. Edwardsson's message had, however, been a minor disappointment. Edward had hoped for the addresses of the former soldier's army colleagues, or at least their full names, but in retrospect he realised that was overly optimistic. It was probably for the best, really – something as intriguing as that might have kept him up all night, and he was a firm believer in the health-giving properties of an uninterrupted eight hours' sleep. Even so, he'd woken uncharacteristically early, and been at the door of the police station when Primrose cycled up at ten to nine.

Should he feel guilty for not involving Le Breton, he wondered? He had swithered about waking him, but this new line of investigation had reinvigorated his spirits once more, and he was damned if he was going to let anyone's negativity dilute that. Besides, if Primrose proved annoyingly obdurate and he found himself in need of John's undoubted abilities to charm, he could always go back and get him. It was only five minutes up the road, after all.

But, as it transpired, Primrose had just had an unpleasant run-in with the powers that be – or with his immediate superior, at least. Something to do with not reporting a single crime for a fortnight, so far as Edward could make out, though he'd not really been listening and had, instead, simply been waiting for a break in the constable's stream of chatter, during which he might impart his own more important information.

In any case, Primrose had proven far more amenable to argument this time around (and really, how was it the boy's fault that there was so little crime in Ironbridge? A matter more for commendation than censure, one would have thought). He had listened relatively quietly to Edward's description of their time in Blackburn, and had quickly agreed to take a look at the Morris Minor Edward remembered seeing in the Byers Road car park.

"I've always wanted to use the skeleton car keys, anyway," he'd said. "And this'll show Inspector Know-it-all, won't it just? He reckoned she must have got a train down, even when I told him there's no parking outside that B&B." He flicked through the keys on the large silver ring he'd carried from the station with evident relish.

"There you go," he said, and slipped a key into the car lock.

Edward heard the door snib pop up and then it was open.

Primrose stood back with a grin, like a conjurer who had just successfully sawn a woman in half for the first time, somewhat to his own surprise. He held out a hand as Edward attempted to step around him and look inside.

"Me first, Mr. Lowe," he warned solemnly. "This is a potential murder enquiry, after all."

Which was a little rich, considering the only reason Primrose was involved at all was because Edward had chosen to invite him along. Though, in truth, he'd actually gone down to the car park by himself before he'd walked back up to the police station, armed with a metal coat hanger that had been hanging unused in his wardrobe since he'd arrived. He only used wooden hangers for his shirts, naturally, but he'd seen a *Dixon of Dock Green* in which a young lout had broken into a car using a twisted metal one, and it was no sacrifice to ruin this one in a good cause.

Sadly, even after unwinding the hanger part with pliers borrowed from the night porter, he'd merely managed to scratch the paintwork down the driver-side door and bang his hand against the wing mirror. There was obviously a trick to it, and he couldn't spend all day learning it. He'd already had a very suspicious look from a man walking a miniature poodle. So he'd thrown the coat hanger into the bushes and gone to enlist the forces of marginally more legitimate authority instead.

He watched Primrose scrabbling about in the back seat, scooping up papers and plastic and shoving them willy-nilly into a carrier bag he'd brought along for the purpose. Edward thought perhaps he should be using a bag of a more official sort (he'd tipped a collection of sweet wrappers onto the ground outside the station before pushing the bag into his coat pocket), but perhaps it didn't matter. They knew who the stuff belonged to, after all.

With a grunt of effort, Primrose extricated himself from the cramped vehicle. He held the carrier bag in one hand, staring down at it with his mouth hanging slightly open, obviously unsure what to do next. In his other was grasped the sheet of paper with *EDWARDSSONS* written in capital letters across the top. He held both out to Edward, uncertainly. "Do you want to take a look now, Mr. Lowe?"

The paper confirmed an order for two gross of model Blackpool Towers, dated the previous week, and addressed to a shop in Lytham St. Annes. Edward indicated the shop name. "Hold onto this, Primrose," he said. "You'll need to give them a ring later and confirm when she was there." He handed the paper back to the policeman and rested the carrier bag on the bonnet of the car.

Inside was a mess of odds and ends, such as might be found in any car. An open pack of tissues, a pen, receipts for cafés and bed and breakfasts. (Edward flicked through them – whatever else might have happened to her, there was no denying Alice Burke had covered the ground on behalf of her father's company. There were receipts from as far north as the Scottish Borders and as far south as Cambridge.) Less common was the set of novelty ornaments – the same three that Edward had seen in Blackburn, plus one new one, a circular Stonehenge in moulded grey plastic.

He dropped them back into the bag and handed it to Primrose. He was disappointed, of course, but he suspected that disappointment was part of the detective's lot. For every idea that turned up a... *hello, what was that?*

As he'd been musing, he'd been staring with unfocused eyes through the windscreen into the car interior. Now, with a pleasing thrill of excitement, he realised the yellow splash on which his eyes had rested for the past few seconds was, in fact, a chunky torch in the passenger-side footwell.

"My God," he said, pushing Primrose out of the way in his haste to get past, "didn't you notice this?"

Primrose's face crumpled in almost comical confusion. "The torch, you mean? Why would we want an old torch? There's one back at the station, if you want to borrow it."

"No, thank you," Edward said, with a patience he didn't feel. "It's not that we want it for ourselves, now; it's that the deceased would surely have wanted it for herself, then."

Primrose stared at him as though he'd suddenly begun speaking in tongues. On reflection, he could have been clearer, he decided.

"Mrs. Burke," he said. "If she'd really intended to go for a night hike across the moors, don't you think she'd have taken her torch with her?"

If they'd been on set, and Primrose an extra in the background, the director would have called a halt to the shot, on the grounds that his exaggerated look of astonishment was too broad even for teatime sitcom audiences.

"You're right, Mr. Lowe," he said in a choked whisper. "That torch is a *clue*!"

Edward nodded, in what he hoped was a decisive, yet matter-of-fact, manner. It wouldn't do to get the young policeman overly excited – if he wasn't already – and he'd discovered while working with Benny Hill that a general air of competence often worked best in calming potentially difficult situations. "That's one way of describing it, certainly," he agreed gravely. "One in the eye for Inspector Know-it-all, eh?"

"In any case, you'll be wanting to do whatever it is you chaps do to take the car into custody, or whatever it's called. And, in the meantime, one quick look around, then I need to get back to the hotel to write up my notes." He held out the torch. "I can rely on you to put this somewhere safe and notify your superiors of developments?" he asked, hoping the uncertainty he felt wasn't too obvious in his voice.

Primrose sounded confident, at least. "I'll get right on it." He dropped the torch into his carrier bag and grinned. "I'm looking forward to it. That inspector said I was 'lacking the basic skills required of a policeman'. This'll show him."

"Did he now? Well, I don't suppose he meant it. He struck me as a highly strung type." Edward ducked back into the car for a final look around, but Primrose had at least proven efficient in packing rubbish into a bag, whatever other failings he might have, and there was nothing to be found, either on the seats or in the glove compartment. He walked around to the boot, but it too was empty, save for a scraper for iced windscreens (now that was the sort of thing Edwardssons should make, he thought idly) and, under the usual cover, the spare tyre. As he straightened up, a happy thought struck him.

"Actually, wouldn't it make sense to drive the car up the police station now?" he suggested.

Before Primrose could object, he slipped into the passenger seat and pulled the door closed. He rolled the window down. "If you could drop me off at my hotel on the way, that'd be most kind," he said, and rolled it back up again.

The torch made all the difference. Even John couldn't deny there was more than a whiff of foul play now.

12

The day's filming passed in a haze of anticipation for Edward.

Just an old shoe, eh? Not what you'd call real evidence, you say?

The thought of what he would say to John was a constant buzzing drone in his head as the entire cast of *Floggit and Leggit* attempted to break into a museum, for reasons which Edward had never quite understood, and continued while he and Clive did a bit of back-and-forth comedy later on involving a ludicrously unrealistic Ming vase that had all too obviously been bought from the nearest Woolworths.

At no point, though, did he manage to get John alone for enough time to tell him his news. Even when they were back at the hotel, and before he could say anything, the other man warned him he could only spare half an hour.

"I'm taking the delightful Madge for drinks at The Crown later – you remember, the wardrobe girl who got us the wellingtons when we went up to the moors? I'd intended to have a good soak after the day's exertions, but all the hot water had gone walkabout, so I had to content myself with a quick wash and brush up, and an earlier-than-expected encounter with a large whisky."

They were sitting in the hotel bar now, pints of bitter half drunk and cigarette smoke curling comfortingly around their heads. Donald Roberts was snoozing in one of the armchairs, and Joe Riley was similarly engaged in the other, but otherwise the place was deserted. There was more shooting tomorrow, of course, so the others would be in their rooms, going over their lines.

Annoyingly, Edward had topped up his bath up so much that he'd fallen asleep in it and missed dinner, and though he was famished – and said as much – the girl at reception had refused point blank to rustle him up a sandwich. He would definitely need to speak to the manager about her, but for now the nicotine was staving off most of the hunger pangs as he listened to John burbling on and waited for his chance to speak.

"The only one here when I came down was old Donald. He was already sleeping then, and that was an hour ago, at least. I had a quick one and was going to head back to my room for a pre-dinner nap, when Joe Riley came in. We were chatting on the coach yesterday, and I told him where we'd been – only very generally, of course – and he mentioned something I thought rather interesting."

He glanced over at the dozing Scotsman. "We were talking about murders and murderers, that sort of thing, you know how he likes all that gruesome what-have-you, and he brought up a part he was offered years ago. It was to play a chap like Jack the Ripper; you know, the fellow that killed all those ladies of the night before the Great War…"

"For God's sake, man, wheesht! If you're going to tell a story, do it properly at least!"

Joe Riley's voice – the finest speaking voice of his generation, in his own generous estimation – boomed across the room like Old Testament thunder. One baleful eye flicked open and glared at the two men, then the other joined it, as the older man pushed himself creakily out of his armchair and walked across to them.

Riley was another one about whom Edward was unsure. He'd had a fine career, of course, but it was all such a long time ago now, and the way he went on about it was a little wearing. Plus, he had a tendency to bad temper and even rudeness, and Edward couldn't abide that in anyone, regardless of whether they'd been in *The Thirty-Nine Steps* or not. Still, if he knew something that might have a bearing on the case, it would be remiss not to hear him out.

He needn't have worried, he realised, for in the short time he'd been thinking, Riley had managed to get himself a drink and pull up a chair at their table.

"The Great War, indeed!" he exclaimed (it was the only word for it) as he slammed his glass down between them. "What did they teach you at yon English private school you went to? Jack the Ripper was the last century, not this one, and the part I was telling you about had nothing to do with him at all."

He twisted around in his chair and tapped a long, bony finger on Edward's knee. "What I was saying to Johnny here is that I read for a part in a movie some years back – och, the late fifties, it would have been, or maybe the early sixties – and it was about a man, sick in the heid mind you, who took his filthy pleasure from slaughtering innocent wee lassies. A *serial killer*, they called him. There was a wee flurry of tat like that at the time, but the twist in this one was this: the police couldnae lay a hand on him, and the reason was that he booked himself into a nuthouse, a mental hospital, ye ken? For he knew fine well that he wasnae right, and he'd no desire to continue his murderous ways. So, into the hospital he takes himself, telling the doctors all the while he's only dreamed of killing, without letting on to the truth of the thing. And he spends ten years in there, undergoing the cure, like, and while he's locked away nae mair lassies die."

He stopped speaking to drain his glass, then smacked his thin lips with pleasure. "Ah, that's a fine drop," he said. "Better than you'd expect from a Sassenach hole in the ground like this." He waved across at the barman for a refill. "Aye, while he was inside there were no more murders, like I said. But this policeman – and this was the part I was reading for – a sergeant at the time, a Hieland man, he can't get the case oot his heid, and he spends all those years poring over the evidence, like an Aberdeen lawyer wi' his hands on the will of a banker wi' nae bairns. Everyone thinks he's a fool, obsessing over this auld case, for they all think the killer must be long since deid, for why else would the killing have stopped? But he identifies the right man from a clue in the files right enough, and discovers he's been locked up all these years. And he breaks into the man's hoose, which is all boarded up, waiting on the day he gets oot, and in a secret drawer he finds cuttings of hair from each of the dead woman's heids, for that sort like their wee games, and will keep mindings of their crimes. So, he knows he's right, and on the day the man gets released from the nuthouse he follows him all over town, and when he tries to kill another woman – as he always was going to, for there's no cure for evil like that – the detective steps in and stops it. I forget how," he concluded thoughtfully, "though I think there may have been a fence involved and maybe the man got shoved over it and into the traffic."

He shook his head, and took a sip from the glass the barman placed on the table. "Not that it matters, really. Yon great ghoul Alistair Sim got the part instead of me, and then the money disappeared, and the damn thing never got made in any case. Good riddance to bad rubbish, I say!"

"You see what I mean, Edward," John said. "Two sets of murders, with years in between, but committed by the same man. And it needn't be a hospital. He could have been in prison, or out of the country."

"*Who* could?" Joe Riley's gimlet eyes flicked between the two men sitting opposite him.

There was no need to have involved Riley at all. That was the most annoying thing. True, his little story might have some relevance, and was certainly enough to suggest some new avenues of enquiry, but John could have waited until later to relay the details, and so left Riley none the wiser. Even if he'd poked his nose in the next day, he could have been brushed off quickly enough with some non-committal explanation or other. But now he would undoubtedly want to be involved, and Edward very much agreed with the old saw about too many cooks. Typical of John, though, making the simplest things difficult. Well, he'd just have to—

"Ach, dinnae tell me, then. I wisnae all that interested anyway." Riley was on his feet, shaking his head furiously. "I've better things to do with my time than waste it on two auld fools like you, creating mysteries where there are none to be found, like a pair of glaikit school bairns." Without another word, he turned his back on them and stomped off towards the stairs.

Edward watched him in silence until he was out of sight, then switched his attention back to his companion. "Perhaps in future, it would be best if we kept the details of the case between ourselves," he snapped. "At least until we have something more concrete to reveal?"

John was immediately repentant. "My dear chap, of course. But in my defence, I never mentioned the" – he smiled crookedly – "*case* to him at all. Still, it is something to consider, wouldn't you say?"

"Find out if any of Edwardsson's comrades in arms have been locked away for the last thirty years, you mean? Add them to our list of suspects, alongside the missing Mr. Menzies?"

"Exactly that. Though I do worry we now have a fairly substantial set of suspects for a murder for which we have precious little evidence and which may never have taken place."

Finally, the opening Edward had been waiting for! "As it happens, the reason I was looking for you was to fill you in on a rather interesting meeting I had with Constable Primrose. One which may cause you to amend your opinion on whether a murder has taken place."

Edward was pleased to see that John was attentive as he described his revelation about the Morris Minor and the discovery of the overlooked torch.

"Why would she have left the torch behind if she were intending to go traipsing about in the dark?" John asked as Edward came to the end of his tale.

"Precisely what I said to Primrose! In my opinion, it proves what I've said all along – Alice Burke never intended to go on a night-time hike. She was either forced to do so by a person or persons unknown, or did so of her own volition, but in fear of her life!"

Edward was aware that, again, he sounded like the hero of a cheap melodrama, but really, it was terribly satisfying to be proven right so conclusively. First the shoe and now the torch. He'd like to see that inspector tell him to stick to acting now.

John's reaction was annoyingly grudging, however. "That's certainly a possibility," he said. From somewhere, he had inexplicably acquired a pork pie, which he began to eat, speaking in pauses between bites. "Or they could yet be totally unconnected. I do think, Edward, we should avoid jumping too readily to conclusions."

The only thing Edward now wanted to jump to was wherever the mysterious pie had come from, but he had no intention of giving John the satisfaction of asking. Instead, he took a long, slow gulp from his pint, peering over the top of the glass as he did so, hoping to catch sight of a tray on the bar. Only when he realised that he'd stopped breathing did he admit defeat and put the now-empty glass back on the table.

"I wouldn't dream of it," he said, trying not to stare at the rapidly disappearing pie. "But you won't deny, I hope, that the evidence increasingly points towards foul play?"

John stroked his chin and made a sound somewhere between tenuous agreement and bothersome catarrh. "Yes," he said finally. "On balance, perhaps you're onto something, Edward. Whether the police would see it that way, well, that's a different matter."

Not for the first time, it seemed that John was determined not to show too much enthusiasm, but that was just his way, so far as Edward could see. And his admission that he personally was coming around to the opinion that Alice Burke had been murdered was definite progress. It would be impossible to carry out the entire investigation alone; he needed John's assistance, for now at least.

"You may be right about the police," Edward agreed in the interests of détente. "But I do think we should speak to the constable tomorrow, and ask him to check up on Menzies. Perhaps he might telephone the camp at Balcon and ask if anyone remembers the case, or the man."

John laid down his fork and wiped his lips with a napkin. "Of course. Whatever you think best."

Edward was quite sure he was no longer paying any notice to what was being said, though. A woman had entered the hotel bar and all of John's attention had instantly switched to her. Tall and well dressed, with her hair in a carefully crafted permanent wave, she smiled and waved across in their direction. Madge the wellington lady, presumably. Edward smiled politely, but John pushed himself to his feet and shot the cuffs of his shirt in a showy manner. "Don't you look delightful, my dear," he said – *simpered* would be closer to the mark, Edward thought, and wondered again what women saw in the man.

"If that's all for now, Edward, we'll be on our way." John took his latest conquest by the elbow and steered her from the room, already turning on the charm – and evidently uninterested in Edward's reply. Before they had disappeared from sight, he heard John's low voice say something witty and the tinkling sound of a woman's laughter.

Truth be told, Edward was grateful for the peace and quiet. He had thinking to do and John's presence would just distract him. He gestured to the barman to bring over the same again and flipped open his notebook. Hopefully Lowell Edwardsson would provide the names of his erstwhile colleagues in due course, but in the meantime, there was a great deal to be added to his case notes.

13

The next few days were taken up in rehearsals for the next episode, in which Wetherby lost a bet with Archie Russell and took a job as a street sweeper to prove he was capable of physical labour. It proved to be unexpectedly arduous, even after the cheap broom snapped in two, and left everyone exhausted and ready for bed almost as soon as they arrived back at the hotel.

Even so, Edward found himself in a considerably better mood than he would have expected. Of course, he would rather be on the trail of the killer, but in the meantime, the scripts had improved – he had quite a moving little speech in the next episode about the bonds of friendship lasting even unto death and, in the final episode of the season, he got to play the hero and disarm a thief – and he and John had at least managed to wangle a late start, and taken the opportunity to speak to Primrose about the mysteriously missing Mr. Menzies.

Fortunately, Primrose's professional problems continued to work to their benefit.

"A proper telling off, that's what it was!"

The constable was pacing about the little cubbyhole at the back of the police station, which doubled up as both interview and tea room. Edward and John were seated at a small Formica table, on which lay a large tape recorder, two mugs of tea in chipped mugs and a white plastic ashtray that advertised Cinzano Bianco. For the moment, the tape recorder was turned off.

"Take a look for yourself, Mr. Lowe!"

He placed the crumpled sheet of paper he held tightly in his fist onto the table, and smoothed it flat with the palm of his hand. He stabbed a finger at a line in the middle of a dense block of typewritten text.

"'…subject to disciplinary proceedings should there be a repeat,' it says, Mr. Lowe! Subject to disciplinary proceedings! And all because I answered a few questions…"

"Answered where, Frank?" John asked.

Primrose blushed and whipped the letter off the table before Edward could pick it up. "Just that interview I gave to the paper," he said defensively.

Edward couldn't have cared less. He'd read the interview in the local rag, of course, in which Primrose had rather exaggerated his own role in discovering Alice Burke's body, but his main thought at the time had been to chuckle at the lack of local news, when two pages could be taken up by the Thoughts of Frank Primrose.

What was important was that the constable was sufficiently

enraged by the perceived injustice of the rebuke that he was more than amenable to persuasion and had apparently forgotten all his earlier objections.

Which was fortunate, as he began with some news that even Edward had to admit was discouraging.

"The letter mentioned you too, Mr. Lowe," he admitted glumly. "About that button you gave me. Turns out it wasn't a button at all, or at least not one anyone would have had on their coat. It's from an old army uniform, from…" He peered down at the letter in his hand. "…a tunic of the Cambridge militia."

"My God, could we be looking for a military man? Perhaps the button comes from the killer, not his victim?"

Primrose shook his head. "Not unless he's absolutely *ancient*, Mr. Lowe. The militia was disbanded in 1881. It must have been lying up there for nearly a hundred years, the letter says. And then it says I'll be for the high jump if I waste any more lab time on fool's errands."

Recalling this fresh insult plainly irritated the lanky constable. "But that doesn't mean that woman up by the reservoir wasn't murdered!" he insisted as he poured milk into his own tea, then added five sugars. "You know what? I hope she was murdered! That'd give me a chance to show *them* whether I'm an embarrassment to the force!" He took a sip of his tea and winced at the heat. With a frown, he added more milk. "Well, I don't actually *hope* she was murdered, not really. But if she was, I'd help you as much as I could."

Edward beamed with pleasure. "Splendid!" he said, rubbing his hands together. "Then perhaps the best thing to do is to bring you up to speed on what we've discovered so far? After that, can we take advantage of your highly trained police mind and experience, and ask your advice on how best to proceed?"

He worried he'd laid the flattery on too thick, but Primrose positively glowed at the description.

"Just say the word, Mr. Lowe," he said, straightening his tie importantly. "I have been in the force for five years next month, you know."

"Really? As long as that." John's voice was soft and enquiring, and fell right on the cusp of outright mockery. "I certainly never would have guessed."

Edward winced. Sarcasm was not the way to get Primrose on side. No doubt John thought he was being wonderfully droll, but it came across as smug and unpleasant, in his opinion.

"We both thought you'd been in the police for much longer than that," he interjected, before John could continue. "You give off such an air of quiet competence."

Primrose's smile widened, and his voice dropped an octave as he invited Edward to describe their problem, so he could "give it due consideration". Edward did so, as quickly and as simply as he could, concentrating on the question of Sylvia Menzies' errant husband, and putting as little emphasis as possible on the potential involvement of Edwardsson's army comrades.

"...and so we wondered if you could possibly contact your colleagues in Cheshire, and ask them if they have any information on Mr. Menzies, and where's he been since his wife died?"

"Blimey!" At first, Primrose had been taking notes as Edward spoke, but by the end he sat with the pencil forgotten in his hand, mouth hanging open. "You've been very busy, Mr. Lowe. And I reckon you're onto something as well."

"So, you'll telephone and see what you can find out?"

Primrose nodded. "I'll do what I can, Mr. Lowe."

"That's all we can ask, Constable. Remember, we need to know why he was away at the time, and where he's been since. Presumably he came back for the child, at least, and I'm sure that sort of thing must have been recorded somewhere, even back then."

"This *is* exciting, Mr. Lowe! You know…" Primrose looked left and right, and leant forward conspiratorially. "You know, this is my first murder investigation. And that inspector thought it was just an accident, too!" He shook his head and tapped his nose. "But we knew better, eh, Mr. Lowe?"

To his right, Edward heard John stifle what sounded suspiciously like a giggle, but he made sure to keep a serious expression on his own face as he met Primrose's eye.

"We did indeed, Constable Primrose," he agreed solemnly. "We did indeed."

14

The crowds of people, some smiling, some angry, all talking at once. The sound of their overloud conversations, mixed with clinking glasses. The smell of spilled beer and cigarette smoke. John adored everything about pubs.

He always had, ever since his schooldays, when he'd celebrated a particularly good batting show against Winchester with a few beers before catching the train back to school. He'd been caught, of course, and lost his cricket colours because of it, but it'd been worth it.

This was his first time in The Grapes, the only pub for miles, however, even though they'd been in the village for a while now. At first, David Birt had been very keen, in his own words, that they "stay focused and keep a tight core" and apparently that precluded visits to the pub. John suspected he was just terrified one of the elderly actors would get pissed and end up breaking his neck on the way back to the hotel.

Very quickly, though, it had become clear that the actors might be elderly, but they were also professionals. David had finally had to accept that even men in their sixties and seventies weren't necessarily one misplaced step away from a sticky end.

"Could you be a dear and put another one in here?" he asked the barmaid, handing over his empty glass. He thought her name was possibly Susan, but there did seem to be a delightfully never-ending supply of pretty, young women who appeared behind the bar one night, then were replaced the next by another, almost identically lovely. "No need to dirty another glass," he smiled. "That one will do fine."

As she poured, he lit a cigarette and looked around the room. A polished wooden bar made a horseshoe beside him, stretching halfway across the room in each direction. In the bar itself, groups of village drinkers sat like small islands which bordered on and overflowed into one another in some spots, and remained in splendid, definite isolation in others. They had all been introduced by Fred the landlord at some point, but John was buggered if he could remember any of their names. Geoffrey rang a bell, and he was pretty sure there was a Ronald out there somewhere, but other than that, he'd be lying. Still, several held up their glasses in a toast as they caught his roving eye and he smiled and half-waved in return; this version of a village/camp coming together was going a good deal better than Lowell Edwardsson's had in the War.

His own colleagues were currently sat in the snug – a separate section to the right of the bar itself, walled off in wood and entered via a frosted-glass fronted door. When he'd been a young man, snugs had been the demesne of women: primarily elderly ladies who drank port and lemon and gossiped about other women's husbands, but also, occasionally, tipsy blondes, who laughed over glasses of something or other and were willing to flirt harmlessly with underemployed actors. Nowadays, the cast used it because it was private, had the comfiest seats and was convenient for the loo.

"There you go, love." Possibly Susan placed a full pint in front of him, along with a two-pence piece. He took the beer and waved away the change. "Just pop that in the kitty," he said. "Much obliged, my dear." (Best not to risk using her name, he decided.)

"Oh, that's bloody bad timing! A minute earlier and I could have got that for you!"

The voice that boomed in his ear belonged to one of the few villagers whose name John definitely knew. Barney Ifeld was about his own age, tall and slim, with sparkling white teeth and wavy brown hair, cut in a style that John thought slightly too young for him. He was also the most successful of the local farmers, though to describe him as merely a farmer was, he gathered (primarily from the man himself), akin to saying of Marlon Brando that he did a little acting now and again. In fact, Ifeld owned a dairy farm that extended halfway across the county and, it was rumoured, was also involved in the hotel trade, luxury car sales, and some form of unspecified import and export. He was loud, ostentatious and vulgar, and John had disliked him on first sight.

However, he was also an important man locally, and there was talk of another series for which local cooperation would be vital, so, when he extended an invitation to join him and a couple of friends at their table, John tried not to make his longing glance at the door to the snug too obvious.

"Of course, my dear fellow, I'd love to stop for a quick one," he said and followed Ifeld across the room.

He was pleased to see he at least knew the other two men as locals, and that they were not business associates to whom Ifeld wished to flaunt his semi-famous showbiz acquaintance. He'd never been a fan of putting on a show away from the cameras. That was one thing he and Edward definitely agreed on. Better to leave that sort of thing to those, like Clive Briggs, who were good at it. But he'd met Bruce Cumming and Alex – was it Alex? – Watson before.

"You know Bruce and Alistair?" Ifeld asked, obviously rhetorically. "We were just talking about that girl who got killed by the reservoir. Bit of a looker, by all accounts, eh?" He nudged John with his elbow. "You were up there, I hear, when Edward found the body? Was she as stunning as they say?"

Oh Christ. It was going to be that kind of chat, was it? It was on the tip of his tongue to make his excuses and damn the state of local relations, but then he remembered Edward pulling him up for making a similar comment at the time. One must make allowances, he supposed.

"She was dead, so it was rather hard to tell," he said. "I've seen photographs of her since, though, and she was certainly a fine-looking lady."

"Told you!" Ifeld rounded on his companions in triumph, as though the attractiveness of the dead woman in some reflected well upon him personally. "Told you she'd be a looker! They only kill the good-looking ones, those types."

"Those types?"

He knew he shouldn't take the bait, but he couldn't help himself.

"Sex killers, John! Perverted molesters of the ladies!"

John raised an eyebrow and gave Ifeld his best, unmistakably doubtful, smile. "What on earth makes you think she was murdered, my dear fellow? The police are saying it was a tragic accident, you know."

Ifeld chuckled and winked with exaggerated care. "Of course they are, John. Of course they are. They don't want to get all the local fillies in a tizzy, do they?" He tapped a finger against his nose (was the man's every gesture copied from television, John wondered?) and leaned in closer. "You were seen, you know. First, Edward in discussion with an inspector from the city. Then you and him back and forward to visit that fool Primrose at the police station. And then your mysterious trip up north, and another visit to the police again as soon as you got back. I hear Edward was back up there again today. Come on man, spill the beans. What have you been up to?" He lit a Tom Thumb cigar and blew smoke over the top of John's head. "Might be I can tell you something, in exchange," he grinned in conclusion.

He would never admit it, but John very much wished that Edward would appear at his elbow and take over his side of the conversation. This sort of thing was far more up his street. For himself, give him a quiet pint or two, some chat about mutual acquaintances, a little mild flirting, and he was perfectly happy. True, he was generally enjoying their little investigation, but that was mainly because he suspected there was nothing actually to investigate. He'd no desire to be involved in cloak-and-dagger assignations with obnoxious farmers, far less to be up to his neck in what he remembered one old script calling "covert information exchange".

He glanced across at the snug, willing Edward to open the door, but it remained frustratingly close. With no idea what to say, he took a long sip of his beer and returned Ifeld's smile.

Unexpectedly, the other man thumped his hand down on the table several times. "Fair enough, John, you sly old fox!" he said with a laugh loud enough to briefly draw the attention of nearby tables. "You play your cards close to your chest, if that's how you want it! But I'll tell you what I know anyway – and maybe later you'll remember I did and let me in on what's going on."

He laughed again and prodded first Bruce and then Alistair (or possibly the other way around) in the arm. "We'll not get a word out of this one, eh boys? He's far too long in the tooth for that." The ash on his cigar tumbled onto his shirt front, but he took no notice. "Well, never let it be said I stood in the way of justice. What I know is that a man was seen up by the reservoir on the night the girl was killed!" He sat back in his chair with enough force that the front legs briefly left the ground, then thumped back down as he grabbed at the table to regain his balance. "What do you make of that?" he asked, triumphantly.

John wasn't sure what to make of it, and said so. "I mean, men do go walking at night, you know. I can't say the idea's ever appealed to me, but it takes all sorts to make a world."

Ifeld's irritation was plain. "Not a local man, John. A stranger!" He turned in appeal to the men at his side. "Tell him, lads. We don't get strangers here. And even if we did, strangers don't go wandering around the reservoir at night."

In unison, the two men shook their heads.

"They don't," Bruce said.

"Not at night," Alistair agreed. "Not strangers."

There was no denying such complete unanimity. "Really? Well, perhaps that does make a difference, I suppose. How did your informant know he was a stranger?"

"Must have been one. When my... let's call him a friend, shall we... shouted to him, he ran off. A local man would have let on."

"He would, would he?" Personally, John thought that'd be the last thing he'd do if one of Ifeld's bruisers called to him across a shadowy field. "Perhaps there are further details which you could share? A description of this mysterious stranger, for instance?"

"I'm afraid not, old son. It's dark as the devil's rear up by the reservoir at night. You're lucky he was seen at all."

"Yes, about that..." In spite of himself, John felt himself being drawn into the role of detective. "*How* was he seen? What was your confidant doing up there at that time of night? And where exactly was it? I imagine the reservoir is quite large."

Unexpectedly, Ifeld seemed uncomfortable with the questions. He paused for a moment before slowly replying. "As to the where, about half a mile from the spot that Edward found the little lady. As the how… well, some things I need to keep to myself for now." He flashed John a wide grin. "When you get to know me better, you'll know I've always got some spot of business or other on the go."

"And you can't say what he looked like at all? Tall, short, fat, thin? No distinguishing features of any sort?" John was rather pleased with the last question, which he could readily imagine an actual policeman saying.

"Well, I wasn't there myself, but tall, I was told. Nothing else, though. But that's something, isn't it? Now you know you're looking for someone tall and not too fat or too skinny. That's a start, I'd say."

Ifeld grinned again, and John wondered if he were being ridiculed. Was this entire conversation a not terribly funny joke?

As though reading his mind, Ifeld shook his head, suddenly at least partway serious. "I'm not kidding about, John. A stranger was seen skulking about up by the reservoir that night. Someone passing through, if you ask me. Stands to reason, doesn't it? If he was still around, somebody else would've seen him since then. Trust me, he'll be miles away by now.

"But I'll ask about and see if I can turn up any more details for you. I've lived here all my days, and my dad before me, and I know just about everyone in a twenty-mile radius. If there's anything to be found out, I'll find it, don't you worry. And in the meantime, remember what I said. Any info you might come across, I'd be interested to know about it." The ever-present smile never left Ifeld's face, but the way he spoke left John in no doubt that he expected his interest to be satisfied.

He reached down into the pocket of his jacket, which hung over the back of his chair, and pulled out his wallet. "Here," he said, handing over a small rectangle of white card. "My office number's on there, and my home number's on the back. Give me a bell."

John examined the card doubtfully. *IFELD DEVELOP-MENTS* it said on one side, with a telephone number beneath, but no address. On the other, as promised, was another number written in black biro.

"If anything comes up in which you might have an interest, we'll let you know," he said carefully. "But I really must be getting back to my friends…" He nodded in the direction of the snug, and rose to his feet with his by-now-empty pint glass in his hand. He was sure he could feel Ifeld's eyes on his back as he made his way across to the bar but, as he handed over his glass to Possibly Susan the barmaid, he glanced back and the three men were deep in conversation.

"Could you be a dear and put another one in there?" he asked, with one hand already on the door handle. "I'll be in the snug, if you could pass it over."

Edward would want to hear what Ifeld had said, he was sure.

15

When he'd agreed to play Wetherby, Edward had been concerned about the need to be away for several weeks of location shooting every year. He'd miss the comforts of home, and he'd be bored. But he needn't have worried.

He'd been pleasantly surprised by the quality of the linen and the firmness of the bed, and though the standard of cooking at the hotel wasn't what he was used to, the food was at least edible, and he'd been given a room overlooking the river.

Equally clearly, boredom was not going to be an issue. Just today, there was the man Ifeld's possible sighting of the killer, which John had shared with him. Edward had been wary of the flashy businessman ever since he'd been introduced to him. More than wary, in fact, though he could not put his finger on exactly what troubled him. Obviously, he had little patience for vulgar new money at the best of times, but there was something in Ifeld's eyes, a dark spark almost concealed by the wide smile and the crushing handshake, which made Edward uneasy. He had the air of a man who might be willing to take things too far, if he thought it in his interests to do so.

But what reason would he have to lie? None that Edward could see.

But Ifeld had said the man wasn't local and that he'd probably moved on by now. Most likely he was right, and it was just some type of itinerant tramp, coincidentally crossing the moors. That being the case, his identification wasn't a priority, if it could be managed at all.

Regardless, any identification would need to be put on one side for the moment, because PC Primrose had telephoned and left a message that morning which, wonder of wonders, the little blonde receptionist had managed both to copy down and pass on accurately. His enquiries in Cheshire had turned up something of interest, it seemed. And there was just time to hurry down to the station with John before the coach arrived to take them off to the day's shooting.

Primrose led them through to the same little room in which they'd spoken to him previously. It looked cleaner than before, and Edward was sure he could smell furniture polish.

As they took their seats, Primrose dropped a buff-coloured folder on the table and sat down opposite them.

"I bet you'll be pretty interested in what I found out," he said, opening the folder to reveal a single sheet of paper.

"So, Mr. Menzies was a conscientious objector, was he?" John drawled unexpectedly. "Well, I can't say I blame him. The War was rather frightful at times, or at least that's how I found it…"

His voice trailed off as though lost in thought.

Primrose was staring at him, his mouth hanging open in comic surprise, but Edward rounded on John in an absolute fury. "You knew that important fact about the man, and you never thought to mention it before now?"

"Oh no, my dear chap, I didn't know it. I just this second read it on the constable's bit of paper." He pointed at the sheet in front of Primrose which, now Edward had a second to examine it, contained only one line, written in a childishly careful hand, and easily read, even upside down.

Eric Menzies was a conscientious objector in the War.

Now it was Primrose's turn to feel the force of Edward's ire. "Is that it?" he asked, acidly. "Is that all you found out?"

"They weren't keen to talk to me at all!" the policeman protested. "They said it was none of my business, and what did I want to know for anyway?"

"Damn cheek! I hope you told them it was related to official business far above their clearance level. You can't let these petty bureaucrats bully you, you know. You have to put them in their place."

"I said that he'd been left a yacht in a will and I needed to tell him about it." Primrose's scowl cleared at the memory. "That got them going. They couldn't have been more helpful after that."

"And yet all you discovered was the bare fact that Menzies had refused to fight?"

"Not at all. I learned loads! I started to write a list of everything I found out, but you arrived before I expected and I'd only got as far as doing a heading." He gestured at the almost-blank sheet of paper, then pushed it aside. Underneath lay another sheet, this time covered in scribbled notes. "Right then, here's what they said in Cheshire." He placed a finger at the top of the page and, jumping from line to line, provided the two men with everything he had learned.

"Eric Menzies was his name, and he married Sylvia Menzies in 1932. He worked as a... wait a minute, I can't read my own writing... labourer on a local farm until 1934, when they had a son. Nobody knew the son's name, but I did say he'd be the one to get the yacht if his dad was dead, so they're going to see what they can dig up. Anyway, around the time the son was born, Menzies got involved with a bad crowd – political and that – and when war broke out and he was called up, he refused to go."

"That must have made things awkward for the whole family," John murmured.

"I'll say! Cheshire said his wife threw him out and he ended up in Scotland somewhere, cutting down trees instead of fighting."

Edward nodded. That sounded right. If he'd been a farm hand, it made sense to use him in the countryside rather than just lock him up.

"Did they say what happened to the child when his mother died?"

"Into care, on account of there being no living family, other than the dad."

"And after the War? When the father returned?"

"No idea, Mr. Lowe. They said they'd check, but they'd lost a lot of the records from back then, so not to get my hopes up."

His finger came to the end of the page, and he sat back with the sort of smile on his face that Edward knew from years of rehearsals with young actors. Keen for praise for a job well done.

"Excellent work, Primrose," he said. "You've uncovered a great deal of very useful – possibly even vital – information." He reached across the table and placed four fingers on the top of the sheet of paper. "Do you mind if I take this?" he asked. "As a crib sheet, in case we forget anything you've told us."

Before Primrose could reply, Edward pulled the paper towards himself and folded it in his hand. "And the police in Cheshire will get back in touch with you if they can uncover anything else? The current whereabouts of either father or son, for instance?"

Primrose nodded overemphatically. "They said they would. And if they find out what the little boy was called." He closed the folder on the table. "And if there's anything else I can do, remember, all you need to do is let me know." His smile was shy and uncertain. "Maybe I could come with you, if you go on another trip?"

"Certainly." Edward's reply was smooth and quick, if not entirely truthful. "If you're not too busy with your duties here, of course. We wouldn't want to take you away from your job and get you into more trouble with your superiors."

"It's not my fault, the trouble I get into," Primrose grumbled, and Edward was struck once more by how young he seemed.

"Well, we must be going," he said. "The coach won't wait for us, you know." He glanced down at his watch. "Actually, we'd better get a move on. We're pretty late already."

He stood and tucked the sheet of paper he had taken from Primrose into his trouser pocket. It was vital they didn't forget any details that the policeman had told them.

He bustled out of the dreary station, bursting with the new information and keen to discuss the implications with John.

They were last on the coach, however, and ended up sitting apart, so it wasn't until later that Edward managed to have a word with John, over a sandwich on a bench by the lunch truck. The bench was hard and none too clean, even after he'd wiped it, and the sandwich itself less than satisfactory, but it was the other man's attitude that was most annoying.

"Just because the fellow didn't fancy getting shot at, Edward, doesn't make him a murderer, you know," John announced as soon as they sat down.

More assumptions. It was still early days, but he'd already heard people comparing him to Wetherby, heard the whispered suggestions that Bobby and David had based the character on the actor. And because Wetherby was bound to despise anyone who wouldn't fight, Edward Lowe must be the same. It really wasn't good enough.

"Did I say that it did?" he snapped, then became even more irritated by John's little shrug of non-apology.

"Of course not, my dear chap," he said. "I was merely making a general observation."

Edward scowled but could think of no useful reply. Instead, he tossed the crust of his sandwich to some of the expectant seagulls who always congregated round the lunch truck. As usual, the birds squabbled and fought over the piece of bread, knocking each other aside in their zeal to get at their prize. There was something about the sight which momentarily caught his eye, but whatever it was, it was lost as John continued to speak.

"I always think seagulls are sinister-looking," he said, watching them with a frown. He rolled the paper bag his sandwich had come in into a ball and threw it in their direction, but it fell short and they paid it no attention. "The way they have of looking at you out of the side of their eyes, as though deciding which part of you they'd eat first. It's unnerving."

He brushed the crumbs from his trousers onto the ground and lit a cigarette, evidently having dismissed the gulls from his mind. "If anything, though, being a conscientious objector makes Menzies less likely to be the killer. If he was so opposed to violence in 1940 that he was willing to risk prison – and worse, being sent to Scotland – then he's hardly likely to have decided, thirty years later, to take bloody revenge on Edwardsson." He paused, watched the seagulls squabbling amongst themselves for a moment. "And the question remains: why did the killer go after poor Alice Burke anyway, and not her father? If anyone was to blame for Sylvia Menzies' death, it was he. The police are always *quite* keen on motive, in my experience."

"That's obvious, surely?" said Edward. "Edwardsson's a big man. You'd not overcome him easily, and if you knocked him into a reservoir, he'd climb back out and chase after you, as likely as not. Plus, there's the symmetry."

"Symmetry?"

"I've mentioned this before, you know. If Menzies believes that Edwardsson killed his wife, then killing his daughter in return might well strike him as fitting."

John's expression was pained. "What a grisly imagination you have," he sighed.

"As for his moral scruples, I give them very little weight." Edward lit a cigarette of his own and blew the smoke into the air. "More often than not, conscientious objection was just a cover for cowardice, plain and simple, in my opinion. And even if it wasn't in this case," he continued hurriedly, for he could see John was about to object, "there's nothing more likely to make a man abandon his scruples than the thought that a loved one has been murdered while he has been sent away."

"All I can say, Edward, is that you've got a more devious mind than mine. It's as though you find common ground with the killer."

Edward suspected there was a hidden insult in there somewhere, but again he refused to rise to the bait. "Be that as it may," he said, "it is a reasonable working theory, I think." He folded up his sandwich bag into a square, walked across to the bin beside the lunch truck and dropped it in. He wondered if it was worth pointing out that the ability to enter the minds of others was almost the definition of acting, but John was clearly one of those instinctive types, for whom acting came as naturally as breathing, and with as little work.

He was about to call over that they should probably be heading back, when the same young man who had come to find him when he had stumbled across Alice Burke's body trotted up and handed him an envelope.

"This was just sent up from the village, Mr. Lowe," he panted. "They said it was quite urgent that you see it."

The envelope was white and unmarked save for Edward's name on the front, in PC Primrose's distinctive, childlike handwriting. He thanked the young runner and, promising he'd be back on set in a moment, sat down beside John again.

"A note from Primrose," he explained, sliding a nail under the gummed-down seal and tearing it open along the top seam. "I wonder what..." His voice trailed away as he read the brief information on the single sheet of notepaper inside.

"What is it?" John asked. "You've gone chalk-white, Edward. What does it say?"

"Lowell Edwardsson tracked down Matthew Peel last night. Peel's daughter has been found dead."

16

"Lowell telephoned the hotel this morning, but the girl on the desk told him we were at the police station. When he phoned there, we'd just left, so he gave his message to Primrose and asked him to let us know."

Edward and John were sitting in the wardrobe van, waiting to be measured for costumes that would be needed for an episode later in the run. As a rule, Edward found these fittings rather trying. Like make-up, wardrobe was a world ruled by women, hordes of them buzzing around like wasps, with hands full of cloth and mouths full of pins, ready to grab any unwary actor in the most inappropriate of places. Still, he'd been looking forward to this one, because he was to be dressed in the uniform of an army captain for the last episode of the current run. He'd always thought he had the sort of robust figure well suited to an officer's tunic, and though he'd not actually read the script in question, he had the idea he'd be wearing the full regalia, complete with cap, Sam Browne belt and even a service revolver.

Now, though, he had darker matters to consider – and discuss – and the wait while the wardrobe girls measured up the multitude of cast members was proving interminable. He and John had at least managed to snag a spot in the corner, sufficiently far away from the others that, so long as they whispered, they were unlikely to be overheard. Though if Clive Briggs continued to fool around in the way he was at present, draping a ballgown over himself and declaring himself Good Queen Bess at the top of his voice, they probably had no concerns in that respect.

"And is he definitely saying she was murdered?"

"Is who saying?" For a second, Edward was confused. The fake Virgin Queen was still bellowing across from him. He shook his head, cleared away the cobwebs. "No, he's not actually saying that at all. Anything but, in fact. Apparently, the claim is that the girl died of a drug overdose." Edward waved Primrose's note in front of him. "When I spoke to Primrose, he said he'd written down Edwardsson's words exactly. 'I contacted Matthew Peel, and his daughter has just been found dead in her university digs. A drug overdose and a lit cigarette set fire to her bed with her in it, according to the police.' And then Peel's number and address."

"Well then, perhaps that's all it is. I know it used to only be musicians who overdosed, but nowadays…"

"You surely don't believe this was an accident? For goodness' sake, John, act your age! Of course she didn't overdose! She was murdered somehow, and the bed was set on fire to cover the killer's tracks!"

"But the police…"

"Those fools!" Edward was scathing. "If this business has taught me anything, it's that the police prefer everything neat and tidy, and have no interest in anything that might require investigative effort."

John nodded, but Edward knew when he was being humoured. "Have you spoken to Edwardsson yourself?" he asked, very obviously changing the subject.

"Only his secretary. She said the news has finished him off. She promised to get him to phone as soon as he was back in the office, but, for now, he's at home and incommunicado."

"Poor man. No matter how she died… for this to happen so soon after his own daughter…" John shook his head. "But there's not much we can do, is there? If the police believe it's a drug overdose, then we can hardly gainsay them from halfway across the country, based on… well, based on nothing at all, when it boils down to it. Time for us to take a step back, wouldn't you say?"

Edward couldn't believe his ears.

"I must say, I didn't expect that attitude from you. To give up at the first sign of danger? To slip away as soon as it looks as though things might get difficult? That's not the way we do things. Once we begin something, we press on to the end." He frowned, suddenly aware his words had actually come from a speech he'd done in a play the previous year in Clacton.

Perhaps a change of tack would work.

"Come now… ah… old man. Think how far we've come, and in so short a time. A few days ago, we knew nothing, but today we have not one but two possible lines of enquiry. We've spoken to several witnesses, taken the advice of experts in the field" – this description of Donald Roberts and Joe Riley was a stretch, he knew but, in the circumstances, a justifiable one – "and have uncovered material evidence, in the shape of a shoe and a torch. We've linked the two deaths to each other and have come up with a working theory. All that in little more than seventy-two hours. Think what we could do in seventy-two more!"

That was a better speech. He was pleased to note the effect it had on John.

"My dear fellow, you shouldn't get yourself so worked up," John interrupted. "You'll do yourself an injury. I never intended to suggest that we should quit entirely. I simply meant it might be best if we take a moment to consider what we know. After all, we need to provide a more substantial link between these women than the fact their fathers briefly did basic training together thirty years ago."

"Well…" Now that he considered it, Edward was forced to concede he had a point. But he was *certain*. He knew, somewhere deep within himself, that whoever had killed Alice Burke had also killed Mary Peel. But if they were to do anything substantial about it – anything meaningful – they'd need at some point to bring the police force (and not just Primrose) onside. And to do that, they would need irrefutable proof. "I'm glad you spotted that, I must say. Very well done. There's no doubt in our own minds that the deaths are linked, but we'll need to convince the authorities if arrests are to follow."

"If we can prove that Mary Peel's death wasn't an overdose, that should do it." John's face froze and the colour drained from it. "My God, if Eric Menzies is killing the daughters of the men who were involved in his wife's death, we need to warn the others that their children are in danger!"

"That thought had already occurred to me. But without their names, how are we to do so?"

"Perhaps Matthew Peel might remember more?"

"Perhaps, and we must certainly pay him a visit. But the address Edwardsson provided is in St. Ives, and that's at least a day's travel there and back from here. We've not got a day off until Saturday, so there's no possibility of going until then. Which leaves the daughter, Mary Peel. Edwardsson's secretary took the call from Matthew Peel, and elicited the information that Mary was a student at Nottingham. I've been turning the matter over in my head, and I think I've an idea how we could get inside Mary's student flat and take a look at her rooms. All it requires is that one of us plays a gas man and the other his dim-witted assistant. We could get your friend Madge to knock us up some sort of disguise."

He gestured through the throng of other wardrobe girls at John's lady friend, but, as it happened, she was already on her way across to them.

"Gentlemen!" she exclaimed, rubbing her hands together as she approached. "What are my two favourite actors doing skulking over here?" She smiled broadly, and

Edward was forced to admit that her whole face, in fact the whole room, lit up when she did so. He was by no means a ladies' man, but just then he could see what had attracted his friend to her, and fleetingly he wondered why he never seemed to do well with women, and regretted that he had never made the effort to do better.

"Johnny, sweetheart, why don't we do you first, and leave the star of the show to relax for a little longer?" She leaned in towards John, but winked in Edward's direction as she did so. "All Johnny needs is to be fitted in a nice dress suit, but I've got something special for you, Mr. Lowe." She spun around and called back across the room. "Eileen, have you got Mr. Lowe's costume there?" She pointed to a rack near the door, and the young girl standing by it trotted across with a polythene-wrapped hanger.

"Here you go," Madge said, as she whipped off the polythene. "One British Army captain's uniform, with all the fixings." From a bag attached to the hanger, she removed a shiny brown belt, a polished and brushed officer's cap and an obviously plastic pistol, a replica of the sort Edward remembered from the War. "We even checked what medals you were entitled to from your own war service and added them." She indicated a short row of campaign ribbons on the front of the tunic and smiled again. Edward, to his surprise, found himself smiling back.

"Thank you," he said, hefting the gun in his hand and trying to hide his disappointment at how flimsy and lightweight it felt. "That's really very thoughtful of you indeed."

"It's a pleasure. Now then, Johnny, let's be having you." She held out a hand and helped Le Breton to his feet. But, before he was led away, he quickly bent back down towards Edward.

"Nottingham University, did you say? You know, there's a fellow I know who's something high up in the Nottingham Police. I'll give him a phone. I'm sure he'll let us have a nose around if I ask."

Five minutes earlier, Edward would have been peeved that his own plan had been so casually tossed aside in favour of John's old pals network – they'd probably been fags together at school, or some such thing – but really, John's idea did sound easier and more likely to succeed. Which was the main thing, of course.

Only as Madge led John away across the room did darker thoughts intrude again.

On some unconscious level, he realised he'd expected their investigation to come to a relatively *comfortable* conclusion. Eric Menzies tracked down by Primrose and his Cheshire colleagues, then safely arrested by the local police. Or perhaps a jilted paramour who had killed Alice Burke in a fit of passion and who, once confronted, would break down in sorrowful confession. It was the kind of thing that happened all the time in plays, especially the more old-fashioned ones on which he'd cut his teeth. Perhaps not quite ending with the guilty party holding out his wrists and saying, "You've got me, guv, I'll come quietly. It's a relief to come clean, finally," but something along those lines.

A second death, however, made that prospect unlikely. A single killing was one thing (he smiled at the inadvertently felicitous phrase, then felt guilty for doing so), but two...

He remembered John mentioning Jack the Ripper, and shuddered. Was this going to end up like that, with girls butchered and left on display, and he forced to examine them, stretched out on the bloody cobblestones?

17

"A drug addict, the university said, and I was shocked to hear it, Mr. Lowe, shocked to me core. Well, you never expect to meet one, do you? Never mind have one living in a place what you does for."

Mrs. Black, the elderly caretaker, led Edward and John up the stairs to Mary Peel's flat at a funereal pace, holding onto the banister for grim death and heaving her substantial frame upwards one careful step at a time. Since she had met them in the street outside the flat, she had kept up an unceasing commentary, moving seamlessly from telling Edward he looked just like that little one off the telly to dissecting the morals of the young students who lived nearby. Even her difficulty mounting the stairs had failed to interrupt the flow of words.

"And she seemed such a nice girl, too. Not like some we get here nowadays, I can tell you. You get all sorts now. Foreigners, even. It was different when I started out, mind.

Back then, the university was for nice people, ones you could tell had been brought up proper. The boys always wore jackets and ties then, and was always in bed for ten o'clock. And you didn't get girls, of course, except if they was doing nursing or teaching, and the university don't teach them subjects."

With a final effort, she pulled herself onto the landing at the top of the stairs. A wooden door lay on either side, each painted the same sickly beige.

"You want that one," she said, pointing to the one on the right and handing Edward the key. "I'll leave you to it, if you don't mind. I told the Dean's office, I said you won't catch me going into that flat until a priest's been round to check it." She shuddered and her face wobbled up and down. "I'll just pop in next door and make myself a cuppa while you do whatever it is you do. The girl who was in there's been moved to temporary accommodation on account of the goings on. Can't say I blame her. What a way to go."

With a final shudder, she crossed herself quickly and went inside, leaving the two men alone on the landing, with Mary Peel's flat in front of them.

Edward had expected the door to be taped off, in the manner of *Columbo* but, to his disappointment, it was unadorned, and there was nothing to suggest to the casual observer that anything untoward had ever happened in the rooms beyond it. He turned the key in the Yale lock and pushed the door open, then stepped inside onto a thin, scuffed carpet that might once have been green, or a pale tan, but was now the colour of dirt. In places, the material was so worn away that the shape of the uneven floorboards beneath were visible as silhouettes.

Thankfully, the air, which he'd feared would still contain the lingering odours of burned flesh and singed hair, merely smelled stale and musty, like the rags cupboard in his parents' house when he was a child.

"Well, this is rather ghastly," John said, glancing round uneasily. "But I don't suppose it'll stand empty for long." He read from a copy of the police report, which his friend the deputy chief constable had helpfully provided. "It says that Mary had been living here since last October, and that these rooms are always in demand."

"God knows why," Edward said, eyeing the stained white walls with distaste. "It's a bit of a hovel. But I suppose there is a housing shortage." He sniffed with disapproval, and pulled at his gloves, so they sat tight against the tips of his fingers. "And this is only a red-brick, when all's said and done."

He flicked on the light switch. The weak bulb, partially hidden by a misshapen brown shade, made little difference to the quality of light, but the act of switching it on acted as a reminder that they didn't have all day to linger. John closed the front door behind him and they stepped inside.

The hall – though only an estate agent would use that term for what was really just a small square barely longer than the front door was wide – opened onto a sitting area, with a window (held ajar by a metal rod that slotted into a raised nub on the frame) on its far wall. Doors, each closed, led to rooms on the left and right.

At random, Edward twisted the handle of the right-hand door and pushed it open. A compact kitchen was revealed, containing a row of cupboards on the wall opposite the door and, behind it and to the left, a cooker, a sink and a fridge, in that order. Two dirty plates lay in the sink and a trail of cereal spilled across the worktop. Edward pulled open the nearest cupboard. A tin marked *Sugar* and another marked *Tea*, two slices of bread, wrapped but hard as brick, and a tin of something improbably called Alphabetti Spaghetti. The other cupboards held mismatched crockery, a few pots and pans, and a bag of potatoes, all eyes and stalks.

"I rented a flat much like this for a bit, just after Sally and I broke up," John muttered from behind him. "If the layout's the same, the bedroom will be through there, with a bathroom off it." He pointed towards the door on the other side of the sitting room.

"I imagine so," Edward replied. "There's nowhere else for it to be, is there?" He walked slowly across to the door and opened it. The room inside was dark, but he strode to the window and tugged open the closed curtains.

The bedroom in which Mary Peel had breathed her last was as tatty and rundown as the rest of the tiny flat. Even with the curtains open, the grime on the windows prevented much light from entering, which added to the gloom of a space barely ten foot square. A cheap chest of drawers that doubled as a bedside table, and a bedframe, minus covers and mattress, made up the entirety of the furnishings. Someone had tried to brighten the chest of drawers by adding stickers of Mickey Mouse and Donald Duck to it, but the effect was more tragic than cheering. The bedframe was iron, rusted in spots, and the springs sagged in the middle. On top of the chest of drawers sat a square crystal ashtray.

The stench of something burned was stronger here. Edward lit a cigarette, hoping to mask the smell a little, but it made no difference. He tugged at the window, managing with some force to edge it open a few inches.

It couldn't really make much of a difference, of course, but even so, Edward was glad he'd made the effort. Perhaps it was only in his mind, but he thought he could feel a slight breeze on his back as he stared glumly across at John, still standing in the doorway. "We're not going to find anything here, are we?" he said.

"In this terrible place? Probably not." With his usual lack of energy, John waved listlessly around the room. "Is there anything in there?" he asked, gesturing at the chest of drawers, but making no move towards it.

There were clothes in some of them: jeans and T-shirts, mainly. Edward pulled out one of the latter and held it up for John to see. "'New Christian Fellowship. Find a friend in Jesus.'" He read the script from the front out loud. "Hardly sounds the type to turn to drugs."

"You never know, Edward," John countered, though without heat. "I knew a priest in Birmingham just after the War who was addicted to opium. He bought it from God knows where. Said he'd got hooked on the stuff in Malaya in the thirties."

Edward didn't bother to reply. He found the flat's air of grubby defeat oppressive. And even if what John said were true – and it had the ring of the sort of tall tale actors told in the bar late at night – he preferred to give the girl the benefit of the doubt. He folded the T-shirt and placed it back with the others, then slid the drawer shut.

"What about through there?" he said, finally. There was one other door in the room, tucked away in the corner, which he assumed contained the usual facilities. Feeling more despondent than he would admit, he pulled open the door, but the interior was clean and bright, white tiled with a matching toilet and sink.

"A trifle basic, isn't it?" John spoke from over his shoulder. "Not so much as a medicine cabinet, or even a mirror."

"No, there's not, is there?" He hummed quietly under his breath. "I'm no expert, but I was under the impression that drug addicts needed to keep needles and whatnot to hand? The tools of their trade, as it were. But there's nothing here, or in the bedroom either."

John flipped open the police report. "It says here the needle she used was taken away by the police. Maybe they removed all that kind of thing, to spare the family? Or to avoid scandal?"

"And then have the university describe the girl as an addict anyway? What would be the point of that?"

"True." John shrugged. "Come on, then. I'll have a poke around the kitchen, and you take the sitting room. Be careful, though. The last thing you want is a stray needle jabbing you."

"Very well," Edward agreed, unenthusiastically, and followed him into the sitting room.

His cigarette was almost finished, and he looked around for an ashtray. There were none visible nearby, and it seemed disrespectful to go back into the bedroom merely to dispose of a cigarette end. John was standing in the doorway of the kitchen, reaching into a high cupboard, so he slid past him and crossed to the sink, where he nipped off the burning head of the cigarette with his thumbnail. He turned on the tap and heard the fizzle as the water hit the burning cinder of tobacco, then watched as it swirled away down the plughole.

He pulled open the door of the cupboard underneath the sink. As he'd expected, in such a small flat no space was wasted, and a plastic bin had been screwed to the back of the door. He lifted the lid and dropped the wet dog-end into the bag, where it nestled on top of hard black banana peels and desiccated teabags.

Wasn't it strange to have no other ashtrays, he wondered suddenly, and felt an unexpected tingle. Had he spotted something everyone else had missed? But perhaps someone had tidied them away?

No, the caretaker woman had said nothing had been touched.

So where were they all, then? He kept a minimum of two in every room at home, and even one in the little toilet under the stairs. Who ever heard of a smoker with only a single ashtray?

"Are you going to turn off that water?"

John's voice cut across his thoughts, startling him. He looked dumbly down at the still-swirling tap water for a moment, then twisted it off, sharply.

"Sorry, miles away," he said, already turning towards the kitchen door. He heard the sound of a cupboard being closed behind him, and an exaggerated sigh, but he had other, more important things on his mind.

The ashtray in the bedroom was a square of faux crystal, with serrated glass edges, divided at each corner by a small, shallow indentation in which a burning cigarette might be laid. The whole of the crystal base was spotlessly clean, as though it had recently been washed.

Which begged the question, of course, when had that happened? And where were the cigarette ends which must have been in it when it was dirty?

He returned to the sitting room and called through to the kitchen. "You haven't come across any ashtrays have you, John? Or any bins, other than the one under the sink?"

He thought there might be protests, but if there were, they were quiet enough that he couldn't hear them. "Not so far," John replied, popping his head around the door frame. "But I've still a few places to check."

"Could you take a look? And see what exactly is in the kitchen bin?"

John raised an eyebrow. "I do wish I'd thought to bring a pair of gloves," he sighed, but he returned to the kitchen without further comment.

It didn't take long for Edward to check the sitting room. There were few places in which anyone might conceal even so small an object as an ashtray. A desk – a table, really – under the window, with a small pile of books stacked on it (all academic religious texts, Edward noted without much interest), and a single scruffy armchair opposite took up almost all the available space. There was no sense that this was anyone's home, Edward considered with a frown. This was a place where a series of people existed, rather than lived, one after the other, with no overlap or connection. Even a theatre dressing room contained more signs of individuality than this sad little flat.

John had had no greater luck. "There's no ashtray in any of the cupboards, and the bin under the sink contains two banana peels, three teabags, a Marathon sweet wrapper and the cigarette end you dropped in there," he announced as he came through from the kitchen. "How about here?"

"Only the ashtray by the bed," Edward confirmed. "Which is rather odd, don't you think?"

John shrugged his shoulders slightly. "In what way?"

"It doesn't strike you as strange that she hasn't got a single spare ashtray?"

"She was a student, Edward. They tend to be short of cash. Perhaps she could only afford one." John laughed and shook his head. "I thought you were hoping to find a clue in the girl's rubbish, not calculating the amount of tableware she owned."

Quickly, Edward explained the anomaly he believed he had spotted in the official version of events.

"The report said she'd taken drugs then fallen asleep with a lit cigarette in her hand. But the only ashtray in the house is spotlessly clean."

"So she never had a chance to use it. The drugs must have had a quicker effect than she expected, and the cigarette had just been lit."

"Then you're saying she'd washed the ashtray since last she used it – but not the dishes in the sink?" Edward could see that one had struck home. He pressed on. "And there's not a single cigarette end anywhere in the house, nor any packets, empty or otherwise."

"That is odd, I grant you."

"More than odd. Impossible. When we speak to the girl's parents, I've no doubt they'll say she wasn't a smoker. Here…" Edward pulled his notebook from his pocket and handed it to John. "I saw a payphone on the wall downstairs. Telephone Mr. Peel just now and ask him. I'm positive he'll confirm it."

While he waited for John to return, he wandered through the rooms again, checking he'd missed nothing, he told himself, but really just marking time until he was proved right. There was nothing to see here, not enough of the dead girl's things for anything to be missed. Except for the cigarettes, of course. That was definitely something. He could feel the same pressure in his chest he'd felt when he'd realised about Alice Burke's absent shoes.

If there were no other cigarettes, or better still, if Mary Peel was not a smoker, then the cigarette must have been placed in her fingers. And presumably after she was dead, or unconscious, at least. Otherwise she'd have thrown it away. The aim must have been to burn the bed, then. But why? To hide something incriminating was the most obvious answer – but in that case, why not use a match? Surely that would have been more effective?

He retrieved the police report from the kitchen where John had left it. Yes, it was as he remembered. The girl's bedding had only caught light briefly, just enough to singe the area immediately around her hand, and then it had fizzled out. A match or two would have done a far better job.

He sat down at the desk and stared out of the window, allowing his eyes to defocus. It was a trick he'd picked up in rep, a way to aid concentration when learning lines. Now he hoped it would help him picture a man standing over a dead girl.

What benefit did a cigarette have over a match? A handful of matches would ensure the destruction of the entire bed, but they'd also risk setting the whole flat, perhaps the entire block, alight. Could the killer have been concerned for the other students' safety?

That seemed unlikely. Killers with a conscience belonged in fiction, not real life. But perhaps it was important to make the fire look accidental? And a dropped cigarette that started a fire was a common enough occurrence not to raise suspicions.

It was the killer's bad luck – and their own good fortune – that the fire failed to take hold.

Edward allowed himself a small self-congratulatory smile. That had to be it. But what evidence had the killer hoped to destroy with his "accidental" fire? And might the failure of the fire to catch have left a vital clue untouched?

So absorbed was Edward in his thoughts that he failed to recognise John was speaking to him until he felt a touch on his shoulder.

"Are you quite alright?" he asked. "You've gone rather pale. You're not feeling peaky, are you?"

"Of course not!" Edward snapped as he turned away from the window. "I was merely deep in thought. Quite productively, as it happens. But before we get to that, did you speak to Mr. Peel? Was Mary a smoker?"

"I spoke to Peel's housekeeper. She says that Mary had never smoked. You were spot on."

Edward wondered if this was why people did puzzles. This small sensation of triumph as a clue was revealed, part of a conundrum resolved. He sometimes watched Joe Riley grunting with quiet pleasure as he completed *The Times* crossword, but until now he'd never seen the attraction. As his theory was confirmed, however, he felt a definite relief, as though a pressure had been lifted from his chest, or he had exhaled after holding his breath too long.

"I thought as much," was all he said, though. No need for an ostentatious show of self-congratulation. "What it does mean is that the thought I just had is even more important."

Quickly, he explained his thinking about the burning cigarette. "Do you think your friend might be able to get us access to the burned covers?" he concluded.

"I've really no idea. But if not, we'll find some other way."

Edward had wondered more than once whether John's heart was really in the investigation, but gradually, as they had uncovered new evidence, he thought he had seen him come around. But only now, as he heard the determination in his voice, did he actually believe they felt the same way, that they'd become a team.

And, possibly, friends.

* * *

"No luck, I'm afraid."

John cupped the telephone receiver in his hand and shook his head. "The chap I've been passed on to says that the sheets and covers have all been destroyed already. No reason to keep them, apparently. Junkies kill themselves all the time, he says." His face twisted in a grimace of distaste. "I've not taken to the man, between you and me."

He paused and turned back to the telephone. Edward could hear the tinny buzz of the voice on the other end of the line.

"What's that?" John asked. "Well, I must say, that's uncalled for." He covered the mouthpiece again. "Now he's saying he's got better things to do with his time than massage the egos of a pair of bored nosey parkers, no matter who they might know."

"Of all the confounded cheek!" Edward exploded angrily. "Give me the phone!"

He grabbed the receiver from John's hand and barked into it in his most authoritative tones. "Now, you listen to me, my man," he began, then suddenly stopped. He pulled the telephone from his ear and peered at it in astonishment. "He hung up on me!"

"He did seem the type," John said.

For a moment, Edward was tempted to telephone back, but he knew it would serve no useful purpose, and he would only end up even more frustrated. Instead, he took a deep breath and returned the telephone to its cradle on the wall.

"What about the missing cigarettes?" he asked. "What did he say about that? I could hear him speaking when you mentioned it, but not what he said."

John winced, his face compressing like a folded washcloth. "Nothing useful, I'm afraid. He just said that the investigation was closed and they were satisfied it was an overdose. I suspect he resented having to speak to me at all. He wasn't interested in the slightest."

A door opened further down the hall and a young man's tousled head popped out. "Are you going to be much longer, mate?" he asked, irritably. "I'm waiting to make a call to my tutor."

"Damn cheek," Edward muttered, but found he couldn't muster the energy to put the student in his place. He could feel the spirit draining from him. What was the point?

"All yours, my dear chap," he heard John call behind him, as he headed towards the entrance.

Outside, in the weak sunlight, he led the way to the car.

"So, where now?" John asked.

"That's the question, of course," Edward replied. A question to which he had no answer – certainly no good one. "If the police here won't help, even now, then I'm at a loss, I have to admit." He sighed, feeling even more deflated. What else could they do? Was there anything young Primrose might be able to root out, now they had linked the two deaths?

As though reading his mind, John asked, "What about back in Ironbridge? Maybe there's something more Primrose could do." He slid into his seat and fiddled ineffectually with the seat belt. "Though I couldn't say what, exactly."

It wasn't obvious to Edward what more they could expect of a village bobby, either, but clearly the only place they had to go for now was back to the hotel.

The energy that had been pushing him on day after day, and which had peaked with his discovery of the absent ashtrays, had drained away to nothing in the walk to the car, and instead he allowed himself to slump forward onto the steering wheel in silence for a moment.

He could feel John's eyes on him. He straightened up and leaned across to lock his seat belt for him, then did the same for himself and started the car. By the time they had emerged from the labyrinthine university car park, John was already sleeping.

Rain began to fall as Edward followed the signs towards Birmingham and the long drive back to Ironbridge. Perhaps John has been right earlier, and it was time to admit they'd done all they could.

18

John was worried about Edward.

He'd been noticeably glum when they'd left the university, which was understandable in the circumstances, but even when they arrived back home, the little man had remained subdued. It wasn't like him; for all his moodiness and prickly nature, he wasn't a man to stay in the doldrums for long.

The reason for his extended unhappiness became clear only once they were seated in The Grapes with a pint of ale and a spot of lunch.

"They've turned out an acceptable steak pie for once," Edward announced first, with a combination of surprise and disinterest that John wouldn't have thought possible. He speared two orphaned peas with his fork and transferred them to his mouth. "I believe it might even be prime beef, not the usual cheap skirt," he went on, but even this fact failed noticeably to lighten his mood. "Not that that makes up for our current predicament, of course."

"Our current predicament?" Whatever the problem was, it was best that Edward said it aloud, John decided. Sally always said it was important to face your problems head on. Perhaps if she'd taken her own advice, they'd still be married...

"This damned dead end we've reached."

"Ah, that."

"I just don't see where we can go from here. We have vital new evidence of foul play, we've linked the deaths of Alice Burke and Mary Peel beyond question... but nobody in a position to do anything about it has the slightest interest in doing so."

"We could have another word with Primrose?"

"What would be the point? He's willing enough, of course, but what's he actually going to do? Canvas the country from the back of his bicycle?"

He swirled the dregs of his pint around the bottom of the glass and stared down at the table. "No, we have to face facts. This is as far as we can go."

He swallowed the last of his beer and made to rise, but John leaned over and placed a restraining hand on his arm. "Don't be so hasty, Edward. Sit down and have another drink." He leaned across and tapped on the bar with the edge of a coin. "Same again here, when you've got a second, Fred," he called over, then, turning back to Edward, went on, "You can surely spare the time it takes to drink a pint before you give up on Alice Burke and Mary Peel? Surely we owe them that?" He smiled. "You can bet old Wetherby wouldn't quit so easily."

For a moment, he thought he'd said the wrong thing and Edward would take offence at the comparison. Then the little man shrugged.

"Perhaps you're right," he said. "But Wetherby is a fictional character, with a writer who makes everything come out right in the end. This is the real world, where inequities are commonplace and bad people often go unpunished." He fell silent as Fred passed over their beer. "But, even so, you're right in one other respect. We owe it to those poor women to continue." He reached over for one of the pints and took a long drink. "So, the question we have to ask ourselves is a simple one. What *can* we do next?"

He was sure he would regret it later, but John had been caught unawares by his own reaction to Edward's dejection. Until that moment, he'd have sworn this whole affair was at heart a lark, a silly, basically pointless way to pass the time while there was nothing else to do, rather like the second feature films he'd made twenty years previously. Of course, there had been times when he'd been more invested than that, but generally, yes, a lark was what it had been.

But not now. He'd stopped Edward from leaving because he genuinely wanted to continue, and to continue with Edward alongside him. The realisation surprised him, and frightened him, just a little.

"One, we can visit Mary Peel's parents," he said with conviction, counting off on his fingers. "Two, we can see if Primrose will make a report to his superiors, detailing the discrepancies we discovered at her rooms – the missing cigarettes and whatnot. Three, we could try to find out the names of the other soldiers. Pop up to Cheshire and do some digging of our own."

It would be an exaggeration to say that Edward seemed wholly reinvigorated by this little speech, but he visibly perked up as he listened to John's plan.

"Bert and Bill, Henry and Bob," he said with a small smile. "I've considered those names so often that I've got them burned into my memory. If only scripts were so easily memorised."

"It's a shame they're so unmemorable generally, though. It'd be a lot easier to find a Rasputin or a Uriah Heep."

Edward laughed, not for long, but with, John felt, genuine amusement. "True. Bob Murray's hardly the most unusual name I've ever heard. There's bound to be thousands of them."

"That there is – there's one just up the road, for starters!"

Barney Ifeld let the snug door swing closed behind him and deposited himself heavily in a seat between John and Edward.

"I heard someone tapping at the bar and thought, old Fred'll have someone's hand off if they keep that up. Then I saw it was you two. Fred won't bother about one of his film people doing that, but he'd have a local out on his ear. You'll be snapping your fingers and shouting 'Garçon' next!"

John blushed. He detested rudeness more than anything, and was ashamed of being so ill-mannered, even inadvertently. And to have this obnoxious blowhard point it out, that was…

Suddenly, he realised what the obnoxious blowhard had said.

"There's a Bob Murray who lives near here?" he asked, just as Edward said the exact same thing, so that their voices ran over one another like a tiny, two-man chorus.

"Oh, aye. And he went round the bend years ago, too, they reckon. Maybe he's the bloke you're after, eh?" Ifeld grinned, exposing a mouthful of big, white teeth, which made John feel a little nauseated, for some reason. "That's what you were talking about, wasn't it? The nutter who killed that girl. Maybe it was him up by the reservoir?"

Edward's voice was cold. It was clear he liked Ifeld even less than John did. "Didn't you say it was a stranger that you saw up at the reservoir, Mr. Ifeld?"

"It's Barney to my friends," Ifeld responded easily. "And it wasn't me who saw anyone. You wouldn't catch me up there, not at night. Bloody freezing it is. The bloke who *was* up there, though, he said it was a stranger, right enough. But no bugger's seen Bob Murray for years. A hermit, he is. Has his food delivered from town, and never leaves that farmhouse of his. Not that I know of, anyway." He grinned again, and John realised why he found the gesture so disturbing. It reminded him of a Lon Chaney poster he had seen as a child, when Chaney had been made up as a wickedly toothsome ghoul. "Until now, maybe."

"Be that as it may, we might wish to speak to Mr. Murray, if you'd be so good as to provide directions to his farm." Edward's voice was no warmer, but he attempted a brief smile in Ifeld's direction.

"It'd be my pleasure! His farm's about a half-hour drive from here. Just follow the road out of town and then take the next turning after you pass the phone box. Bob Murray's farm's at the end of the track." He scratched at his chin, the sound of his nail running across stubble loud, like a match striking. "He's a wrong 'un, though, and always has been. If you go up there, you be careful. Bob Murray's the local monster, that's what he is." He laughed, though whether he was joking or not, John couldn't tell.

"A monster?" he asked. "In what way?"

"Burned in the War. Got himself stuck in a tank that took a direct hit from Jerry. Got out, but left most of his face behind."

"My God." John had known men who'd been in burning tanks. The stories they'd told of their less-fortunate colleagues, the ones who hadn't got out in time, had been enough to make his blood curdle. "And he's locked himself away in his farmhouse ever since?"

"That's the story. But could be he comes out at night, eh?" He deliberately held John's gaze for longer than was comfortable. "That's the second time I've given you useful information, John. Isn't it about time you returned the favour? What happened up there?"

"Why are you so interested, can I ask?" Edward had been watching Ifeld silently, but now he spoke up. "I wouldn't have thought a busy man like yourself would have the time to get involved with our little investigation."

Ifeld looked thoughtfully at the little actor. He said nothing, obviously considering his next words carefully. Finally, he gave a small shrug, a far less dramatic gesture than John was used to seeing from him. "Fair question. But before I tell you anything, I'll need you both to give me your word that none of this goes beyond us three."

The two men nodded.

"OK, then. What it is, I've got… an interest, let's call it… in a development on the north side of the reservoir. We're going to build a retirement home up there beside the water; a big, modern place, with colour tellies in every room, teasmades, flock wallpaper, the lot. Room for fifty well-off pensioners, I reckon. Lakeview Manor, we're calling it."

"What a pretty name," John said, and winced as he caught Edward's irritated look.

"Thanks. It was a company down in London came up with it, but we think it's got a decent ring about it. But it's all about perception in the retirement game, and it wouldn't be helpful if it gets out that a woman got herself murdered right about where we're going to plant an ornamental garden for the old dears to sit in."

"No, I imagine not."

"Though, saying that, murders happen all the time, and the papers are so full of them that they soon get used to wrap chips. It might actually be trickier to sell Lakeview Manor as a place for your old mum to spend her twilight years if some silly cow managed to fall in the actual lake and drown. Old folk have accidents all the time; they don't get murdered *all* that often." Again, his teeth flashed whitely in a wide grin. "So, you see the predicament I'm in. Whether it was a murder or an accident, it's not ideal for me. But if you boys could give me a bit of advance warning, I can get a head start on smoothing things over, decide how to handle it…"

Once, during rehearsals for an utterly forgettable play of the week, the star, an actor who had been quite well known in his heyday, but was by then sliding down to booze-fuelled anonymity, had turned up drunk as a lord. He'd refused to say his lines properly, dissolved into giggles at every opportunity and generally caused the entire day to be ruined. The director, furiously aware that every minute counted, had grabbed the inebriated lead by the collar, dragged him to a water trough which was being used as set dressing, and held his head under for so long that John had begun to fear he was witnessing a murder.

But his anger was as nothing to Edward's.

"Decide how to handle it!" His voice rose in volume with every word, until he was all but shouting. Fred the landlord stuck his head round the corner of the bar, but withdrew it hurriedly. Edward, for his part, evidently realised he was calling attention to himself, and continued in a quieter, but no less vehement, tone.

"A woman may well have been murdered, and all you can think about is the effect that might have on some tawdry business opportunity of yours?"

Ifeld was unabashed. "Pretty much, yes. It's not like it makes any difference, does it? No matter what I do, she'll still be dead and I'll still be building up by the reservoir. I don't see what difference it makes if I get a quick heads-up about what happened to her."

Without another word, Edward stood up and walked out of the snug, ignoring Ifeld, but casting a quick glance across at John.

"I do believe it's time we were going," John mumbled awkwardly, also getting to his feet. He quickly drained his glass and placed it alongside Edward's still half-full one on the bar.

He could feel Ifeld's eyes on his back, and hear his soft laugh, as he pushed open the door and wandered outside.

"Remember, keep this to yourself!" he called after them, still laughing.

"Did you believe his story?"

"That he's only interested in Alice Burke's murder to the extent it affects him? Yes. That he's building a retirement home by the reservoir? I've no idea. Perhaps."

Even with the advantage of his far longer legs, John was struggling to keep up with Edward as he strode down the hill towards the hotel. He was quite impressed that the shorter man was able to keep up a conversation as he did so.

"Does it really matter?" he asked, as they turned off St. Peter's Street onto Abbeygate.

"No, I suppose not." Edward came to sudden halt. "Though now that I think about it, wasn't David very pleased that he didn't need to get any special permission to film up there? Didn't he say that the Ministry of Defence owned all the surrounding land, but the local council had responsibility for the reservoir?"

"Did he? I must admit, I rather tune out when he starts talking about the logistical side of things. But, even if he did, what difference does that make? The council are perfectly at liberty to sell the land to Ifeld for development. Isn't that the sort of thing councils do all the time? I'm no expert, but it does sound like their kind of thing."

"I'm sure it is. But it begs the question – who in their right mind would build a retirement home surrounded by MOD training grounds and firing ranges?"

"Someone hoping to sell accommodation to elderly gun nuts and ex-army officers?"

Edward was not amused. "Do try not to be facetious, John. It doesn't become you. No, there's definitely something off about Mr. Ifeld. Let's file it away for now, but we mustn't forget that he's still not explained exactly how he came to know about this mysterious stranger wandering about in the dark."

"So, what do we do next? Do we go and visit Farmer Murray, or take a train to Cornwall and spend an hour or two with poor Mr. Peel? We've only got tomorrow off filming, so we can't do both."

"Perhaps we need to split our investigations in two, then," Edward suggested as they climbed the steps to the hotel entrance. "I telephoned British Rail about trains to St. Ives, and it's impossible to get there and back in a day in any case, so there's the necessity of staying in Cornwall overnight. I also spoke to David, and apparently you're not needed for morning filming on Tuesday, so you could shoot off to visit the Peels first thing in the morning, and be back here for lunchtime the following day. Meanwhile, I'll borrow a car and pay this chap Murray a visit. We can then compare notes during the lunch break on Tuesday. How does that sound?"

It sounded, in John's opinion, as though Edward was taking a quick spin in the countryside while he spent hours trekking down to Cornwall along dirt tracks and mucky lanes to spend the day in the company of a grief-stricken family – but, even so, it was good to see the little man restored to his usual overbearing self.

He could see one problem, though.

"I'm not sure you should be going up to see Murray on your own, you know," he said. "He's a suspect, and from Ifeld's description, could be dangerously unhinged."

"That's true," Edward conceded reluctantly. "You don't doubt that he's our man, though? You heard Ifeld – caught in a burning tank, just like Lowell Edwardsson said. It's too much of a coincidence for it not to be the same man. But even if we wait to speak to this particular Murray until after you get back, I still can't go with you to Cornwall. I'm needed first thing on Tuesday morning for a fitting for the captain's uniform I'm wearing in the last episode. But I won't approach Murray in your absence, if that's what you want."

He couldn't ask for more than that, John decided. "Fair enough," John said. "I'll go down to St. Ives and we can decide what to do about Murray when I get back. Perhaps Matthew Peel will have some useful information, something which would weaken or strengthen our suspicions about Murray."

Edward nodded. "Perfect," he beamed, and skipped up the stairs to his room, the spring completely back in his step.

John followed at a more sedate pace, wondering what to pack for his trip to Cornwall, and whether the lovely girl on reception would be willing to do it for him. It was wonderful that Edward had regained so quickly his zip and brio, but it was also quite, quite wearing.

19

John remembered seeing the pictures in the newspapers, just after the War. Grainy, indistinct greys and blacks and dirty whites, British prisoners of the Japanese, smiling uncertainly at the camera as though unwilling to believe they were free, all recently released from starvation diets and back-breaking toil in the murderous heat of the jungle.

Matthew Peel had, it seemed, been one of those men.

Margaret Hunter was her name – "Call me Meg," she'd said – and she was small and slim and fair-haired, a little younger than he'd expected. When he'd telephoned from the train station, after a journey that had actually turned out to be rather pleasant, she'd apologised she couldn't pick him up. "Matthew does all the driving," she'd explained, "and he's not up to it at the moment" – and for a second he thought he knew her voice, only to realise that she reminded him of a landlady he'd had a youthful (on his part) and all-too-brief fling with many years previously. It was the combination of affection and apology in her voice.

She'd met him at the door, and after the awkwardness of explaining that, yes, he was the same John Le Breton who played the posh antiques chap on the BBC, but that also, yes, he was currently helping the police with their enquiries, unexpectedly hustled him into the kitchen, barely letting him stop long enough to remove his coat. She'd explained the reason as soon as she'd safely shut the kitchen door behind him.

"I just wanted to prepare you," she said. "Matthew was a prisoner of the Japanese for three years, you see, and when he came home, he wasn't the man who left for the War." She'd been crying, he could tell from the redness of her eyes, but he guessed this was a strong woman, and not one to give in easily to public weakness. Even so, there was no missing the pain in her voice. "He was always a slim man, but when he walked off the ship that brought him home, he was skin and bones. And he never bulked up, not so you'd notice."

He wondered exactly what the relationship was between her and Peel. She'd introduced herself as his housekeeper, and explained that his wife had died years ago, before the War. But all this talk of *Matthew* this and *Matthew* that was what his own father would have called *over-familiar* and his mother *taking liberties*. And then there was the crying. Perhaps she'd just been working for the family for a long time? Did that *mean* something, he wondered, then chided himself for being so suspicious. It really wasn't like him.

While he was thinking, Meg sniffed and opened the cupboard behind her, reaching up for a teapot on a high shelf. "But that wasn't the worst of it, Mr. Le Breton. Physically, he recovered, eventually, but mentally…" She dropped three teabags into the teapot and added hot water from the kettle. "Mentally, he's been an angry, bitter man from that day to this. Before, he was jolly as can be, the life and soul wherever we went, but after… I think that if it wasn't for Mary, he'd have given up on the world completely."

"Mary was an only child?" John wasn't sure if that was the right thing to ask, but it had been one of the questions he'd agreed with Edward, and he wanted to keep asking questions here in the kitchen for as long as he could. Peel would be the second bereft parent he'd spoken to in little more than a week, and he didn't even have Edward with him this time. He could think of innumerable places he'd rather be than in this kitchen with this grieving woman, but the room next door was not one of them.

Fortunately, it seemed it *was* the right thing to ask. Meg smiled, and for the first time since he had arrived, he was sure he saw happiness reach as far as her eyes.

"She was. Their one and only. We cosseted her, Matthew always said, and I knew it was true, but… do you have children, Mr. Le Breton?"

"Do call me John," he replied. "It seems only fair if I've to call you Meg. But, yes, I've got two. Both boys, though."

"It's all the same, I expect. I never had any, myself. I never married. But Mary was as good my own, and I tried to fill the space where her real mum should have been.

Maybe me and her dad spoiled her too much. But she was the only child in the house, you see, and I think you keep them closer when there's just the one. That's why she didn't go to university until she was a bit older."

"Mary was a quiet girl? What Sally, my ex-wife, would call a homebody?"

Meg half-smiled. "That's as good a description as any. She liked to be here, with me and her dad, more than she liked anything else. And we liked it too, there's no denying it. She said I was her best friend, which I loved when she was little – well, who wouldn't? – but, as she got older, I did wonder if it was healthy."

From a drawer, she selected a red tea cosy and laid it on the table. "Don't misunderstand me, John, she wasn't strange or anything. She had pals, from the church, mainly, and she was still close to a couple of girls from school too. But she never had a boyfriend, not a serious one anyway, and she wasn't one for going out at the weekend. Matthew thought that was a good thing, but I wasn't so sure. Everyone's got a little bit of the devil in them, I think, and it does no harm to let it out now and again. I'd have liked Mary to get in trouble, just a little, now and again. Does that make me a terrible person?" she asked suddenly.

He shook his head. "Far from it. Some minor devilment never did anyone any harm." He chuckled. "I could tell you some stories of my younger days…"

He stopped, uncomfortable with himself, with the way in which he so easily slipped into casual, harmless flirtation. *Remember why you're here*, he said to himself, fiercely.

"But never mind me and my dissolute youth," he said, and this time his laugh was clumsy and forced. "Mary wasn't one to misbehave? Not even a little? You said on the phone she didn't smoke?"

Meg was firm. "Never. She signed the pledge at church, not to smoke or drink, when she was about fourteen."

"And no boyfriends at all?"

"Nobody serious. Dr Cummings' son Grant took her to a couple of church dances, but they were just friends."

There was a wobble in her voice. John reached across and placed his hand over hers. She smiled with gratitude, and John was pleased the gesture had been the right one.

"That's why I was glad when she decided to go to university, and in a different city too. It was a real jolt, don't get me wrong, and I missed her terribly, but it's not right for a girl of nearly thirty to spend all her time in church or at home. She needs to get out and meet new people, make a life for herself. That's what I thought, then. I'd give everything to change that now."

"I wasn't around as much as I should have been while my boys were growing up," John admitted, more to keep the conversation moving than from any particular desire to swap experiences. "I left all that sort of thing to Sally. But I imagine even one is a lot to handle."

"Not Mary, no. We always knew where she was and what she was up to. You could set your clock by her, even when she was little."

"You've been with the family that long?"

"Since Mrs. Peel died, God rest her soul. Mary was just one past, barely able to walk. Matthew's little sister and me had been friends at school, and he knew I was looking for a position. I'd always admired him, you know, in the way young girls do of their pals' older brothers. A crush, they'd call it now."

She stirred the water in the teapot and stared down at it, watching the bags swirl around in the water. Avoiding his eye, John thought.

"I don't know why I'm telling you all this," she said finally, without looking up. "It must be because I've seen you on the television. It makes it feel like I know you, somehow."

"I've been told I have one of those faces," John said. "Though a director also once told me I looked like an undertaker who didn't care much for his job."

She looked up and smiled. "I wouldn't say that. And anyway, when Matthew had to ship out quicker than expected, I agreed to stay on and look after little Mary."

The conversation always came around to where it needed to be, if you were patient.

"That's actually part of what I wanted to speak to Matthew about," he said, and hoped she wouldn't ask for details just yet. If she did, and she decided that his questions would be too upsetting, he knew he wouldn't be able to insist, and the trip would be wasted.

"About the War?" Meg was puzzled, he could see, but no more than that. He realised she was operating entirely by instinct, obeying the polite niceties of having a visitor in for tea. She'd no energy spare to wonder about the questions he had to ask. Hardly surprising, given what had happened.

She crossed to the fridge and poured some milk into a china jug. "He'd probably rather speak to you about the War than... you know. But Mr. Edwardsson said that you and Mr. Lowe had been very helpful with his daughter..." Again, her voice broke, and this time she turned away.

"I thought Mr. Edwardsson knew about Matthew," she said over her shoulder as she fussed about, opening and closing cupboard doors with her back to him, apparently looking for something. "But I suppose he assumed Matthew had gotten better. Well, you would, wouldn't you? But he hasn't, not even after thirty years..." She turned with an open packet of Digestives in her hand and John could see the love, and the sadness, in her eyes. "I thought it had broken him, the jungle... but then when the police phoned... phoned about Mary..." Her voice faltered and a single tear rolled down her face, only to be ground beneath the palm of a defiant hand. "Sorry about this carry-on," she said simply and arranged the Digestives on a plate in a circle. "When we got the news about Mary, that was when he really broke."

She laid the plate down on a tray, along with three cups and saucers and, a moment later, the cosy-covered teapot, the milk jug and a bowl of sugar.

"He seems a bit better today," she said. "The sedative pills the doctor gave him have helped. I think he'll be OK to talk to you, though he might fall asleep – but do be careful what you ask him and try not to upset him." She smiled as she thought of something. "He'll not recognise you, by the way. The only television he watches is *Songs of Praise* on a Sunday." She clucked her tongue and pulled open a drawer. "Almost forgot the teaspoons." She smiled again, but now John fancied that all he could see was pain. "Shall we go through and see him?"

He held the kitchen door open and followed her through to the sitting room, to the broken Matthew Peel.

Peel was exactly as Meg had described.

He sat in the only armchair in the room, its high back and wide arms dwarfing his own slight, skinny frame. Net curtains obscured the view through the window, but, though he faced it, it was obvious he had no interest in whatever was outside. His eyes were wet and red, and he seemed never to blink as John took a seat on the sofa opposite him.

Meg laid the tray down on a low coffee table and sat beside him. She poured John a cup and handed it to him. "I'll let you put your own milk and sugar in. Matthew says I've got a heavy hand with the milk." She smiled again, and this time the smile was all courage. The courage she needed to control her own grief in front of this stranger, and courage for Peel, as she carefully placed a cup in his hand and curled his fingers around it, making sure he had a good grip before she relinquished it.

"This is Mr. Le Breton, Matthew," she said quietly. "Remember, Lowell Edwardsson said he was going to come around to ask a few questions about Mary."

Now, Peel blinked and his eyes slowly focused on John. He said nothing, just stared at the interloper in his home as if unsure which of them had the right to be there.

"And the War," John added. "If you don't mind. The camp you were in."

"The camp?" Peel's voice was querulous and thin. He wore dark trousers and an open-necked white shirt, through which John could see the almost translucent skin of his throat. His Adam's apple bobbed like a duck egg as he spoke. "What about the camp?" He shivered and turned to look at his housekeeper in obvious anger. "I don't talk about the camp. I *never* talk about the camp. Didn't you tell him that, Meg?"

John realised his mistake and inwardly cursed his stupidity. "No, not that camp, old chap. The one you were in before you shipped out, when you were still in England. In Cheshire, weren't you? It's a lovely bit of the country, isn't it?" John turned to Meg, inviting her to join the conversation. "Sally and I spent a month there, many years ago, a sort of working holiday."

She nodded encouragingly, but said nothing, and he turned back to Peel. "You were based in Balcon, I think? That was the camp I meant."

"Balcon?" Peel spat the word out with unexpected vigour, as though it pained him to have it in his mouth.

Now, that's quite a reaction, John thought.

"Yes, I was in Balcon." Peel's gaze held John's own for a moment. His voice, when he next spoke, was cold and, somehow, even sadder. "At one time, I thought Balcon was the worst place in the world, you know. That was before Singapore, though. And Singapore was before now, before sitting here in this spot. This…" He thumped his fist weakly down on the arm of the chair. "This is the worst place in the world. The worst place there'll ever be. I know that now."

John had no idea what to say to that, and no desire to intrude on so raw a grief, and so fell back on his usual approach when in an awkward social situation. He continued as though the awkwardness did not exist.

"When you were in Balcon, when you were training on the base there, there was a spot of bother, I believe?"

At first, it seemed Peel would not answer. Then, as though coming to a decision, he nodded once, slowly. "You could call it that. Yes, you could call it a spot of bother." His laugh was sharp, mirthless, almost cruel. "Not that it matters, not now, but it was that spot of bother that led me to Singapore and three years…" He trailed off, sipped from his cup, then placed it on the table with a shaking hand. "But, yes, there was a girl that died, and we all got our marching orders. Is that what you mean?"

"It is." John put his own cup down, the tea untouched. He'd have preferred something stronger. "I'm sorry to trouble you just now, but we – I – believe that what happened then might have something to do with your daughter's death."

"I'd guessed that. What other reason would you have for asking about it?" There was a hint of steel in the way he spoke, which suggested there was an intelligent mind housed in his fragile body. "Plus you spoke to Lowell, and the only thing we have in common, other than what happened to our children, is those months in the countryside all those years ago…" He grimaced and indicated a photograph of his daughter that John only now realised sat on a small shelf to the other side of his chair. "I have other, more important things to consider than the distant past, Mr. Le Breton, so what would you like to know?"

"I won't keep you any longer than I need to," John promised with conviction. "I'd just like to know what you recall of the night Sylvia Menzies died."

Peel considered the question carefully. John saw his lips begin to move more than once, apparently about to speak, then fall still. Finally, he said, "What happened to her was the inevitable result of the brutality of the army, or at least the army as it existed in Balcon. Hundreds, thousands of young men pulled from their lives, removed from the system of checks and conventions that kept them from running wild and deposited together in the countryside, given access to guns and alcohol and women, and encouraged all day, every day, to think of battle, destruction and the imminence of their own deaths." He shook his head. "Is it any wonder that terrible things happened there?"

"You didn't enjoy your time in the army?"

"I hated every moment of it, and it ruined my life." He paused. "I intended to enter the Church, you know, but Balcon and the War put paid to that."

"You lost your faith?"

"In a manner of speaking. I never lost my faith in God, but I did lose my faith in His creations. How could I minister to a flock of parishioners, when I'd seen the cruelties men inflict on one another?"

"I believe it was terrible in the Far East…"

"Not just in the Far East!" Peel's voice was sharp but brittle, like the edge of a piece of flint. "At Balcon too. You asked about the night Sylvia Menzies died, and I said it was inevitable, and so it was. Not that unfortunate woman in particular, or even a death necessarily, but something terrible was bound to happen, sooner or later. With so many vile people in one place, how could it not?"

John remembered his own training days with relative fondness, but he knew that had not been everyone's experience.

"But you had your group of friends, at least," he said. "That must have been some comfort to you."

"Friends? The thugs and drunkards with whom I spent that night? Those were no friends of mine, Mr. Le Breton."

"Surely Lowell Edwardsson at least was a friend? That's how he described you when we spoke to him."

"Lowell was the best of them, but not one of them was a good man. All they thought about was women and drink, and where and when they could get their hands on one or other. That night was no different. I'm no drinker, neither then nor now, but I was young and weak and foolish, and I wanted to fit in. I'm not made of the stuff of martyrs, Mr. Le Breton, and I taught myself to stomach beer, so I wouldn't be ostracised. I taught myself to stomach the presence of loose women, too, though there at least I retained enough self-respect not to become involved personally.

"But the others – Lowell, Bob Murray, Bill and Bert – that was all they thought about. Every time we got a pass, we headed down to the public house in the village, and we would meet up with Sylvia Menzies and her slattern of a friend. I forget the friend's name, but she was as much of a harlot as Sylvia. No better than prostitutes, the pair of them."

"Prostitutes?" John had intended to keep quiet, so as not to distract Peel, but the word was out of his mouth before he could stop it.

"Perhaps not literally," Peel conceded reluctantly. "I doubt they made enough to do the job professionally, but they were always happy to take drinks and trinkets, even money when they could, from the soldiers. It was young Henry's birthday and he'd had a small amount from home, so Sylvia was all over him. I remember that particularly, because Lowell wasn't happy; he thought she was his girl, even though she was a married woman."

"Not happy? How so?" John couldn't deny that he was starting to enjoy himself, just a little. While they stayed on the subject of the War, and away from that of Peel's dead daughter, he could see why Edward liked this so much.

"Nothing serious. Just Lowell telling Sylvia to stop making a show of herself, and her telling him she'd do whatever she wanted. As though that wasn't obvious to anyone who looked at her! And Bob Murray was doing his best to make everything worse, like he always did. He was a nasty piece of work, was Bob. Always whispering in people's ears, stirring up trouble where he could, starting fights and then melting back into the crowd to watch. One minute he'd be goading Lowell, telling him to keep his girl in check; the next he'd be at the woman, reminding her that her husband could come home any time."

"Did you know the husband?"

"No, I never met him. I don't think any of us did. There was talk in the camp that he'd got a temper on him, and that, when he came back, he'd kill anyone who'd taken liberties with his wife, but there was always talk of that sort, and we thought nothing of it. Out of sight, out of mind, when you're that age."

To his annoyance, John realised he hadn't thought to bring anything with him on which he could take notes. "I wonder," he asked Meg, "could I trouble you for a sheet of paper? Would that be a terrible nuisance?" He reached into his jacket pocket for a pen, but he had forgotten to bring one of those, as well. "Perhaps a pencil too, if that's not too much bother?"

She returned quickly. John wondered if she was worried about leaving Peel on his own for too long. Clearly, whatever he had been given by the doctor had done its job; Peel was mainly calm, if glassy-eyed, and though his eyes betrayed the pain of his grief, it was masked by the effects of the medication and the anger he plainly still felt about his time at the training camp. Meg's hand trembled as she passed him the pen and paper; Matthew Peel was not the only one in need of artificial assistance, in John's opinion.

The best help he could give the pair of them, though, was to find out who had killed Mary Peel.

"I wonder, could you tell me the names of everyone in the group that night?"

Peel nodded. "There was me and Lowell, Henry Anderson, Bert Smith and Bill Carmichael – those two were regulars, not conscripts like the rest of us – and Bob Murray."

"And Murray was a troublemaker, you said?"

"He was. Bert and Bill were great friends, they went everywhere together, and so did me and Lowell, and we all looked out for young Henry, of course. But Bob was one of those men, you know the sort, always on the outside looking in, always sniping and snipping away, telling tales and spreading rumours. I don't even know why he was with us that night. He didn't usually hang around with us. Maybe something to do with the other woman, I don't know. He thought himself a great ladies' man, I do know that, but only the roughest ones would entertain him."

John scribbled all of this down. Edward would be delighted with confirmation of everyone's names and the news that Bob Murray had been a bad lot. Time to move Peel along, though. His eyelids were drooping a little and John remembered Meg's earlier warning about the effect of the sedatives.

"Was Murray violent at all?"

"They all were, at heart. We were there to be trained as killers, after all. But Bob was no worse than anyone else, no."

"And everyone was there when the jeep was stolen?"

"That was Bob's idea too. If I'd been in my right mind, I'd have had nothing to do with it, but like I said, you had to drink to fit in, and I'd had more than was good for me. So we piled in, all of us plus the two women, and they were drunker than the men and slobbering all over anyone they could get their hands on. It was a disgusting spectacle."

"You drove out into the countryside?"

"We had a sort of picnic, I suppose. Some coats on the ground, the bottles we'd brought from the pub, and a fire to keep out the worst of the cold. Sounds quite nice, doesn't it? It wasn't. Sylvia Menzies started dancing in the light of the fire, flaunting herself in front of everyone." He scowled at the memory and shook his head. "That got Lowell's dander up again. He told her to sit down, but a couple of the others told him to shut up; someone shouted they were enjoying the show. Anyway, there was a bit of a row, a couple of punches were thrown, and then Lowell announced he was leaving, and since he was the one who knew the guard on duty who might let us slip into camp after hours, we could either go with him or face the C.O. on a charge in the morning. Sylvia Menzies said she was having a good time and wasn't going anywhere, and she and Lowell screamed at each other a bit, and then she slapped his face and stormed off."

"There was some fighting before Sylvia stormed off?" John asked, and underlined this in his notes. This wasn't quite how Lowell Edwardsson had described the night. "Can you remember who was involved?"

Peel shook his head. "No, I'm afraid not. Fighting wasn't uncommon back then, when they'd been drinking. It never came to much that I know of, and was usually all forgotten by the morning, but I couldn't say for sure who was involved that night. Lowell, certainly, but as to who with? Your guess is as good as mine.

"Anyway, we couldn't leave the woman out there, much as she deserved it, so we all had a look for her, but she was nowhere to be found. We couldn't stay there all night either, though, and pretty soon we decided we'd have to go, regardless. Maybe the walk back to town would teach her a lesson."

"And she was found dead the following day." John regretted the words as soon as they left his mouth. What was he thinking, saying something so thoughtless to a man who had just lost his own daughter? He heard a stifled sob at his side and felt the little housekeeper hurry from the room before he could apologise. Though what use would an apology be? If he'd wanted to avoid upsetting these poor people, he should have stayed away.

Hard to credit he'd been so pleased with himself only minutes previously.

Thankfully, Peel himself seemed not to have noticed, or at least was sedated enough for the remark to cause him no visible pain.

"She was," he said simply. "Frozen to death, they said, but only God knows the truth."

"You don't believe that's how she died?"

"I didn't say that. I don't know. All I know is that one day we were in basic training, with months still left to do, and the next I was on a train heading for Southampton, and on my way to the fighting in Malaya." He reached forward for his cup, then thought better of it and sat back in his chair. "Do you know how long it was between that night and my first night as a prisoner of the Japanese, Mr. Le Breton? Nineteen days exactly. Less than three weeks before I entered that hell on earth, I was tucked up in bed, writing letters to Meg, planning my next forty-eight hour pass and the chance to spend some time with my little girl."

In the silence that followed, John picked up Peel's cup and offered it to him, but he shook his head. "Thank you, but no. I think I'd like to sleep now." He settled back in his chair, and his eyelids fluttered once or twice, as he struggled to stay awake a little longer. "Three weeks from a night in a village pub in England to a night on open ground in a Jap POW camp. That's not something that happens because some drunken harlot dies in an accident, even if there were some soldiers nearby." His eyes finally closed completely, and his voice faded to a whisper. "It takes much more than an accident to get the British Army moving that fast, even in wartime," he murmured so softly that John had to lean in close to hear.

There was obviously to be no more from Peel. His head fell to the side, and he began to snore quietly. John slowly rose to his feet and looked down at the sleeping man. Nestled between the high wing backs of the chair, he looked even smaller and more frail, closer to a child than an adult. He wondered when the sedatives would wear off, and hoped it wouldn't be for a long time yet.

He tiptoed from the room, closing the door softly behind him. From the kitchen, he could hear the muffled sobs of a woman in the most terrible pain. For a moment, he glanced at the front door, but he knew there could be no immediate escape that way. Instead, he straightened the cuffs of his shirt sleeves and walked towards the sound, with what he hoped was a comforting smile on his face.

20

The rain had settled into a steady rhythm by the time Edward reached the hilly path leading to Bob Murray's farm, and when he realised Bobby McMahon's car could go no further and he'd need to walk the rest of the way, he nearly gave up.

Fields stretched out on either side of the increasingly slippery mud of the path, though none were currently in cultivation, despite the season. The sight of a rusting farm machine of some sort, large and hulking in the half-light of dusk, suggested the fields had been left fallow for longer than just the current summer. Two dead crows, tied by their feet to the fence, were grisly indicators that someone was still at work nearby, however. He hurried past them, averting his eyes from their black wings slapping back and forth in the wind.

Perhaps he should have waited until John got back? But it had seemed such a good idea back at the hotel. A pleasant after-dinner drive in the countryside, combined with a quick recce of the Murray farm. Kill two birds with one stone, he thought, then glanced back at the dead crows with a shudder.

Luckily, after a few hundred exhausting uphill yards, the path flattened out and arrowed straight for a collection of buildings that had until now been hidden behind the hill. A moss-covered mile marker stone by the side of the road (once covered by a handkerchief) offered Edward a chance to sit and take stock, as well as catch his breath.

Primrose had said that Murray was a hermit who never left his house, but he could presumably look out of his windows. Which meant it was vital to keep out of the line of sight of the farmhouse, whichever that was.

He stood up on his tiptoes, but it was impossible to make out which building was which, even as the rain tailed off to a light, if wet, haze. He tried balancing on the mile marker itself to gain some much-needed height, but only succeeded in slipping off and barking his shin through his trousers. He cursed loudly and rubbed at the offending area, then hobbled towards the hedge, which he was able to follow along its length to a wooden five-barred gate.

Fortunately, the gate was held closed only with a loop of rope. Even more happily, it didn't creak when pushed ajar, as he'd expected it would. He squeezed through the smallest gap he could manage and carefully closed it behind him.

In front of him, another short stretch of path opened out into a large, muddy yard, constrained on two sides by long, low hangar-style barns, and at the other end by what was obviously the farmhouse. Edward quickly ducked into the shadows of one shed and peered up at the house.

It was exactly as he'd expected: two storeys of dirty stone, with a door dead centre, flanked on either side by a plethora of windows. At the far left-hand side, an extension had been built at some point in the past; its door had not been closed properly and it moved in the wind, banging gently but steadily against its frame. Otherwise, the scene was deathly quiet.

Now he was here, Edward found himself uncharacteristically cautious. It was one thing to sit in the cosy snug of The Grapes and lay out plans on the back of handy napkins, quite another to stand in an unfamiliar farmyard in the failing light and decide which enormous rusty barn to investigate first, all the while under what could easily be the deranged eye of the murderous owner of said barns. For all he knew, the man could have a gun aimed at him right now.

Until that moment, it hadn't crossed his mind that Murray might be armed – but farmers all had shotguns, didn't they? And rifles for killing crows, he thought, remembering the gruesome sight at the bottom of the hill. Nervously, he pressed himself flat against the barn wall…

…which immediately gave way behind him.

He tumbled backwards, with a cry he was certain echoed and rebounded across the yard, and smacked his head against something hard.

Not absolutely my finest hour, he had time to think, and then everything went black.

* * *

"What the hell are you doing in my barn?"

The voice was harsh and rough, and contorted in some way, so that Edward had difficulty making out what was being said. Something – a boot, presumably – connected with the side of his leg, but without much force.

"Get on your feet!" the voice commanded. "And don't try anything. The dog'll be on you before you can take a step."

As though on cue, a dog growled softly in the darkness near the voice. Edward slowly pushed himself into a sitting position and fumbled in what he hoped was dirt for his glasses, which had gone astray when he'd fallen.

"If you wait a moment until I find my spectacles, I can explain everything." One questing hand nudged against something cold and metallic, and he gratefully slipped his glasses back on his nose. Unfortunately, the left lens had cracked, but at least now he could make out the figure standing over him.

There was no doubt this was Robert Murray. Tall, but thin, he wore wellington boots and a coarse black jacket over striped pyjamas, and held a shotgun pointed roughly in Edward's direction. But it was his face that made the identification certain.

Ifeld had said that Murray had been burned in the War, but, in Edward's opinion, the businessman's description had been wholly inadequate. The right side of the farmer's face was – as might be expected from a farming man of his age – weather-beaten and lined, but otherwise unremarkable. The left side, however, was another matter.

From the top of his crown down to the end of his chin, the skin was smooth and completely devoid of hair, the flesh twisted in tight folds, like a waxwork that had partially melted. His left eye was smaller than the right and half-closed by healed skin which stretched down to his nose – or where his nose would be, were it not for the fire that had destroyed much of it. His mouth, too, had been damaged by the flames, and was pulled into a fleshy knot at one side.

Edward recoiled and shuffled back on his haunches, away from the burned man. He grabbed onto a wooden barrel and pulled himself to his feet. His glasses fell to one side where a metal arm had bent in his fall, and he was forced to hold them in place with his hand.

"Right then," Murray rasped. "Out with it. What're you doing on my land?"

"It's perfectly simple, Mr. Murray," Edward replied, with as much confidence as he could muster. He was aware he wasn't looking the farmer in the eye, but hoped the condition of his glasses would make that less obvious than would otherwise be the case. "My name is Edward Lowe. Perhaps you've seen me on television? I was on Corrie a year or two back?"

Murray grunted. "I've got no television. Never felt the need. But even if you're George Formby, that doesn't explain what you're doing skulking about my barn."

Edward could feel his carefully constructed cover story unwinding around him, but realised he had no choice but to press on. He spoke quickly, before Murray had a chance to say anything further.

"Of course, if you don't have a television… are you at least aware there's a TV series currently filming in Ironbridge and the surrounding area? No? Well, anyway, I play the lead role in that, and I was hoping to scout out possible shooting locations for future episodes."

He had been quite pleased with this when he'd rehearsed it in front of the bathroom mirror, but now he came to use it in the field, he wasn't so sure.

Neither was Murray.

"Is that right? Without telling me what you were up to?"

He took a step closer and the dog snarled at his heel. The shotgun, which he had allowed to drop until it pointed at the ground, now swung back up. Edward did the only thing he could and shuffled away from the farmer until his back pressed against the wall.

"Now, I don't know what you're up to, Mr. Lowe, but I know a liar when I see one. I had that skinny halfwit of a policeman up here the other day, asking questions about things long since dead and buried, and now there's you, creeping about my land like a burglar. I reckon I'll give you thirty seconds head start, then I'll set the dog on you. And maybe blast a round or two of this buckshot in your direction, too. Won't kill you, but, by Christ, it'll sting your behind. Now go on – get!"

Edward didn't wait for a second invitation. Desperately ignoring the growls of the dog, he pressed his glasses into his face with one hand and pushed himself into a run with the other. From behind him as he rounded the corner of the barn, he heard Murray's harsh laughter and an incomprehensible command to the dog, which howled its bloodlust in response.

Terror gripped him by the stomach as he stumbled over a tyre lying in the yard and measured his length in the dirt. As he scrambled to his knees, he caught a glimpse of another, smaller shed, until then hidden by the bulk of the barn. It had what appeared to be a new metal hasp and padlock on its door, in marked contrast to the dilapidated condition of everything else on the farm.

"Time's nearly up, Mr. Lowe," he heard Murray shout from the behind him, then a loud bang and flash as he fired the shotgun. Whether he missed or merely aimed high, Edward had no way of knowing; he put the new lock out of his mind and, abandoning his glasses as they fell in the mud, clambered painfully over the farmyard gate and staggered off across a field with Murray's laughter ringing in his ears.

Only when he reached the main road again did he feel safe to stop. He slumped to the ground, retching painfully as he struggled to catch his breath. He squinted back up the hill, but quickly had to admit that, without his glasses, Murray could be three feet away with the shotgun pointed directly at him and he would have no way of knowing.

He knew Bobby's car had to be close by, but everywhere he looked was a blur. In broad daylight, perhaps, he'd be able to distinguish a car from a phone box, but at the moment, in the summer dusk half-light…

A phone box! Of course! He'd passed the familiar shape of the phone box just before he'd parked. It couldn't be more than a hundred yards down the road, and even half-blind he could distinguish a bright-red metal box if he got close enough.

Now all he had to do was get close enough.

Carefully, with his hands outstretched in front of him, he edged slowly along the side of the road. If he remembered correctly, there was a small ditch that ran alongside the hedge. It wouldn't do to miss his footing and fall in; the irony of ending up dead in a ditch, given Sylvia Menzies' fate, would be all too painful.

He stopped and extended one arm out as far as he could to his right, until the tips of his fingers found the leaves of the hedge. Thankfully, the summer growth meant it was bushy and easy to locate. Surely an arm's length was sufficient distance to ensure he didn't tumble into the ditch? He moved forward slowly, shuffling his feet along the ground, with his left arm straight out in front of him and his right brushing comfortingly against the hedge.

"What you doin', mister?"

The voice was curious rather than impertinent, but clearly young. Edward desperately squinted in its general direction and was gratified to be able to make out a slightly paler blob of colour in the surrounding darkness.

"Are you blind?" the voice continued, in an interested tone; then, before he could answer, "Are you blind *and* deaf and dumb?"

"No, young man, I assure you I am neither."

"Have you hurt your back then? Did you fall off a wagon? I saw my Uncle Tommy walking like you once, and my mum said it was cos he fell off the wagon again. Fancy going back on a wagon, if you keep falling off it." He gave a soft grunting noise which Edward took to indicate a general distaste for the behaviour of adults. "My Uncle Tommy gets drunk a lot, though, so maybe that's what makes him keep falling off."

"No, I've not hurt my back either," Edward said, before the boy could describe any more of his family. He straightened up, and groaned as pain flared in half a dozen places. He would be bruised all over in the morning. "Or, at least, if I have, that's not why I'm walking like this."

By dint of closing one eye and screwing the other almost closed, he could just make out the rough features of his interrogator. A boy, he was certain, with a mop of dark hair and wearing a white shirt and shorts. Beyond that, he remained invisible. About ten years old, he would have said, which prompted a thought.

"But never mind me," he said sternly. "What on earth is a boy of your age doing wandering the country lanes at this time of night? Do your parents know where you are?"

"They don't mind. So long as I'm home before it's dark, that's all right."

"But it is dark," Edward protested.

"Not *full* dark," said the boy airily. "And besides, I've not got a watch, have I?"

"I'll have to take your word for that, I'm afraid."

"Are you sure you're not blind?" The boy seemed genuinely concerned, but then added in a far less pleasant tone, "Here, you're not a tramp, are you? Mum says I've to stay away from tramps, on account of they steal children."

Edward grimaced. To be mistaken for a tramp by a small boy was not something he'd be sharing with John and the others later. "I am not blind, not injured – much – and nor am I a tramp, young man. My name is Mr. Lowe, and I wonder if you could help me?"

"Mine's William," the boy said. "What do you want me to do?"

"I've lost my spectacles," Edward explained.

"How did you do that? I lost a half crown the Christmas before last, but Dad said it would teach me to be more careful. I expect you weren't being very careful either, were you?"

In spite of himself, Edward chuckled. There was something appealing about the boy. "Not very, no," he conceded. "I was up at Mr. Murray's farm, and I fell and they got broken."

"Oh, him." William clearly knew Murray, and equally clearly had a low opinion of the man. "All my pals are terrified of him," he confided scathingly, "but not me. I met him by myself last week and I just said, 'How do,' nice as anything. You won't catch me running away from him, just because he's a… whatchamacallit… a bogeyman."

"Quite right," Edward agreed approvingly. "He sustained his injuries fighting in the War, so that youngsters like you…" As the implication of William's words struck him, he came to a sudden stop. "Wait a minute, you saw him, you say? Why were you up at the farm?"

William's laugh was short and sharp. "Catch me up there. Not likely. I said I wouldn't run away from him, not that I'd go looking for him."

"But if you didn't see him at the farm, where did you see him?"

"Along the road a bit. Just up there."

Edward had an idea that the coloured blob which was William changed shape, but he had no idea in which way it pointed. William obviously noticed his trouble, for his apology was immediate.

"Sorry, I forgot how you were good as blind. I met him up the road, back towards the village."

"I was under the impression that he never left his farm," Edward said. "Are you telling me I've been misinformed?"

"Must've been," William replied seriously. "I've seen him a few times when I've been out exploring at night."

"Do you ever go exploring up by the reservoir, on the other side of the village?"

"I wish! I mainly have to stay round here. Mum doesn't like me going too far."

It was a shame, but it would have been too much to expect that the boy might have seen Murray at the reservoir on the night Alice Burke was murdered. True, the description Barney Ifeld had given John had been thin to the point of emaciation, but the one definite thing he had said was that the man was tall.

Something to consider later.

"My car is somewhere over there," he said, waving over the boy's head, "but I need to telephone a colleague to come and drive me home."

"Oh, is that all?" William sounded disappointed, but rallied quickly. "If you put your hand on my shoulder, I can walk ahead of you like an Indian guide. I saw someone do that at the pictures last week."

Edward peered at the boy as he stepped in front of him, then placed a hand gingerly where he thought his shoulder should be.

"That's it," William confirmed. "Now, if you follow me and don't walk too fast, we'll be at the phone box pretty soon." He coughed in a forced manner. "If you could phone my parents after you phone your friend, and let them know I'm helping you and that's why I'm late home, that'd be good too."

Edward smiled in agreement. He was filthy, sore and about to be led along a country road in the dark by a small boy, and that was before he had to ask someone to come to his aid. But he had met Bob Murray and, more importantly, had one or two matters of potential importance to tell John about.

21

He shouldn't have been surprised, he supposed.

From the very beginning, Edward had been aware that John was less convinced by the idea of foul play than he had been himself. But recently – especially over the last few days, in fact – he had thought he'd seen a real thaw in his attitude, a definite move towards engaging wholeheartedly with the investigation.

Which made the rather sour look John gave him on his return from Cornwall all the more galling.

"That's all very well, Edward," he said, "but just because the man happened to be away from his farm one night, and happens to be taller than average, doesn't necessarily mean he's up to no good. I'm quite tall myself, and you don't know what I was up to the night Alice Burke was killed, but you don't suspect me, now do you?"

Edward ate a mouthful of crisps to give himself time to craft a response that was less confrontational than his initial, irritated *don't be so sure of that.*

They were walking down the hill from the hotel to the little village green, on the evening of John's return from Cornwall. The sun was just beginning to slide behind the nearby hills, and there was a nip in the air. Edward zipped up his coat and stuffed the empty crisp packet into a pocket, then stopped and turned to John.

"Don't be ridiculous," he said, but without heat. "And I'm aware that Murray's attitude proves nothing. But we're not likely to stumble across cast-iron proof of anyone's guilt, are we? So what I propose is that we establish who's most likely to be the guilty party, and then keep an eye on him until he makes a mistake." He gripped John's arm in a dramatic gesture, then thought better of it, and let it go. "We're so close, John! I can sense it!"

To his surprise, John nodded. "I agree," he said. "Things do seem to be moving along. Which makes it even more important we cover every eventuality. Eric Menzies remains as plausible a suspect as Murray. More so, I'd say. He was your original suspect, after all."

That was true, of course. But surely John could see his initial suspicions had been based on pure conjecture, whereas now they had concrete evidence that implicated Murray?

"I'm all for thoroughness," he said finally. "Of course I am. But I do think we need to focus our attentions on one suspect at a time. And, on the balance of probabilities..." He savoured the phrase, which had just popped into his head but which he thought had a nicely scientific sound. "...Robert Murray is the likeliest suspect."

Even though the last rays of the setting sun still cast a long slice across the grass of the green, a light, almost imperceptible drizzle had begun, and moisture hung in the air in a damp mist. Edward stopped beneath the single oak tree that dominated one end of the green and turned to John.

"We have to think like the police do," he began. "Though less idiotically, obviously. Who has a motive, who had the opportunity and who has..." He stopped, and tried to remember the third thing. "And who has the means?" he concluded, triumphantly. He held out his hand and began to count on his fingers. "First of all, Murray certainly has a motive. He ended up going off to war before he had to, and came back horribly disfigured, to the extent he's forced to hide himself away. Who wouldn't be angry at that? Secondly, he had the opportunity every time. Unlike everyone else we've considered, Murray's been free to come and go as he pleases, with not even a neighbour to notice his movements. Why, if it hadn't been for the inquisitive young lad I met in the lane that night, we'd never have known he ever left his property. And, finally, he has the means. His disability is purely cosmetic, after all. There's nothing in his injuries that would prevent him from killing three women, especially if he came on them unawares. Add to that the fact that he fits the description given by Ifeld, and I think his status as our main suspect goes without saying."

John had listened quietly as Edward spoke, and now, as he fell silent, he nodded slowly. "That's rather a good summary, Edward," he said, approvingly. "There's not a part of it I disagree with. Though I do wonder how you imagine a recluse like Murray managed to track down all these women. But" – he waved a hand in Edward's direction to forestall any objections – "in any case, I do think everything you said applies as well to Eric Menzies. He lost his wife due to the soldiers who are now being hunted down, he's been in the wind for decades and, for all we know, he might be a complete madman." He shrugged. "Or perhaps not. But you know what I mean. And besides, what you said has given me a thought. Could we not ask your young friend to keep an eye on the Murray farm while we seek out the missing Mr. Menzies?"

Edward had no doubt the lad would be willing to act as their spy (he would be delighted, in fact, he suspected), but he could see one serious flaw in John's plan.

"I take your point," he said, "but there's the minor inconvenience that Eric Menzies is, as you say, missing. We've no idea where he might be or how he might be located."

"We could ask Primrose to check in with Cheshire? They did say they'd continue to make enquiries."

"Very well," Edward conceded. "We'll do that. And if they're able to come up with an address, I'll speak to the boy's parents and check they've no objection to their son doing a bit of work for us. Perhaps I could convince David to use him as an extra or something. But, in the meantime, we can concentrate on Robert Murray."

He was happy enough to offer these concessions, because even though he was certain Menzies could not be the killer – was a man unwilling to kill to defend his country from the Nazis likely to take up murder as a hobby later on? – he was equally certain that Primrose was more likely to be appointed chief constable than he was to unearth the missing man.

Of course, he said nothing of this to John, and though he felt guilty for deceiving his friend, he reasoned that no harm could come of following the correct course. It was John who was happy to pin their chances of success on Primrose, when all was said and done, and well-meaning though the lad was, Edward doubted he had ever done anything genuinely useful in his life.

As though summoned by this uncharitable thought, the reedy voice of Primrose rang across the village green, calling his name. John held up a hand in greeting and Edward turned to see the constable running across the green towards them.

"Mr. Lowe, Mr. Lowe," he was shouting, waving a sheet of paper in his hand like a flag of surrender. Breathlessly, he reached the two men and came to a sudden halt, doubling over and gripping his sides as he sucked in long, painful breaths. "I've got two messages, Mr. Lowe," he panted, finally. "Important ones." He straightened up and held out the paper. "Cheshire got back in touch. They haven't been able to trace the man you were looking for, but they've found the couple who adopted his son. Tom, the son's name is. That's their name and telephone number on there."

"That's excellent work, Primrose," Edward said, hoping his disappointment was not too obvious. He glanced at the paper and passed it to John. "We can telephone the… eh… Donaldsons in the morning and arrange to meet them. If we can speak to the son, perhaps he can shed some light on the whereabouts of his father."

He still thought Eric Menzies a distraction from their main goal of building a case against Bob Murray, but he supposed it was important to definitively rule the man out. Besides, he had agreed that was their immediate plan of action only minutes previously and he could hardly change his mind now.

John, at least, was delighted.

"Jolly well done, Frank!" he said, pumping the policeman's hand. "That's enormously helpful! This could be the just the break we've been looking for!"

That was going a bit too far, Edward decided. "You said you had two messages, Primrose?" he asked.

The constable nodded. "The other one's for Mr. Le Breton, actually," he said. "Someone called Margaret Hunter phoned. She said, can you call her back? It's urgent."

22

John trotted back to the hotel, certain he knew why Matthew Peel's housekeeper had telephoned. Peel, his body prematurely aged by his years of captivity, his spirit crushed by the loss of his daughter, had finally succumbed and gone to join the rest of his family in whatever afterlife there might be. John was not himself a particularly religious man, but he suspected Peel would not have been sad to go.

It came as a surprise, therefore, when Meg Hunter answered his call and told him that Peel was sleeping peacefully, and that she had phoned with entirely different news.

"I've found something, John," she said. "Another one of the girls."

Well, that was unexpected. When he'd last seen Meg Hunter, she'd been sat in her kitchen, drying her eyes and promising to look after herself better. There'd been no indication she intended to do anything else, and John hadn't thought to ask.

"The daughter of one of the Balcon soldiers?" he asked finally.

"A niece. Bert Smith was her uncle. But her parents were killed in the Blitz, and he brought her up when she was young."

"And you tracked her down? How did you manage that?"

Meg laughed at the other end of the line. "Actually, I was quite cunning there. Matthew's regiment have an old soldiers' organisation, and he always kept up his membership, though he never attends reunions or anything like that. So I telephoned them and said I was arranging a surprise birthday party for my husband, and that he'd lost touch with some of his old comrades in arms, and did they have contact details for them?"

"Your husband?" John hoped the good humour was clear in his voice, and that Meg would not think he was being unkind.

"Yes." She laughed again. "A bit cheeky of me, I know, but I wasn't sure they'd tell his housekeeper anything!" The warmth left her voice as suddenly as it had arrived, and she went on more soberly. "They only had contact details for a couple of the names Matthew told you. A lot of the regiment died in the War, and some of the others didn't keep in touch after they were demobbed. But when I asked after Albert Smith, the chap said he only had contact details for his niece, as Smith had emigrated to South Africa some years ago. Apparently, he prefers to pick up his mail from her when he's in the country."

Suddenly, Meg Hunter's voice trembled, and John could hear the effort she was making not to cry. "The chap on the phone had heard about Mary. He said he wanted to offer his condolences on behalf of the regiment. He said they liked to think of themselves as one big family." Her voice broke and John heard her give a terrible, heaving sob.

He felt a lump form in his own throat and swallowed heavily to shift it. "This must be so difficult for you," he said, waving away Edward, who hovered at his shoulder like a short, round ghoul, mouthing questions and gesturing towards the telephone. "Take your time. Go and get yourself a drink of something strong, and have a good blow, and I'll wait here until you're ready."

He cupped his hand over the mouthpiece. "She's found Bert Smith's niece."

"Does she have an address? We need to get to her before the killer does!" Was there an eagerness in Edward's voice as he pulled his notebook from his pocket? Surely not. "Find out where she lives, and we can check how far it is from Murray's farm."

"John? John? Are you still there?" Meg's voice in the earpiece drowned out anything else Edward had to say.

"Yes, I'm here. Feeling better?"

She sniffed. "Yes, much. I knew when I phoned that I'd get upset. It couldn't be helped, though. Now," she went on, in a brisk, businesslike tone, "what else do you need to know?"

"I'm not sure, really. The girl's address, of course." He considered for a moment. "Actually, her name would be handy, if you have it. That'd probably be useful if we need to speak to her."

"Rebecca Boyce. She's an artist, her uncle said, lives on her own in a cottage outside Cambridge. But that's all they knew, I think. She's not on the phone, but they did give me Albert Smith's number in South Africa. I hope you don't mind, but I telephoned him straight away. God alone knows what the charges will be – I don't know what came over me! Maybe it was that I felt like by helping you, I was helping Mary. But, in any case, I explained who I was, and told him about Mary and about Lowell Edwardsson's girl, and he was very keen that you and Mr. Lowe speak to his niece."

"Oh, jolly well done!" He kicked himself at the feebleness of his response. He wasn't congratulating her on the quality of her scones, for God's sake. "That really is incredibly helpful. It's so good of you to have arranged this, Meg."

"Not at all." She brushed away his thanks with a briskness that was almost fierce. "The police aren't interested in either this poor girl or Mary. Only you and Mr. Lowe have lifted a finger to investigate. Anything I can do to help, I will. Now," she went on, and John thought he sensed a smile in her voice, "do you have a pen and paper? I'll give you the address and directions, and you can write it down. Mr. Smith said it's a bit out of the way."

As it happened, both pen and paper were supplied by the hotel and lay to hand, but John said, "I usually rely on you for pen and paper," and laughed in self-mockery, just to hear Meg do the same. A tiny thing, but it felt like thanks of a sort for her efforts on their behalf.

Edward stared at him as though he'd taken leave of his senses as, still chuckling, he repeated the address Meg read out to him and gestured for his colleague to write it down.

"We'll head down there first thing in the morning," he assured Meg. "We will get to the bottom of this whole horrible affair, I promise."

He regretted the last two words as soon as he said them; they felt like far too much of a commitment.

He could only hope that, somehow, he could keep his promise.

23

John stared at the gated entrance to Rebecca Boyce's home, and tried to imagine it at night, in the dark. The house stood by itself on a country road to nowhere, a mile or so outside town, behind an unkempt hedge that rose well above his head and hid the building from casual view. A metal plaque set into the leaves read *Gatehouse Cottage*.

Somehow, given the reason for their visit, he expected the gate to creak when pushed open, but it swung back smoothly and silently. Behind the hedge, a wide but poorly tended lawn spread out on either side, with a pebble path leading in a long, ruler-straight line to the front door.

Approached from the road, the house had a surprising grandeur about it that John liked. For one thing, it came with a far greater number of cornices and buttresses than he would have expected for somewhere called either a cottage or a gatehouse. It reminded him of a place he'd once rented with some school pals during half term, and he stopped for a second to consider what might have become of the main house it had presumably once served. But Edward grunted at him to stop daydreaming and he pushed the thought out of his mind as he hurried up the path to the front porch.

An ornately carved wooden door frame reached almost to the mid-point of the upper windows – though, fortunately, a smaller door inset in the larger frame provided a more manageable entranceway. As John stepped closer to the door, he could see the decorative brickwork was not in the best of conditions, a missing wing on one praying angel, a smoothed-over face on another, but these small imperfections merely added to the comfortable aspect of the place. It was the type of house he could imagine retiring to some day.

A step ahead of him, Edward clearly had no interest in the masonry. He rapped firmly on the door knocker and stood back, waiting for Rebecca Boyce to answer.

There was no response. With a loud tut, he cupped his hands against the frosted-glass panel at the top of the door and attempted to peer inside, then banged the knocker again.

"I told you she might not be home," John remarked mildly after a few minutes of waiting, shivering in the cold wind that whipped across the garden from the open fields surrounding the cottage.

"That would always apply," Edward snapped.

John glanced at him out of the side of his eyes. Edward had been in a foul mood ever since Meg Hunter had telephoned, complaining that John had failed to ask the right questions on the phone and then, when David Birt insisted they complete their scenes in the morning before driving down to Rebecca Boyce's cottage, accusing the producer of deliberately hampering their investigation. He'd bitten John's head off twice in the car and once almost put them in a ditch in his haste to overtake a caravan on a blind corner.

Waspish, John would have called him, had the idea of a wasp the shape of Edward not been so ridiculous. *Desperate* was a more accurate description, perhaps. Desperate to achieve something concrete; desperate to save Rebecca Boyce. He'd admitted as much as they pulled up to the cottage.

"This is our last chance, you see, John. We've been chasing our tails up until now, always a step behind our quarry. But this time I'm certain we can get in front of him. All we need do is alert Miss Boyce that she may be in danger, then deliver her into police custody."

It had been on the tip of John's tongue to suggest they should involve the police before, not after, they spoke to Rebecca Boyce, but he'd known it would be pointless. He'd suggested the same thing before, and Edward had made it clear that whatever faith he once had in the authorities had long since evaporated.

"And we can always leave a note, or wait in the car for her return, if she's not at home," Edward went on and rapped again, harder than before.

The sound of knocker on door was loud in the otherwise silent garden, and John found himself wondering how the house's occupant could fail to hear it, if she was inside.

Edward shuffled from foot to foot impatiently and banged the door again, then once more.

The sound was beginning to give John a headache. "I'll go and take a look around the back, shall I?" he said. "If you want to keep knocking?"

Without waiting for a response, he set off towards the corner of the building.

He peered through the front window as he passed it, but it was too dim inside to make out anything except dark clouds reflected in the glass. There was no window to the side of the house, but he followed the path to the rear and was rewarded by a handy back door, which swung open when he tried the handle. For a moment he stood in the doorway, suddenly conscious that, technically speaking, he was about to commit the crime of breaking and entering, and that it might be more sensible to rejoin Edward at the front door. He took a half-step backwards, then stopped, rocking on his heels, the door handle still held loosely in his hand.

After a lifetime of avoiding making any important decisions, somehow this felt like a very important one indeed.

On the one hand, they had no actual reason to think anything had happened to Rebecca Boyce. She might be at the shops, or simply have fallen asleep in an armchair (something he did increasingly often himself). She might be at work or visiting friends. She might even be on holiday.

On the other hand, there was a killer on the loose and they were here specifically because they believed she was in danger. Perhaps it would be better to err on the side of caution and check?

He remembered the promise he'd made to Meg Hunter the night before, and the commitment he had felt then. And though he would never admit it to Edward, the little man had been right about one thing – this *was* their last chance. Alice Burke had already been dead when Edward discovered her body and Mary Peel had been killed before they knew it, but Rebecca Boyce was someone they might save.

He pushed the door open and stepped inside the house.

He found himself in a long, wide kitchen, the walls fashionably covered in pine planking. A poster advertising a concert by a rather attractive young lady named Sandy Denny had been pinned up on the back of the closed door that led to the rest of the house, but otherwise the room was plain and utilitarian. An old-fashioned, cast-iron range and deep Belfast sink to the right dwarfed the more modern shiny white refrigerator that sat between them, but the room was still big enough for a table and chairs. A small pile of correspondence lay on the table alongside a copy of the *Woman's Own*. Sally had taken that magazine for a time, if he remembered right, or one very like it. He twisted it around with one finger and smiled at the headlines on the colourful front cover, then remembered why he was in the kitchen and guiltily pushed it away.

With a start, he realised he'd been tiptoeing about, and the memory of a charming little dancer once telling him he was always playing a role popped into his head – was he unconsciously playing a gentleman burglar this time? He was supposed to be making himself known to the house owner, not skulking about. He opened the kitchen door and moved through into what was presumably the hall, calling out, "Hello? Anyone home?" as he did so.

He just had time to see Edward's face pressed up against the frosted glass of the front door before the words died in his throat and he felt the taste of bile replace it.

Lying at the foot of the stairs to his left, crumpled in an untidy, unnatural heap, was what could only be the body of a young woman.

For a moment, John froze in place, his brain preventing any movement that might take him closer to the corpse. His mouth opened and closed wordlessly, and the fingers of his right hand pressed so tightly into his palm that he could feel the nails digging into his flesh. He blinked several times in quick succession then, finally, slowly, as reluctant to move as he had ever been in his life, he walked across to the stairs and knelt down.

The girl was dressed in pink pyjamas and matching mules, one of which had come off and lay alone on a higher stair. Her face was almost entirely obscured by long, dark hair that curved down along the line of her jaw and a black sleeping mask which covered her eyes.

Aware that he shouldn't touch anything, he resisted the urge to push down the mask, which seemed too big for the girl now she was, presumably, deceased. Instead, he reached through the thick coils of hair and pressed two fingers to her neck, checking for a pulse. He knew at once that the effort was wasted; her skin was ice-cold and unnaturally mottled. Though he was no expert, he thought it likely she'd been dead for some time.

The thought caused a brief panicked flutter in his chest, as he considered for the first time whether the killer might still be in the house. He clambered to his feet and rushed to open the door.

"Edward, we need to telephone the police," he managed to say, before pushing past him and slumping against the door frame. To his surprise, Edward said nothing, and made no attempt either to assist him or to enter the house, only stared into the dimly lit interior.

"Is that Miss Boyce?" he said finally, without meeting John's eye. "Is she… is she dead?"

John nodded, then, realising Edward couldn't see the gesture, added, "Yes, I'm afraid so."

"If we'd come this morning…"

"No, I don't think so, Edward. I think she's been dead a while. It would have made no difference if we'd arrived a few hours earlier."

Edward's response was indistinct, more sound than words, a choked cough John couldn't decipher. "There's nothing else we can do here," he said eventually. "We need to find a telephone box and phone the police."

Edward still said nothing. He turned away and walked back to the car just as the rain began to fall. John took a last look at the crumpled figure by the stairs and pulled the door shut, then followed him into the rain.

* * *

The ambulance had been and gone, and John and Edward found themselves seated across from a uniformed police constable in Rebecca Boyce's kitchen. He could not have been less interested.

"So that's about it," he said, folding his notebook. "The doctor's satisfied that the lady fell down the stairs approximately forty-eight hours ago and broke her neck." He gestured backwards with his head. "There's a fuse blown in the fuse box, and the lights upstairs are still out. I reckon she was coming down to change it, and she tripped at the top and took a tumble." He dropped the notebook into his jacket pocket. "And, like I said before, the station has been on the phone to the lady's uncle, and he confirmed you were expected here today, so you're in the clear." He smiled as he stood up. "What a story that would have been, eh? Telly stars bump off young woman!"

John understood this was intended as a morbid joke, but, really, it was in very poor taste. Edward obviously agreed; he glowered balefully across the table but, thankfully, said nothing.

In any case, the interview was clearly over.

The two men followed the constable out of the house and stood in the road as he got into his police car.

"You might get a letter asking you to appear at the Coroner's Court, if there's an inquiry, but I can't see that, if I'm honest," he said through the car window. "It's an open-and-shut case, as far as I can see."

They watched him drive along the lane, then turn right at the intersection and disappear into the early evening mist. Only then did either man say anything.

"Why did you tell him we only saw the body through the letterbox?" John asked. "Why not tell him the truth?"

"And let him know the back door was unlocked?" Edward snorted and glared at the spot where they had last seen the police car, glad the idiot constable was finally gone. "You heard him – an open-and-shut case. The exact phrase that inspector used about Alice Burke. No, John, this is down to us now, I'm sure of it."

The realisation had come to him as he looked at Rebecca Boyce's body. From the start, the authorities had made it clear they had no interest in investigating the deaths of these young women. Time and again they'd contacted the police, and on each occasion, they'd been given the brush-off. He'd allowed that to anger him and then he'd allowed it to depress him, but he realised now that each of these emotions had been both selfish and not at all useful.

The thing was, he'd recognised in that moment a significant reason for poking his nose into this whole business had been to uncover something missing in himself. He'd spent his life being the second man, he saw now, the loyal pal left on the sidelines while others stepped forward and reaped the glory. He'd never married and never really made many friends, and he'd spent his professional life as a supporting artist, in the background or on the edges of the action, more often than not.

At some unconscious level, then, much of what he'd been doing – this criss-crossing of the country on the trail of a killer, desperate to be some woman's saviour – had been motivated by a desire to show he could be the leading man in his own life. Not all of it, of course – he genuinely hated to see injustice and detested guilty men going free, he allowed himself that much. But a lot of it. He wanted to be the hero, and that was the most selfish thing of all.

And so he had decided, as he'd turned away from the body by the stairs and stepped out into the rain, that he'd tell the police nothing. And that he would no longer allow his personal failures to hinder the investigation. They might not have saved any of the girls, but they could still catch their killer, and allowing his emotions to rule him made that less likely.

"You take my point?" he went on. "If we leave everything to the police, nothing will get done. This way, we can look around the scene of the crime far more closely than they ever would, and they need never know."

He half-expected John to object, but something seemed to have changed in him too, and he simply nodded and began to walk back up the garden path towards the house.

Inside the cottage, everything was much as Edward would have expected from his brief glimpse of the hallway; it was wooden-beamed with whitewashed walls, warm and cosy but little of it new and much of it worn. Where the paint had flaked off the walls, patches of bare plaster were exposed, and in one corner of the long hallway, a dark patch indicated dampness. For all that, it was a pleasant little bolthole.

"She lived here alone, I think your friend said?" he called across to John.

"Yes, I believe so. She was left the place when her parents died."

"She presumably never married, then. I wonder if the killer knew that? That she'd be alone, that is."

John shuddered. "Are we sure he's gone?"

"The police doctor said Miss Boyce had been dead two days," Edward reminded him. "I doubt he's within a hundred miles of here now."

He gestured towards the stairs. "The stairs are steep enough that a tumble down them could break your neck, wouldn't you say?"

"I imagine so." John's tone of voice made it clear he didn't care for the question, and there was no denying it was a macabre one. But it needed to be asked – it was important they consider all alternatives, so they didn't waste this opportunity to examine the crime scene while it was untouched.

"I mean, the killer would only need to push Miss Boyce down the stairs," he clarified, "rather than needing to sneak up and break her neck himself." He grimaced. "It's an unpleasant thought, I know, John, but we can't allow ourselves the luxury of avoiding unpleasant thoughts."

John shrugged. "I suppose so. It just seems a terribly long way from our visit to the police station with that shoe, when Primrose frightened us by slamming the door."

There was an open door to the left, and John wandered through it without saying anything more. Edward followed, unwilling to remain in the hallway by himself.

At some point, Rebecca Boyce had converted the rear portion of her sitting room into an office and placed a wide desk in front of two French doors, through which the sun would no doubt stream on summer mornings. For now, with clouds massing across the sky, it was in shadow, but it was easy to imagine her at work. Edward walked around behind the desk and, after a momentary uneasy pause, sat down in the chair.

Arranged neatly before him was a wooden board with clips on each corner to which drawing paper could be attached and held in place. A pot filled with coloured pencils had been positioned to the top-right corner, and another containing paint brushes to the left. Along the top of the board, lined up precisely parallel with its edge, lay a ruler, rubber and fountain pen, with a pot of black ink immediately behind them. A plastic tray to the left-hand side of the desk held neatly stacked sheets of blank paper, and on the opposite side, an identical tray lay empty. It was the desk of a meticulous, tidy worker.

A single drawer ran the entire width of the desk. Edward pulled it open, but all it contained was more paper, longer and wider than that in the tray and, tucked neatly to one side, an appointment book. He flipped it open, but the writing was tiny and spidery, and he could barely make it out in the poor light. John was poking about in the bookcases on the other side of the room, so he called across to him to switch on the main light. Even with the bright illumination that provided, he had to hold the book up close to read it, but all it contained were entries for meetings and notes of deadlines. The final entry was for the day she had died, and read: *Publisher. London office.*

8.30am. She'd already been dead by then, Edward realised. The sense of anticipation unfulfilled and opportunities taken away added to his feeling of despondency, and he closed the book and laid it on the desk with a tired sigh.

"Nothing important?" John asked. "Nothing here, either." He looked across at the doorway. "I suppose we should go and take a look upstairs?"

It was obvious from his expression and the half-hearted way he phrased the question that he hoped the answer would be no, but Edward wouldn't allow his earlier resolve to dissipate quite yet, so he mentally shrugged off the miserable feeling that had swept over him and followed him upstairs.

"Over there, I should think," John said, waving a somehow weary hand from the top of the stairs, where they took a sharp turn to the left, so that the two men emerged onto a small landing. There was an open door opposite and slightly to one side, and another to their right, with a sign reading *The Smallest Room* on it. The light was better here than downstairs, but even so, in the absence of electricity, they obviously had a finite time to look about.

Edward tutted and pulled the bathroom door closed, then pointed across the landing. "Yes, by process of elimination, that must be Miss Boyce's bedroom." He considered the distance from the door to the top of the stairs. "Presumably, she's meant to have come from there and crossed this landing, misjudged the distance and fallen down the stairs." He frowned. "Of course, we know that's not what happened at all, but it's like everything else. Unless we figure out what did happen – and prove it – well…"

He marched across and went inside, and John reluctantly followed.

Rebecca Boyce's room was large and colourful, and overflowing with stuffed animals. There seemed to be a floppy-necked giraffe or an improbably pink elephant on every available flat surface, and a small mountain of assorted lions, monkeys and parrots spilled in a heap at the near side of the unmade bed. Even the dressing table behind the door and the top of the large wardrobe that faced the only window were covered in soft toys.

"Obviously an animal lover," Edward remarked, as he opened the top drawer of a chest of drawers, then hurriedly pushed it shut again. He stood and considered the room for a moment, then nodded to himself. "According to the constable, Miss Boyce would have been in bed when she realised the fuse had blown, and fell while making her way to the fuse box downstairs."

"Probably under the stairs," John suggested. "That's where mine is."

"Very probably, but we can check later. The first question we need to ask ourselves, though, is this: how did she know the fuse had blown?"

John pointed to a book, lying face-down on the bedside cabinet beside a little yellow lamp. "Perhaps she was reading and the light went out."

Edward nodded. "That would make sense. So, she's lying in bed, reading." He lay down on the bed, picked up the book and held it in front of him. "The light goes out, she knows it's the fuse downstairs. Probably happened before, so she throws the covers back…" He mimed the action and swung his legs over the side as he spoke. "Gets up and heads for the door…" He took a step forward, trod on a purple hippopotamus and fell back onto the bed as he lost his footing. "Damn toys!" he cursed under his breath. His glasses had been knocked askew in the fall and he righted them before he spoke again, glaring at John, daring him to comment.

John held out a hand instead. "Can I help you up, Edward?"

"Thank you." Edward struggled to his feet and the two men took a step back and squinted down at the bed.

Edward was the first to speak.

"If some of those damned teddy bears had been lying at the top of the stairs, I could understand how she might have tripped. They're treacherous underfoot."

John peered into the hall. "No, there's nothing on the floor out there."

"Which does beg a very obvious question. How do the police think she came to trip and fall?" He walked over to the door and waved towards the hall outside. "It's no more than half a dozen steps from her bedroom to the top of the stairs. She's hardly likely to misjudge the distance in her own home."

"Unless she was pushed."

"Indeed." Edward squinted up at him and frowned. "Which means someone else was definitely upstairs that night. Surely we can find some evidence of that?"

However, though they spent the next hour scouring the rooms in the dim afternoon light, crawling about on their hands and knees, and rooting around in cupboards and drawers, peering beneath beds and under sinks, they found nothing that seemed out of place in a young woman's home. Finally, grubby and tired, Edward called a halt to proceedings.

"I rather think we're done here," he said. "We had to look, but now it's getting too dark to see properly, and anyway, it's obvious there's nothing to be found."

John gave a shrug and nodded. "That's fine by me. To tell the truth, I've felt uncomfortable since we arrived, but all this raking about the poor woman's possessions… well, it's getting us nowhere. I feel like a grave robber."

Edward pulled a handkerchief from his pocket and mopped a thin veneer of sweat from his head. "I won't say that we're done, however. It may seem – again – we've hit a dead end, but what we can't allow ourselves to do is give up. If recent events have shown us anything, it's that new avenues open up all the time."

"Does that matter, if every avenue which opens up has a dead girl at the end of it?" John was already turning towards the stairs as he spoke, so Edward was sure that he had no idea of the pain his words caused.

It wasn't like the man to be so callous, Edward allowed, but evidently they were both feeling the pressure of being in the murdered girl's house.

"It seems to me that all we're really doing is criss-crossing the country," John went on, "visiting the gruesome scenes of horrible tragedies." He rubbed ineffectually at his filthy hands.

He'll be doing speeches by Lady Macbeth in a minute, Edward thought uncharitably.

"Perhaps she really did trip," John said. "You did say her parents were dead, after all."

"So they are. What of it?" Edward's question was harsh, he knew. Belligerent even. But the suggestion that he was no better than some kind of morbid dilettante had aggravated him.

"Well, we've been working on the assumption that someone is killing the children of the Balcon men as punishment for their actions at the camp. But if Rebecca Boyce had no living parents, who's her death supposed to hurt? Her uncle?"

"Why not? He did bring her up like a daughter, according to your lady friend."

"Maybe. But how did he know that? The killer, I mean?" John frowned and shook his head. "Perhaps I'm over-thinking things. He obviously did know where to find Rebecca, of course, so perhaps it's not as difficult as all that."

"Two different things, surely? To discover an address is hardly an impossibility, but God knows how you'd find out if someone's parents were still alive. It's not like there's a list somewhere. Though..." Edward's voice tailed off and he stared into the middle distance for a time, marshalling his thoughts. Finally, "Though yes, perhaps there is," he said slowly. "You remember you asked once how a hermit like Robert Murray could track down his victims? Well, one group of people who might be able to find out about Bert Smith's family life would be former members of his regiment. After all, if Matthew Peel's housekeeper can speak to the regimental society, an old soldier like Robert Murray certainly could. And once he knew the details of Smith's life, a morning spent looking through phone books at the library would have given him the address of his beloved niece!"

That was it, he was sure of it. Did they have motive, opportunity and now means for the old soldier? Was this idle thought the final piece of the puzzle?

"A trip to the library, Edward? When would Murray do that, do you suppose? For someone who never leaves his farm, you do seem to have him roaming the country rather a lot when it suits you." The peevish quality in John's voice pierced through Edward's happy daydreaming. Some of the dismay he felt must have shown on his face, for John smiled and attempted to take the sting out of his words. "Though, perhaps it's as you say. Who knows what lengths a killer might go to."

Edward shook his head. John was right about the library. He had to remember that getting carried away with enthusiasm was just as unhelpful as excessive anger. "No, that's a very good point," he admitted. "But just because Murray couldn't easily get out and about, doesn't mean he couldn't find the address some other way. And the fact remains that he's very well suited to have discovered Miss Boyce's relationship with Bert Smith." He frowned, but when he spoke again, his voice remained positive. "We've done good work here today, John. But it's been a long day and I, for one, would appreciate some supper."

John smiled again, then made his way back downstairs. Edward took a moment to tidy the dead woman's bed before following him.

By the time he caught up with John, he'd already opened the front door and was staring out at the torrential rain that had started while they were inside. He quickly closed it as water whipped in on the driving wind. "We should have brought an umbrella with us," he complained. "I wonder if we might borrow one? We can always post it back."

Edward was keen to get back to Ironbridge, where they could regroup and consider how best to approach Robert Murray. Plus, he'd almost forgotten they'd arranged to meet Tom Menzies' adoptive father in Ironbridge in the morning. The sooner they were out of this place, the better. If the price of leaving was the borrowing of an umbrella, so be it. "I think I saw one hanging up," he said, pointing to a coat rack by the door. "If you want to grab it, I'll just switch off the light in the sitting room."

He heard John grunt his agreement as he crossed the hall and reached around the sitting room doorway to flick the light switch. As he did so, the room – the entire ground floor, in fact – was plunged into darkness. Not quite dark enough to prevent him getting back to the front door, where John stood with an umbrella in his hand, but enough to force him to move very carefully.

Only when John put his hand on the front door handle and pulled it open, allowing a barely greater amount of light to enter, did he realise what this darkness might signify.

"Why on earth was she wearing an eye mask?" he asked.

"Eye mask? What are you talking about? Who was wearing an eye mask?"

"Rebecca Boyce! She was wearing a black eye mask." Edward pointed to the foot of the stairs, as though expecting to see the girl's ghost hovering there.

John shrugged his eyebrows, confused but interested. "So she was, my dear chap. But what of it?"

"Look how dark it is just now, John, and it's only mid-afternoon. There are no streetlights out here. It'll be pitch-black by dinner time. And remember the appointment book I found. I could barely read it without a light on, but it said she had an early morning meeting in London the next day. She'd have needed to get up early to catch a train."

"When it was still dark," John said, with dawning realisation.

"Exactly. So why was she wearing a sleep mask?" He coughed awkwardly and looked down at his feet. "I actually used to wear one sometimes, when I was on Corrie and had to drive to Manchester at the crack of dawn. In the summer, I had to go to bed while it was still light outside. The damn things were terribly uncomfortable. Not the sort of thing you'd wear if you didn't have to. Plus," he went on, growing enthusiasm colouring his words, "that mask was far too big for her. Remember how it covered most of her face. It would have slipped down as soon as she stood up."

John closed his eyes in recollection. Raindrops spattered the side of his face and he hurriedly turned his back on the door and pulled it half-shut.

"I do believe you're right, you know. It was much too big. And, besides, wouldn't she have taken it off when she got out of bed, if she was going downstairs to check a fuse? I know I would."

The thought of John in a lace-frilled black eye mask was a ridiculous one, but Edward knew it was neither the time nor place for foolish jokes. "So it didn't belong to her. Someone must have put it on her after she was dead," he suggested, with a sick excitement building in his gut. "Though why would anyone do that?"

"Your guess is as good as mine," John replied. "But there must be a reason, if only we can winkle it out."

There was nothing else to say. John stepped out into the rain and popped the umbrella open. Edward closed the door behind him and stood in the shelter of the larger frame for a second, watching the other man walking towards the gate.

The sky was black, and the rain heavy enough to have already formed puddles on the path, but John strolled past each one as though unaware of its existence. He walked like he did everything else, Edward decided: in the certain belief that all would somehow work out well and someone would look out for him. He wished he could be like that, but without goals and focus, he always felt a little lost. They were very different sorts, but between them they seemed – almost inadvertently – to have become a good team.

The thought brought a small smile to his lips, as he turned up the collar of his coat and gingerly stepped into the downpour, taking care to avoid the puddles. Being focused was all very well, but he did hate wet socks.

24

Though it was something John preferred not to discuss, it was fairly common knowledge that his ex-wife Sally had run off with the insurance man. For a while, he'd tried to stay friends with her, hoping she might come back to him. And, on a couple of occasions, her new man had allowed his drinking to get the better of him and she had come home for a bit, at least until the swine had sobered up and snapped his fingers, and she'd gone running back to him.

Each time, he'd made a point of dropping Sally off and staring at the bastard when he appeared in the doorway. God knows why; physical violence had never been his forte. But there was something in Tom Menzies' adoptive father that reminded John of him and immediately got his hackles up.

Perhaps it was Mark Donaldson's receding hairline, or his pale-grey eyes, set too close together beneath heavy eyebrows. Even his voice was similar, incongruously deep and low and faintly sepulchral, more suited to a funeral parlour than the brightly lit little tearoom in which he'd agreed to meet John and Edward on the day after they'd visited Rebecca Boyce's cottage. John had half-expected Edward to cancel, now that he had Robert Murray fixed so firmly in his sights, but to his surprise the little man had been insistent that they must cover every possible avenue. "No stone unturned, John," he'd said as they entered the tearoom and Donaldson had waved them across to his table.

"Tom was nearly five when we got him," Donaldson was saying now, shifting his weight on his hard, wooden seat. "It was just before his birthday, I remember, and we drove down overnight to get him, because Enid wanted him to be settled at ours before his birthday party. From that day to the one he upped and left, Enid did everything she could for that boy. She put him before everything and everyone." He laughed – a hollow, unconvincing thing, the laugh of a selfish man still annoyed that there had once been a time when he wasn't the most important person in his wife's life.

John cautioned himself not to let a chance physical resemblance colour his impressions of the man – he had travelled all the way to Ironbridge to meet them, after all. But he wasn't warming to Donaldson, he admitted to himself, even though he had introduced himself by saying how much he'd enjoyed the first series of *Floggit and Leggit* ("Mind you, it helps that Enid's always thought you were a handsome man, Mr. Le Breton," he'd said, and winked in an unpleasantly familiar manner.)

"Did the people at the home tell you about his life before you adopted him?" asked Edward loudly, jolting John from his irritated reverie. He started guiltily and turned his full attention back to the conversation.

Donaldson shrugged. "Only what they had to. That the mother was dead, and the father had done a runner. Some sort of deserter from the army, they said. We didn't ask for any more. Well, you don't, do you? You want a clean slate; you don't want to know." He frowned. "What if there'd been something... *off?* We didn't ask, and they didn't offer to tell us."

"Did Tom ever mention his parents?"

"*We* were his parents," Donaldson chided, but there was neither conviction nor heat in the correction.

"You still *are*, of course," John said, and was rewarded for this small maliciousness with a grimace from Donaldson.

"Of course. Still are. That's what I meant. Not that Tom was ever grateful. Not that he ever showed it."

Edward caught John's eye and raised his eyebrows, all but imperceptibly. "He wasn't a happy child?"

"He was trouble from the start, that's what he was. And maybe this'll interest you: he never shut up about his dead mother. He called her that, too: 'My mum,' he said, and Enid standing right in front of him, the ungrateful little sod."

"What did he say about her? Can you remember?"

"I'm not likely to forget. He said it over and over for years. 'They took my dad away, that's why my mum died.' Enid would ask him what he meant, but he had no idea; it was just something he said. And that wasn't the half of it."

He sighed and nibbled at one end of the biscuit that had come with his tea. "They had us down at the school more times than I care to remember, for fighting, playing truant, screaming at the teachers… all sorts.

"I blame myself, of course. A woman like Enid couldn't be expected to control a boy like Tom. He needed a man's hand. But I was so busy with my work…"

"Your work?"

"Well, I say *work*." Donaldson was suddenly coy. The effect was not attractive. "It's more of a calling, really. A vocation, even." He pulled out a black wallet and flipped it open, extracting a folded piece of paper from within it. "This is me," he said proudly.

Edward reached across and took the paper. He unfolded it and smoothed it out on the table so John could see.

Even so, he had no idea what it was. An advertising flyer of some sort – the words *Donaldson's Portable Orchestra* were printed in bright-red at the top – but what exactly was being promoted was unclear.

"It's a complete orchestra that you can carry about," Donaldson explained, his face lighting up with enthusiasm for the first time. "This…" He traced a finger around the object at the centre of the page, which John had taken to be a wholly abstract shape, but which he now realised contained alternating white and coloured keys. "…is a piano keyboard, and this…" He ran his finger along a long pipe that extended from one end of the piano. "…is what I call the modulator. By flipping these toggles on the side of the modulator, you can get the piano keys to mimic other instruments."

He beamed with pride. "It's still patent pending at the moment, but I'm sure I can trust you gents not to steal my idea."

John couldn't see the point – he could think of few things less likely than that he would one day be seized with a desire to carry an orchestra round with him – but he feigned enthusiasm. He knew Edward favoured Bob Murray as the killer, but he wasn't willing to give up on Eric Menzies just yet.

"How fascinating," he said. "Does it mimic many instruments?"

"Only the kazoo and the xylophone at present," Donaldson admitted, "but I'm working on adding others."

"So more of a one-man band than an orchestra," muttered Edward, but John coughed quickly to cover the comment. Was he trying to sabotage the interview?

He quickly folded the advertisement back up and returned it to Donaldson. "Your work on this prevented you spending as much time with Tom as you would have liked?" he asked. "Well, you shouldn't blame yourself for that, my dear fellow," he went on, though he rather thought he should have. "There are only so many hours in the day, after all, and I'm sure your orchestral whatnot needed most of them."

"Exactly!" Donaldson shifted in his seat so that he was speaking only to John. "Ten years I've been working on this – it was mechanical back then, you understand, but it's electrical now – but I got no support from Tom, though the little blighter would have been happy enough to reap the benefits later, I bet."

"I'm sure he couldn't wait. But he continued to cause trouble, you were saying?"

"He did. He had Enid at her wits' end, more than once. And that was no help to me, either. Well, you're an actor, you understand that an unhappy home life plays havoc with the creative mind."

John thought again of his own failed marriage, and other relationships which had proved tumultuous, to say the least, but said nothing. They were here to find out what they could about the Menzies family, not to judge Mark Donaldson, tempting as that might be. "Well, quite," he said encouragingly. "It must have been very trying for you. I know how it was when my children were younger and I was trying to work, and one of them interrupted. What sort of things did Tom get up to? I'll bet Stephen has been up to the exact same."

He laughed, inviting mutual solidarity, but Donaldson scowled in return.

"I doubt that, Mr. Le Breton. I doubt that very much indeed." He twisted his mug around on the table, picked it up and blew on the tepid liquid inside, then placed it back, undrunk. "It was when the police got involved that I had to do something," he finally said in a low voice, glancing nervously at the disinterested girl behind the counter as he did so. "They came to our door. In broad daylight. I've never been so embarrassed." The memory clearly still rankled, for he flushed an angry red as he spoke. "I mean, I'm in the Rotary Club. I was treasurer the year before last. Assault, the policeman said."

"That's more than Stephen's ever got up to, I have to admit. What age was Tom then?"

"Just turned eighteen. It was the day after his birthday, actually. Third of February, 1959. His father had been in touch again. That happened now and then, even though it shouldn't have: a card in the post, or a phone call to the house."

"You heard from Eric Menzies?" Try as he might, Edward couldn't keep the excitement from his voice.

"Well, Tom did, once in a blue moon. And, as sure as chips is chips, he would start acting up straight afterwards."

"Because of something the father said to him?"

"I reckon so. I don't know, mind. He never told us what was said."

"Did you ever speak to the father?"

"Never. It was always Tom who answered the phone. We'd sometimes get a call beforehand, where the bloke on the other end would hang up as soon as Enid or myself answered. That'd be him trying to get hold of Tom."

"And you mentioned postcards? You never saw them?"

"Ah well, I did manage to get my hands on one or two of those, but there was never anything on them."

"How do you mean, nothing on them?"

"Nothing interesting. Just a line to say that he'd telephone on Tuesday evening, or whenever it might be. That's how we knew it was him hanging up on us. But what could we do? We couldn't be there every time the telephone rang."

Now, Edward's disappointment was plain. "That is a shame. But you said that Tom was charged with assault soon after hearing from his father?"

"That he was. He attacked some kid in the pub. He'd gone with some pals to celebrate his birthday. His first pint and all that. I reckon it was too much for him. A sniff of the barmaid's apron, as my dad used to say."

"Was he convicted?"

"No, we were spared that shame, at least. The other lad wasn't interested in pressing charges, and the police thankfully took the view that it wasn't worth ruining a young man's life for the sake of some drunken tomfoolery."

Some things never change, John thought, as Edward scribbled in his notebook. "I think you said on the telephone that your son left the family home several years ago and hasn't been back since then. Was that connected with this?"

For no obvious reason that John could see, this seemingly innocent question caused Donaldson some agitation. He fidgeted with his mug again, raising it to his lips and sipping from it, then tutted in an exaggerated manner, as though only now realising it was no longer piping-hot. He looked over Edward's shoulder and beckoned to the girl at the counter.

"I'll have another tea, miss," he said, and pushed his mug to the edge of the table. That done, he brushed some crumbs to the floor, and turned his attention back to the two men.

"Please understand, gentlemen, this is all very personal, and if the details were to get out, it would cause Enid no end of upset. She suffers with her nerves, and it's taken all this time for her to get over Tom's behaviour that night."

"That night? So matters did come to a head, then?"

"About a week after we heard there'd be no charges," Donaldson confirmed. "Those were among the worst days of my life, I can tell you, and as for poor Enid... You see, I heard Tom on the telephone that night, after we'd gone to bed. He was whispering, so that nobody would hear, but, with all the unpleasantness, I'd taken an ill-advised third bottle of beer, and had to get up to use the loo. Anyway, the bathroom is at the top of the stairs, and the telephone at the bottom, by the front door, so when I heard whispering, I crouched down at the top, out of sight, and listened."

Just then the mug of fresh tea arrived, and as Edward paid for it, Donaldson kept quiet and stared down at the table. Only once the girl was safely back at her counter and out of earshot did he take up his tale again.

"I couldn't make out much, but he was talking to his father, I was sure of that. It was all *Dad* this, and *Dad* that, and him that hadn't ever called me that, even though I took him in and gave him a good home, and this other bloke just disappeared on him. Well, I was livid, there's no denying it. I'm not a hot-tempered man generally, but to hear him saying that, it made my blood boil. Maybe it was that, or maybe it was the three bottles of beer, but whatever it was, I flew down the stairs, grabbed the telephone off him and started shouting all sorts down the line."

He stopped and fumbled in his pockets for cigarettes. "I'm trying to give up," he said. "But I reckon I deserve a smoke."

John reached across the table, lit his cigarette and watched him inhale deeply.

"Well, Tom didn't like that, as you can imagine, and he tried to get the receiver off of me, and there was a bit of a barney. That was enough to wake Enid, and she came running down the stairs, hoping to calm things down, but as bad luck would have it, she reached the bottom step just as Tom got the telephone off me. He pulled it away with enough force that his hand shot backwards over his shoulder and caught Enid square in the face.

"Next thing I knew, I'd picked up the whole phone and was smacking Tom with it, and he was screaming that we weren't his parents and never would be, and Enid – and she didn't mean this, it was just the shock, and the hurt he'd caused her – she shouted back that his real mother was a whore who got sliced up by some soldiers."

He ground his cigarette out in the silver-foil ashtray on the table, half smoked, and immediately lit another.

"That was the first I'd heard of any of that – like I said, the home only told us the mother was dead – but later on, Enid told me she'd got in touch after he'd started playing up, and got the whole story out of them. How Tom's mother was some kind of good-time girl, and squaddies killed her in the War.

"I could see that Tom didn't know about it, either. Or, if he did, he hadn't heard it put like that before. He went white as a sheet, and we all stopped dead, with the telephone receiver in his hand and the rest of the telephone in mine, like we were playing some sort of kids' game. Then he let go of the receiver and walked out the door.

"And we haven't heard from him since."

Edward had been busily taking notes while Donaldson was talking and, as he stopped, he laid his pen down. "And you've no idea where he might be now?"

"Actually, there I can help you. At least, I know where he *was*. I wasn't joking when I said he walked out and never came back. He left everything, just took the clothes he was stood up in. All the postcards from his father were in a box in his room – and they all had the same return address on them." From inside his jacket, he pulled three small card rectangles. Flipping one over and laying it on the table, he indicated a line at the bottom.

2/4, EH8 1PY

"I went along and checked with the G.P.O., and that's a flat in Edinburgh. That's where he went after he left us, I'm sure of that."

"This is very helpful, Mr. Donaldson," Edward said, copying the address into his notebook. "I wonder, do you happen to have a photograph of Tom?"

Donaldson frowned and shook his head. "Not a recent one, no. But I thought you'd ask, so I brought the last one Enid took before he left." He opened his wallet and slid a small photograph across the table. "We were never much of a photograph sort of family," he muttered apologetically.

Evidently not, thought John as he picked up the photo and peered at it. It showed a boy of ten or eleven at most, viewed side on and partially obscured by a pot plant of some sort, thick green leaves covering the bottom half of his face.

Other than the fact he had dark hair and pale skin, it would be of no use for identification.

Still, he smiled his thanks as he handed the photo back. The man had been helpful in other ways, after all.

"Will you go to see him?" Donaldson asked suddenly, gesturing with the photograph in his hand. "In Edinburgh, I mean?"

It was on the tip of his tongue to ask what concern it was of his, but there was a look on Donaldson's face – could it be guilt? – that made him pause for a moment and then nod.

"I think we'll have to," he said, glancing across at Edward, who said nothing.

"Right. Good," Donaldson said. He seemed unsure of himself and repeated the word "good" twice more into his teacup, then looked back across at John. "You could tell Tom we're sorry how it ended up," he said quietly. "If you find him, that is."

John nodded. "Of course. We'll be sure to pass that on," he said, though if they were right about Eric Menzies, he doubted his son would wish to exchange pleasantries.

It seemed that was enough for Donaldson. He tucked the photograph back into his wallet, then solemnly shook each of their hands. As he walked away, Edward was already muttering to himself about speaking to Primrose and trains to Edinburgh.

25

The Castle, perched on black volcanic rock, looming over the city like a protective mother, always caused Edward to stop for a moment when he arrived in Edinburgh. He'd played the theatres here many times after the War, and knew the place as well as any north of Manchester, but he'd never ceased to be impressed by its skyline. If there was a city with a more beautiful and majestic silhouette in the country, he had yet to see it.

The contrast with the dilapidated block of flats directly in front of them, only a ten-minute walk from the Castle Esplanade, could not have been starker.

Misshapen black stains like slicks of oil discoloured the chipped and cracked front of the building, and several windows were entirely covered by wooden boards. A broken overflow pipe dripped water onto concrete slabbing that was itself cracked and overgrown with weeds and wild grass. Indeed, it seemed there was grass everywhere except on the bare square of brown earth in front of the flats marked by a small warning placard that read *No Ball Games*.

On the corner of another block, a group of men stood in a huddle, smoking hand-rolled cigarettes and passing around a bottle of something alcoholic. Each of the men was in early middle age, heavy set, and had a shaved head. One or two of them glanced across at the two actors and laughed, but other than that, they demonstrated none of the hostile intent Edward had feared when he first noticed them.

"Layabouts," he muttered disdainfully, stepping towards the block in which they hoped to find Menzies. "I doubt they've ever done an honest day's work between them."

The glass in the main door to the block had been smashed at some point, allowing the two men an unobstructed view into the dark stairwell inside. The smell of urine wafting sourly through the hole did nothing to make the prospect of entry more appealing.

"Couldn't we just write Eric Menzies a letter?" John asked plaintively. "Or send him a telegram?"

His nervousness wasn't helping. Best to nip that in the bud straight away.

"Hardly. If he is the killer, then he's not likely to hang around and wait for us to pop around with the police, is he?"

"If he is the killer, I'd feel a lot more comfortable if we had the police with us now."

Edward sighed. They had gone over this more than once. "And if the police were at all interested, we wouldn't need to be here at all. But they're not, so it's down to us."

In truth, he had been a little disappointed by Primrose's reaction when they'd asked for help in approaching Eric Menzies.

"Edinburgh?" he'd said, as though they'd suggested a jaunt to the moon. "The one in Scotland?"

Even when assured it was only a few hours on the train, he'd refused every suggestion that he accompany them in an official capacity.

"I've got no authority abroad, Mr. Lowe," he'd insisted.

In the end, Edward had lost all patience, called him a blithering idiot, and stormed out of the police station. Which had undoubtedly been the right thing to do at the time, but in retrospect did seem a trifle foolhardy.

"What if he's armed?" John asked suddenly. "I don't know about you, but I did rather think my days of being shot at for real ended in 1945."

"If he had a gun, he'd have used it to shoot Miss Burke and Miss Peel," Edward pointed out patiently. "Whatever else might occur upstairs, I hardly think we need fear gunplay."

John pursed his lips and murmured, "I still wish we weren't blundering in blind like this," but left it at that.

In truth, they were not as well-prepared as they might have been. After Edward's disastrous encounter with Bob Murray, they had agreed that, in future, they would confront nobody alone. Which was all very well, but they'd not considered whether, even acting together, they were capable of overcoming a man who had potentially already killed several times. He would be an old man, of course, but so were they, and there was no saying what sort of physical condition he might be in. Plus, the son might also be there.

As though reading his mind, John grimaced and said, "And what if there are two of them? Eric *and* Tom?"

"What of it? So long as we stick to the plan, there's no reason why anyone would be suspicious. Remember, we're researching a story about conscientious objectors in the War, and we were given Eric's name."

"That's all very well, but what if we bugger it up? You have been known to forget your lines before now, Edward." John was uncharacteristically snippy, but Edward was willing to make allowances for the tense situation they found themselves and said nothing. "What if they're both in on it," John went on, "and they realise we're onto them? What then?"

It was a thought. What if both father and son were involved in the murders? He'd been so focused on Eric Menzies, he'd never considered Tom as a suspect.

There was only one way to find out, and standing in the street bickering was not it. Edward took a deep breath, pushed the broken door open and began to climb the stairs. "Come on, if you're coming," he called back over his shoulder.

John caught him up just as he reached flat four.

They had agreed the approach they would take with Menzies, but now, with only a flimsy plywood door between himself and a potential multiple murderer, Edward hesitated. Perhaps John was right. After all, if the police weren't interested…

He knocked on the door. *Someone* had to be interested.

The man who answered could not possibly have been Eric Menzies. He was thirty years too young, for a start. In his late twenties or early thirties, Edward guessed, of medium height, with wavy, shoulder-length brown hair and large brown eyes.

Tom Menzies, presumably.

The man stared at them for a second then, when neither Edward nor John spoke, said, "Can I help you?" in a polite but challenging tone.

Edward cleared his throat. "We're looking for Mr. Eric Menzies."

"You're a bit late then. He died seven years ago last month."

It seemed ridiculous to Edward, standing mutely in the stairwell, that they had not considered the possibility Menzies might have died. They had thought it possible – probable, even – that he no longer lived at the same address, but that he no longer lived at all...

Edward looked across at John, but he offered nothing save a tiny shrug. No help there, then. He turned back to the man in the doorway, but the discovery that their quarry was dead had left their plan to get inside the flat in tatters, and he had no idea how to proceed.

"Christ, I'm so sorry." Unexpectedly, the stranger was full of apologies. "I can't believe I just blurted that out like that. Are you pals of my dad's? From the movement?"

Edward had no idea what he was talking about, but at least that confirmed the young man's identity.

"You must be Tom?" he asked. "We've heard a lot about you."

"That's me," Tom Menzies grinned, "and sorry again for forgetting my manners. I don't get many visitors. Come on in."

He stood back and waved the two men inside. "The living room is just along and to the right. Grab a seat and we can have a chat. I never met many of Dad's pals, you know."

The room was small, with a ceiling so low that the top of John's head was only a foot or so from scraping along its artexed whorls and jagged points. The walls were covered in cheap white woodchip, and the floor was wooden floorboards with, here and there, rugs of some Eastern pattern. Along each wall, save the one which held the only window, were long bookcases, each packed two deep with paperbacks. As John took a seat, Edward glanced at the nearest one: the books were arranged neatly in alphabetical order and seemed all to be non-fiction. Politics, religion, history, economics – even in the small stretch he could see, there was enough reading to last years.

"Mainly Dad's." Tom Menzies' voice was quiet behind him. "He was a great reader."

"Was he?" Edward said, and cursed inwardly. There was no way he could pretend to have been friends with Eric Menzies now. The *late* Eric Menzies. He felt a momentary flutter of alarm, then remembered he had never actually claimed that he did. Not in so many words.

Fortunately, Menzies seemed not to have noticed anything amiss. "Yeah, anything to do with the way the world's run. That sort of stuff fascinated him."

He hovered above them, seemingly unsure what to say next. "So, how did you know my dad?" he asked finally.

What to say? Edward knew he was staring, but he would be the first to admit that improvisation was not his strongest suit. And what John had said was playing on his mind. Tom Menzies had as much cause to hate the Balcon soldiers as his father had. More, perhaps. He'd lost both mother and father, after all. Why had they never considered that the son might be avenging his parents?

"Oh, we met Eric as part of the movement," John interposed smoothly, filling the lengthening silence. "We've been members since the early days, and Eric got in touch after the War."

Menzies whistled softly. "You knew him longer than I did then. We lost touch when I was a kid. We only got back together a few years before he died."

"We've known your dad for absolutely ages." Now that John had an audience, all the hesitation he'd shown outside had evaporated. "We first met Eric, oh, back in the late forties it must have been, wouldn't you say, Edward?"

Edward nodded – what else could he do? – but said nothing. He knew he lacked John's easy facility for storytelling, though he wondered how long even he could keep up a conversation about a man of whom they knew so little.

"Was that when my dad joined the movement? He never really spoke about the past much. 'It's all about the future, son,' he used to say. But I know he went back down south for a bit, after the War, and he was living in Manchester when he joined the Peace Union."

Luckily, it seemed that Tom Menzies would supply all the details John needed.

"God yes, the old Peace Union," he said, with the faintest of fond smiles. "Happy times. Edward here was shop steward at a metalworks that switched to the manufacture of weapons, and got sacked when he refused to be a party to capitalist aggression. Little Teddy Lenin, they called him, you know. I'm afraid I was a bit less active, but my father was an army man, and when I wouldn't sign up to fight, he threw me out of the house."

"Like my dad! He refused to fight as well!"

"Eric was an example to us all. It wasn't so bad for me. I was a single man, and a spell driving a truck was no great hardship. But for poor Eric, being forced to leave his wife and son behind... well, you can imagine how that affected him. He told us how much he loved your mother." John's voice broke with emotion as he mentioned Sylvia Menzies, then reached over and took her son's hand in his own.

Edward wondered if he was laying it on a bit thick, but it seemed John had judged his audience to perfection. Tears formed in Tom Menzies' eyes and spilled over onto his cheeks.

"Did he?" he asked, and there was so much longing in his voice that, had he not been a suspected multiple-murderer, Edward might have felt sorry for him. "He never really talked about my mum, either. But I always knew he loved her, deep down." He scowled suddenly, and wiped his hands across his face, then bunched them at his sides. "But they never stood a bloody chance. Those army bastards made sure of that." He banged his fists angrily against his legs. "Army bastards," he repeated.

Edward was sure he could hear the boy's teeth grinding together.

It was alarming to see Menzies' mood change so quickly. Edward shuffled forward in his seat, ready to take evasive action if required, but John simply pulled out a packet of cigarettes and offered Tom one. He lit both cigarettes with a silver lighter and gestured to the sitting room door. "You couldn't rustle up a cuppa, could you, dear boy? It's quite a walk from the train station, and I'm not as young as I once was."

If John had hoped that the request would shift Menzies' mood to something a little less intimidating, he was destined to be disappointed. The young man simply stared at him, his face still flushed with anger. Only after an uncomfortable length of time spent in silence did he pull a small table across and place an ashtray on it. He stubbed out the cigarette John had given him, unsmoked, and nodded sharply. "Tea," he said. "OK, I'll stick the kettle on. Then you can explain why you're here and what you wanted Dad for."

Edward watched him leave, and only when he heard the sound of water running, nudged John.

"My God, I thought we were done for there. That young man is several biscuits short of a full tin," he whispered, glancing nervously at the door. "You realise what this means, of course?"

"That we've tootled up to the wilds of Scotland for no reason? Yes, the thought had occurred."

Edward glared at John. Surely he wasn't really this obtuse? "No, not that! What I mean is that you might have been right, outside. Rather than confronting an elderly killer in his own home, we might be confronting one half our age. You remember what Donaldson said Tom Menzies used to say? 'They took my dad away, that's why my mum died.' And now his father's gone too. More than enough to push a nervous lad over the edge, I shouldn't wonder."

"His father died seven years ago," John reminded him dryly. "If that pushed him over the edge, it's been quite a protracted fall." He reached across and pulled a book from the nearest bookcase. "*Soviet Agriculture Since the September 1953 Reforms*," he read from the spine. "More likely it was being surrounded by this sort of thing that was the final straw. I'm certain it'd drive me to murder."

But Edward was no longer listening. He had seen something which changed everything.

The corner of a newspaper, peeking out from the top of the nearest row of books.

Had John not dislodged it when he pulled out the guide to Soviet agriculture it would have remained safely hidden from view. But it had twisted around just enough that the first few letters of the newspaper's name were visible, and Edward was certain he knew that typeface.

He reached for it, then stopped as footsteps in the hall announced their host's imminent return.

"Quickly," he hissed, "go and keep Menzies occupied and out of the room."

For once, John wasted no time in idle questions. Without a word, he jumped to his feet and shot through the living room door, just in time to stop Menzies from entering.

Edward heard him apologetically say that actually he despised tea and wondered if coffee might be available, and then thought no more of him as he pulled the newspaper, and another which lay underneath it, from the bookcase.

It was as he'd thought. A copy of the *Ironbridge and District Times*, the one that contained the interview with Constable Primrose which had gotten him into such trouble with his superiors. He folded back the front page to check and, sure enough, a blurry photograph of Primrose standing outside his station dominated an inside page.

Edward's mind reeled at the implications, but the second newspaper was enough to stop him from breathing. The *Nottingham Post* was one he remembered well for a series of flattering, if short, reviews early in his career, but the edition he held in his hand had been left open at a far more immediately interesting page.

New drug death at University! the headline declared with, underneath that, an unpleasantly melodramatic description of Mary Peel's death and subsequent discovery. The text contained nothing new, and one or two things which were patently false, but its very existence in Menzies' home was enough to make his blood run cold.

There was no reason except one for Menzies to have either of these newspapers. Mementoes, Joe Riley had said. A murderer's reminder of his terrible crimes.

They had caught their killer.

Edward was no coward, but neither was he a fool. The half-formed plan he and John had come up with on the train had really only taken them as far as accusing Eric Menzies of murder, with a tacit understanding that, once bearded in his den, the nerve of the guilty old man would at once collapse and he'd willingly give himself up to justice. Now, though, faced with irrefutable proof that the younger Menzies was the killer, he realised this had always been an unlikely outcome.

They needed to get out of the flat and return with police reinforcements, but he knew that none would be forthcoming without proof. He cast about for some way to get the newspapers away with them, and was on the verge of – regretfully – secreting them down the back of his trousers when the sounds of a kerfuffle in the hall made him first hesitate, and then panic. He tried to stuff the newspapers back on the shelf, but the top one caught and bent over in his hand just as the living door burst open and John was propelled into the room by the sole of Menzies' boot. He stumbled forward and crashed into a bookcase, which rebounded against the wall with a bang and a shower of books. Edward gripped the newspapers as books fell from the shelves onto John's head and shoulders. He had just enough time to push himself to his feet before Menzies was in the room and standing before him. In his hand he held a long bread knife, which he pointed at Edward's face.

"You thought I didn't recognise you," he spat angrily. "You thought I was just some bloody idiot you could make a fool out of. But I know you. I know you both. I've seen you before somewhere. I remember now. I've seen you about. I don't know where, but somewhere."

"Actually," John began from his position on the floor, "that's because we're on—"

"Shut up!" Menzies was clearly in no mood to be reasoned with. The bread knife swayed up and down in his hand like a cobra Edward had once seen in a fakir's act in India. "You've been following me, I know that. Spying on me. Were you spying on Dad too? Is that why you asked about him?" He frowned. "When you said you didn't know he was dead, was that just an act?"

He poked Edward in the shoulder with the tip of the blade and pressed hard. Edward felt the serrated edge of the blade tear his coat as Menzies pulled it down and away.

"Maybe you killed him! No, not you. And not him either," he said, gesturing down at John. "You pair couldn't have managed to kill him. Dad could take care of himself. He had to, didn't he, after what you lot did to him. You were there, you said, during the War, when he was sent away. When you sent him away. 'I made a stand,' he used to say. 'I made a stand and they didn't like it, so they took the ground away from under my feet, and left me nothing to stand on.'"

A fine spray of spittle had been expelled from his mouth as he shouted, and he wiped his free hand across his chin. For a moment, Edward considered grabbing for the knife, but the distraction, if it could even be called that, was too brief, and he was too old and slow. Instead, he took a step back while Menzies continued to speak, though in a quieter voice now.

"We watched him go, you know, me and Mum. From the window at the top of the stairs, we watched him walking away, out of town, with his clothes in a sack over his shoulder. It was raining, but nobody would give him a lift to the station. Folk he'd known years, and they turned their backs on him as he walked past. Me and Mum watched until he was out of sight, then she sent me to my room and I heard crying all night. Next day, she said that since there was no man in the house anymore, she needed me out the way until she found a new one. I stayed at a neighbour's most nights after that."

It seemed to Edward that Menzies had almost forgotten he was there. The bread knife was still aimed roughly in his direction, but Menzies' grip had loosened and the tip now pointed downwards. Again, he wondered if he should grab it, but the length of the blade meant he'd need to lunge significantly forward, and he wasn't sure his knees were up to it.

"I mean, I understood," Menzies continued in a flat, unemotional tone. "There was nobody in that bloody village who'd give her the time of day, and nobody to put food on the table now Dad was gone. There were only the soldiers down the camp. I didn't see her much; she slept in most days and only got up at teatime. But there was usually something in the cupboard she'd brought in, and bits and pieces off the ration. We got by alright. But I knew Dad wouldn't like what she was doing. He wouldn't like what those soldiers were making her do."

It was difficult not to feel sympathy for the child Menzies had been, and, having made that connection with the child, almost as difficult not to feel some sympathy for the man he had become. His voice had dropped to barely a whisper and there were heavy tears filling his eyes.

Edward was surprised to discover that the fear he'd felt at first was beginning to fade. Clearly, Tom Menzies was a troubled young man, and very probably he was a murderer. But his story was a tragic one, one in which – at first, at least – he had been far more sinned against than sinning. Perhaps if Edward just asked for the knife and promised to get him help?

"Why don't you give me that knife, Tom?" Edward said in what he hoped was a reassuring tone. "Give me it, and we can sit down and talk."

It was obviously the wrong thing to do. As soon as he spoke, Menzies' head snapped up. "And then the soldiers killed her! Killed her and left her lying by the side of the road, like rubbish. That was you. You sent Dad away, and that's why Mum died! That was you!"

He slashed forward with the knife, forcing Edward hard against the bookcase at his back. "No, no, you've got it wrong, Tom," he cried, throwing his hands up to defend himself. To his horror, he realised he was still holding the incriminating newspapers and had just thrust them into Menzies' face.

For an instant, everything stopped. Then Menzies' eyes widened in recognition and he raised the bread knife high above his head, ready to bring it down in a final stabbing attack.

Edward's mind was entirely blank and his body appeared to have closed down completely. There was no strength in his legs with which to flee, and though his arms extended before him, still foolishly holding the newspapers, they felt utterly detached from him. Without conscious thought, he inhaled deeply and held onto what was sure to be his last breath.

And then John was shouting something and Menzies was falling backwards, the knife flying out of his hand as he landed with a crash, flat on his back. His eyes rolled back in his head and closed, and he groaned loudly but made no attempt to move, only lay there, his breathing ragged and heavy.

"Come on," John grunted, as he used the bookcases to lever himself back to his feet, the rug he had just pulled from under Menzies' feet still gripped in his hand. "He's out for now, but he'll not stay like that forever. They never do. Probably best if we made a daring escape and came back later with some burly policemen, don't you think?"

Shoving the newspapers into his jacket pocket, Edward nodded. The sooner they were safe in a police station, the better, so far as he was concerned.

With John hobbling a little from his fall, and Edward's back aching where it had banged against the bookcase, they could not claim to have hurried from the flat. But even so, they made it down the stairs and got the attention of the group of shaven-headed loafers just in time for the latter to grab Tom Menzies as he stumbled into the square after them, carving knife still in hand.

26

To Edward's undisguised irritation, the Scottish police proved far more helpful than their English counterparts. It doubtless helped that, in the words of the desk sergeant at the local station, Tom Menzies was "known to the authorities".

"His dad was a harmless old bampot," he explained as they sat in an interview room at the station and waited for news of Menzies' arrest. "But as soon as he arrived in Edinburgh, the laddie got himself in bother."

"I can't say I'm surprised. He was obviously imbalanced." Edward prided himself that he was willing to give any man the benefit of the doubt, but even so, there were limits, and attempting to impale him on a bread knife was well beyond them. He chewed without enthusiasm at the unappetising cheese-and-pickle sandwich the sergeant had rustled up from the station canteen, and wondered how long they would have to wait.

In fact, it wasn't long. Edward had barely finished his sandwich and was looking hopefully at John's, which still lay untouched on his plate, when the interview room door swung open and a tall, slim man entered and told the sergeant he'd take over.

"Inspector Rush," he said, dropping an envelope on the table. "And you're Edward Lowe and you're John Le Breton," he continued with a wide grin. "We get the telly up here, you know. Though I can't for the life of me figure out what the pair of you are doing in Edinburgh, tracking down nutters."

He fell silent but remained standing over them, inviting them to explain themselves. Fortunately, Edward had been waiting for just such an opportunity for some time.

"…and so we extricated ourselves from Menzies' clutches and made our way straight to the nearest police station."

"And very well done on that." The inspector waved his hand at a fly which had entered the room with him. "You'll be pleased to hear we've brought Tom Menzies in for questioning concerning the murders of Alice Burke and Mary Peel, though we haven't charged him yet. However, as well as the two newspapers you removed from his flat, we also discovered these…"

He flipped open the envelope he'd brought in and tipped the contents into his hand. They were photographs, Polaroids, dozens of them, which the inspector passed across the table. Edward took them and slowly examined them, one after the other.

Like those slideshows at the pier, he thought. *Put in a ha'penny and see what the butler saw.*

But they were not the sort of pictures anyone would pay to see.

The top-most photograph was murky and dark, and Edward had no idea what it might show. But the second was unmistakable.

Sprawled across an unmade bed lay a young girl. Behind her head, a cheap chest of drawers decorated with stickers of Mickey Mouse acted as a blurry backdrop. The girl was obviously dead. Her eyes stared blankly up at the camera, and her mouth hung slackly open.

Fighting back a sudden urge to vomit, Edward turned to the next photograph. It was no better: a close-up of the girl's face, tight enough in that it was slightly out of focus. Each of the others showed the same scene, taken from a variety of different angles.

Mary Peel on her deathbed, exposed obscenely for the gratification of the photographer.

Carefully, the inspector took back the photos and dropped them into the envelope. "Obviously, Mr. Menzies has a lot of explaining to do. At the moment, he's refusing to say how and why he has these photographs, but he'll talk eventually, I can promise you that."

"They all do in the end, I imagine," Edward said, though whether he intended it to be a statement or a question he couldn't say.

The inspector shook his head. "No, not really. Most criminals know it's not in their best interests to admit to anything, so what usually happens is they say nothing until their lawyer arrives, and then he tells them to say even less. But Menzies is a chatty soul, bless him. If he's got anything on his conscience, I reckon he'll tell us without much prompting."

"I do hope so." Edward wasn't sure how he'd expected to feel at this moment, now the investigation was over. Not this flat nothingness, though. It was the photographs, of course. Up until he'd looked at them, it'd all been rather jolly, for the most part; he and John play-acting policemen. Like acting, he thought – just dressing up. Games without consequences.

But the pictures of the dead girl, the amount of them, the *detail* in them, made everything horribly real. He'd thought they'd been at the sharp end, facing murderous horror full on. But, like silly old men riding horses back to front, they'd just been making fools of themselves.

They'd caught the killer, of course – and there was something on which to congratulate themselves in that – but they'd been too late, had never once managed to get ahead of him, not when it really mattered. Not when a life could have been saved.

He glanced across at John, but he was apparently engrossed in watching the fly flitting about the room, and gave no sign of emotion, one way or the other.

"Is that us done, then?" he asked, suddenly wanting nothing more than to be away from this place.

"I think so." Inspector Rush stood and ushered the two men towards the door. "I've got the phone number of your hotel and I'll be sure to let you know if anything comes up. And I'll give you my direct line, in case you think of anything else.

"And thank you again. You've done good work here."

But Edward wasn't sure that they had.

Not really.

The trip back to Ironbridge was a quiet one. As usual, John had gone to sleep almost immediately, and Edward had found that his black mood wouldn't lift. He had heard it said that the competition was the important thing for some people, not the winning, but had always thought it an asinine conceit, and one presumably only claimed by those who'd lost. But as he sat and smoked and watched the countryside from the train window, he was forced to admit he had enjoyed these trips across the country for themselves, divorced from their purpose, and he would miss them – and that left him even more despondent.

There was another thing, too. There was something niggling at the back of his mind, something not *exactly* untoward, but faintly worrying even so, if only in a general, non-specific way. He couldn't begin to say what it was, far less put his finger on it, but he had a nagging sense he had missed something very obvious, and very important.

Perhaps it was simply his mind trying to keep the race going, like one of those round-the-world yachtsmen who, rather than cross the finishing line, decide instead to continue sailing. He spent the rest of the journey racking his brain in an effort to dislodge the hidden thought, but to no avail. And, by the time the train pulled into Ironbridge, all he had to show for his efforts was a headache and a sore neck.

* * *

Over the next few days, he tried to push whatever it was that had been bothering him – if it was anything at all – out of his mind as he concentrated on the more mundane matter of preparing to film the last episode of the series. Further fittings for his captain's uniform had distracted him to some degree, but it had certainly helped that John, to his surprise, had refused any suggestion of acclaim, even when Bobby McMahon let it be known that they had been instrumental in capturing a dangerous criminal.

He'd actually become uncharacteristically snippy when Clive Briggs had tried to propose a toast to them in the hotel bar. "No, no, nothing of that sort. It'd be absolutely grotesque to celebrate three dead girls and a disturbed young man spending the rest of his days behind bars." Then he'd ordered a round of drinks for the entire company and forced everyone to join in a singsong until they'd all forgotten Clive's toast. Quite out of character, but perhaps a sign that John too had found the end of the investigation an unexpectedly bittersweet occasion.

It was good to get back into the normal routine of working on the show, Edward told himself as he prepared for bed the next evening. The day had been spent shooting scenes in village halls and auction rooms, barking orders at John and the others, then back to the hotel for dinner and drinks before an early night in which to recharge the batteries. Far more sensible at his age than charging about the country willy-nilly.

He was musing on the humdrum banalities of life as an actor as he swirled toothpaste around his mouth and spat it into the sink. "It's all very well traipsing about the country on the trail of murderers," he said to his reflection, "but probably best to take things easy for a bit."

He cleaned his toothbrush and put it back in its little travel case, screwed the lid tight on the tube and pulled on the string that turned off the light built into the mirror. Then, edging slowly across the floor (foolishly, he had kicked off his slippers by the door), he made his way to bed and settled back into the pillows.

Almost immediately, he began to dream.

As was often the case, his mind at first simply replayed the key moments of the day, going over points of particular aggravation and, satisfyingly, slightly tweaking events so that what he should have said and done were now what he had said and done. A minor disagreement with Bobby about a line in the script now concluded with an apology from the writer, rather than the exasperated declaration that the words were fine and they had no time to change them. A dropped vanilla slice was now no longer dropped, but instead caught and very much enjoyed. John Le Breton gave a humorously exaggerated grimace and drawled, "The seventeenth-century chamber pots are ready for display…"

Edward stirred in his sleep, half awake and half sleeping. The air in the room was too close, too stifling, and he hazily considered getting up and opening the window, but it was never a serious thought, and within seconds he was asleep again.

It was, he gathered, the day of the annual shopkeepers' cricket match, and his turn to bat. Well, he was team captain, and it was important they put up a good show. Honour of the regiment and all that. He looked down the crease at Archie Russell, who stood rather sloppily leaning on his bat and waving to someone in the crowd.

"Pay attention, Russell!" he called, but in the spirit of good-natured joshing, he felt. It was a friendly game, after all.

Behind Russell, he could make out that hideous little greengrocer from the High Street running towards him, ball in hand. Friendly or not, he was damned if he would be bowled by a man who sold turnips for a living. He made a tiny adjustment to his stance, and peered at the approaching figure as the ball left his hand.

One half-step forward, pull the bat backwards, then let it flow forwards. Don't rush it, let the natural momentum of the swing create the appropriate force. One, two… and bat met ball with a satisfyingly solid smack.

Without looking, he could tell it was a beautiful stroke. He pushed off with his right foot and began the run down the wicket, even though he was certain the ball was heading for the boundary. Russell ran too, and Edward was grudgingly forced to admire his style, which ate up the ground to such an extent that they passed one another some distance from mid-wicket.

"Don't feel too bad about falling behind, old boy," Russell murmured as they crossed paths. "It's my longer legs, they give me rather an unfair advantage."

"Nothing of the sort," he replied testily, but out of the corner of his eye he could see Russell's strangely elongated body stretch like elastic, so that in a single step he was beyond the wicket and almost in the clubhouse.

No doubt that's the kind of thing they teach them at public school, he thought, and hoped a second wind would kick in soon.

Again, Edward shifted in bed, and his eyes flickered half open. The covers had wrapped themselves around his legs and he was far too warm. With a grunt, he kicked himself free, then flipped his pillow to the cooler side. Part of him worried that he was about to wake completely, but not for long. He rolled on his side and fell asleep once more.

Now he dreamed of sipping drinks on a fancy yacht, and of waving friends on board for a party. Then, as is the way of dreams, the yacht became a sailing ship and he was at the helm, turning an old-fashioned wooden steering wheel, like something from a movie concerning the navy under the Virgin Queen. The rest of the cast were there, all dressed as jolly jack tars, and even the oldest of them implausibly scurried up and down the rigging like agile, if elderly, mice. He worried briefly at Donald Roberts in the crow's nest and put his hands to his mouth to shout him down, but before he could do so, John Le Breton appeared at his side and tapped him on the shoulder.

"We really shouldn't be here, you know," he said, frowning. "We should be much further on."

Edward was having none of it. No defeatism here; they would be the first men to cross this great ocean.

"Nonsense!" he snapped at his cowardly first mate. "England will rule the New World, or Her Majesty will want to know the reason why!"

John held out his hands in a calming gesture. "Very well, if you say so. It's just that we've been becalmed for a week, and the Spanish…"

"A week? Nonsense!"

Sea spray splashed across his face, and when he blinked the water away he was in his cabin, sluicing shaving cream from his chin. Only, rather than his own face in the mirror, it was that of Wetherby which stared back at him.

"Not nonsense at all, Lowe," the face in the mirror snapped irritably. "Check your dates. It was a week if it was a day."

Suddenly, with a start enough to bring him completely awake, Edward sat up in bed. Wetherby was right. It had been a week.

He needed to speak to Inspector Rush as soon as possible.

He was pleased to discover that Rush was at his desk when he telephoned at eight the following morning.

"Good morning, Mr. Lowe," the inspector said, with no indication that he objected to a call as soon as he arrived in his office. "What can I do for you at this early hour? I hope you've not uncovered any more killers for me?"

It was tempting, and would have been easiest, to blurt everything out, but it was possible that lives were at stake. Clarity was vital.

"It's actually to do with a dream I had last night. About cricket. And a sailing ship."

Not as clear as it might have been, he realised.

"By which I mean, while I was in bed last night, I realised that Tom Menzies is unlikely to be the killer of Alice Burke – or, if he was, he wasn't acting alone."

He heard the whistle of air through teeth from the other end of the line. "That's quite a claim, Mr. Lowe," Rush said after a moment. "Especially since he's up in court for a preliminary hearing in about two hours. I assume there's more to this than just a particularly vivid dream?"

"Forget I mentioned dreams. They're not important. The important thing is the interview that Constable Primrose gave to the local rag about Alice Burke's murder. The one in the paper I found in Menzies' flat? Well, that didn't happen until a week after the poor woman died."

"Well, yes, we had noticed that, as it happens. We're not entirely incompetent, you know."

"I wouldn't dream of suggesting such a thing. But you haven't been down here, Inspector, so you're not to know. There's no way that someone like Menzies could have killed Alice Burke then hung about the place for a week to buy a copy of that newspaper."

"People do stay in places for a week at a time, Mr. Lowe, even killers. It's not a crime in itself, that I'm aware of."

"Not a crime, perhaps, but it doesn't happen here, apparently. They don't have strangers here at all, or if they do, then everybody knows about them straight away. A local man told John that, in almost those exact words."

Edward heard what sounded suspiciously like a sigh, though one quickly bitten off, from the other end of the line.

"I'm sure he did, sir, but still, the opinion of one man is hardly evidence. As you say, I've not been to Ironbridge, but didn't you say you're staying at one of the two hotels in the place? That hardly argues for a tiny hamlet, does it? And in my experience, killers do like to revisit the scenes of their crimes. It wouldn't be a great shock to me to discover that Menzies hung around for a while. And if he didn't, how do you suppose he ended up with the newspaper in his flat?"

Edward could feel his enthusiasm draining away as the inspector spoke. (He noted, too, the way that Rush had slipped from *Mr. Lowe* to the far less convivial *sir*. That was surely not a good sign.). He had been certain he was right and had, he was forced to acknowledge, anticipated this conversation running along completely different lines.

Plus, he now had another thought. If Menzies was not himself the killer of Alice Burke – and he did have to admit that, in the cold light of day, that seemed less certain than he'd thought in the middle of the night – then the disfigured farmer, Bob Murray, was once more their chief suspect. Which in some ways was a good thing – he had championed Murray as the killer, after all. But if he was, why had Menzies had those newspapers? Could Murray and Menzies have been working together?

If they were, the remaining children of the Balcon soldiers were still at risk.

"Is that everything, sir?" Rush interrupted his thoughts in a tone that made it clear he hoped it was.

"Why yes, I think so." Edward forced himself to sound both sincerely apologetic and pitifully grateful, just an old actor who had gotten carried away with his amateur detective work, and who appreciated a hard-working professional humouring him. "I'm sorry to have bothered you so early, but the thought struck me overnight, as I said, and I felt I should let you know. But of course, you chaps know your business far better than I do. I'll stick to acting from now on!" He laughed, and the sound made him wince. Needs must, though. "I wonder, by the way, did you manage to rake up the other children of the soldiers who were involved in Sylvia Menzies' death? I'll bet they're astonished by how close they might have come to a killer, if you hadn't taken him so promptly into custody."

If that line had appeared in one of Bobby's scripts, Edward would have circled it and suggested that it came out of nowhere, but – perhaps because he could sense the unwanted conversation was coming to an end – the inspector seemed to think it unremarkable.

"As it happens, I had someone check that list you gave us, and none of the other soldiers we managed to locate have any children, or any close female relations for that matter." Rush coughed, and cleared his throat. "But I'm afraid I have to get going. Lots to do today. I'm sure you understand."

"Of course." Now, it was Edward who was keen to end the conversation. If there were no other children to worry about, they could concentrate on Murray. Rush's failure to take him seriously did have the benefit of meaning that Tom Menzies would remain safely behind bars for now. "Sorry again to have bothered you so early."

He hung up before Rush could say anything further. He had a great deal of thinking to do, and the first of those thoughts necessitated a meeting with the young lad, William.

The boy was prompt, Edward was pleased to see, but he was behaving very oddly. Almost as soon as he and John had taken a seat at one of the benches in the beer garden to the rear of the hotel, the youngster had popped up from behind a parked car and sidled across to them – and *sidled* was the only word for it – making the most preposterous movements with his head, whipping it back and forward, while at the same time occasionally spinning around on the spot and glaring at various bushes and litter bins.

In this way, he crossed the car park and slipped into a seat beside John. Edward was surprised to see he was wearing what appeared to be a pair of oversized ladies' sunglasses, which he only slid from his nose once he had settled low in his seat.

"You can't be too careful, Mr. Lowe," he said seriously, catching Edward's look. "Who knows who might be following me?"

Ignoring the smirk on John's face, Edward nodded with equal gravity. "Quite so," he said, then, after a decent pause, went on, "but who do you think might be following you?"

William snorted, indignantly. "Old man Murray, of course! Who else?"

He glared across at Edward as though he'd taken leave of his senses, then bent forward, inviting the two men to do the same.

"He's nearly caught me twice, you know," he whispered, shading his eyes with his hands. "The last time he shouted that he'd had enough, and if he saw me again, I'd pay for it with my hide. With my hide!" the boy repeated, with a mixture of fear and fascination.

"Did he now?" asked Edward. "When was this?"

"Yesterday morning," said the boy. "I've been in hiding ever since then, I can tell you! Why, I didn't even go out to play football last night, even though it was my turn to be captain and pick a team."

"Very wise," murmured John, but Edward had spotted a problem.

"But that means Murray wasn't watched last night!"

"S'OK," William assured him. "My pal Robin took over for the night." He brightened. "You owe him a shilling for that, but I'll take it and give it to him, if you like."

Absent-mindedly, Edward pulled several shillings from his pocket and passed them across. "Did either Robin or yourself see anything suspicious, then? Did Murray stay on his farm both nights?"

William nodded emphatically, as he secreted the coins inside his jacket pocket. "He did, but he won't be staying for long. Last night, Robin went right up to the window of the farm and looked inside, and he says that old man Murray was packing a suitcase!"

For the second time in a week, Edward knew they had their man. What other reason could the reclusive hermit have for packing a case? He was about to run.

But what if he'd already gone? What if he'd already made his escape?

There was no time to lose. They couldn't even wait for Primrose to return from wherever he had vanished to (the police station had been locked and bolted when they'd passed, with a sign pinned to the door stating that Primrose would return that evening). If Murray had been packed and ready to go the previous night, surely the latest he would wait would be that night? Edward glanced at his watch. It was a little before midday, and he was due on set for filming at three. David and Bobby had been very good in turning a blind eye to his occasional disappearances, but they'd made a point of how important this particular scene was.

They would have to go to the farm right now and stop Murray themselves.

27

This time Edward was determined to be properly prepared. He shooed the boy away, and quickly wrote a note to Primrose explaining where they had gone and why, and left it behind the reception desk, to be handed over to the constable should they fail to return by nightfall. He borrowed a stout walking stick from Joe Riley for protection ("Against a shotgun?" John enquired acidly), and warned John that, as soon as they arrived at the farm, they should let Murray know that people knew where they were.

"He's a dangerous man, of course," he said, as John bumped Bobby McMahon's borrowed car along the rutted lane he'd walked only a few days previously. "But I doubt he'll do anything once he knows he's a suspect, and we've told the authorities we've gone to confront him."

He could tell John was unconvinced; really, he hadn't seemed overly keen on recommencing the investigation at all. Hs reaction to Edward's dream had scarcely been more positive than Inspector Rush's, and even the news that Murray had packed to flee raised little more than an eyebrow. In the end, Edward had been forced to say that he intended to challenge the farmer by himself if need be, and suggest that, if he was killed, the blame would lie squarely with Le Breton.

Bloody idiocy, John had called it, but he had agreed to come along.

In truth, Edward wasn't certain John wasn't right. But, damn it, there came a point when the time for discussion ended and the time for action began.

"If you say so, Edward," John said doubtfully, as he pulled the car to a halt just inside the farm gates. "I do think we might have been better to actually bring some of the authorities along with us, though."

"Possibly so, but as they weren't available, would you have preferred that we simply allow a guilty man to walk free?"

Edward gave John no opportunity to reply. He quickly opened the car door and stepped outside, almost planting his foot in a pothole full of dirty water. Only a last-minute hop and jump saved his shoe from a soaking, and by the time he'd manoeuvred his other foot onto dry land, John had joined him, facing the farmhouse at the end of the yard.

They did not have long to wait.

The front door swung open with a long creaking sound, and Murray stepped out of the darkness inside. He carried the same shotgun as he had on Edward's previous visit, and the same dog hugged his heels as he strode forward and stopped before the two men.

"You again!" he spat. "I thought I told you to stay away! I've had enough, more than enough, of you and that bloody copper! And them kids, sneaking about on my land, watching me all the time! I've had enough, you hear! Enough!"

He raised the shotgun to his waist and pointed it in the direction of Edward and John. But it was a curious thing. Perhaps it was simply that it was daylight this time, or that they had driven up to the farm in plain sight, rather than skulking about like thieves, but Edward realised he was no longer afraid of the big farmer.

Seen clearly, the burns on his face were less horrific; the skin was stretched and smooth, yes, but the face of the soldier from Balcon could still be made out beneath his injuries. Only he was older now, and far more decrepit. Tall but painfully thin, and slightly stooped. His rheumy eyes watered in the sunlight.

And his hands holding the shotgun were shaking with fear.

Even the dog, viewed without the filter of terror, was no ferocious killer. Instead, it appeared to be a young collie, with all the boisterousness and energy of its kind, but nothing more. Edward doubted it would rip his throat out on command.

He took a step towards Murray and held out his hands, palms upwards.

"I'm sure you've had enough, Mr. Murray," he said slowly. "It'd be too much for any man, to have your peace and quiet shattered like this. But all we want to do is talk, I promise, and then we'll be on our way."

Edward had never seen action during the War, but he'd spoken to a lot of men who had, and some of them had mentioned the peculiar way they'd felt in moments of extreme danger. How time slowed down and stretched, so it seemed as though they were moving through treacle, not air. How the world became brighter and more vibrant, the detail in everything they saw becoming finer and clearer, as they came close to losing it all.

Unfortunately, all Edward felt was an unpleasant trickle of sweat down his back and an overwhelming desire to vomit.

"If I talk to yous, you'll leave me in peace?" Murray asked. The tip of the shotgun dipped, and Edward felt a sigh of relief escape him. "You, and that constable, and them boys?"

"If you'll answer two questions to our satisfaction, I promise you we will."

Murray's eyes flicked nervously between Edward and John. "You best come in, then," he said.

He turned and pushed open the door, holding it until the two men had passed inside. For the briefest of moments, Edward worried they might be walking into a trap, that Murray might blast them in their backs, but instead he followed them inside and hung his cap on a hook.

The interior of the farmhouse was basic, but tidy and clean. A large wooden table took up much of the kitchen, with an old-fashioned dresser against the back wall, and stove and sink to the right. Doors in the left-hand wall, and to the side of the dresser, presumably led deeper into the house. A closed suitcase sat in front of the dresser, Edward noted.

"Are you going somewhere, Mr. Murray?" he asked.

Murray followed Edward's gaze and shook his head. "I were thinking of taking a trip, aye. Get away from folk like you prying into my business. But it were a stupid idea. Where would I go?"

He broke the shotgun and dropped the shells into his hand, then laid both on the table. "You better sit down," he said. He poured water into a heavy iron kettle and set it to boil. As he moved about the room, it was impossible to miss his dragging gait, or the slowness with which he carried out the simplest of tasks. Even carrying the kettle from the sink to the stove was a painful process, and Edward heard him grunt with effort as he dropped it on the gas.

Was this the man everyone described as a monster? The man they'd been sure was a killer?

Though Murray was presumably about the same age as himself, he looked far older and more frail, a danger to nobody, certainly incapable of overpowering a young woman. Edward was sure of that now, and also unexpectedly ashamed of himself. Not for running away that night – anyone might have done the same, in similar circumstances. No, he was ashamed for thinking himself so right that he'd been unwilling to consider any other point of view.

Murray poured them each a mug of tea before taking a seat across the table from them. The dog lay down at his feet. Edward could hear its tail thumping on the floor as the old farmer reached down and stroked its head.

"Was it you that set them lads to spy on me?" Murray asked before Edward could pose any of his own questions.

"We did," he said.

"Why?"

"We needed to keep an eye on you while we were… otherwise engaged." Edward was certain now that Murray was not their man, but that didn't mean he need share details of the investigation with him. He hadn't yet had time to consider what the revelation of Murray's infirmity meant to the case, but he knew that discussing it now was not a good idea.

"Because of something that happened up by the reservoir?"

"In part, yes." Edward frowned. "You do know what happened up there, don't you?"

Murray shook his head. "All I know is that bloody policeman came up here and asked if I'd been near the reservoir one night, and I chased him off."

"Had you been? At the reservoir that night, I mean?"

"I told him I hadn't…" He shifted in his chair, looked up at the ceiling before continuing. "…but that's not true. I don't even know why I told him that; mebbe because I just didn't take to him. But there's no harm in telling the truth, I suppose. I weren't anywhere I'd no right to be, in any case. So, aye, I were up there that night."

"Can I ask why?"

"Looking for my dog." Murray had gained a little colour as he described Primrose's visit, but now his voice broke and his eyes brimmed with tears again. "Not this one," he went on, nodding at the animal under the table. "Her sister. She'd gone missing."

"And you were looking for her at the reservoir?"

"Nearby. She'd more sense than to go right up to it, but we'd been on the moors round there some nights, and I were running out of places to look."

"But you didn't find her."

"She weren't there. Leastways, I didn't find her. Not that I got much chance to look, not with that Ifeld one there, him and his boys."

"You saw Barney Ifeld?"

"Aye, I saw him, and he saw me, though I reckon he never knew it was me. Dunno what he was doing up there, but he didn't want anyone to find out. His boys chased me off as soon as I got near. Drove a jeep at me, they did. Reckon they'd have caught me easy, if there was more roads up there. But I cut across the moor and they had to leave me alone."

"You couldn't see what they were up to?" Edward turned to John. "Didn't Ifeld say that he wasn't at the reservoir, that it was some employee of his who saw the stranger there?"

"That's what he said."

"Stranger's about right," Murray interrupted with a short, barking laugh. "I keep myself to myself. Have done since I came back. No bugger round here knows me nowadays. Nor anywhere else, if it comes to that. But I never saw what they was doing. Something that took three of them, and they didn't want anyone to know about it."

Edward felt a strange tingling in his stomach, an increasingly familiar sensation falling somewhere between nausea and anticipation. Part of him was excited at the potential consequences of this new information, and part of him recognised that uncovering new suspects was becoming a regrettable habit.

"Did you ever find your dog?" John asked unexpectedly.

Murray's face fell. "I did, aye. She'd managed to get herself stuck in an old shed down the hill. I dunno how she got stuck, nor why she didn't let on when I shouted her name, but there she was. Poor girl had nowt to drink for days by time I found her." He sniffed and reached down to reassure the dog under the table, who had begun to whine, perhaps sensing her master's distress. "I brought her back here, but she were too weak. She didn't last the night."

"Was this in the shed you can see from the farm gate?" Edward asked, pointing through the window at the farmyard. "Have you put a new padlock on it?"

"Aye, I did. Too late, I know, but if I'd done that before, she'd never have gotten stuck in there in the first place."

Another mystery explained, thought Edward. A minor mystery, admittedly, but Murray's explanations were entirely believable, and completely mundane. Increasingly, he wondered how he'd ever thought this man was a cold-blooded killer.

"Two questions, you said." Murray pulled out a handkerchief and wiped his eyes. "That's one answered, what's the other?"

What was the other question? Edward had gone blank momentarily, but he covered by noisily clearing his throat until it came back to him.

"Tom Menzies," he said flatly, hoping to catch the old man out, but there was no flicker of recognition in his eyes as he shook his head in confusion. "Or how about Sylvia Menzies, then?" he asked, conscious this interview was not turning out as he'd hoped, that what certainty he'd had was slowly ebbing away. "The woman who froze to death in the War and led to you and your pals being sent into action."

Lowell Edwardsson had seemed almost indifferent to Sylvia Menzies' fate, and John had described Matthew Peel's anger when asked about that night, but Bob Murray unexpectedly flushed bright-red as soon as he heard her name. Edward recognised the look on the old farmer's face.

He was ashamed.

"You remember her, of course?"

Murray fumbled for his mug of tea, spilling some of it on his hand. If it burned, he gave no sign as he raised it to his lips and took a shaky sip. Slowly, he lowered it to the table and only then looked across, at a spot over the heads of the two men.

"Aye, I do. I won't ever forget her, either."

It seemed that was all he had to say.

The silence stretched on for a full minute, but Edward made no attempt to fill it. John, too, for once, seemed to recognise the importance of keeping quiet.

Finally, Murray spoke again. His voice was low and difficult to make out, but Edward pulled his chair closer to the table, the better to hear the old farmer's words.

"You wouldn't have called me and the other lads at Balcon *pals*. I didn't have many pals, never have done. I never had the knack of making them, even when I were a kiddie. But we was all thrown on top of each other in the camp, what with all of us being away from home for the first time. We sort of knocked about together, seeing as we had to. Me and a couple of other lads. We'd go into the town, sup beer, chat up the girls, such as there were. But I knew I weren't really liked. That I were only tolerated on account of being from the country, same as them.

"Anyway, one lad, Lowell his name was, he got himself a regular girl, and he'd meet her every chance he got. She were a woman really, not a girl… Well, you know all this, don't you? If you didn't already know most of it, you wouldn't be asking about the bits you don't, would you? That night, that's what you're interested in, isn't it?"

It was as though, after his many years of solitude, Murray had finally found an audience on which to unburden himself. His voice grew stronger as he went on, in a rush of words. His hands fluttered across the table as he spoke, a fist now and again rapping down to punctuate certain words, while a full hand of fingers beat an incessant light rhythm on the wood.

"Thing is, I saw her first. Sylvia Menzies, I mean. Long before Lowell took up with her. I were too slow though, didn't say anything, and he got in there before I could.

"But that night they had a row, a right to do, going at it hammer and tongs they was. We was all drunk, we'd been at it all night, but she was in the worst state, thinking she were dancing, but really just falling about, and shouting and laughing too loud. You could see Lowell didn't like it; he grabbed her arm and pulled her away, told her to behave herself, that she were showing him up. And then they was screaming at each other, and I think she might've slapped him, even. Anyway, off she stormed, and the rest of us were laughing and finishing off the booze. Lowell went to look for her, and when he came back and he hadn't found her, well, we couldn't leave her, could we? So, it turned into all of us – all of us who could still stand, anyways – going off after her. It was pitch-dark as soon as you were away from the fire, but we was all shouting her name, and with all of us out there, I reckoned she'd come back quick-smart."

Murray's hands stopped their incessant movement. The silence in the room was so complete that Edward could hear a car backfiring from the main road. Murray sighed heavily and slowly before he took up his story again.

"She never shouted back, though. After a minute or two, my eyes got used to the dark, and I could see a lot better. So, I kept walking in a straight line, thinking I'd give it a few minutes. Because, even drunk as I were, I'd been thinking, and I reckoned that if I found her and had a word with her, maybe I'd have a chance with her, instead of Lowell. I'd never had a girl either, you see, but I reckoned Sylvia Menzies weren't too fussy which soldier she was with, so long as he had a bit of spare money to spend on her. And if I played my cards right, taking her side over Lowell's, then maybe I could be that soldier for a while. I'd heard him say some nasty things about her, when we were back at camp, that she was easy and would go with anyone for a half crown, the kind of things young lads say to each other, and I thought I'd tell her a couple of those, put her right off him."

"And did you find her?"

"Aye, I did. She was heaving up her guts, leaning against an old drystone wall, and being sick over the back of it. 'Sylvia, love,' I said. 'You alright?'

"Well, she turned round at that, and wiped the back of her hand across her mouth. I can see her now, clear as day, wobbling a bit and holding onto the wall with her other hand to stop her from falling. 'Do I bloody look alright?' she said, and it was vicious, the way she said it, but I'd been drinking all night, and I had it in my head that she was bound to want me, if I just put her off Lowell.

"'He's an idiot, that Lowell,' I said. 'He doesn't know when he's got a good thing.' And I reached out and put my hand on the back of her head and sort of pulled her towards me. Like they always did in the pictures. I was sure she'd kiss me, but she went for me instead, called me a creep, and slapped me and punched me. I didn't know what was happening, only that it was going wrong, and that she'd tell the other lads I tried it on and she'd knocked me back. And I didn't mean it, I swear I didn't, but before I knew it I'd belted her back."

Matthew Peel had called Murray a nasty piece of work, and as far as Edward was concerned a man who raised his hands to a woman was beyond the pale. But just how nasty was he? Edward was certain he didn't have the strength nowadays to kill a young woman, but he certainly would have done back then. One glance at John's face confirmed he was thinking the same thing.

"Did you kill her, Bob?" he asked.

"No!" Murray's denial was swift. "She were still alive when I left her. But she did fall." He had looked Edward square in the face when denying killing Sylvia Menzies, but as he continued to speak, his eyes dropped to the table again. "She fell back and must have stood in a rabbit hole or something. She hurt her ankle, anyways. She sat on the grass, rubbing it and crying and calling me a bastard. It'd be even worse if the lads heard I'd thumped her for knocking me back, I knew that. They'd have been done with me if they heard about that. So I just walked away and shouted that she weren't to be found. I were the last one back at the jeep, so we all piled in and drove back to camp."

"And she was found dead the next day," Edward said, as flatly as he could manage. "Was the injury to her ankle the reason she didn't walk home?"

Now Murray was crying, tears running down his ruined face and dripping into his mug. "I reckon so," he said. "It can't have helped, can it? I as good as killed her. I didn't mean it, I swear, but I did it, right enough." He looked up and met Edward's eyes, his own swimming in tears. "I were a different man back then. A weak, stupid lad who thought he were something special, and that it were everyone else's fault that nobody recognised it. And a coward too, aye. A coward terrified to go to war. But after they found Sylvia Menzies, I changed. I wanted to go to fight, to make up for what I'd done. And I thought this…" He waved his hand towards his face. "…was mebbe my punishment. I've been locked away in here for all these years, trying to forget what

I did. But now you're here, and you're right. I can't hide forever. I'm ready to pay properly now."

He stood and carried the mugs across to the sink. "Somebody'll look after Annie?" he asked, without turning around. "They'll not have her put down? She's done nothing wrong, and she's a good dog."

He ran some water into the sink and swilled the mugs in its stream. "There's nowt else, though. I'll get my coat and we can be on our way."

The poor man thinks we've come to arrest him for Sylvia Menzies' death, Edward realised. "No, it's not like that," he said. He had no idea whether there might legally be some case to be made against Murray for Sylvia Menzies' death, but it seemed unlikely. Even if there was, it was none of their concern. They had come to unmask a murderer, but in the end had only revealed a sad old man who had spent half a lifetime hiding from a mistake he'd made thirty years previously. "We're not here to accuse you of killing Mrs. Menzies," he went on, as Murray stared at him in confusion. "It's far more likely that she was just too drunk to make her way home, rather than any actions of yours – however reprehensible they might be – stopping her. But we're not really investigating her death at all, in any case. We just think it might be linked to the murders of three young women this year."

Murray slumped down, and Edward half-rose from his chair, concerned that all these shocks had been too much for the old man. But rather than fall, Murray lowered himself to his haunches and pulled the dog towards him. Saying nothing, he pressed his face into its fur and stayed that way for long enough for John to eventually ask if he was alright.

"Aye, I am," Murray replied, grabbing the table edge to pull himself to his feet. He resumed his seat and stared across at the two men. The revelation that he was probably not to blame for Sylvia Menzies' death, and that he wasn't about to be taken into custody, seemed to have given him some strength, and he held their gaze as Edward explained about the deaths of the children of the Balcon soldiers.

"We thought perhaps you were taking your revenge for being sent away to war too early, but obviously that wasn't the case," he concluded, tactfully omitting his doubts that the elderly and infirm farmer could have killed the women, even if he'd wanted to. "Which means we've come to the end of our investigation."

It was a depressing thought. There was whatever Ifeld and his men had really been up to by the reservoir, of course, but that could be anything or nothing, and suddenly he felt bone-tired, and saw himself as the police must always have seen him. A foolish old man, nearing the end of his mediocre career, jumping from one outlandish theory to the next, desperate to convince himself he was still relevant, that he still had something to offer.

But all his efforts, all his theories, had, in the end, come to nothing. They had failed to stop the killings, or to find the killer.

As though reading his mind, John sighed and said, "We've not done terribly well, have we? We're further away from uncovering the killer than we were at the beginning, everyone we suspected has been wrong and those poor girls died, all the same." He shook his head, and his long face fell. "Not that it matters now, I suppose. It's not like there are any other children left to kill."

There was nothing else to say. They both knew it to be the truth. Edward lit a cigarette and they sat in unhappy silence.

"Well," said Murray. "There's still Henry Anderson's girl."

28

Murray had spoken so casually, in such a matter-of-fact tone, that it took a moment for Edward to grasp the importance of what he had said. But John was quicker on the uptake.

"What do you mean?" he asked. "Are you saying that Henry Anderson had a daughter?"

Murray nodded. "Aye, he did. Did you not know that?" The old man smiled, and it was a sour, unpleasant smile. For a moment, Edward could see the sneaking young troublemaker Lowell had described. Then Murray's face settled back into its by now familiar smooth lack of expression, and the disagreeable impression was gone.

"He told me about the bairn when we was doing our training. Confided in me, like. That was one knack I did have, back then. Not many friends, but people would tell me things sometimes. Or I'd find them out for myself.

"But Henry himself told me about the girl he'd got in trouble back home. He'd hurt his shoulder the day before, you see, and been signed off the ten-mile hike every other bugger was on. He were lying on his bunk, crying like a lass, thinking he were on his own, but I'd not fancied tramping across the moors either, and I'd got the doctor to believe I were poorly. Henry got a right fright when I asked him what the matter was."

The old man's eyes were sparkling as he remembered the events of decades before, and his voice had grown louder and stronger, as he relived a sliver of his distant youth.

"And out it all came. How he were in love with this lass back in London, and how they'd wanted to get married when she found out she were in the family way. But he came from money, he said, and she weren't good enough for him according to his mam. So, he joined up, to spite them like, and ended up in Balcon. He'd got a letter from her that morning, to say she'd had a baby girl."

Murray pulled a battered tin from his pocket and began to roll a cigarette. His hands were no longer shaking, but even so, his fingers were weak and the process was a slow one. Edward and John waited impatiently until he finished the job and had lit his cigarette, but it seemed there was no more to the story.

"Is that all?" Edward prompted. "That girl could be in the most terrible danger. Do you remember the mother's surname at least?"

Murray picked a stray shred of tobacco from his tongue and nodded. "I can do you better than that. They gave the lass a funny name, French-sounding. It were a family name, Henry said; he were pleased she'd got the name. Marguerite, it were. Marguerite Kenyon."

Now it was John's turn to surprise Edward. "My God!" he exclaimed, slapping his hand down on the table. "We know her! It's Madge. My friend Madge Kenyon! She works on the show. She got us the boots that time, you remember?" He tutted at Edward's apparent failure to recall the woman, though in truth he was babbling so quickly that it was impossible to get a word in. "I took her out a couple of times," he went on excitedly, his hands flapping before him as he described her. "Quite tall and well-built, with an adorably coquettish smile and terribly striking eyes. Very blue and piercing." He frowned as Edward continued to stare blankly at him. "She called you the star of the show when you were being measured for your captain's uniform! Oh, come on, Edward, you must remember her."

He did, of course; he doubted he would ever forget that wonderful smile. But it hardly mattered whether he did or not. He let John rabbit on, describing the woman in ever more esoteric fashion, but Edward's mind remained elsewhere. Surely it could not be coincidence that Marguerite Kenyon was nearby? The murderer, whoever he was, must have been aware of her location all along... my God, could that be why Alice Burke was killed where she was, to provide a ghastly symmetry to the whole affair? Edward had an idea that was exactly the sort of thing these types got up to. Hadn't Joe Riley mentioned patterns when he was talking about serial killers?

The sound of a chair scraping across the floor as John pushed himself to his feet snapped Edward back to the room. For the first time in their acquaintance, the tall actor appeared genuinely alarmed.

"For God's sake man, stop daydreaming!" he barked. "That bloody madman's bound to go after Madge!"

Which was a very good point, Edward agreed, but only if the killer knew about Marguerite Kenyon. Because something had just occurred to him.

"Wait a minute, John," he said. "Are we sure he actually knows about Miss Kenyon at all?" He turned his attention back to Murray. "Did anyone else know about the baby? Either then, or since?"

Murray shook his head. "Only Barney Ifeld. He come into our barracks on the scrounge, like, thinking we was all out on the hike. It were just when Henry were spilling his guts, and he heard the lot."

"Barney Ifeld was at Balcon at the same time as you?" If the news that Henry Anderson had a daughter had rocked him, the revelation that Ifeld was another of the Balcon soldiers caused Edward suddenly to feel sick to his stomach.

"Aye, for a bit. Different barracks, right enough, but the same regiment. Is that important?"

"It might be," Edward replied, the sick feeling in his guts worsening as he looked across at John. It was plain he'd had the same thought.

"Would Ifeld have any reason to want to wish any of you chaps harm?" John asked quietly.

Murray gave the matter some thought, but when he spoke, he addressed himself to Edward.

"Like I said, I weren't the most popular man in our barracks, but Barney Ifeld were hated by everyone. There weren't a soldier in the camp who'd give him the time of day, unless he were ordered to. He were a born thief, you see, and soldiers can ignore a fair bit, but not a tealeaf. When you ain't got much, what you have is worth a lot to you, and woe betide the man who takes it away.

"Thing is, he couldn't help himself. It was in his nature. He'd always been that way, ever since he were a boy. Likely you don't know, but him and me was at school together, on the other side of the town, and we knocked about a bit as kids. We even joined up at the same time, but just by coincidence, like. I'd fallen out with him long since, and I was surprised to see him when I arrived at the camp. I could tell straightaway though that he'd been up to his old tricks, and I never let on I knew him from home."

"Ifeld was ostracised?"

"No bugger'd speak to him, if that's what you mean. We all knew the kind of man he were. He had a nasty temper, and he were a dirty fighter, too. And sneaky. He'd not come at you if you did something he didn't like, not right away. What he'd do is wait until you were by yourself and had a drink in you, then he'd do something to get a fight started. Provoke you, like. He leathered a couple of the lads that way, and people learned to stay out of his way, if they could."

"You didn't report him?" Edward said. "That kind of behaviour isn't acceptable, even in wartime."

Murray laughed, the same harsh bark Edward remembered from their first meeting. "We were young lads," he said. "Young lads don't go complaining to the boss about a bit of a knock about, even if they do come off worst. They either get their own back or they let it go – and there comes a time when you reckon that mebbe you've let it go enough."

Was there a hint of pride in his voice, Edward wondered, as he remembered his younger self?

"It were a week or two later, money had gone missing from the hut, and someone saw Ifeld take it. So, we waited till we were out on manoeuvres, and we knocked seven bells out of him." He frowned suddenly, the action barely registering on the smooth section of his face. "Truth is, it got a bit out of hand. He ended up in hospital, lost all his front teeth, broke his arm, he were in a right mess. He said he fell onto some rocks, and by the time he got out, we was all away to the War."

Unpleasant, but it hardly sounded enough to justify the deaths of several young women three decades later, Edward thought. But who knew what motivated someone like that? He said as much to John, while Murray watched with undisguised interest.

"It doesn't matter why he's doing it! For God's sake, Edward, it doesn't even really matter *if* he's doing it. Perhaps he's got nothing to do with the murders at all, but it makes no difference either way. What we need to do just now is find Madge Kenyon and keep her safe."

He was right, of course. There would be time later to consider Ifeld, but, for now, the priority must be to get the girl to safety. It was not the primary concern, naturally, but if they could save one young woman from the insane killer who was after them, then their investigation would not have been entirely unsuccessful.

"Do you have a telephone?" Edward asked Murray, who shook his head.

"Never seen the need," he explained.

Edward checked his watch. "It's one forty-five just now, so the coach will have dropped everyone off. We're shooting outdoors, today," he said to Murray. "It's the final episode for this run, and they've pushed the boat out a bit. My character is a judge at one of those military-enactment affairs, and it involves a bit of dressing up, so I need to be there early. Anyway," he muttered, suddenly aware he was wandering off topic, "it's at somewhere called Hill Top. Is that far from here?"

Murray shook his head. "No more than two miles."

"Well, I'm due on set at three, so I can check for Miss Kenyon there. But what about the hotel? It's more than likely she stayed behind; I don't imagine she'll be needed – I was fitted yesterday for the captain's uniform I'm wearing at the enactment."

"As it happens, I'm not needed today either," John piped up. "Archie's at a school reunion," John explained, then, for Murray's benefit, went on, "I play Archie Russell in the show, you see, he's a... well, it doesn't really matter, I suppose..." He trailed off as he caught Edward's unimpressed glare. "Anyway, I'm not on set today, so I can go back to the hotel. What about transport, though? We've only got the one car."

"That's a point." Two miles was not that far, but Edwards doubted he could make it on foot.

"I've got the tractor," Murray offered unexpectedly. "It's not been out the shed for, oh, must be five year now, and last time I used it, it got proper mucky, but it'll get us to Hill Top, I reckon."

Edward was hoping that Hill Top would prove to be further away than Ironbridge, but annoyingly it turned out that the village was another mile and a half from the farm. Much as he would have liked to claim otherwise, it made sense for him to hitch a ride on the tractor, and John take the more reliable car back to the hotel.

He couldn't deny that, of course, but still – he would rather have ridden in to save the day on a white charger than the filthy, smelly brown-and-green tractor that Murray eventually reversed, steaming and grunting, out of one of the farm's many ramshackle sheds. John had already left in the car, which was something, he supposed. At least there would be no immediate witness to his humiliation. "Up you come then, if you're coming!"

Edward suspected strongly Murray was enjoying his discomfort, and as he clumsily heaved himself into the cab, narrowly avoiding putting his hand into something unpleasant, he began to see just why nobody had a good word to say about the man. He glanced across with what he thought was very pointed irritation, but between the cap which he had pulled down over his eyes, and the heavy scarf wrapped around most of his face, he doubted Murray could even see him. He settled for nudging him in the ribs with his elbow as he squeezed himself into a space not designed for two young men, far less two older, and – in Edward's case – more portly ones.

"Well, go on then," he snapped. "We don't have all day. There *is* a killer on the loose, you know."

Murray just grunted in what might have been a chuckle and, with a grinding noise reminiscent of a boat hull scraping the bottom of a canal, sent the tractor on a slow path down the hill.

29

A BBC television programme doing extended location filming involved far too many people for one small country hotel to handle, and so the bulk of the crew had been billeted in the village's second hotel, The Crown, just down the road from The George.

John raced along the road from Murray's farm at what he later recalled as an extraordinary speed. He was not, everyone admitted, a particularly good driver, and indeed, preferred to be driven wherever possible, but the thought of dear Madge Kenyon in danger had motivated him to a degree that surprised even him.

As a result, barely fifteen minutes had elapsed before he pulled to a halt in Bellevue Road and rushed inside The Crown.

He'd only met the slightly brassy woman on reception once before, but she smiled as he raced up.

"Hello John! What brings you here, love? Missed me, did you?"

"I'm afraid I can't stop to chat, my dear," John said, with reluctance. She really was a very attractive thing for her age and… with a start, he remembered the errand he was on. "I must find Madge Kenyon. You know who I mean? The girl with the lovely eyes? Works in wardrobe? It's rather urgent, you see, she's…" It probably wouldn't be a good idea to have the whole village aware there was a killer in their midst, he decided. Bound to cause panic. "…needed to fix a terrible wardrobe malfunction on set," he concluded, with barely a pause.

"Ooh, sounds painful!" The receptionist giggled and pulled across a ledger. "She's in room seven… but if that's the one you mean, she went out about five minutes ago. Said she was going down to the shops for ciggies." She pointed towards the door. "If you run, you might catch her."

John was already on the move, shifting with an uncharacteristic burst of pace towards the street. Fortunately, as soon as he turned the corner into St. Luke's Street, he saw Madge not ten yards ahead, peering over the wall of the next-door churchyard. She looked rather glamorous, in a cream raincoat, belted at the waist, and black high heels. The fringe of a red skirt hung down below the bottom of the coat.

He was on the verge of shouting her name when another, far less welcome, figure hove into view. From the little lane that ran along the back of the church, Barney Ifeld stepped into the street and looked along it, thankfully in the wrong direction.

Quick as lightning, John stepped into the shadows of the nearest doorway, a newsagents, and peered across the road through the tangle of children's fishing nets which were, inexplicably, hanging there.

Madge had obviously seen enough of whatever she was looking at. She stooped to retrieve the bag at her feet and swung it over her shoulder, then headed straight towards Ifeld, who remained where he had first appeared, making a great show of lighting a cigar.

John had never thought of himself as a martial sort of chap, and though he and Ifeld were of a similar vintage, the other man had clearly kept himself in better shape. Even so, he was about to step out and confront him when Madge stopped, quickly examined something in her bag, and turned on her heel, back the way she had come.

To his surprise, though, instead of turning back towards the hotel, she turned right and headed up the hill towards Bridge Street, in the opposite direction.

In an ecstasy of indecision, John hovered in the doorway. He could follow on foot, but if he did, Ifeld was bound to spot him. And even if he could somehow manage to stay out of sight, how could he get Madge to safety, back past Ifeld, short of confronting the man directly? Which he wasn't keen on, given he'd potentially already killed three people. But if he went back to the hotel for the car, he risked losing sight of Madge or, worse, Ifeld making his move while he was away.

What to do for the best? Why had he and Edward not both come to the village? It really was the most ridiculous—

"Excuse me!"

The little man who ran the newsagents – Frank, was it? – was glaring up at John, who suddenly became aware there was a family standing in front of him, trying to squeeze past and get inside the shop.

"Oh, I do beg your pardon."

Involuntarily, he took a polite step forward into the street, and with that movement, the decision was made.

Without further conscious thought, he nipped across the road, grabbed Madge Kenyon by the arm and, before she could utter a protest, hurried her across the junction and into Bellevue Road, out of sight of Ifeld. They were in his car and pulling away from the kerb before his brain began to work again. As it did so, Madge's mouth did likewise.

"What the blazes do you think you're doing, Johnny?"

Her voice was clipped and precise, with a surprising lack of concern in it. More like irritation, John considered, which was impressive, given an actor she'd gone out for a drink with once or twice had just snatched her off the street without a by-your-leave.

"Well, it's rather complicated, actually." He smiled what he thought of as his most helpless smile, one that always seemed to make women feel protective towards him, and therefore less likely to become upset. "You remember that girl who was found dead by the reservoir? Well, we – Edward and I, that is – think she was murdered. And we think the man who killed her is now intending to kill you."

Actually, now he said it out loud, it wasn't all that complicated. He turned the car onto the road that led back out of town, and checked behind to make sure Ifeld wasn't following them. To his relief, there was no other car in sight.

He glanced across at Madge, but she seemed fine, calm even, though he noticed that her knuckles, where they clasped the top of her handbag, were white with the pressure she was exerting.

"I know this must come as a bit of shock…" he began, but she let him get no further.

"It has, I must admit," she said, and John was impressed again by her composure. "It's not every day that someone tells you you're to be murdered, after all." Her smile was polite, rather than warm, but that was understandable, in the circumstances. As she went on, though, a tiny note of alarm began to creep into her voice for the first time. "I'm sure you have very good reason for believing what you've just told me, but I wonder if you could provide just a smidge more detail? And perhaps stop the car while you do so? While I certainly don't doubt your good intentions, it's a little unnerving to be driven to an unknown destination by, with respect, a gentleman who recently manhandled me into his motor vehicle."

John hadn't considered that aspect, but now that she mentioned it, he felt wretched with embarrassment. She hid it well, but of course she *was* frightened. How could she not be, when someone who was basically a stranger had to all intents and purposes kidnapped her, and was even now driving her to what could well be his fiendish lair?

There was a layby just ahead, and he pulled the car into it.

"I really am frightfully sorry," he murmured. "The thing is, the chap we believe is at the back of all this was just behind you, and I had only a second to do something. Bundling you away like that seemed the best solution."

Now the car was parked, Madge had regained her composure. The hands gripping her bag relaxed and the blood returned to her knuckles. She nodded as John pulled on the handbrake. "Thank you," she said. "Now, perhaps if you tell me everything, from the very beginning, I'd understand your actions better? It began with the woman who fell into the reservoir, I think you said?"

There was still the worry that Ifeld had spotted them, but the road remained empty, and John couldn't deny he owed her a proper explanation. He checked behind them one last time and came to a decision. He switched off the car engine and began to explain as quickly as he could. He suspected that time was of the essence.

* * *

"Can't this contraption go any bloody faster?"

Edward was beginning to think he could have walked to the set more quickly than they were managing in Robert Murray's ancient tractor. It was only two miles, but he doubted they'd covered more than half of that in the past fifteen minutes.

Murray tugged his cap more firmly onto his head as he gave the question serious consideration, which annoyed Edward even more. It was obviously rhetorical, surely? More and more he was coming to dislike the old farmer; a large part of him was disappointed he wasn't the killer, if he was honest.

Finally, with another of his irritating barking laughs, Murray deigned to reply. "No, it'll not go any faster. Tractors in't designed for speed. They're not really what you'd call road vehicles. But you was wanting Hill Top, you said? Well then…"

With a sharp twist on the wheel, Murray guided the tractor off the road, down a short grass- and pebble-covered track, and through a gap in the trees. Before them stretched a wide expanse of meadow with, in the distance, more trees and a low hill.

"…we can take a shortcut, can't we?"

Edward felt his bones jar against one another as the tractor shuddered into the field, to begin its slow, bumpy progress across the uneven ground. All in a good cause, he told himself, but still… it was hard to maintain his enthusiasm, sitting half on and half off a seat made of a single plank of wood, with one leg swinging alarmingly in space.

He could only hope John was having better fortune.

* * *

"…and of course I hurried after you, and saw you by the churchyard, with that dreadful fellow Ifeld almost on you, and, well, you know the rest."

Now he'd said it all aloud, John thought it hung together pretty well. It had taken them a while to get to this point, perhaps, but well… they weren't detectives, were they? And they had saved this delightful lady from certain death, which was something. More than something, in fact, he decided, and bathed in a sudden rush of personal pride.

"It really is quite…" he began, turning to Madge with a smile, but the words died in his mouth as he saw the gun she was pointing at his midriff.

In the face of this unexpected turn of events, John was surprised – and secretly rather pleased – to discover that his main emotion was an amused curiosity. What could he possibly have said that would elicit such a reaction? He'd been slapped in Tangiers by a lady he'd tipsily described as a delicious tootsy pop, but other than that, ladies tended to adore him more often than not. So what could have caused the attractive woman before him with her immaculate make-up and pretty little teeth to turn into some kind of gangster's moll?

"Don't you believe me?" he asked plaintively. "It's all true, I promise you. If we go up to the set and see Edward, he can explain it far better than I ever could." He could feel his smile weakening and a growing nervousness in his belly. He'd obviously told the tale far less well than he'd thought, but was it possible to tell it so badly that the poor woman should feel the need to defend herself at gunpoint?

It was only then that he paused to consider why exactly she would be carrying a gun in her bag at all. Sally was right, he could be infuriatingly slow on the uptake at times.

"I'm sorry it's come to this," Madge said, and where the calm in her voice had previously been impressive, now it was entirely unnerving. "I did enjoy our little dinner dates, I hope you can believe that." She smiled. "I saw you years ago, you know, at a gala in London. Frightful tosh, of course, but you were wonderful, wandering about the stage as though every word had just occurred to you. I was only eighteen at the time, and I fell a little bit in love with you, I think."

"Isn't that sweet of you to remember," John said. "I never think the stage really suits me, if I'm honest, but it's nice to know that someone thought it worth watching." Then he recalled the gun and frowned. "But, you know, the pistol… I'm not absolutely clear where that comes into things."

The weapon was actually familiar to him, he realised with surprise: an army revolver from the War, of the sort every officer wore back in the day. "It's just it's so unexpected," he sighed, and attempted a fresh smile, inviting her to reveal the joke, but she merely twitched the thing like he'd done himself, time and again, in awful B-movies decades previously.

"Start the car," she said, but though his brain was screaming to do as she said, because if he didn't she looked more than capable of blowing a filthy great hole straight through him, his hands refused to play ball, and instead he sat, staring at the gun blankly. Sally had also often said his idleness would be the death of him.

"Start the car," she repeated, "or I'll be forced to shoot and…" She joined the fingers of her free hand together, then released them and made a *pooft* sound, like a puff of air. "… you'll be as dead as all those silly women. And I'd hate to have to do that."

Was it a sign of his own self-regard, John wondered with one small part of his brain, that he believed that to be true? She would regret killing him, he was certain. He could see it in her blue eyes and in the way she ran the tip of her tongue over her lips. But best not to test that theory, another, more sensible, part pointed out, and instructed his hands to turn the key in the ignition.

With what sounded like a nervous cough, the car pulled out of the layby.

"Just drive along this road for about a mile," Madge said. "I'll tell you when you need to turn."

With little other choice, he did as he was asked, cheering himself – though only slightly – with the thought of Edward's face when he found out how wrong they'd been.

* * *

"Over there!" Edward scowled, and poked Murray in the shoulder. He pointed at a spot where the field rejoined the road. There was a slow rise in the ground there which he supposed was the hill, though it was hardly deserving of the name. A hillock, at best. Still, at least it meant he could walk the rest of the way and wouldn't have to face any idiotic comments from certain of the crew, which he certainly would have done if he'd turned up on the tractor. "Stop there," he said. "I'll walk from here."

Obviously, it was important that he get to the set as quickly as possible – but the tractor went barely faster than walking pace, after all. In any case, if the Kenyon girl was here, she was certainly safe; Ifeld could hardly wander through the cast and crew without being noticed and challenged.

He lowered himself gingerly to the ground, feeling every muscle in his body protest as he did so. His stomach was rumbling too. Would it be too reckless to stop at the lunch wagon on the way to finding the girl, he wondered?

Probably best not.

"Thank you, Mr. Murray," he called up. "Your help has been invaluable." He had worried on the way over that the old farmer would want to come all the way to the set, prompting God knew how many asinine questions, but thankfully he seemed keen to be on his way. With a grunt, he heaved on the steering wheel and began slowly to turn the tractor around. Edward stood for a bit, not wishing to appear rude, but finally his rumbling stomach – and the urgency of the situation, of course – overcame his good manners, and he turned his back on Murray and began to tramp up the grassy incline.

Not for the last time, he cursed the luck which had bestowed on him this dreadful, mucky slog, while John got to speed about the countryside like some geriatric James Bond.

* * *

"In about two hundred yards, just around the next bend, there's a little turning on the left. It's almost hidden by the hedge, so it's easy to miss, but take it slowly and you'll see it."

Madge never took her eyes from John as she spoke. Her voice was polite, as though she were providing directions to the village fête, or helping a particularly slow actor with his buttons, but her hand was steady as a rock and her finger remained curled on the trigger of the gun.

"Turn in there," she went on, "and continue along the road to the farmhouse at the very end. It's a narrow road, but don't worry, you won't pass anyone else. Nobody ever goes there."

That was the kind of seemingly innocuous, yet actually quite sinister, line which suave men in shiny suits and spats uttered in the movies, but coming from Madge's pert and impeccably lipsticked mouth, perhaps it was just helpful information? It was so hard to take her seriously as a kidnapper. But that was definitely what she was, he reminded himself firmly. He wasn't sure quite how it all fitted together, but obviously he and Edward had got it all wrong. Whatever else she might be, Madge Kenyon was no helpless victim.

But was she Ifeld's accomplice, he wondered – had he, in fact, interrupted a clandestine meeting, rather than saved her from certain death – or was she acting alone? The latter possibility made little sense so far as he could see, but by now, he was thoroughly confused.

"That sounds snug," he said finally. "Quite lovely, in fact." He signalled to turn off the road and encouraged the car to roll slowly onto the rough country lane. Ahead, tucked into the hillside, was a farmhouse rather less rundown than Robert Murray's. Madge gestured to a spot at the side of the house, hidden from the road by a copse of trees, and John brought the car to a halt.

"Will we be meeting Ifeld here?" he asked casually.

"Ifeld?" There was a mocking tone to Madge's voice as she uttered the name, but more tellingly, there was no sign of familiarity. With a sick sensation, John realised she had no idea who Barney Ifeld was. Which was exactly what he had believed half an hour previously, of course, but circumstances had changed, and what had then been a consequence of her innocence now felt like the confirmation of her guilt.

He glanced down at the gun and up at the forbidding bulk of the farmhouse, and felt his heart flutter in his chest. Unless Edward somehow contrived to figure out what had happened and where he had gone, this could well be his final resting place.

* * *

Edward was feeling altogether better. Hill Top had turned out to be less steep than he'd thought, and within five minutes he'd found himself on the outskirts of the shoot. Gratifyingly, he'd immediately been spotted by one of the crew, and a great fuss had been made of him, especially when he'd explained his mission and the lengths he'd gone to get there.

There was a moment of concern when, as soon as he was settled with a cup of tea and a sustaining egg-and-cress sandwich, he'd discovered that Marguerite Kenyon had been delayed at the village and would be following on later, but even that had swiftly been soothed by a telephone call to The Crown Hotel.

"Le Breton has her!" he announced triumphantly to the rest of the cast as he replaced the receiver. The spontaneous applause this simple statement generated was almost enough to bring a manly tear to his eye, and he found himself beaming with pleasure as first David, then Bobby and the others, gathered around him in congratulation.

"The receptionist at The Crown saw him pick her up in the car and drive off. Unfortunately, she doesn't know Barney Ifeld, so she can't say if he was sniffing around, but even so, having snatched his victim from his clutches, all we need do now is alert the authorities to take him into custody."

That was a thought. Much as he'd have liked to be the one to tell that idiot Inspector Ewing they'd cracked the case, it would be more fitting – and do the boy's career no harm, either – to give the honour of the arrest to young Primrose. Which made it all the more annoying when there was still no reply from the police station. He left a message on the machine, telling him everything, but that was hardly the same.

Was he supposed to sit on the news until Primrose deigned to show face?

"David says your costume's waiting for you in your tent," someone said from behind him. "He says he's looking to start shooting in half an hour, if you could be ready for then?"

Edward sighed and picked up the script for today's shooting. He supposed it was time to get back to work, but he would have liked just a *little* longer to savour their triumph.

30

The interior of the farmhouse was much nicer than Robert Murray's, too, with a grand fireplace (sadly, unlit), a sideboard containing a reasonable selection of decanters and glasses, and a selection of stuffed animal heads mounted on the walls.

Madge saw him looking around. "I rented this place as soon as I knew we'd be filming in the area. The hotel is all very well, but sometimes privacy is terribly important, don't you think?"

He supposed that was true, though, at the moment at least, he would have welcomed more company. He glanced towards the sideboard and felt himself relax just a tiny bit when Madge invited him to pour himself a drink. Everything was more bearable with a single malt, and he slopped a generous measure into a glass, trying not to let his hands tremble too much.

"And for you?" he asked politely, but she shook her head and indicated that he should step away from the bottles.

"Nothing for me. I think I'll keep a clear head." She motioned with the gun towards a wooden chair, tucked under a small round kitchen table. "If you could be a dear and pull that across to the middle of the room, that'd be lovely." She nodded at the spot she meant; the gun never wavered from its position aimed at John's heart. "Face it towards that wall."

John picked up the chair and, just for a moment, recalled the happy way in which the bad guys invariably collapsed, unconscious, when smashed over the head by chairs in the movies. He doubted it was the same in real life. For one thing, he doubted he could lift a chair over his head.

Even so, something about the way he held the chair, some tensing of what passed for his muscles perhaps, must have communicated itself to Madge, for she took a step back and tightened her grip on the gun.

"I'm a very good shot," she said, "so please, John: no foolishness. You are such a handsome man, and I should hate to have to spoil your looks."

Very carefully, John lowered the chair. He tossed back the whisky he'd poured himself and felt the reassuring burn in his throat. He needed it, too – now he could take a better look, he recognised the gun as a Webley, a Mark VI. Funny how that sort of detail stuck in one's head, when whole years had disappeared from memory. But like every other officer, he'd been issued with the exact same one during the War. He knew that a bullet fired from a Webley at this range would certainly kill him.

He was pleased to discover, however, that the fear he felt was not overwhelming. "I shouldn't care for that much myself," he said, and if his smile was lacking in a certain enthusiasm… well, it was a loaded gun, after all, and – contrary to popular opinion – he didn't entirely live in a dreamworld of his own devising. He'd seen a lot of damage done with guns, once upon a time.

Madge seemed to appreciate the effort, at least. "That's the spirit," she laughed, and indicated he should sit in the chair.

"Put your hands around the back, please," she directed, and he did so.

He felt something encircle his wrists then quickly tighten, so his hands were trapped. An experimental tug indicated he'd been securely tied to the chair.

"Funny how there's always a piece of rope when you need it," Madge said, unbelting her raincoat and dropping it on the table. "I'll leave your legs free, though. With every respect for your manly pride, you're in no physical condition to overpower me without the use of your arms."

She wasn't wrong. He doubted he could do anything more threatening than topple sideways from his current position. Instead, he waited to see what she would say next. Perhaps, if he could keep her talking for long enough, someone might notice his absence and track them down. It didn't seem likely, even in his own head, but you never knew, did you? People had unexpectedly proven awfully helpful in the past. There was the time he'd collapsed on the plane from Tangier to Gibraltar (if one must die, best to do it inside the Empire, at least) and that lovely little stewardess had helped him from the plane and commandeered a taxi to take him to the hospital…

"My mother's heart had been broken once too often, you see," Madge said loudly, and he realised he'd allowed his attention to drift. Maybe he did live in a dreamworld, after all.

He smiled blankly up at her for a moment, and slowly the annoyed grimace on her face softened into what he recognised from long experience as a look of exasperated fondness.

She tutted and shook her head. "If you could pay attention, John…"

"It must have been very difficult for you," he said hopefully.

Thankfully, it was the right thing to say. "It was the final straw." Madge nodded and, for the first time, he saw a crack in her icy composure. She sniffed and pulled a tissue from her pocket.

"The final straw?"

She turned to face John, but he was unsure if she had even heard his question. Her voice was quiet and her eyes disconcertingly unfocused. *The thousand-yard stare*, John thought, recalling a distinctly creaky script his agent had sent him earlier in the year.

"It was only after Mother died that I found out the truth," Madge said. "She left me a parcel, you see. It was the first thing in her will, apparently. All that she owned came to me, naturally, but the solicitor said she'd placed particular emphasis on this one parcel. I was to be given that by hand, he said, as he pushed it across the table.

"I took it, of course, but I didn't open it, not immediately. I was numb, I think. *I'm an orphan now*, I remember thinking, and that seemed to be the only thing that mattered, really, so I threw it on the back seat of my car, and forgot about it, would you believe? Strange the way our minds work. I wonder if, unconsciously, I thought that, if I didn't deal with it, Mother would still be here, in some fashion.

"Anyway, it was only after a week, maybe ten days, that I remembered it was there. I had some boxes of paperwork to move, and I went to put them in the back of the car, and there it was: the parcel."

Abruptly, she turned on her heel and walked across to the dresser on the wall. Without taking her eyes off John, she reached behind herself and pulled something from a drawer. It was a large, padded envelope of the sort sold in every stationer in the country, unsealed at one end.

"As well as my father's army revolver, this is all that was inside," she said.

There was an occasional table by the dresser, with the remnants of a sandwich on it. She swept the sandwich to the floor in a grand, exaggerated gesture, and dropped the envelope in its place, then laid the gun alongside it.

Hands now free, she upended the envelope and allowed the contents to slide onto the table. John, who was not quite in the right position to see easily, craned his neck to get a better view. She noticed and moved the table further to one side.

"How kind of you," he said automatically, but his attention was focused entirely on the little table.

At first, he was unsure what he was looking at. Two more envelopes, each smaller than the large one she now held in her hand, one manila and one cream. And a metal circle, like a cog from some giant machine. Only when he noticed the small strip of film protruding from it did he recognise its true purpose.

"A film reel?" he said, turning the statement into a question halfway through. Best to let her feel as though she were in charge. *She is in charge*, he reminded himself.

"Exactly. A film reel. Of course, I had no way to play it, but I *could* read the letter and examine the photographs."

As she spoke, she picked up the two envelopes and took a seat directly in front of him. The gun still lay on the table beside the film reel. Madge placed the envelopes on her lap and reached across for her cigarettes and lighter. Her hands shook a little as she held the flame to the cigarette tip, but otherwise she gave no sign she was engaged in anything more unusual than afternoon tea with an old family friend.

"Best to read the letter first, I think. It provides context for the photographs and the film. And context is so important, isn't it?"

She opened the cream envelope and slid out the letter it contained. The paper was of good quality, heavy and thick with something embossed at the top, John noticed, then felt a queasiness in his guts. It was too late to be looking for clues.

"'Dear Marguerite,'" Madge read, without further preamble. "'This package represents both an apology and an explanation. An apology first, because I never summoned up the courage to tell you any of this while your father and I were alive. That was a failing on my part. I should have trusted your good sense more, but I hope you will forgive me once you know the full story.'"

Madge snorted, and took a long draw on her cigarette. "'Secondly,'" she continued to read, "'an explanation; one which will, I hope, provide answers to certain questions you once asked me, but which I felt unable to supply at the time.'"

Madge ran a finger down the page, then flipped it over, with a small tutting sound. "And then there's a load of stuff I don't even remember asking. About genetics and eye colour and Lord knows what else... let's skip past all that. Let's see... yes, here we are. She gets back on track here... 'I can think of no clever or kind way to say what I have to say, my dearest Marguerite, so I will simply say it quickly. I did not meet, far less marry, your father until you were four years old.'"

She stopped and glanced, almost coyly, at John. If she was expecting to shock him, she was likely to be disappointed. He had been an actor for too long to be surprised by any of the many failings of humanity, far less a simple affair of the heart. He'd been involved in more complicated matters himself, and if he'd not handled them as well as he might, well, there was no point dwelling on that now.

"What do you make of that, John?" she prompted, when he failed to respond.

Not for the first time in his life, John found himself wishing he had a writer to tell him how to react in real-life situations. Having to come up with responses all the time, especially clever ones, was really quite tiresome.

"I'm afraid I don't quite understand," he said after a moment's thought. "Were you and your father very close?"

This time he had plainly said the wrong thing. "He was not my father!" she snapped. Her face flushed and she crumpled the letter a little in her hand.

"No, no, of course not." John's voice was placatory. He felt an unpleasant finger of cold sweat trickle down his back as she reached across and picked up the gun again. "I meant the man you'd thought was your father. But I don't know his name," he concluded, with a burst of sudden inspiration.

It seemed to be enough. The redness left Madge's face, and she relaxed her grip on the weapon. "His name was Cuthbert Snodgrass. I know – how ludicrous! We were never close, and when he died, I started using my mother's maiden name. Marguerite Kenyon sounds more exotic than Madge Snodgrass, don't you agree? But I always felt there was a distance between us, even if I could never understand why. Mother's letter answered that question for me." She gave a small smile, but there no mistaking the pain behind her eyes. "She was right about that, at least."

She smoothed the letter out carefully where she'd crumpled it, and read on.

"But let's see what else she had to say, shall we? Yes, here we are… 'Your biological father's name was Henry Anderson. I met him in the early days of the War, when I was fifteen and he sixteen, and we were both living with our families in London. We fell deeply in love. It should have been a glorious time, in spite of the bombing, but his family were unhappy that we were courting. They were very traditional, and had already decided on his future bride, so they forbade him to see me. And when we disobeyed, they sent him away, evacuated him to the country. He never knew that I was pregnant until it was too late. I didn't know myself until almost the day you were born. In my defence, I can only say that those were more innocent times.

"'I begged my parents to find out where he had gone, but they refused, and instead sent me away too. I wrote to him after you were born, but I don't know if he ever received the letter.

"'By the time I returned to London, I was a young mother and the War was over. And Henry was dead. He had been dragged into some sort of trouble by a group of local ruffians and forced to enlist long before he need have done. He was killed in France.'"

She looked up, and a single tear rolled down her face. "Mother was wrong about that. He'd already joined up, without telling any of his family. He didn't have to, but he did. That's the sort of man my father was." Her voice broke and, to hide her pain, she bowed her head over the letter and hurriedly read what were evidently the final lines from her mother. "'I have enclosed the few photographs I have of Henry, and a film reel, which was given to me some years later by a fellow from the War Office. When you watch it, you may wonder why I have not destroyed it, but when you have so little…'"

She folded the letter in two and placed it back on the table, picking up the second envelope as she did so. She pulled a handful of photographs from inside, then held them up, one at a time, before John's face.

The first showed a group of young men, all in uniform, grinning awkwardly at the camera. John recognised the large man in the centre as Lowell Edwardsson, and thought the stiff figure at the far right might be Matthew Peel. The others were unfamiliar, but there was no doubting this was the group of "young ruffians" the letter had mentioned. He wondered if their names had been handily pencilled on the back.

Madge dropped the photograph to the table, then stared for a long moment at the next one before flipping it around for him to see.

So, this was Henry Anderson. Young Henry. He peered at each of the photographs as they passed before him. A short man, a boy in fact, barely an inch or two taller than the girl beside him in each picture.

"Your mother?" he asked.

She nodded. "My parents. Four photographs, that's all I have of him. Four photographs from their summer together. And one hundred and ninety-two seconds of film from his final day."

The tears were flowing now. She looked like she was about to break, John thought. Despite everything, he found himself feeling sorry for her.

"Can I see the film?" he heard himself asking. "I'd like to understand."

She stared at him over the top of the last photograph. She blinked once, heavily and slowly, then nodded.

"I do believe you would. How sweet of you to ask."

She slid the photographs back into the envelope and laid it on the table, covering the gun. "I just need to get the projector. It's in the other room." She stood and smiled down at John. "You needn't get up."

He watched her walk across the room and heard her open a doorway behind him. Now was his chance. *Time for some British pluck and ingenuity*, as George Wetherby would doubtless have said, if this were a scene on the show.

He'd have had a point, too. Surely there was something within reach that could be used to cut himself free. A jagged edge to a handy length of metal pipework, or a forgotten kitchen knife. Even a glass bowl that might be nudged to the floor, and its smashed remnants used as an improvised blade. All it needed was a little time and—

"Here we are!" The thump of the projector banging on the table by his elbow caused John to flinch.

So much for that. He'd let his mind wander again, and the opportunity – if it had ever existed, he consoled himself – was gone. He composed his face into an expression of keen interest and watched Madge as she fitted the reel to the projector. Satisfied it would run true, she caught his look and returned it with a small, knowing smile. He couldn't say exactly why, but he felt oddly as though he had just been bested in some way.

"It's dark enough in here, I think," she announced. A lock of hair had slipped from the knot on top of her head and bounced against her ear as she resumed her seat. She must have been a pretty thing when she was young, the type he'd taken to dances a hundred times. Edward would say it was typical of him, to be thinking such thoughts at a time like this, but it was just the way he was made.

He could not say, later, if it was the thought of his friend or the mention of the darkness of the room which caused him to glance across at the window at that moment. Whatever the reason, the action was instantly rewarded. For a second, a face was framed by the glass, and then it was gone. He couldn't be sure, but could it have been Edward? He did hope so. The cavalry – even cavalry as unconventionally shaped as Edward Lowe – would be a gladsome sight round about now.

Without further warning, Madge flipped a switch and the projector whirred into life, casting a flickering off-white square of light on the far wall.

The film began.

31

A second or two passed, then a title of some sort – capitalised and in German.

Something something forbidden, it said.

Typically German. They were never happier than when they were forbidding things, thought John. It was why he'd never gone there on holiday, even when Sally had her heart set on a Rhine cruise.

"There's no sound, I'm afraid," Madge said, then blushed; at the incongruity of the apology, he supposed.

The film was indeed soundless, and grainy and rough, reminiscent more of a home movie than a professional one. But no professional movie would ever show anything so terrible as this.

As the images flickered into life against the wall, the surface coloured from white to grey and black. Three indistinct figures emerged from the haze to the right and crossed the screen to a wooden post at its centre. The central figure of the three staggered as he walked, and the other two had to steady him and help him move forward. Any thoughts John might have had that these were the first man's friends lasted only as long as took him to realise they were wearing the uniforms of the German army, and the stumbling man was not.

It's a firing squad, he realised, with a dizzying sickness in his stomach. *It's a damned firing squad.*

There was no doubting it. As he watched the two German soldiers tie the third man to the post with leather straps at his ankles and around his chest, he felt his stomach turn in horror.

One of the Germans turned and shouted towards the camera, beckoning the cameraman towards him. Unsteadily, the camera closed in on the execution party, until it was near enough that John could make out the terrified face of the young man being tied to the post.

He was barely more than a child, eighteen at most, thin and smooth-faced rather than clean-shaven, with dirty blond hair that had matted to his forehead with sweat. A nasty cut ran across one cheek, and one eye was swollen shut. Even so, there was no doubt this was the man from Madge Kenyon's photographs.

It must have been a sunny day, for he squinted with his good eye as the camera framed him and what was obviously a German officer. The officer turned to the camera and smiled, spoke again, then bent down out of shot. When he reappeared, he held a white paper circle, the size of a tea saucer, which he pinned in the centre of the condemned youngster's chest.

"My father had been in France for three days, John." Madge's voice was sharp and bitter behind him. "He spoke fluent French, but he wasn't prepared for the job he'd been given. He didn't have a chance."

He might have replied – though what exactly could he have said? – but his attention was focused on the film before him. The German officer pressed a hip flask to the lips of the British soldier. (*Henry Anderson*, he corrected himself angrily. The least he could do was give the man the respect of his name.) A little liquid trickled down his chin, and he coughed. The German laughed and lit a cigarette, then held it so Anderson could smoke.

A white circle. A final drink. A last cigarette.

Of course.

"You re-enacted your father's execution, didn't you? All those women you killed… each one was one part of… *this*."

There was a click behind him and the film came to a halt. Madge stepped in front of the still image. "Jolly well done, John!" she said, clapping her hands in congratulation. "A little theatrical, I grant you, but then again, theatre has been my life." She gestured towards the figure of her father, cigarette hanging limply in his mouth. "He didn't smoke, you know. And neither did the Peel girl. I did think that was a nice touch, if a smidge risky. Don't you agree?"

The question was unexpectedly bright and breezy, as though the sight of her father, even in so desperate a condition, had lifted her mood. When John just stared up at her, she gave a little moue of mock displeasure. "No? Perhaps I do myself too much credit. But I did think that would raise eyebrows amongst the boys in blue. I thought it might even make them do a blood test, and then they'd have found the remains of all those horrid tablets I crushed in her drinks." She laughed, but there was a sharp edge to it. "She was such a sweet girl, too, and so keen to please. She was studying drama, did you know that? She wanted to be an actress... and when an old friend of her poor, dead mother got in touch, one who actually worked in television, well, she was delighted to invite her over for a bite to eat and a few drinks."

"The police didn't seem to care," John said dully. "We – Edward, anyway – noticed there were no ashtrays in her flat, but when we told them that, they rather told us to bugger off."

Madge nodded. "Yes, the constabulary were such a let-down; I thought they'd be far more on the ball. It seems laughable now, but at the beginning I wasn't certain I'd even get away with the dog."

"The dog?" John asked, confused again, just as he thought he'd got a handle on things. Life was so often that way, he found.

"The one belonging to that hideous farmer." She grinned and clapped her hands together like a schoolgirl who'd been told there would be cakes for tea. "Oh, don't tell me you missed that? The very first thing I did was to lure the farmer's little doggie away and lock it up in the dark. Just like the Germans did with my father."

Her voice now was flat, with a lack of emotion that was almost an emotion in itself. She shook her head and smiled thinly down at John. "The fact he was so close was what made my mind up for me, I think. Even after reading Mother's letter, I might have done nothing. Well, you don't, do you? You imagine all kinds of terrible revenge, but you don't actually go through with any of them.

"But someone mentioned him to me, in the village shop. A local war hero, so badly injured that he never left his farm and had only a dog for company. Robert Murray, they said his name was, and I thought, *oh, it can't be the same man.* But it was. Fate obviously meant me to do *something.* It'd have been rude not to, really."

"So you killed Murray's dog?"

"Well, he had nobody else worth killing, you silly man!" Her voice was childish and gleeful, amused by his failure to grasp the obvious. "The dog didn't suffer, though." Her face fell. "I'm not a monster, John. I fed it some sausages laced with enough sleeping tablets to kill a horse before I locked it up. I'm sure it wouldn't have known what was happening.

"And nobody suspected a thing. Not a thing. What was funniest of all was that ridiculous constable coming round to the hotel to ask if anyone had seen it. 'I do hope it turns up,' I said, and did my best to look awfully worried." She tucked away the loose strand of hair and shook her head. "The police really are so dim."

Watching her father's film had done something to her, John realised. It had caused something to change in her. Before the film had started, she had obviously been a troubled soul, but, for all her sadness, and even though she had kidnapped him, she had essentially been rational, even composed. Now, though, he realised that any sanity she retained was only skin-deep, and that something basic inside her was broken.

"Not you, though, John," she went on, snapping open a compact mirror and carefully reapplying her lipstick. "You're not dim at all. You and fussy little Edward. You seem such a pair of simpletons, too: Edward, the grumpy little toad, and Johnny, the overgrown schoolboy, always looking for Nanny. And the police seem so competent, don't they, with their shiny cars and their jazzy radios and their smart uniforms? But they missed everything. They'd have kept missing everything as well, if it hadn't been for you two, poking at things which really shouldn't have been of any interest to either of you.

"It was quite a disaster for me that it was Edward who tripped over Alice Burke…"

She sighed dramatically, then immediately brightened to a dazzling smile. "But hey ho! Let's not be Gloomy Guses! If you hadn't gotten involved, nobody would ever have known what was happening, would they? I'd have known, of course, and I did think once that that would be enough. But now… oh now, I think this is much better. Now all those daddies and uncles know that the one person they loved the most in the whole world didn't just die. No, they were taken away from them.

"Just like my poor, dear father."

Her voice trembled, and John thought she might break down, but she rallied and continued with barely a pause. "And not just mine, either. I wasn't the only one who lost a parent because of those monsters, you know." She tapped a finger on the side of her nose and cocked an eyebrow, exaggerated gestures which reminded John of the vaudeville stars of his childhood. "There was the Menzies boy, too. It wasn't his fault his mother was a disgusting tramp, was it? I sent him some souvenirs, copies of the local newspapers, and photographs, just to let him know someone was doing something." She smiled again. "I'm sure he appreciated that."

"I'm sure he did." Best to keep on her good side as long as possible. "We met him, you know. He kept the papers you sent. Edward found the one with Primrose's interview about Alice Burke in it." He shook his head. "We should have realised then that you had to be local."

"Wasn't it lucky for me that you didn't! That would have ruined everything!" Madge wagged a finger in John's face like a schoolteacher chastising a wayward child. "But it doesn't matter now."

An odd look crossed her face, and a tremor rippled on her lips that could be either the beginnings of a smile or the precursor to tears. John thought it was probably quite important to keep her talking; if she decided she'd said all she needed to say, it was unlikely to lead to a very cheery ending for him.

"How did you get her to come to see you?" he asked. "Alice Burke, I mean."

Madge brightened at once. "Oh, that was simple. Everybody wants something wonderful to fall into their laps, John. There's nothing better than unexpected good fortune, is there?"

"And nothing worse than bad?"

"Perhaps."

"Like the bad fortune your father had?"

Madge's jaw snapped shut with the audible sound of teeth coming together. All warmth disappeared from her face. She stared down at him for a long second, then stepped out of his line of sight and restarted the film.

On the wall, the other German, a private, checked the knots which tied Henry Anderson to the post and stepped back to salute. The officer nodded. He removed the unsmoked cigarette from the young Englishman's mouth and handed it to the private, who nipped it and tucked it in his pocket. From his own uniform, he pulled a strip of black cloth.

It's a blindfold, he thought with a shudder. *Like Rebecca Boyce*.

In the film, Anderson's eyes were covered, and the two Germans stepped out of sight, leaving only the condemned man in view. The cameraman backed away along with them, until Anderson was framed in the centre of a long shot. A dirty grey wall stretched out on either side of him, but otherwise the scene was empty.

Again, something clicked behind him and the image froze.

"My father was eighteen when he died. Just a frightened boy, with no idea why he was dying. But you know, John, don't you? You know exactly why he died. And that luck had nothing to do with it."

She picked up the second envelope from the occasional table.

"Here it is in writing," she said, holding up the letter it contained, so that John could see it. Cheaper paper this time, thin and tinted very slightly blue. He recognised the type from the War. Official army stationery.

"This is the letter from father's commanding officer to his divisional superior, regarding the Menzies Affair – see, it's even capitalised, *The Menzies Affair*, as though they were discussing important international stratagems, and not some stupid dead whore. And this bit is his recommendation." She held one manicured nail against a line halfway down the page and read the words aloud.

"'Public knowledge of military personnel involvement in this matter can in no way reflect well on His Majesty's forces, nor would it be conducive to morale, either within the camp or in the country in general. Since thorough investigations have been unable to come to a definitive conclusion regarding guilt in the death of Mrs. Menzies, it is my recommendation that justice would best be served by immediate overseas postings for the soldiers involved, and a formal verdict of death by misadventure.'"

As she read, her hand shook enough to cause the page to fold forward on itself, but she obviously knew the words by heart.

"What do you think of that?" she asked, slipping the letter back into the envelope and laying it carefully down.

What could he say? He had the feeling that the wrong word now might be the end of him. Where *was* Edward?

"Your father was fast asleep, overcome with drink, long before Sylvia Menzies was left to die," he ventured hesitantly. "He had nothing to do with her death."

"I know that!" It was not a shout filled with rage and fury, as he would have expected, but rather a sad, broken cry, the sound of someone themselves lost, grieving the thing they have lost, and the unfairness of losing it.

Tears like fat raindrops filled her eyes but didn't fall as she looked at the wall and the grainy image of her father on it.

"When I was planning to kill the dog, I thought that might be enough. I was sure it would be, actually. Just to do something, to make one of them pay for what they did to my father. And it was only a dog, when all's said and done. But afterwards, I bumped into that silly constable, and he told me the dog had been found dead, and how upset the old man was. And it felt good. No, more than that. It felt right. *Fitting*. The innocent paying for the crimes of the guilty.

"I had all their names, didn't I? And one of them was unusual enough that he wasn't hard to find."

"Lowell Edwardsson," John murmured quietly.

Madge nodded, running her palms across her wet cheeks. "It took five minutes at the library to find him, and then another five on the phone to discover his daughter worked for him. I wrote to her on BBC notepaper, saying we were considering contracting out the manufacture of our plastic prop modelling. Well, that was enough to have her packing her little rucksack and driving all the way down here, lickity split. She was perfectly happy to lie to her father about it, too – we couldn't have word of this getting out, I said, there'd be such a fuss, with the BBC license fee always under scrutiny. 'No problem,' she said. 'I quite understand.' Oh, you've never met such an ambitious young lady as Miss Burke."

"She didn't suspect anything?"

"Not even when I said we needed to meet out by the moors. We couldn't risk being seen together, I said."

"We found one of her shoes. On the moors. It was the fact it was a dress shoe and not a boot that convinced Edward something skew-whiff had taken place."

"That was a little annoying, I must admit. Frankly, I hadn't planned things out very well, when it came down to it. I'd intended to offer her a drink first, to put here at her ease, then kill her and leave the body in the car park with the paper circle glued to her. But, as I was waiting for her to arrive, I suddenly realised I'd never considered how to do the actual killing. I suppose I'd a vague idea I'd hit her on the head and that'd do the trick, but beyond that..." She shrugged. "In any event, this lack of method was still playing on my mind when she did arrive, and something I said must have made her suspicious. She wouldn't take a drink and said she was going back to her hotel and I should phone there in the morning and we could arrange another meeting. I lost my temper a little then, I'm afraid. She was about to get back into her car, so I grabbed her hair and banged her head down hard on the roof."

She glanced across at the still image of her father on the wall and stood there silently, as though she had forgotten John was there. He craned his neck around to look out the window but all he could see was the yard and, in the distance, the point at which the fields met the overcast sky.

"Which goes to show that a bang on the head isn't enough to kill anyone. I stepped back, thinking she'd collapse onto the ground, but quick as a flash, she was on her feet and past me, and I had to run after her. I actually thought she might get away, but she wasn't dressed for the occasion, and it wasn't hard to keep up.

"What was annoying, though, was that I'd cut out a paper circle exactly like the one those swine pinned to my father, but I dropped it in the chase. Luckily, I had some white make-up from the show in my jacket pocket and I drew a circle with that. It wasn't perfect, but close enough, I think.

"And it worked out alright generally, in the end; it was black as pitch out on the moors, so there was no chance of being seen, and when we got to the reservoir and I banged her across the head with the brandy bottle, well, what better way to kill her than to dump her in the water? It felt like a sign, almost. A sign that what I was doing was the right thing and I should carry on.

"Still, I was shaking, I was so nervous when I tipped her over... actually no, not nervous, that's not right. *Elated* might be a better word. I had a drink of the brandy, to calm me down, but my hands were shaking so much that I spilled it all over myself. I had to mop it up with a hankie, and then I dropped the bottle and it smashed, and I didn't know what to do... oh, it was like French farce, it really was. In the end, I just left the bottle – and the hankie, though I didn't discover that until later." She laughed. "I got quite a shock when one of the girls told me that Edward had stood on the damned thing. Otherwise, the fat little fool would never have gotten involved."

Without thinking, John found himself defending Edward. "He's a damn sight cleverer than he looks, you know. He was onto you from the off for one thing, wasn't he?"

Not the wisest thing to say, he realised, but it had just come out. Madge frowned down at him and he felt his stomach twist into an acidic knot, then she suddenly turned back to the projector. With a click, the film ran on for its last few seconds.

There wasn't much left to see. For a second nothing moved and then, in grotesque silence, Henry Anderson jerked once, twice, and slumped forward, held against the post only by the straps which bound him. The German officer's back filled the frame as he stepped into it, and then, in a jumble of identifying letters and numbers, the film abruptly ended and the wall returned to its previous pristine whiteness.

"He was supposed to be a kind of spy, I think, but Mother wasn't very clear about it. Apparently, someone at the camp, someone senior, had approached him... before he got involved with those terrible people. Lord knows how she knew that. The same chap at the War Office who got her the letter, perhaps?

"In any case, my father *was* fluent in German and French, so perhaps there's some truth in it. But whether it was or not, he was betrayed – or betrayed himself – almost as soon as he arrived. And as an Englishman, out of uniform in occupied France, he was beaten, left without food or water in a dark, filthy room, then taken outside and shot. The officer that sent him might as well have pulled out his gun and shot my father himself. The result would have been the same, and it would have saved my father all of this."

As she was speaking, John could hear her moving about behind him, and when she reappeared in front of him, he could see what she had been doing.

She had changed clothes, swapping the red dress and heels for the sensible woollen skirt, matching jumper and flat shoes in which he'd often seen her on set. She unclipped her golden earrings as he tried to see the far window over her shoulder, hoping that Edward might make another appearance. He strongly suspected he was running out of time.

After she'd pulled on a shapeless brown coat, she bent down and picked up the gun.

She cocked an eyebrow at him, and looked down at the weapon in her hand with a sly half-smile.

"What to do with you, John?" she said.

He could think of several things, all of them involving her leaving him alive and well, but he didn't really see how she could. The bad guys never left witnesses alive in the movies, and he doubted it was much different for the bad girls. Still, better to keep her talking than to leave a silence she might decide to fill with a bullet.

"Don't you think you've behaved rather awfully?" he asked suddenly. "I mean to say, what were you thinking of, going around pushing people into reservoirs and down flights of stairs?"

"Down flights of stairs?" she asked, her face creased in thought. "Oh, you mean the Boyce girl? No, you have that wrong, I'm afraid, Johnny. I didn't push her down the stairs." She shook her head and smiled. "Actually, I pulled her as she ran *up* the stairs away from me and she just happened to fall back down them. The sound her neck made as it snapped was actually quite unpleasant, between you and me. Much better if she hadn't seen me lurking in the darkness and I could have sneaked up and strangled her as I'd intended."

She was still smiling as she talked. John knew he should try to humour her, but the words were out of his mouth before he could bite them back. "You really are a frightful monster, aren't you? You disgust me, frankly – and if your father was still alive, I bet he'd feel the same way."

What he said was true, perhaps, but it was also inadvisable. Still, there was no denying it kept Madge's attention.

Unfortunately, while he held her attention, she held a gun.

She raised it slowly until it pointed directly at his head. Very deliberately, she pressed the barrel against his forehead.

He had known that her seeming good humour and bright laughter was merely a brittle cover to a deep madness, but he would much have preferred it to the cold fury he now saw behind her eyes.

"I knew as soon as you and Edward got involved that I'd need to end this by killing one of you. Are you volunteering, John?"

Even in the War, he'd never been so close to death. Unexpectedly, the image of a restaurant in flames popped into his head. The name eluded him, though it was on the tip of his tongue, but he remembered the night a Nazi bomb had destroyed it, and he'd rushed to help the wounded. He'd tried to hand the wrong arm to a man missing his own, and suddenly he felt clammy and sick, and wondered if he'd faint before Madge could shoot him. He blinked slowly, willing himself unconscious, but he remained stubbornly aware of the pressure of the gun barrel against his skin.

Slowly, Madge took her finger off the trigger and allowed the gun to fall to her side.

John realised, without surprise, that he was holding his breath. With a long sigh, he exhaled.

As though on cue, something smashed through the window behind Madge, and somewhere out of sight he heard a crashing sound he recognised from innumerable TV effects as a door being kicked open.

He just had time to shout a warning – *"Edward, watch out! She's got a gun!"* – before he was cuffed hard on the side of the head.

As his eyes closed in shock, he saw a window being thrown open and the shape of a woman silhouetted against it. With a supreme effort, he pushed his feet down hard and thrust himself forward, still attached to the chair, so he was launched into a stumbling, barely controlled run.

Head down, unable to see where he was going, he felt his shoulder collide with something, and then his head cracked against the wall and the effort to remain conscious became too much.

With a final groan, he gave way to the darkness.

32

"Wake up, Mr. Le Breton, wake up…"

Reluctantly, John pulled himself away from a delightful dream about him and Sally – why was it always Sally he dreamed about? – taking the boys to the zoo, and opened his eyes. He was disappointed, but not surprised, to be confronted by a close-up of Constable Primrose's moon-like face. That voice was unmistakable.

"What happened?" he asked, realising his head was aching like he'd emerged from Ronnie Scott's in the wee small hours the night before.

"I saved you!" The pride in Primrose's voice was terribly sweet.

"Did you now? Well, many thanks for that. It's very much appreciated."

With a groan, John pulled himself to his feet, wobbled alarmingly as his head swam in dizzy circles, and he stumbled to the same chair to which he'd recently been tied and slumped down.

"Did you get her?" he asked. "Madge Kenyon? Did you get her?"

Rather than reply, Primrose grimaced and turned away. Unsure how to react to this, John reached up to tug at his sleeve but, as he did so, he realised the young policeman was calling another man over, a man with sergeant's stripes on his own uniform. Primrose, it seemed, had not come alone.

"Mr. Le Breton," he said, "I'm Sergeant Oliver, and it's a pleasure to see you're none the worse for your ordeal." He frowned, coughed, and John realised he was embarrassed for some reason. "We'd have been here sooner, but there was a bit of a mix-up with the message from Edinburgh."

"Edinburgh?"

"Yes…" The sergeant dragged the word out slowly, clearly wondering how best to phrase whatever it was he had to say next. "Seems there's a lad up there, name of Menzies, you helped the Jocks take into custody? Well, he's been talking, looks like, and the name he gave them was Marguerite Kenyon. Says she's been sending him newspaper clippings of a suspicious nature. So, their inspector phoned down to ours, but somehow Inspector Ewing missed the message." He reddened. "That was a few hours ago. It was only when young Frank here telephoned in to say he'd passed you on the road outside town and that some woman was pointing a gun at you that someone remembered the message from Scotland. It took us a while to pick up your trail after that, but there's only so many farmhouses in the area."

"We did rather go off the beaten path," John offered with a smile. The sergeant seemed a decent chap, and it was hardly his fault his superior was an idiot. "But what happened to Madge? I rather think she might be a killer, you see. Did you catch her? Or did she get away?"

"Both, you could say, Mr. Le Breton. And then again, neither." Again, he frowned, as though hesitant to give troubling news. "She tried to jump out the window after coshing you on the head, but you threw yourself at her and caught her on the back just as she jumped. Looks like she fell head-first on account of that. Broke her neck, the doctor says. Dead as a doornail."

John slumped down in the chair with a sudden, aching tiredness. Until that moment, he'd not realised how tense he'd been. Which was ridiculous really. He'd been kidnapped, tied up, forced to watch a gruesome execution and had a gun pushed in his face. The surprise was that he wasn't a babbling wreck on the carpet.

He laughed suddenly, involuntarily, a strange, gargling sound, wholly unlike his usual chuckle, and for a second, thought he might cry. The two policemen were looking at him, he realised. Primrose laid a hand on his shoulder and patted it awkwardly.

"You saved me," John said, for something to say.

"I helped," Primrose replied shyly. "I was on my bike and I waved when I went past you. But you never looked up. Neither did the lady, which was lucky." He smiled. "I nearly came off my bike when I saw the gun!"

"I bet you did! Thank you again, Frank."

The sergeant plainly had other things to do. As Primrose's smiled widened, he made his apologies and turned to go. "Take Mr. Le Breton back to his hotel, Constable," he said before leaving. "He's had a hell of a shock, and someone'll need to keep an eye on him for a bit."

The sooner he was out of the farmhouse, the better, as far as John was concerned. But he wasn't sure he wanted to go back to the hotel either. Unexpectedly, he had no desire for a drink. He could still taste the whisky he'd drunk when he arrived, and it was sour in his mouth.

"We could go up to the set," he said suddenly. "We need to tell Edward what's happened, and I'd prefer to do it in person. This has been his baby all along, and he deserves to hear it's over, face to face."

"If you want, Mr. Le Breton. I'd better go with you though. You heard what the sergeant said."

John nodded and pushed himself to his feet. Physically he felt back to normal, he was pleased to discover, but something was nagging away at the back of his head. *It's the disappointment*, he thought. *Tripping and falling out of a window. It's all so... anticlimactic.*

It would never do as the ending of a movie, that was certain, not even a Danziger seven-day quickie made in a back room in Bermondsey. A shootout, with bullets pinging off the walls, or a car chase through the country lanes – that's how it should have ended. Not this.

Glumly, he followed Primrose out into the yard. He glanced across at the broken window and, underneath it, just visible through a ruck of policemen, the still figure of

Madge Kenyon. A shudder ran through him and, again, he felt tears prick his eyes. It wasn't that he wanted her to be alive instead of him, but she had been broken in ways which were not all of her own doing, and he had been fond of her once.

"Come on," he said to Primrose. "Let's get out of here."

He opened the car and slid into the driver's seat before Primrose could protest. The boy might have saved his life today, but he wasn't risking it all over again at the hands of his driving. He'd seen Primrose on a bicycle.

"Let's go and see Edward," he said, and started the engine.

To John's delight, it had turned into a glorious day. The clouds had cleared and the sun, weak but bright, was beaming down on the damp hedgerows which lined the road. Fields stretched around them in all directions, and though it wasn't warm, he rolled down the window and flicked cigarette ash out of it with the sense that all was basically right with the world.

He even continued to think reasonably kindly of the woman who had, only half an hour previously, threatened to kill him. It did help she was safely dead, to be fair.

Mad as a brush, of course. But she'd been dealt a rough hand in life, hadn't she, and had some pretty shocking and unexpected news. That sort of thing was bound to have an effect. And she did have such pretty little teeth.

She'd obviously taken a shine to him, too. Why else would she have bopped him on the head with the gun, rather than just shoot him when she had the chance?

"I was just thinking," he said, turning to Primrose, "that it was lucky Madge decided to knock me on the head with her gun, instead of shooting me with the thing."

"With this gun, you mean? Shot you down like the lousy dog you are?"

Primrose, the awkward, lanky, incompetent policeman, the butt of everybody's jokes, the one man nobody would suspect of involvement... Primrose leered evilly and pulled the revolver from inside his jacket and pointed it at John's chest. For the second time in the same day, he watched as a finger curled on a trigger and knew there was nothing he could do to save himself. His head swam in panic but his body froze in place. He closed his eyes, confused and terrified, and pictured Sally at the Players, on the day they met, and felt a little better as he waited for the end to come.

"Oh, she couldn't have done that, Mr. Le Breton. Not with this."

He heard the click of the trigger being pulled and flinched backwards with a cry, his hands thrown up before him as though to ward off a bullet which, to his surprise, never arrived.

"Bang bang!" Primrose laughed, and flipped the gun around in his hand, so he held it by the barrel. "See, it's just a plastic replica," he said, handing it across. "You couldn't shoot someone with this, even if you wanted to."

Sure enough, as soon John closed his hand around it, it was plain the revolver was nothing but a cheap plastic moulding, designed to look like a Webley but only at first glance. He turned it in his hand, surprised at how light it was, and pulled the trigger, the only moving part, once or twice. If he'd ever had the chance to take a good look at it, he realised, he'd have recognised the deception at once. Even under the most cursory inspection, it was obviously just a toy.

Or, he thought suddenly, a prop.

Later on, sitting ashen-faced and alone, giving his statement to the police, John described the next moments as being a mixture of nauseating, dizzying sickness and astonishing, blinding clarity. The details were all of a blur in his head, but he remembered swinging the car off the road and into the nearest hedge, then putting his hands over his ears to block out Primrose's continuing chatter about his collection of books on World War Two. His head was suddenly awash with words and images, snippets of conversations and frozen tableaux from the previous weeks.

He knew now what had been nagging away at him, ever since he'd heard Madge Kenyon was dead. It wasn't disappointment at her anticlimactic end at all; it was, in fact, two very simple questions.

Where had she gotten the gun? And why had he recognised it so easily?

He'd known it from his own service days, of course, but that was decades before, and he'd been an officer, even if a lamentably incompetent one. Only officers were issued with sidearms, not teenage boys playing spy in France. Henry Anderson would no more have had a Webley to pass on to his daughter than he'd have had a Sherman tank. So where would Madge have gotten it?

Only officers were issued with sidearms … or those play-acting as officers.

Oh God.

Edward.

33

The last episode of the series was one Edward had been looking forward to. For once, Wetherby – so often the butt of foolish jokes and asinine slapstick – behaved quite well, and even a little heroically.

This thought, combined with the success of their investigations, left Edward in an excellent mood as he changed from his mud-spattered civilian clothes into the captain's outfit he was to wear throughout the next scene.

He took a moment to admire the flow of his jacket in the mirror – he did suit it, there was no denying it. Funny to think that he and John had probably saved the life of the woman who had made it.

Still, he reminded himself, a smart appearance would count for nothing if he didn't have his lines down pat. It couldn't hurt to skim over the script one last time.

The entire episode revolved around the Groat Street pensioners' involvement with a local military enactment society, and Wetherby's role as judge of the Best Uniform competition at their annual fête – for which purpose he was to be dressed for the day as a captain in the light infantry.

In this, the final scene, he had to walk into the dealers' tent, discover the rest of the cast standing with their hands in the air, then react as an unseen hand grabbed the dummy army revolver from its holster at his waist. Whip around and find a burly ruffian threatening to shoot him with his own gun if he didn't join the others. Ask what's going on, react to the news that the ruffian was now robbing the place of the day's takings and that he'd now swapped the knife he'd been carrying for Wetherby's gun.

Then a line... damn, what was it again? Oh yes, *Not too antique to deal with the likes of you!*... and step forward, grab the barrel of the gun just before it fires and sock the ruffian in the jaw with the other, knocking him out cold.

Accept the others' stunned congratulations on his tremendous bravery and ignore Joe Riley's whispered observation that he knew the gun wasn't loaded. *Whae's ever heard of a re-enactment gun bein' loaded wi' real bullets?*

Straighten tie. Reholster revolver with a small smile.

Run credits.

Yes, that was very decent. He must remember to congratulate Bobby later. It was only right to tell him when he'd done well, and it might encourage him to do more stuff of that nature and a bit less of the *whoops, my trousers have fallen down again, Vicar* rubbish he'd been churning out up until now.

A head appeared around the doorway. "Everything's ready for shooting, Mr. Lowe," it said.

He pushed himself to his feet, placed his hat on his head and checked his gun was in its holster, flap button unfastened.

All present and correct, Wetherby confirmed contentedly, and followed the runner back towards the set.

* * *

"That must be the dummy gun Edward's supposed to be wearing in this week's episode!"

John wrenched the steering wheel to one side and whipped the car around the corner fast enough to make Primrose squeal in fear. "So what's he got in his holster just now?" He glanced from the road for a second. "Are you sure, Frank – all it takes to turn a decommissioned gun back into a working one is to replace the firing pin?"

"It's easy, Mr. Le Breton," Primrose wailed. "I read about it in a magazine. Anybody could do it."

I need to end this by killing one of you.

Madge's last words echoed through John's head as he slammed on the brakes at a junction, then pressed on the accelerator and sent the car haring down yet another lane. They were a good fifteen minutes from Hill Top, and about the same distance from anywhere with a telephone. He could only hope they got to Edward in time.

He should have realised earlier, he cursed himself. Madge hadn't changed into clothes for going back to work, but into nondescript ones in which to make her escape. Whatever she had planned was already in place and didn't require her presence.

I need to end this by killing one of you.

He'd assumed she meant him, but now he was certain she'd meant Edward. He could see the script, as fresh in his memory as when his eyes had flicked over it a few days before. The robber chap pinching Wetherby's gun and Edward retrieving it even as it was fired at him.

Something else Madge had said came to mind.

The officer that sent him might as well have pulled out his gun and shot my father himself.

John leaned all his weight down on the accelerator pedal, though it was already pressed against the floor.

God knows where she'd actually acquired a working gun, but if he didn't get there before they shot that scene, Edward was going to be murdered in front of everyone.

* * *

"It's all pretty straightforward, Edward. You see your chaps with their arms in the air, standing against the back wall. In you go, wanting to know what the hell's going on, and before you know it the chap's stolen your gun."

"Yes, yes, I know," Edward snapped, a little peevishly probably, but he had acted before, and had no need to be nurse-maided by David. "It's hardly Ibsen, is it?"

He thought David was going to respond in kind, but all he actually did was laugh. "At least it's not in Norwegian,

Edward," he said, shaking his head. "Right then, places everyone," he went on, stepping back behind the camera.

The set was a simple one: a doorway through which Edward was to enter a set of flats made up as the interior of a tent, complete with a handful of stalls, on which lay medals from the War, and a trestle table with a till on it. The other actors were already arranged against the far wall, opposite the door, with the crew and the cameras to the right. The young actor playing the ruffian was hidden to the left of the door.

As David spoke, the actors got into position and everything took on the peculiarly deep silence that always came over a set just before the cameras rolled.

There was a pause, and then he called "Action." Edward squared his shoulders and walked through the door and into shot.

The others all reacted on cue, gurning and grimacing in a tiresomely broad manner as he took his first steps forward. He had mentioned to Bobby and David before that there really was no need for such pantomime shenanigans all the time, but apparently audiences liked it and thought it funny, so it was unlikely to change any time soon. Which went to show how lowbrow the viewing public could be, in Edward's opinion – but since the show was hardly likely to be one that lingered long, either on screen or in the memory, he didn't suppose it really mattered. A pay day was a pay day, and the fact it had got to a second season was surprising enough.

Automatically, he glared at the motley crowd before him and muttered an exasperated "What on earth are you playing at, you damn fools?"

He had to admit there was something pleasing about the way they responded, each man, old troopers that they were, doing his level best to out-stage his immediate neighbour in an impressive range of twitches, tics and goggle-eyed glares designed to warn him of the robber just behind—

He's gone too early! Edward thought irritably as a hand grabbed at his waist and he felt his gun being lifted from its holster. He spun around with a blustering snort. For a moment he was stopped in his tracks by the sight of the gun pointing at him, then he took a step forward, an Englishman undaunted by wrongdoers, regardless of the odds.

"Stop right there, Granddad, or you'll get it!" The young actor was presumably local and his snarl was more extravagant than it needed to be, but subtlety was hardly *Floggit and Leggit*'s forte, Edward supposed.

"Give me that gun!" There was just the right mix of indignation and fury in his voice, Edward was pleased to hear. "I brought that from home, you know!"

The ruffian – Smith, the script imaginatively called him – was a big lad, who almost filled the doorway. He snarled again and raised the revolver to shoulder height. "Well, it belongs to me now, Granddad."

The snarl was a little less pronounced this time, and all the more effective for that, and Edward felt a tiny flicker of alarm as he stared down the barrel of the gun.

He glanced over at a stall that contained a selection of imitation army knives and plastic pistols, then unsure if the camera had caught that, twisted himself around and made a deliberately clumsy movement towards them. On cue, the cast began to offer advice in their own various, inimitable styles.

"Last warning, you old antique," Smith growled, but this was Wetherby's big moment, and Edward had judged the swing of his body as he moved in the direction of the shelves just right. A quick pivot on the soles of his feet, a step forward and a swift uppercut to the jaw. That should do the trick. Now, what was the bloody line?

"Not too antique to clip your ear!" he barked and swung around, pulling back his arm to launch his fist at Smith, while the other reached for the barrel of the revolver. The young actor, playing his part damn well now, recoiled and began to shout a warning, even while his thumb pulled back the hammer of the gun and his finger whitened on the trigger. The click of the hammer was loud in the small space, and as Edward registered it, rather than concentrating on getting his swinging punch just right, another set of images went through his head.

An imitation sword bending in the middle, caught on the wind. A photograph of Guernsey in a plastic frame. A cheap broom snapping in two as he pressed down on it.

So, it was true what they said about facing great danger, after all. Time did slow down and the world did become more vibrant, the details so much clearer. There was no way that the tiny budget for *Floggit and Leggit* would stretch to a revolver with working parts, he realised, not one where the hammer moved and engaged so noisily, or where the light glimmered off the barrel in a manner that indicated metal not plastic.

The last thing Edward heard, before the loudest sound in the world obliterated all sense in the little room, was one of the cast's puzzled cry...

"What are you doing, you daft bugger?"

...and then there was blazing agony in his head and everything went black.

34

John ate the last of the grapes and stared moodily out of the grimy hospital window. Outside, the rain was hammering down in sheets of grey.

"It's lucky David's abandoned filming and sent everyone home. We'd get nothing done in this weather, in any case." Edward frowned across the top of the bedcover. "Have you finished *all* those grapes?"

In response, John crumpled the brown paper bag in his hand and threw it inexpertly towards the wastepaper bin at the side of his bed. It was petty of him to have eaten all the grapes, he knew, but damn it all, it was him stuck in this tedious hospital with a buggered leg, wasn't it, not Edward? All because he'd been in such a hurry to save his friend's life that he'd missed a corner, skidded across the road and deposited the car on its roof in a field.

On the plus side, he thought with a smile, coming to and finding himself dangling upside down a few scant feet from a set of cow's udders was going to make a wonderful story for pals over drinks at some point. That it was all for nothing somehow made it funnier.

Good humour entirely restored, he lit a cigarette and blew smoke at the ceiling. "So, the bullet skimmed your temple and went straight into the camera, did it? Who knew you had such a good eye for firearms…"

Edward nodded. "It's rather ironic, really. If *Floggit and Leggit* was a better show, with a decent budget for props and whatnot, I'd never had noticed that the gun was the real thing, instead of the usual cheap tat. I mean, I saw enough Webleys in the War to recognise what a real one looked like, but you know as well as I do that a bigger show would have paid for a decommissioned one."

John laughed. "That's all that Madge did, apparently. Bought an old army revolver using BBC stationery, claiming it was to use in the show, then had the firing pin replaced. She didn't even have to pay for the gun she tried to kill you with!"

Edward frowned at that, and John would have said of another man that he looked furtive, but that wasn't really a word you could use to describe Edward Lowe. Irritated, annoyed, indignant… all of those, yes. But *furtive* implied a degree of stealth and dishonesty of which he doubted Edward was capable. Still, there was something troubling him. He flicked ash onto the hospital floor and waited for him to say something.

"It's a strange feeling to come so close to death," he eventually said. "A second later or a few inches to the side and that bullet would have gone right through me. But what would have bothered me most is that if that *had* happened, if I *had* been killed, she'd have won. She'd have completed her little pattern, and we'd have achieved nothing. The injustice of that would have haunted me beyond the grave, I think." He smiled then, a rueful sort of a smile, which almost but not quite managed to convince. "I wonder what that says about me?" The smile faded to a tight, constipated scowl. Obviously, he wanted to stop talking about it.

Fair enough, thought John, who found that sort of philosophical musing a bit tedious anyway. "It says nothing at all," he said firmly, then, changing the subject, asked, "What about Barney Ifeld, though? What was his role in everything?"

The look on Edward's face was almost comical in its vindictive glee. He rubbed his hands together and smiled, genuinely this time. "Ah, now, it turns out we were barking up the wrong tree there. Mr. Ifeld had nothing to do with the murders. What he did want to hide, however, was the fact that much of his surprisingly large fortune was made by means of moving quantities of..." Edward's voice fell to a whisper and he leaned close to John. "...marijuana."

John whistled. "Was it now? Well, well..." He frowned. "But what's that got to do with him being up at the reservoir?"

"That's where he kept his... ah... *stash*. Big bundles of the stuff, wrapped in plastic, apparently, and buried all around the moors, including a spot not far from the reservoir."

John had tried a funny fag now and again – it was quite common in the London jazz clubs – but he preferred a drink, given a choice. He could tell by Edward's face, though, that he viewed it in the same light as devil worship and Fray Bentos steak pies in tins.

"How did all of this come out?" he asked. "I assume Ifeld didn't volunteer the information?"

"No, no – it was young Primrose, would you believe? After you and he had been picked up from that field, you were a bit dozy, and you'd injured your leg, so they brought you here, but they dropped Primrose off at the police station. I'd left a message earlier, asking him to be on the lookout for Ifeld, before we knew the truth, and he decided to go out and find the man. No idea why – perhaps he still thought he was involved in some way – but, in any case, he went out to his house, and caught him red-handed. He'd dug up all his drugs in a panic, and there it was, piled up all around his living room. You couldn't see the sofa for it, Primrose said."

John laughed, then winced as he remembered he also had a cracked rib. Whatever painkillers they'd given him were wearing off. What he wouldn't do for a whisky right now.

As if on cue, Edward reached into the nylon bag he'd brought with him and pulled out a quarter bottle and two shot glasses.

"Now the case is closed, perhaps we could allow ourselves a small celebratory toast?"

He placed the glasses on top of the bedside cupboard and filled them, then handed one to John.

"To a return to a quiet life!" he said as the glasses clinked together.

"And no more adventures!" John replied, and drained his glass.

Though, really, would more adventures be so terribly bad?

ACKNOWLEDGEMENTS

This book had a more difficult birth than usual and, while it was being put together, I was immensely grateful for feedback from Simon Bucher-Jones, Alex Douglas, Dave Hoskin, Scott Liddell, Paul Magrs, George Mann, Dale Smith and Nick Wallace. My agent Piers Blofeld and Sophie Robinson at Titan were both hugely helpful, and my editor, Rufus Purdy, was a wonder at spotting the ghosts of previous drafts and suggesting ways to improve the story. Without him, this book would make far less sense!

Finally, thanks as ever to my wife Julie and my children, Alex, Cameron and Matthew, who have put up with me wandering about the house for the past year or more muttering things like, "When were answering machines invented?" to myself.

ABOUT THE AUTHOR

Stuart Douglas, the creator of the Lowe and Le Breton mysteries, is an author, editor and publisher, who has written five Sherlock Holmes novels for Titan Books, and contributed stories to the anthologies *Encounters of Sherlock Holmes*, *Further Associates of Sherlock Holmes*, and *The MX Book of New Sherlock Holmes Stories*. He runs Obverse Books and lives in Edinburgh with his wife, three children and a dog named after Dusty Springfield. Follow him on Twitter/X: @stuartamdouglas; and on Instagram: @stuartamdouglas

For more fantastic fiction, author events,
exclusive excerpts, competitions, limited editions and more

VISIT OUR WEBSITE
titanbooks.com

LIKE US ON FACEBOOK
facebook.com/titanbooks

FOLLOW US ON TWITTER AND INSTAGRAM
@TitanBooks

EMAIL US
readerfeedback@titanemail.com